Alanna Knight was born in N[...] parentage. She has lived in Aberdeen since her marriage, with her scientist husband and their two sons.

Her first novel was published in 1969 and since then she has written fourteen others, including six historicals, numerous short stories, magazine features, and radio material, including two documentaries, a stage play, and an encyclopedia on R.L. Stevenson.

Alanna Knight enjoys travel, painting and classical music. She also plays an active role in many writers' associations including Society of Authors, Writers in Scotland and P.E.N.

Also by Alanna Knight and published by Futura

THE BLACK DUCHESS
COLLA'S CHILDREN

THE CLAN

Alanna Knight

Futura

A Futura Book

First published in Great Britain in 1985
by Macdonald & Co (Publishers) Ltd
London & Sydney

This edition published in 1986
by Futura Publications, a Division of
Macdonald & Co (Publishers) Ltd
London & Sydney

ISBN 0 7088 2936 8

Printed and bound in Great Britain by
Collins, Glasgow

Futura Publications
A Division of
Macdonald & Co (Publishers) Ltd
Maxwell House
74 Worship Street
London EC2A 2EN

A BPCC plc Company

To
Sheena Macdonald
with love,
and to
Macdonalds and Campbells
everywhere
who bear a proud name and live
in peace
this book is respectfully dedicated

Prologue: 1666

'No more.'

He could take no more killing.

Even as he said the words, the snow began to fall. Softly, as if not to disturb those who died. And the stars that had watched him, a million accusing eyes were mercifully hidden as they folded into the shadowed hills.

Liam watched the snowflakes gratefully, this shroud divinely sent to hide the dead. A gentle goose feathers' flutter, too soft and white in angel purity to be associated with the black carnage around him. Snow? Surely an omen of God's sorrow, for the glen still blazed golden in October's bright melancholy.

Melancholy autumn indeed. For at his feet lay the man he had slain, his face already waxed into still death. If only he could put back this night into the womb of time unborn and, as in many a childhood game, draw his 'slain enemy' to his feet again. If only he could find once more that lost boy brandishing a wooden sword with nothing deadlier than a shrill war cry on his lips.

Now faced with grim reality, he vomited at the sight of his bloodied sword. Seventeen years of boyhood fascination with the *seanacchie*'s legends, of death to the Macdonalds of Ardarroch — vermin on the face of God's earth — the Campbell of Glencorrie's holy quest, was a pack of lies. Reared to believe in sweet vengeance, he had never until this hour known that outside legend, Death wore not the face of glory but of gore. Death was not honour but a foul stain upon the soul of a man.

Liam Campbell dashed a hand across his eyes. Useless to tell himself that this was the enemy who had murdered his kin in Glencorrie and left the Campbells homeless. Had he not been visiting his cousin Sir Robert Campbell of Glenlyon at Meggernie Castle, he too would have perished in the raid. The young man at his feet was no older than himself. He should have been repulsive, old and verminous, not young and beautiful in the glory of youth. Black-haired, white-skinned, the slightly parted full red lips looked as if they were ready to smile and the Macdonald eyes in death were still wide in the surprise of it, dark as spring violets, fringed by a curtain of sooty eyelashes, and gentle, unreproachful as a girl's. Liam shuddered, certain those eyes were etched deeply upon his immortal soul. And he bowed his head before the inevitable truth that they would remain with him until his own eyes closed in death.

A dark shadow hovered. Liam swung round, sword upraised.

Red Alistair, his father's henchman, his *late* father's henchman, Red Alistair Campbell nan Creach of the Many Forays, a warrior in the stature of folk heroes, swaying from a sword thrust in his shoulder and upper arm, his plaid dyed red — oh, dear God — would it never end, this senseless killing, and maiming. But his bloodied hand on Liam's shoulder had lost none of its strength.

'You have done well. Himself would have been proud of his son this day. You have proved yourself worthy of the name of Glencorrie.'

Proud? – Brave? The words meant nothing. Proud of still slain bodies, sprawled and huddled in untidy death. Proud of a sudden raid that had taken their enemy completely by surprise, for they had spilled out of the Tower of Ardarroch, bewildered, hastily armed.

God's mercy. He longed to cry out: What was there in this sight for pride, in this mortal sin committed in revenge. It did not bring back slain Glencorrie, his Campbell kin hastily buried. The thought sobered him that a million Macdonald deaths could neither cancel out Campbell deaths nor resurrect them, nor lessen his grief.

Do unto others – had the words been spoken or were they a whisper in the rising wind, with its snow flurries, no longer gentle, but stinging his face, like the needles of a thousand avenging angels.

Christ Jesus – forgive me. But he must not cry before his

8

Clan. He was now their chieftain and it was unmanly to shed tears, to show weakness of indecision before the thirty armed men and boys who awaited his command. In their eyes, he was a hero and the *seannachie* would sing his praises in a ballad of glory. A boy of seventeen, Liam Campbell had proved himself a warrior lord this night. None would ever know that henceforth in his own heart he would carry the killer brand, the mark of Cain.

He looked up into the face, seamed with age that towered above him, saw cheeks that were wet, hair that streamed water. Thank God for the elements, now he could cry and no one suspect the difference.

'We await your orders, lord.'

'Back to Glencorrie –'

'Glencorrie, lord?'

'No, Glenlyon, a slip of the tongue.'

For there was no longer a Glencorrie. When the Macdonalds of Ardarroch had sacked the glen and murdered most of his kin, they had run off cattle and sheep, destroyed crops, what could not be lifted and carried away was ruthlessly burned. The Campbells were left destitute without food or roof. Sir Robert Campbell of Glenlyon, their overlord and Liam's kinsman, had come to their assistance with the offer of whatever ramshackle hovels could be found on his land. Any place where their women and children might survive the coming winter and gather strength to rebuild the broken glen, to build homes where they could breed again, more warriors to fight the accursed Macdonalds.

Until we rebuild. The words were a mockery with scarce twenty trained fighting men and a scattering of old men, women and children. As Liam mounted his waiting horse, Red Alistair's pain stricken face was level with his own. 'Will you manage back all right?'

The old man drew himself up to his full height, a movement of pride which cost him agony from his sharp intake of breath: 'I have managed back on worse, lord. This is one more scar that I am proud to carry, one to add to the many I wear for the sake of your late father and grandfather.' And Liam remembered that Alistair who seemed incredibly old, had been his grandfather's cousin and boyhood friend.

'I mind it well. We were no older than yourself when we

made our first raid, when we rode out together and drew our first blood of the Macdonald vermin.'

'How many did we lose tonight?' demanded Liam impatient of the old man's tendency to babble on about the glorious bloody battles of his youth.

'Three only.' Liam ignored his reproachful look at this interruption. 'Three only – Hamish, Angus, Duncan.' The names already sounded impersonal, Liam thought, as if they had never belonged to living flesh and blood men, whose bodies hurt as they died. Hamish and Angus were two boys with whom he had run the hills of Glencorrie. Duncan, the older man, his father's crony who constantly teased and tormented him. Guiltily, Liam remembered how he had hated those mocking black button eyes – now they were closed for ever. Two loved, one hated – death the great leveller.

But life would go on unchanged. There would be no widows and sorrowing mothers, sisters, or sweethearts to give him reproachful looks for this afternoon's work. Campbell women – and he supposed Macdonalds too – accepted as their lot, loss of their beloved menfolk from their first cry when they bore them into the world in pain, to the last farewell of even greater agony which bore them out of it again. Rare indeed for any to survive the allotted Biblical span of three score years and ten. For those who survived the perils of infancy's sickness – childbearing took its toll of the women, and violence carried off the men. Brief, sad life and back into the dark again. There was a bitter price for those who loved their kin too well, the deeper the love, the deeper the loss.

Suddenly as if he had been transported up into the air and watched the scene from treetop level, Liam looked down on the glen of their Macdonald enemy. Ardarroch, devestated by fire and sword. Smoking pitiful hovels, whose rapidly disintegrating thatched roofs cast merry sparks hissing into the snow, serried ranks of bright dancers whose upward flight suggested celebration rather than sad *coronach*.

Smoking thatches. And a tall gaunt tower. The Tower of Ardarroch, unassailed – as yet.

'It grows late, lord, we should be back in Glenlyon, this storm – ' When Liam made no move, the old man's eyes followed his brooding gaze.

'The men await your orders, lord.'

Orders? Lord? Liam was unused to being addressed other than as lad. 'Lord' was still his grandfather's title, the one his father did not live to inherit.

'Orders?' he repeated bleakly.

Before him, the old man cleared his throat, a delicate sound from so large a frame. 'That is so, lord. The men will make no move, no more killing, until their chief raises his sword and gives the rallying cry.' He jabbed a finger towards the tall tower. 'Now, is it your will, lord, that we burn out the rest of the vermin from yon place?'

'No. No more burning. It is enough.' At the frown of disapproval, he added, 'But let them take what they can carry and whatever livestock is in the fields.'

'That alone?' Red Alistair was perplexed, a child deprived of a treat. 'Scant pickings with empty, burned-out hovels, except for yon tower,' he grumbled, chewing the ends of his long moustaches impatiently. 'And the wood.' The Glencorrie men were whispering among themselves, perturbed at their young laird's indecision, grumbling that in raids, speed of attack and quick thinking were the essence of success.

Liam saw that they now gazed hungrily upon that dark and silent wood. Drunk on blood, other brutal senses required satisfaction.

There were Macdonald women in that wood. Comely young women for sport. Women with hands clasped tightly over the mouths of terrified babes, stifling with their plaids the cries of those too young to know that their lives and those of all who crouched beside them depended upon not uttering a single sound.

'Women – and children, Alistair nan Creach?' asked Liam gently.

'Women breed, lord. We could wipe them out now, put an end to the vermin for ever, wipe their hated name off the face of God's good earth.' The old man spat. 'We need only your command, lord.'

'I am thinking about it,' said Liam sulkily, wishing he had someone less warlike to advise him as reproach and doubt hung tangibly between himself and the old warrior. Even to his own ears he sounded more like a querulous schoolboy

11

than a lofty warring chieftain. He could guess at Alistair's thoughts on the matter: Was this a milksop who had succeeded as their leader? Was it for this lint-haired laddie that he had taken the sword thrust that drained his life blood away?

Alistair's painful sigh expressed his feelings. He had thought to die gloriously, serving a leader whose courage, strength and cunning equalled that of the boar, the Clan Campbell emblem he wore in his bonnet.

'No more killing.'

'Is that wise, lord? It is usual to root out the vermin, put all over the age of seven to the sword.'

'Usual be damned. No more. That is my command.'

Alistair stared across at the dark tower, in his eyes a question that Liam could not ignore.

'And I will see to that,' said Liam harshly, pointing with his sword, which he fancied had turned suddenly heavy in his hands.

'I will accompany you, lord.'

'You will not. You will make all haste back to Glenlyon. Man, you have blood everywhere. Get someone to bind you up before you bleed to death.'

Alistair continued to regard him doubtfully. 'You take care, lord.'

'What do you think I am? Simple-minded or something?' And summoning a devil-may-care grin which was agony to his soul, Liam swung his horse's head round in the direction of the tower. He would have liked to whistle nonchalantly as he did so, but his dry lips could not manage the sound. As he dismounted and proceeded stealthily on foot into the courtyard, he prayed that he would not meet a Macdonald as brave as the one he had killed, whose solitary eagle's feather declared him Ardarroch. He had sold his life dearly. Already wounded he had fought Liam with the desperate strength of a dying lion, doubtless to protect those who still remained within this dark Tower.

He pushed open the oak door which creaked heavily. Standing on its threshold, he deeply regretted forbidding the old man to accompany him. While he had no stomach for more killing, old Alistair would have cheerfully despatched any lurking Macdonalds with no more qualms than disposing of a vixen's litter.

Liam tried to tell himself that Alistair was in the right. If the remaining Macdonalds were allowed to live, they would grow up as full of hate for the Campbells as their fathers before them, always ready and waiting the chance to avenge this day's work. So were feuds perpetuated, generation after generation.

Once inside, Liam listened warily, hardly daring to breathe. But over all there reigned the empty hollow silence, the curious stillness he now recognised as the absence of life. He sped up the twisting stone stairs with heart-hammering dread, knowing that he was vulnerable, for the ring of his spurs on stone would have had any living Macdonald rushing down upon him, with the advantage of the narrow spiral stair cunningly constructed in the defender's favour. Even an indifferent swordsman, or a woman, could cut down an intruder.

The stair continued to unwind upward and endless. But the silence beyond his own footsteps remained unbroken. No fighting men, that for sure. He swallowed deeply, hoping there were no lurking terrified women or servants either.

The scene into which he emerged was so unexpected and bizarre that it halted him in his tracks. Amazed, he saw that a table stretched the full length of the great hall.

A table set for a banquet. There was food everywhere, plates with half-finished contents pushed aside, wine goblets spilt like the premonition of blood. Although it was not yet dark, the hall gleamed bright under the extravagance of many wax candles, the food still permeating the air with delicious odours, the huge fire beaming a welcome of warmth and hospitality. For a moment Liam fancied that he was hungry, snatched a small roast fowl, but at the sight of his bloodied hand he cast it angrily into the fireplace. Before this onslaught, a huge log toppled, shattering the sorrowing frozen silence.

He took the next flight swiftly and sword at the ready, kicked open closed doors. Before his onslaught bedchambers yawned empty of all but images of the crucified Christ, staring down at him reproachfully from their walls.

Papists too. The Macdonalds had deserved to die for that heathenism alone. From a corner turret, knotted bedsheets

13

trailed towards an outhouse roof. The powdering of snow dotted by a flurry of footprints vanished in the direction of the wood.

There was a new sound. The jingle of harness as the Campbells rode out and then the silence folded back.

That wood, so dark and secret, drew his attention. He thought of the Macdonald women, creeping around the edges of the snowy fields, weeping women with shocked, cold children clasped in their plaids, then finding their menfolk dead. He should destroy this tower. Many would seek refuge within its strong walls.

He should not feel compassion. God should not give warriors hearts that ached with pity for their enemies. Angrily he snatched a brand from the fire in the great hall and hurled it at the table, watching with some satisfaction that flood of light from end to end, consuming the banquet that would have provided for needy Glencorrie for a month. For a moment, he considered carrying some of the meats with him, but the thought of such ill-gotten fare would choke him and he feared, bring naught but sickness upon his hapless clan.

At the door he looked back, realising that as walls, ceiling and floor were solidly stone, the Tower would not burn for long, the burning was a gesture of his defiance rather than destruction.

Now another faint sound alerted him.

A distant cry? A small animal whimpering from the solar near the great hall? He had inspected the room and dismissed it as empty. Curious, the sound came from there. A trapped kitten perhaps?

He put his head round the door. No kitten, but surely an infant crying.

But where? The curtained bed was rumpled, empty. He seized a torch from the wall and in a dim recess which he had dismissed as a Papish oratory with candles and crucifix, he twitched up the altar cloth.

A girl lay in the shadows, half-hidden. At first glance it seemed that she slept, then he backed away from the stench of blood. She was dead, the linen around her soaked in blood. Dead but not murdered. Dead in the business of childbirthing.

About which he knew nothing.

Yet. By the time he reached Glenlyon, Mairi, his wife had promised him a fine son. Mairi, his bride of a year, in premature labour thanks to the rough handling of these same devils of Macdonalds.

God forgive me, but if some ill fate befalls her this night, I have ample reason for any revenge I care to take.

Thrusting the torch into the wall-sconce, with some reluctance he dragged the girl from her hiding-place. She was indeed dead and clasped in her arms, roughly hidden by a plaid, a new born child, still as a waxen effigy. By the torch flame he saw with fleeting pity that like Ardarroch, whom he had despatched, the dead mother was young and beautiful.

And suddenly he knew the reason for the feast laid out in the hall and why the Macdonalds had been taken unaware. They had been celebrating the birth of an heir, little knowing that as they did so, the mother and child were already dead — or dying. Realising that they could not carry them in their flight down the roped sheets, they had thrust them out of sight in the oratory. His lip curled, doubtless with a prayer to the Virgin Mary for divine protection, in their Popish fashion.

Now it was clear to him why Ardarroch had so desperately defended this Tower with his life. For the sake of his wife and child.

And the child who seemed dead, now lived and moved, whimpering like a blind kitten, flourishing small pearly fists, as if in defiance of him. Ah, here was revenge indeed. Ardarroch and his lady dead, but their spawn lived. Celebration, and their extreme youth indicated a first child. Kill it and one nest of Macdonald vermin would trouble Glencorrie no more.

Seizing the child in one hand, sword upraised in the other, he murmured: 'This is for Mairi — '

And then a strange thing happened, so unexpected that his resolve was shattered.

The crying ceased. The infant eyes opened wide and looked directly into his, with uncanny recognition. And from among all the carnage surrounding him this night, the Macdonald brat smiled.

Liam shuddered. Had he held the devil himself, he could

not have struck that fatal blow. He had stained his immortal soul in the name of revenge. There was not enough forgiveness in heaven or in Christ's blood to blot out all his sins but he could not add infanticide to them, or leave the child to roast in the fire which now roared angrily behind him in the hall.

As he hovered indecisively, from out of the corner of his eye in the region where vision ends, a shadow moved. And he knew with the one warrior's instinct he had inherited, that he was no longer alone. The fire's raging hid all extraneous sound but even as he swung round, still clutching the infant, the shape fluttered and dissolved into the darker shadows beyond. Should he pursue, seek out and destroy?

He shuddered. No. Not again. No more blood – ever. Angrily, he thrust the babe against his naked breast, where its tiny shape was almost invisible inside his plaid.

Red Alistair awaited him at the edge of the wood.

'You should have gone with the others.' The old man bowed his head stiffly and said nothing. Not even his chief or the pain of his wound could make him desert.

As they rode out, Liam looked back only once. The snow had turned to sleet which might well douse the fire he had started. Why had he not left the child back there in the courtyard, for some of the women to find? Was it too late to go back?

'Something amiss, lord?'

'Nothing.' Was it compassion or was it the more primitive fear, the sight of the dead mother, filling him with superstitious dread that such might already be the fate of the wife he had left in childbed in Glenlyon.

Murmuring about fixing a stirrup, he followed the old man swiftly. Too swiftly.

'Have a care, lad,' shouted Alistair as his horse stumbled, almost throwing him. 'Little sense in breaking your neck now, lord. Especially when there will be a fine son awaiting to welcome you home at Meggernie.'

Inside Liam's plaid, the small burden was ice – and he hoped dead already. But as they rode swiftly before the gathering dusk, the snow ceased and the stars rose again above the shrouded hills, in that eternity of accusing eyes, he knew his burden still lived. Restored by his warmth, he was sickeningly aware of the blind instinct that turned its face against his bare flesh, searching for the soft comfort of its dead mother's breast.

A fine son, a fine son, chanted the horses' hooves as they trooped into the courtyard of Meggernie Castle, where Liam hastily dismounting, raced up the steps to the upper rooms Sir Robert had set aside for his wife and himself. There he found the fine son Mairi had promised him born, and dead long before he had set foot in Glenlyon.

'Mairi?' he croaked, hardly daring to speak her name.

Eunice Stewart, Mairi's step-sister who desired him, scowled. 'Aye, she still lives – just. But no thanks to you,' she added spitefully, wanting to torture him, for thinking so little of her that she was pushed roughly aside from the bed, where Mairi's face was white as the pillows on which she lay.

He sank down and took frail bird-boned hands to his heart. 'Mairi.'

She stirred, her eyes wide but dazed, like one called back from the shores of a far distant land, her feet moving beneath the sheet as if impatient at this summons, and unsure of their change of direction.

'Liam – oh Liam.'

Cradling her in his arms, his tears mingled with her own. Tears that went far beyond the loss of a bairn, tears shed for the savagery of a world that bound him to cruelty, senseless and endless as long as he lived. Such was the first law of Campbell survival, dinned into him since birth. Kill or be killed.

He thought that their shared grief was silent, then he heard that other sound. The whimper of the child in the plaid he had thrust aside and forgotten.

Mairi heard it too. Her eyes brightened with sudden hope. 'The babe? Eunice told me – it was dead. She was wrong, *wrong*!' Her weak voice soared with delight as she clutched his hand. 'Liam, Liam. He lives – our son lives.'

Liam pressed her face against his heart. 'No, my dearest, it is not our son.'

She gazed at him in shattered realisation. 'Then, then you brought back – one of *theirs*?'

17

'Aye. There was a fire. I could not leave it – alive.'

'You should have done. Left it to roast in hell, where it belongs,' shouted Eunice, inspecting the writhing bundle. Liam rushed over and seized her bodily, even as she raised her foot to crush the tiny skull.

'Kill it, kill it,' she screamed struggling against him. 'One of *their* brats. For God's sake, Liam Campbell, have you lost your senses? To bring it here. Kill it, I say,' she shouted, hanging on to his arm, as she had called him to kill a rat in the cellar at Glencorrie.

He looked at the ground. 'No. I *cannot*.'

'Then I will. I will show you. Give it to me – '

As Liam swung the bundle away from her, she leapt upon him with clawlike hands, the red murder-light blazing in her eyes.

'Sister, sister – leave us for pity's sake,' moaned Mairi.

'Then kill it, do as I say.'

'There will be no killing, unless my husband says so, sister. You are in his house, remember and this matter is for him alone to decide. Please go now, Eunice.' As the door closed, she turned to Liam and asked: 'The child's mother?'

'Dead. They were having some celebrations. For its birth, I expect. But the mother, just a girl – she was dead when I found her.' He shuddered. 'Of a bloody flux.'

Mairi nodded, so her own mother died, herself the only witness. She had been eight years old and it was a sight she would never forget. She was haunted by the fear of bleeding to death in childbed. Terrified, with none to reassure her, only her overwhelming love for Liam had made her close her eyes to this inevitable sacrifice. And yet miraculously she had survived the agony. She was still alive. But Liam's son was dead.

'The father?'

'Dead too. In the fight.' Ashamed he closed his eyes against the memory of Ardarroch's eyes.

Mairi frowned. 'What shall we do?'

'Since our babe was lost because of what they did to you, it is now your right – and only *yours*, to decide whether this Macdonald brat lives or dies.'

'Kill it, kill it,' chanted Eunice from the doorway. 'Kill it, you great fools. Kill it now or you'll rue the day. I warn you,

Glencorrie, its presence under your roof, will bring naught but ill luck.'

'Sister,' said Mairi wearily. 'Go away. It is a bairn you speak of, not a wild animal.'

Eunice nodded vigorously. 'It will grow into one, mark my words. Vermin it is, like all that accursed clan.' When the door closed again, Mairi said: 'You must forgive her, husband, she has been sick in her mind since her man's death.'

Liam was always surprised by this ready excuse for Eunice's inexplicable violence, her murderous rages over trifling matters. Especially as she had treated the elderly husband forced upon her by Mairi's tight-fisted father, with derision and contempt. His sudden death had only freed her, thought Liam, knowing where her true desire lay. In the later stages of Mairi's pregnancy, she had pressed her body whorishly against him, offering herself. He had recoiled, horrified at the idea of physical union with any woman except his wife.

'You decide, wife. Does it live or do we let it die?'

Mairi smiled wanly, stretching out her arms to receive the bundle he had carried next to his heart over the miles from Ardarroch. 'Give it here, husband.' And pulling aside the folds of the plaid she stared at the tiny crumpled face, the blind eyes and feebly threshing fists. 'Better a live babe than my empty arms this night. Hand me clean linen.' Then smiling, 'Your wee mannie is a wee lass, Liam Campbell. God bless her, poor wee mite.' And kissing the dark downy head, she bared her breast and pressed nipple to questing mouth. With a sigh that was almost content, she whispered: 'We have had enough of killings. Perhaps this one will change the tide. Maybe God willed this one born for life, for love instead of death.'

And Liam was amazed that she accepted the babe readily as any stray dog or kitten, or fledgling bird, loving it all the more for that. Longing to give her the whole world, he watched her daily gather hope and new strength from this enemy's child she suckled: 'See how well she has settled with us,' she said stroking the tiny velvet head, 'I can scarce believe that I did not bear her, that she is not our own flesh and blood. I have decided we shall call her Caitlin – '

'Caitlin?'

Mairi smiled. 'Caitlin, for your own mother. Anyone can see already she will be dark like the Irish.'

Caitlin. Liam looked down at the sleeping babe, but could not yet bear to touch her. 'So be it. She is ours. To all outside this room, and that includes you, Eunice Stewart, Mairi Campbell bore a healthy living daughter.'

Eunice sorting out linen, scowled and turned her back on them. Liam took her by the shoulders, swinging her round to face him. 'That includes you,' he repeated. 'Do you understand? The child you see lying there was born to Mairi and myself.' When she evaded his eyes, he shook her gently. 'You are to swear that you will never breathe a word of what happened in this room to a living soul – '

'But, but – '

'Swear. Swear, Eunice, for if you refuse, if you break your promise by as much as a whisper and word reaches my ears, I will know at once from whence it came. And if God does not put his curse upon you for breaking your oath, then I surely will. And you will leave my roof, wherever that may be, for ever. You and your children. Do you hear me?'

'I hear you,' she said sullenly.

Liam held out the Bible and his sword. 'Then swear.'

As she swore she told herself that her sweet but stupid stepsister was unlikely to survive another childbirth. Then Liam Campbell would be hers. For that, she would have damned her immortal soul and promised anything.

Caitlin: 1681-82

Chapter I

The Sighe Stone which hid her from Eunice Stewart's wrath was vast, older than time. Overlooking Fortingall, impervious to the frail span of mortal life, it brushed the fleeting generations away with the same indifference that Caitlin Campbell swept aside a midge cloud on a summer's day. An army could not move it and most wise men were too superstitious to try. Even the Roman legions who prided themselves on their own immortality had marched through Glenlyon and left only their Latin carved upon the Fairy Stone. And before the Romans came and went, somewhere lost in the shadowy land where legend and reality merge, great Fionn's Celtic warriors had sharpened their swords upon its side.

The Sighe Stone was at once Caitlin's refuge and her terror for it possessed in certain light, helped by her ready imagination, a secret existence of its own. On such days, it whispered of another time, when all of Glenlyon, the Campbells and the hated Macdonalds would be but a fleeting shadow from the past and the clachan's turf-roofed houses a rubble of stones. When even the laverock's song was mute, still the Stone would remain.

Caitlin clung to such permanence, her only security in a world which in her fourteen years had twisted and changed, so that she wanted to thrust out her hands against the relentless tide of events. All of her life had been a battle to hold on to the intransient as indeed had been her own nativity. According to Red Alistair, the way the wicked Macdonalds had treated her mother on the very eve of her birth, it was surprising that she had been born alive at all, let alone strong and healthy, for Mairi Campbell had never borne another living child.

Caitlin sighed. The Sighe Stone could not stretch out warm arms to comfort the anguish of having seen her beloved mother laid in the kirkyard beyond the yew tree, in a grave like a black open wound upon the greensward three summers past. The grass that had regrown brought no healing to the aching emptiness of her own heart. Mairi had died of the son she had borne Liam after many barren years and he carried his broken heart, his bitter sorrow, to his mother's family away across the sea in Ulster. His mission was to raise funds from the O'Rourkes to re-establish his Clan and rebuild the glen that the Macdonalds had destroyed.

Caitlin had long ago learned the folly of tears shed against the cruel indifference of destiny. She had also learned in her short life that weeping availed her nothing with her father. A father incapable of loving his only daughter, it seemed.

This, Red Alistair assured her, was but his indifference to womankind in general and because she was not the son a chieftain needed. But Caitlin's yearning, her desperation for her father's love became more intense as with each passing year, he scarcely seemed aware of her presence. Even while her mother was alive, as Sir Robert's kinsman, tacksman and rent collector, he had never been at home each day like other fathers. And Meggernie Castle was twenty-five miles away.

'Take me with you, take me with you,' she had pleaded, but he had merely looked at her dully and impatiently pushed her aside. 'Take me – please. After all, I was born at Meggernie.' But she had no power to cajole or persuade him. Beside, she was curious, since she could remember not a room nor a window, nothing of that castle, either inside or out.

'No. Your place is here with your aunt.'

How could she tell him that her aunt too hated her, treated her not with his painful indifference but with vindictive cruelty. That in this house she, Glencorrie's daughter, was the meanest slave and would have been more ill-used had it not been for the presence of Alistair nan Creach and her cousin Jean. Always ready to soothe with excuses, Alistair decided that as Eunice could do little with her simple daughter who idolised Caitlin. It was natural for her to feel sorely tried by this affliction of God's will, resentful of Caitlin's sharp mind and her bonny looks too. But only the fact that the old man might whisper of cruel treatment to Liam, kept the full brunt of Aunt Eunice's malice in check.

When Caitlin had heard of Liam's plans to go to Ulster, she had seized his hands, cried: 'Take me with you. Don't leave me here alone, I beg you.' She pleaded that she longed to meet her grandmother's family. According to Red Alistair, who well-remembered Caitlin O'Rourke, her dark looks, her black hair, white skin and eyes, mirrored the woman whose name she bore. She never wearied of his tales of that other Caitlin who had captivated her stern warrior grandfather Peter Campbell.

'Please, please, take me to Ulster. I will be no trouble.' But Liam did not even seem to hear her, deaf and blind as always to her presence.

'If I had been a boy, you would have taken me – would you not – would you not?' She shouted after him, as he prepared to leave.

He had swung round in the saddle and looked down at her in bewildered amazement, as if such an idea had never entered his head. But there was no hope for her in that look. His face took on its closed-in look. Dear God, she sobbed into her pillow that night, what had she done in her short life, so warily walked, to earn his cold looks, his lasting displeasure. She tried so hard to be good, a dutiful daughter, to please him. Although he was never cruel and never struck her, he did not seem to see her at all. Perhaps that was worst of all.

When would he come home again? Three years was a long time, even though she thought of him each day. She closed her eyes, touched the Sighe Stone and willed him to appear. One day, its magic would work for her and bring back her father who could not love her because she was only a lass.

A shadow moved far below in the doorway of the tall square tower house. Its stone walls and glass-filled windows were far grander than the clachan's houses, as befitted the cousin of Sir Robert Campbell.

Caitlin recognised the figure who emerged by the billowing plaid as he staggered up the hill towards her.

'Caitlin, are you there, lass?'

Her heart went out in love to the once proud warrior, Red Alistair nan Creach of the Many Forays. The fiery hair which had struck terror into his enemies, was now sparse and white for he had carried his sword for three generations of Glencorrie Campbells and had lost an arm on the night she was born. Everyone knew he was now almost blind from an earlier skirmish, although he tried in his pride to conceal this, and Caitlin felt the pity of the young and strong for the aged and infirm, as well as the sudden sweet surge of her own immortality. This would never happen to her. Unthinkable that age could ever overtake her young strong legs as she kilted up her skirts and ran down the hillside to meet him.

His eyelids blinked rapidly in her direction. 'Caitlin, there is news, a messenger from Meggernie. Your father is on his way home.'

At last, at last. She closed her eyes. The Sighe Stone's magic had worked. All she had needed was patience. But before she could assimilate the miracle, another figure appeared in the square doorway.

'Caitlin, I want you at once.' Even at that range, the venom in Eunice Stewart's voice was unmistakeable.

Never a soft word or a tender glance for the lass, nothing but blows and ill-concealed hatred, thought Alistair, as he felt the tremor in Caitlin's small work-hardened hand. If it rained, Caitlin was to blame, if the fire died down or the hens escaped, Caitlin was at fault. True, Eunice's own lass was simple-minded, but Stephen made up for his sister Jean's deficiency by an abundance of brains. Why in God's good name should she hate this bonny black-haired lass, warm-hearted and caring, when she had so loved Mairi, nursing her delicate stepsister since Caitlin's birth?

There was another reason for that devotion. Alistair suspected, as did many others, that Eunice Stewart's widowed heart had long yearned for the love of Liam Campbell.

Fortingall gossips and his tavern cronies considered it right and proper, as well as a prudent matter of economy, that after a decent interval had elapsed, Liam Campbell should marry his late wife's stepsister.

'Glencorrie has never recovered from his wife's loss.'

'That is all very well, Alistair nan Creach. But for the lass's sake – '

He said nothing to that. Not one of them had the least idea of how Caitlin was treated behind those closed doors. Small wonder that for all his reassurances, her family were extraordinarily hard to love, even with a heart as overflowing with humanity as Caitlin Campbell's. And not even an old man with rapidly failing eyesight could fail to observe that on Liam Campbell's rare visits home, it was never his daughter he took on his knee, but his little step-niece, Jean. While her step-aunt regarded Caitlin as if she were plague-ridden, Alistair also had seen the child brusquely thrust aside by her own father.

What was wrong in that house, he wondered? To him love and duty owed to parents by children, and vice versa, were simple uncomplicated issues dictated by the Ten Commandments and maintained by fear of God's wrath. What had the lass done to be treated so? Other men had learned to love daughters when sons were not forthcoming. That too, was the will of God, and Liam Campbell would do well to abide by it.

Ah well, as long as I live, she will know only kindness and gratitude from me. And the old man smiled to himself, knowing how he bored everyone with his tales of yesterday. Not so Caitlin. There indeed he had a willing and eager listener.

'I mind it well – ' With those tempting words, so all his tales began, slowly, puffing at his clay pipe.

'Tell me again, tell me how it was.' Now that his days of fighting were over, his life had recently taken on new purpose in the ceremonial role of *seanacchie*, the poet and wise man of Fortingall. But for every day he needed no greater audience than one eager listener. And for Caitlin, he discovered, he could indeed resurrect the past, relive his days of glory. As the tale progressed, so did the clouds of smoke dramatically increase. And Caitlin watched them with considerable anxiety in case the pipe went out before the end. Filling and lighting was a slow process for a one armed-man, which she must bear with patience, for his pride must not be offended by any offer of assistance.

'I remember fine the night you were born. We had been raided by Ardarroch,' he paused and spat as if to clean out his mouth at the mention of such an obscenity. 'Your grandfather, murdered by those vermin, your father's grandfather, the chief himself, murdered. Your father but a lad of seventeen – God was good to him, he was far away, safe at Meggernie when they fell upon us. How bravely he led us to avenge them. How well I can see it all.'

And so could Caitlin through his eyes. He was careful now to omit any details of the actual killings for she had a sensitive nature this lass and could weep for a dead bird, or for any living creature. Sometimes he feared that even the death of their mortal enemy might cause her grief, strange child that she was.

'Tell me again about the part where Father went into the Tower alone,' she shuddered.

'Aye, brave he was, tackling that grim devil's cauldron single-handed.'

'What was it like?' she whispered, picturing occupants who were scarcely human, according to the old man's account.

'I could not tell you that, for I was never inside. Your father would not allow me to accompany him, seeing that I was sore wounded.' Delicately, as if it still hurt, he touched the stump where his arm had been. 'You must ask himself.'

And so she would, some day, when her father had forgiven her for not being a son. But she shivered, as she always did at that part of the story. She could see it all so clearly, just as if she had been there: her father running up the spiral staircase, spurs clattering on stone, sword in hand. She closed her eyes. That particular dream had recurred all her life. It differed from Red Alistair's version in only one slight particular. In her dream Liam Campbell was not her father. He was her enemy. He intended her death.

'And then,' she said, knowing the story well.

''Twas a wonder you were born whole.' He looked at her proudly. 'Your mother had been roughly used by the vile Macdonalds. When they came in to take the old chief, who had been long ailing and was like to die in his bed, your mother tried to protect him but they lifted her, threw her bodily against the stone wall, heavy with child as she was.'

But Caitlin although she nodded sympathetically could never visualise that part of the raid as clearly as the grim Tower of Ardarroch itself.

She dragged one curl over her shoulder and regarded it critically. 'Is it because I'm not like our Clan, because I am black not gold. Is that why he hates me, and because Mother was hurt?'

'Who hates you, lass?' asked Alistair innocently, pretending to misunderstand but knowing full well.

'My father.'

The words shocked him, so coldly uttered. 'Never, never, you must not even think such a thing,' said Alistair. 'He loves you – why, of course, he does.' But even Alistair wasn't too sure about that and he saw by her face that she didn't believe him either.

'He does hate me,' she said, without rancour. 'Aunt Eunice told me, because I'm a useless girl and black-haired, like, like – ' She couldn't say the hated name, but saw that she had shocked the old man. What was getting into the lass? One thing for others to speculate about her father's attitude, but quite another for her to take it so calmly.

'You must not sully your innocent mind with such ideas.' Laying aside the pipe, gravely he stroked back the shining curls. 'Your colour, you know fine well, you take like your name, from your granddame.'

And as Alistair nan Creach puffed a great cloud of smoke into the sky, he beheld there in the vision of the late Caitlin O'Rourke, with whom he had been a little in love, or perhaps more in love than he thought at the time. Like every man who had set eyes upon her he had fallen under her spell, too shy of womankind to declare himself, he had watched her go to his young kinsman, Liam's father, Peter.

'Tell me again,' whispered Caitlin.

'I mind it well, as if 'twere yesterday. She was a beauty, cousin to the Earl of Antrim.' He sighed. 'Those were troubled days in Ulster but we Campbells were loyal to Oliver Cromwell. Caitlin O'Rourke now, she hated the English and the Scots hardly better, with good reason. 1648 it was,' he sighed, 'your grandsire a young man then and

27

myself scarce forty – '

Caitlin's expression told him how old forty sounded to a lass not yet fifteen. 'We were both soldiers, eager to fight, even in a war that was not of our making. It was this way – '

Peter Campbell had been a younger son, eternally restless for action, a born soldier and leader. Leadership came to him unexpectedly when the sweating sickness carried off his elder brother and the riding accident that left his father bedridden for fifteen years, left him as Glencorrie's heir. But ignorant of that destiny, Peter had gone as a mercenary to Ulster with Red Alistair, his second cousin, sent to watch over him.

As he told her the story, Alistair saw again, vividly, Ulster soft and green, its undulating hills and rivers making a man feel that he might be in his own homeland, like Perth itself with the muted colours of a summer haze, gentle and soft. Aye, but such things were a savage bitter contrast to the terrible pain and hatred in the faces of those who stood by the roadside and watched them ride past. People who had borne the brunt of General Cromwell's insatiable cold rage and lust for destruction. Tortured maimed bodies, broken, ruined castles, but under the surface of defeat, the fierce burning pride of race. It told Red Alistair, who was not a fanciful man, that the blood spilt by the conquering General might cry out down all eternity for revenge.

He sighed. Peter Campbell had contemptuously dismissed the O'Rourkes as 'black bog Irish', scarce better fitted to live in their pigsties than the vile Macdonalds of Ardarroch.

Until he set eyes on Caitlin O'Rourke. For there in the castle by the lake whose waters forever sighed like the souls of lost drowned maidens, Caitlin O'Rourke had bewitched him, singing at the window, a harp in her lily lands.

When he was wounded in ambush, those soft hands had been gentle, caring, a swallow's breast upon his pain. Tough, passionless man of action, that he was, Peter Campbell had fallen under her spell. And although Red Alistair could never have believed love possible between such a pair, Caitlin O'Rourke had melted before that rough soldier's wooing and her strange black-haired wild beauty, her gentle acquiescence to his demands had touched a heart unused to any emotion.

Liam Campbell was the fruit of those nights of bewildered ecstacy, born in February 1649, on the same day that King Charles of England was beheaded away across the Irish Sea at Whitehall. But for Peter Campbell this event meant no more than a melting snowflake as he stared desolately over the once-magic lake with its frozen waters. Ill tidings had reached him from Glencorrie. His brother was dead.

He must return with all haste. But Caitlin was too frail to survive the recent birth, so swiftly followed by that wild sea journey to Glasgow and across Scotland to Perth. Before April touched the frozen glen with the promise of resurrection, Peter Campbell sat alone by his son's cradle. The house around him echoed emptily. The beloved wife who was to share it with him now occupied the bridal chamber in icy solitary death.

Then a strange thing happened, for all trace of Caitlin O'Rourke seemed to vanish entirely with the earth that closed over her grave. Day after day Peter Campbell stared hard at the son she had given him, twisting the tiny face this way and that in his big shovel fists, searching for some token of Caitlin's immortality, that she still lived, in a smile from eyes he remembered, the reassurance of God's promise of a meeting in Paradise. He searched in vain. The features of the child revealed naught of the wife he had briefly loved and lost, not even the hint of an endearing smile or dimpled chin that had beguiled him.

Peter Campbell put his head in his hands and wept. His beloved was indeed gone for ever, but the son she had left him was wholly his. His living image, he knew from the steel mirror on the wall, his every detail, down to the very set of his toenails, he thought in disgust.

And Peter Campbell could not love this creature who had, he reasoned, by his birth, murdered the only precious being in his barren life. For that murder there was no forgiveness. To Red Alistair who knew him as did no other he confided his horror: ''Tis as if I created him from my own flesh, without any assistance from my lady, as if she never existed, except in my imagination.'

And Red Alistair's comforting words, that as the lad grew older, he would no doubt resemble his dead mother, fell on deaf ears. Soon Peter ceased to visit her grave in Glencorrie.

He could not believe that she lay there in the quiet kirkyard beneath the headstone, with the heather blowing and the elegaic requiem of the mavis singing in the branches above his head. For Peter the world had emptied, grown cold and deserted. Once, in his cups, he told Alistair that he often dreamed in those early days of opening her grave and finding only an empty coffin.

Soon it was Alistair's turn to feel compassion for son instead of father. Poor young Liam, he did not realise as he grew alarmingly in Peter Campbell's image, that his father would have been less hard on him had he resembled his dead mother; Peter Campbell would never have struck his fist against Caitlin's mouth and made it bleed, or shouted down angry curses into Caitlin's eyes. Peter Campbell felt cheated in his only son. Cheated that this flesh of his flesh bore no mark of the great and only love of his life. For Peter there were no more women, other than tavern whores used to cool the heat of a soldier's blood, a necessary purgative bringing no solace to an aching heart.

If there was no love left in the world for Peter Campbell there was still hate. For the Macdonalds of Ardarroch. Hate, to be fed, cherished and enjoyed. Hate that was bred in the blood and bone of the Campbells of Glencorrie. And that was more enduring than any mortal woman's love.

And now when Liam's lass asked old Alistair: 'Why do we hate them? How did it begin? Tell me – ' he could only murmur that it had always been so. But such an explanation was not enough for Caitlin Campbell.

She shook her head. 'It could not just happen, someone had to begin it all.'

Sometimes Alistair wondered what was wrong with these kinsfolk of his, father hating son and that same son hating his daughter. And neither with any just cause to do so. For Liam had asked the very same question in his childhood. He had been rewarded for such an intelligent and thought provoking question, instead of answer, with a furious clout across the ear from his own warlike parent.

'There is no why,' Peter had shouted. 'You hate them because they are foul, worse than touching human excrement. To even think their name is to sully your mind with filth, to put in jeopardy your immortal soul. You hate them because they are Papists and because you are Protestant and a Campbell, and it is your solemn duty to your clan to do so.' But this reply would never do for Caitlin. All that Alistair or any of the Glencorries knew for sure was that, like Mother Eve, a woman began it all. The details were vague, but the feud had retained its initial ferocity.

'There was a Campbell woman abducted way back,' said Alistair sternly.

Caitlin smiled. 'And not altogether unwillingly. Did she not in fact marry the man who carried her off?'

Alistair frowned. 'That is so. But I dare say they were not happy together.'

Caitlin nodded sadly. The mysteries of marriage were beyond her.

'There were other things too, concerning land and cattle lifting and then the troubles between the chiefs of the Macdonald and Campbell clans spread to us, their lesser septs. Aye, and not too long ago, in living memory, lass, there was an Ardarroch man among the thirty-six Macdonalds hung by our Sir Robert's grandfather, mad Colin Campbell, on the braes of Meggernie. And he watched them die from his very window, old devil that he was,' he added with a crow of delighted laughter.

Caitlin considered for a moment and then said: 'All that for one woman.'

'Aye,' said Alistair grimly. 'One woman.' He did not question what God had ordained: that Campbell must fight Macdonald until the end of time. The minister so preached from his pulpit each Sunday and who was Alistair nan Creach to question the word of God. He was just a soldier and accepted the divine order of things he could not understand. As he grew older and looked back over the long and often sad pattern of his own life, sometimes his dreams were troubled with the faces of the Macdonalds he had killed. Such matters had caused no sleepless nights in his young days but now that youth's fever had been usurped by a body that ached with old age's creaking bones and dim sight, he gave more thought to the matter of eternity. This lass with her unending questions regarding the universe, and her uncanny knack of seeming to read his mind had helped to unlock doors in his soul that led into secret gardens wherein strange flowers grew, the dolorous dark flowers of repentance.

Caitlin was silent at his side. Along the road from Meggernie, a dust cloud no bigger than a man's hand grew and grew. The pounding of her heart identified the horseman.

'Father, it's father – '

Chapter II

Liam rode towards Fortingall along rough roads familiar to him as home, down wooded paths and leafy lanes where once he had wandered with a tranquil heart and Mairi at his side. Now their budded gentle green hung with sorrow from every bough. For him the early evening, bland as skimmed milk in lazy sunshine, held only the treachery of a fool's welcome. How could he bear to face that grey stone house empty of his love?

As he reached the gate he saw old Alistair. Even with the sun behind him, the giant frame was more stooped than he remembered. A figure hovered at his side, with wind blowing long dark hair over her face. Liam frowned. A newcomer to Fortingall. Some friend of his step-niece Jean, perhaps?

As he dismounted the girl came forward, shy, reluctant, holding back her hair with one hand. And Liam saw that time which had set one kind of seal upon the old man had set quite another upon the girl curtseying before him.

Caitlin.

'Welcome home, Father.'

'Caitlin, I would not have known you.' He shook his head. 'You have grown. You are quite changed.' There was surprise but no welcome in his chiding smile, as if by growing she somehow failed to please him, she thought. He made no move to touch her, turning hastily to embrace the old man, slapping him on the back unaware of the pain in Caitlin's eyes.

She looked on, like a stranger, thinking he had not changed at all. He was still the god-like creature of her fantasies, for every hero Alistair told her of, every angel, bore the countenance of Liam Campbell. His face was broad of forehead, strong of chin, the gold hair on his cheek bones

33

sparkling with a million grains of sunlight. The straw-coloured Campbell hair had darkened to the same dull gold as his eyes, surprisingly light under thick dark eyelashes and eyebrows, their tawny colour identical to the buff leather jacket he wore with the Campbell plaid slung over his shoulder. And, as a hint of new riches at Meggernie Castle, fine Spanish leather thigh boots and a fine full-sleeved cambric shirt with lace at the collar. Although he was shorter and more lightly built than Red Alistair he was magnificent in her sight.

She watched the two men who no longer noticed her. Just as well for merely being near him, breathing the air he breathed was a feast to her love-starved senses. Present or absent, he filled her every waking moment, with the burning quest of how to shine in his sight, to please him, to do something splendid, noble and self-sacrificing, that would have him smile upon her and say 'Well done'. Sometimes she thought it would be worth dying, worth leaving this world that was just beginning to unfold its wonders to her, for the sake of having him weep at her death bed. In her whole life she had never heard one word of praise from his lips. Not one word. For she would have remembered each precious syllable of praise.

I would not have known you. She turned it over and over in her mind as the two men talked. Could it possibly be construed as praise, she wondered eagerly, as she watched Liam's horse handed to the old servant who had served three generations of Glencorries, and observed his greeting of old Jock, considerably warmer than her's. Was it possible to love anyone so much, with every thought and action directed towards him, while he remained stonily indifferent to her existence? Mutely, she followed the two men still talking with such delight, glowing with mutual admiration, into the house where her step-aunt waited to receive Liam Campbell. A strange unfamiliar Aunt Eunice, modest and smiling as befitted Glencorrie's housekeeper and stepsister-in-law attending to her lord. A pleasant, gentle-browed woman, scarcely recognisable in tranquility.

Caitlin's astonishment increased. There was surely enchantment abroad this night. Where was the shrew who but an hour ago had screamed and railed at her and who now politely asked for her assistance in the kitchen? Could this be the same virago who rained curses and blows upon every moment of her waking hours? This almost pretty, docile creature in her second-best gown?

And Caitlin understood many things in that moment of revelation. Eunice had been secretly, impatiently awaiting his home coming. Eunice too was a dreamer who loved Liam Campbell.

But what of Liam? Only Caitlin knew why his step faltered at the threshold of his own kitchen, why he gripped the door and stared round the room through dazed, half-closed eyes, as if to deaden the pain of that empty chair by the fireside. For a moment their spirits touched in a common bond, both searchers for a loved face that was no more. From the depths of her own desolation, Caitlin knew the scene intimately that Liam had lived with during these three empty years. The last time he had set foot in this house was the day they carried Mairi out to lie in the green kirkyard with his only son at her side. With their deaths, the light that Liam Campbell carried in his heart was quenched for ever and provided a convenient reason for Caitlin to excuse his subsequent coldness towards her. She had survived, they had died.

Now she watched Eunice curtsey, her eyes shadowed. Liam clasped both her hands in his and greeted her warmly. But he did not kiss her although he felt her green eyes caress his face, her mouth an invitation. 'Little Jean' was the recipient of his effusive welcome. Jean Stewart who was now sixteen years old but remained the child he had left in Fortingall.

Unlike Caitlin.

His eyes sought her.

Caitlin. The child he had dismissed all these years was suddenly a woman. A woman, he had not expected that and remembered guiltily how seldom she had entered his thoughts during his absence from Glenlyon.

A woman. He rubbed his chin. How very tedious, now he would be faced with the task of finding a husband for her. At least such would remove the burden of her presence in his life. A husband, yes. A Lowlander, preferably from far away, who would not care one way or t'other if she was

Macdonald or Campbell. He sighed. He must talk to Sir Robert about a dowry.

Around him everyone talked at once; Red Alistair shouting questions without giving him a chance to answer them, while familiar smells and sounds swirled into his thoughts stirring old memories into life. The house had grown shabbier. Smaller too, after the splendours of Meggernie Castle, twenty-five miles down the glen but belonging to that other world of fine houses, the homes of wealthy Campbell gentlemen in Glasgow, Edinburgh and Perth.

He looked around. This huge kitchen in which the waking hours and daytime activities of the women's lives were spent. No drawing room or withdrawing room for them. That great scarred oak table had seen many generations of Glenlyon tenantry blossom into youth, flourish for a season and then fade into old age and oblivion. An air of sad neglect pervaded and he realised why. No two pieces of furniture matched. All had been hastily assembled when he became Sir Robert Campbell's tacksman and one of the tenants' turf roofed hovels was not considered right and proper for the dispossessed lord of Glencorrie.

Fifteen years ago, come autumn; he and Mairi, newly wedded were full of plans. One day they would rebuild the Glencorrie that the Macdonalds had destroyed and, there in peace, Mairi would bear him many fine sons and daughters. But she never recovered from the internal damage of that first premature birth. A few weeks of hope throughout the years and finally a triumphant certainty which became a long weary pregnancy wherein Mairi had grown frailer, paler as the child bloomed inside her. Their child, his son – his only son – dear God, and not the babe they had carried over this threshold, who was none of their making, but the spawn of their hated enemy.

Caitlin.

He watched her as she helped Jean set the table, spreading the white cloth as they did on Sundays and setting out the Bible for his reading to them after supper. Beyond the window the day darkened into the wild glory of a spring sky, unfurling banners of gold and rose that whispered of unsettled weather and promised storms to come. The conversations rode over his head unheeded, although he smiled attentively while he watched Eunice remove the tallow dips that were for every day. These, she proudly replaced with costly wax candles, candles that were saved for celebration and now glimmered brightly on the chimney piece. At his questioning look, shy-eyed, demure, she curtseyed: 'Nothing but the best, Glencorrie – nothing but the very best for our laird's safe return to us.'

Liam smiled wryly. Glencorrie? A hollow title without land or fortune to go with it.

Glencorrie. His mind slipped away to that deserted glen over the hill. Glencorrie, silent in the dark of a long despair, a black, burnt-out ruin, haunted by only the corbies' desolate cry. Glencorrie, he thought bitterly, that had stood strong and proud, the home of his clan since the days of King Robert the Bruce.

Until the Macdonalds of Ardarroch came and took them unawares, the men in the field at harvest, peaceful, unarmed –

Again his eyes turned to Caitlin.

Caitlin. Obeying Eunice's instructions, she brushed past him almost apologetically, to shut out the first bright star in the darkening square of window. One of the shutters jammed and as he sprang to his feet to assist her she stopped, stepping back wild-eyed as if, he thought, she expected a curse and a blow for her clumsiness.

'The hinge is broken,' he said.

'I will attend to it tomorrow.'

'You will do no such thing, Glencorrie, that is menial work. Jock can mend it.' Eunice's voice held a note of suppressed outrage.

Liam smiled. 'Come, mistress, I am but a tacksman.'

'You are no tacksman in this house – you are Glencorrie.'

Liam ignored her interruption. 'Nevertheless, mistress, this tacksman is dependent on his laird's charity. And if he cannot keep his own house in order is hardly worthy of his name.'

'Do not be belittling yourself, lord.' Red Alistair came to Eunice's defence. 'Sir Robert Campbell's secretary, and his cousin, are you not?' he added proudly.

Alistair had been proud when young Liam who had gone

to the University of Aberdeen, not without protest, but because his father, that inarticulate, warlike Campbell, was a stern believer in education. Was it out of some wistful sense to prove himself in the matter of Caitlin O'Rourke's odd choice of husband? That gentle cultured and aristocratic lady who had chosen a man whose conversation was as coarse as his rudimentary table manners and whose ideas of culture went no further than the *seannachie*'s ballads? The University was a bewildering experience for Liam, whose capacity to absorb Latin and the philosophies was stumbling and unequal. But he had a good hand at writing and a good head for figures and law, abilities which Sir Robert was to find very comforting when he scratched about for someone competent to sort out the tangle of his extragavance and Meggernie's muddled finances.

'All this fuss over a broken shutter,' Liam shook his head good-humouredly, wondering at the same time if they were always like this, fretting over trivialities, the substance of their lives contained within the confines of four stone walls. He did not miss Eunice's scowl in Caitlin's direction either, and the fear in the girl's face, as if the fault was her responsibility.

As she slipped past him round the table, he smelt the warmth of her hair, the intimately female body smell he associated with Mairi, but with no other woman.

'A blessing, Glencorrie.'

Bewildered he looked at their expectant faces. They were waiting for him to say grace. A solemn moment and then the pleasure of food on the table fit for a hero's return although the growing season had not yet begun. He guessed that in many houses in the glen the dearth of winter and near starvation had already taken its toll of the sick, the old and the very young. But here was plenty, for one of the conditions of his employment with Sir Robert was that the carter passing through Glenlyon each month dropped off supplies at Fortingall. Come winter and bad weather, even these grew scarce, he thought, grateful for broth, thick with early vegetables followed by mutton, from a brax ewe, dead in the lambing. ''Tis all that is left,' said Eunice when he praised the flavour of the stew. 'We would have killed a hen, but there are few and needed for the eggs.'

He murmured consolingly that there was naught for any man to complain about, with only the homes of the dominie and the minister similarly favoured by Sir Robert as well served. And the inn, for there was profit to be gained from the few travellers who might pass through Glenlyon. The meat was followed by home brewed ale and honey cakes made from the produce of last year's bees.

Liam sat back and stretched out his long legs. 'No more, no more. A feast I have had.' And at their request his reading from the Bible was the return of the prodigal son.

'Amen. Amen.'

''Tis good to be home,' he said with a sigh.

'God be thanked,' said they, well-pleased. Amid smiles from all around the table he relaxed content in the one high backed carved oak chair, cushioned in gold velvet. In common with the rest of the furniture it was at once too grand, incongruous for the kitchen of the tacksman's house.

During the meal, Alistair had led the questioning. He did not consider this amiss as the eldest relative who considered himself in loco parentis to the young man who would always be laird to him.

In answer to his question, Liam explained that he had been on Sir Robert's business in Glasgow, Edinburgh, and Argyll.

'Tell us about Ulster, lord, for I mind it well,' interrupted Alistair with a wistful sigh.

Caitlin too listened intently.

'Ulster. Aye, and my O'Rourke relatives.'

'Were they in good health?'

'They were, but not overeager to part with money to help Sir Robert, or provide for the rebuilding of Glencorrie. Understandable, since times go hard with them, there is great trouble politically which has left them scarcely less impoverished than ourselves.' When Alistair tut-tutted this statement, Liam smiled. 'Besides, why should they make a sacrifice which bring no benefits to themselves.'

'What, not even for their own kin?' roared Alistair in disgust.

'What of Meggernie Castle, uncle?' Jean interrupted eagerly. Her thought processes were slow and she was apt to take up conversations long after they had been abandoned. 'I have never been there and I will never go there and my

Caitlin,'' she paused to look fondly in her direction, 'my Caitlin is too young to remember. But she was lucky to be born there.'

Lucky? Eunice's eyes sought Liam. When are you going to tell her the truth, they demanded, tell this vile Macdonald brat we have sheltered all these years that she has no right to the name of Caitlin or Campbell. In that glance and Liam's defiant stare, it was as if the entire subject had been raised and dismissed between them.

Caitlin.

Liam looked at her. Her eyes were downcast over her plate and he wondered how many nights she had sat at the table thus, remote and detached from all of them. He was aware acutely that he had never liked her, had never even considered her as part of his family, treating her, even while Mairi lived, like some small domestic pet, rescued and brought home, against his better judgement. A presence either ignored or tolerated with extreme caution. His enemy's child, who might any day turn and rend her foster family. In those first eleven years, before his long absence from Fortingall, he had many times regretted the impulse which made him snatch her from the Tower of Ardarroch and place her in Mairi's arms that night. Had their own child lived, he knew he could not have done so and his resentment knew no bounds when her insistent demands summoned Mairi from his arms at night, for food and comfort. Helplessly, he watched the child capture her affections, become her child in every way but the accident of birth. Her child, but never his.

As time passed, he consoled himself with secret thoughts that she might succumb to the perils of infancy which carried off so many well-beloved children from other homes in the glen. But strong, lusty and indestructible she seemed to be made, as Mairi had prophesied, for life and not for death, surviving where others sickened. Then later as querulous demanding toddler, talking early, clutching at him eagerly, all toothless smiles, he learned to avoid any contact with her except in Mairi's presence, and hardened his heart to winsome ways others found so irresistible.

'Da, da,' she yelled after him, a cry that became 'Father' in later years. But her infant tears aroused no tenderness when he could not forget that, but for her vile family and the damage they had done to Mairi, he might have fathered a string of live Campbell sons. Father indeed, he thought in disgust, he was as like to enjoy having a beast of the field call him by such a name. She was no flesh of his and never would be.

Or so he had thought.

He looked up to encounter Eunice's mocking glance, as if she read his thoughts. Through the years, he had tried to conceal his true feelings from Eunice.

'And now I have presents for you,' Liam said and from the depths of his saddlebag he produced clay pipes for Red Alistair and a leather pouch to carry his tobacco.

'This is for Stephen.' He saw Caitlin's eyes suddenly wistful for the leather-bound volume of Milton's poems.

'He will be pleased, Glencorrie. You should be proud of your nephew for he has done well at the University,' said Eunice with motherly pride. 'He would make a fine Clan chief,' she added reminding him that once he had said that should he not remarry, Stephen would be his heir.

'And this is for you,' he said handing her a lace fan with ivory handle.'These are the fashion in Edinburgh, where all ladies carry one. No, no, you hold it thus, see?'

Eunice followed his directions. Smiling over the fan, she gave him adoring, languishing glances, fluttering her eyelashes like a lovesick girl, thought Caitlin. Her eyes widened at this transformation, watching lips normally thinned in anger, blossom suddenly into a woman's mouth, rosy and seductively curved.

'A lace kerchief, oh, how grand, Uncle,' said Jean.

'It is for Sundays. There is another also.'

And as Jean screamed her thanks childishly half-strangling him with hugs and kisses, he remembered that he had no gift for Caitlin other than that second kerchief.

Caitlin, who sat there quiet and composed, so different from all of them, expecting nothing.

'And, Caitlin, this is for you.' He handed her a crimson velvet box. As she opened it he was conscious of Eunice's angry gaze as she mentally compared its value to her own gift.

Caitlin withdrew a miniature of a girl with black hair,

41

white skin and smiling dark eyes. Caitlin looked up at Liam, lips trembling: 'Is it, is it?'

Liam nodded. 'Yes, it is Caitlin O'Rourke.' He could not say 'your grand-dame', and added hastily: 'I brought it from Ulster.'

'Thank you. Thank you,' she whispered and tears unbidden, overflowed. This, this, the first present she had ever received from him.

Almost reluctantly she passed it over to Red Alistair who was holding out his hand, murmuring excitedly. He held it to the candlelight, hoping to recognise the face that he had long since loved and lost. But poor sight, turned the picture into a mere blur. Undefeated, proud still despite his disappointment, he smiled and nodded encouragingly:

''Tis her image, the very spit of her. And did I not always tell you, the mirror of yourself, Caitlin Campbell.'

There was a sudden stillness. Eunice, her good temper vanished, remarked coldly: 'It is time you lasses were in your bed.'

Liam stood up and bowed gravely, not as a man at his own hearth, but like some polite guest, thought Caitlin, not realising that such manners were the fashion in polite society. To remain seated while ladies took their departure, was considered boorish. The Scottish lairds, Liam had soon discovered as he moved in Glenlyon's charmed circle, had a lot to learn, their rough and ready manners and often uncouth speech were a source of amusement and cruel behind-hand derision in the town-houses of Edinburgh and Glasgow.

Liam remained standing, clearly expecting Eunice to depart also. Chagrined, she curtseyed gracefully. She was still smarting over that miniature of Caitlin O'Rourke but when she looked up at Liam, he recognised in her eyes that if he chose to visit her room this night he would find the door unlocked, her bed warm, and her arms ready to welcome and ease his loneliness.

Suddenly embarrassed, he was glad when Jean darted forward thanking him all over again, leaping upon him with all the eagerness of a young puppy. Eunice watched this behaviour with good-natured tolerance before hustling her daughter upstairs.

He watched them depart and replenishing his glass saw that Red Alistair sat by the fire, asleep in the sudden unpredictable way of those at the beginning and, he thought sadly, at the end, of their lives.

Caitlin.

He had forgotten her presence. How silently she moved. Turning he saw that she stood with one hand on the balustrade, the other clasping the velvet box so tightly that her knuckles grew white.

'Thank you, father,' she said. 'And I am glad you are home again with us.' The words sounded like a carefully learned but difficult lesson.

He bowed. 'I am glad to be home.' Even as he said the words he knew that he also meant them. On impulse and because the warmth of *usquebaugh* filled him with further generosity of spirit, he put his arm about her shoulders very gently, almost nervously. Bowing his head, his lips brushed her cheek. A woman's cheek, to his astonishment. Soft and warm, it conjured up a sudden vision of love in his sterile heart.

'Goodnight, Father,' she curtseyed.

'Goodnight, Caitlin.' He watched her run upstairs, lissom and light-footed, slender long-legged but small-boned, she was going to be taller than the Campbell women. For a long time he stood tapping his fingers on the balustrade, moodily watching the dark shadows at the top of the stairs and wishing she would return. Return and fill a sudden void of aching loneliness that yawned within him for the hours of the night still to be endured.

Caitlin, come back. Come back and smile at me.

But no one came and only the tick of the clock on the chimney piece and Red Alistair's rhythmic snores filled the emptiness. With a sigh Liam snuffed the candles, the old man would doubtless find his way to the *culaist*, his box bed on the other side of the room, by firelight.

Upstairs in his own room, he undressed slowly, reluctantly, eyeing the once familiar marriage bed with its closed curtains wherein nostalgic memories of arms and white flesh that were no more, threatened to suffocate him. An hour later knowing that sleep was still far away, he sprang out of bed and opening the shutters watched the sky

43

with its thousand glittering stars, surveying the dark glen.

While he sat there, taunted by his sweet ghosts, a young moon, no more than a crescent hung trapped in the old yew tree's branches, and an eagle's dark wing span hovered. Then somewhere close at hand, a dog-fox barked once and was silent. Cold drove him back to bed where at length he slept and dreamed of Mairi. For the first time since her death, his dreams were uncommonly sweet as if her ghost watched over him in this bed they had shared. No longer was he filled with dread, no longer did her shade torment him, but instead the bitterness drained from his soul, and he awoke feeling hopeful, that now he might begin to live again.

To live again with hope renewed.

With hope renewed, Caitlin opened her eyes to a May morning whose pale beauty held the promise of summer. The sun wavered like an invalid emerging from a long winter indoors, cautious and blinking before the wonder of this world whose earth, long dead, now thrust forth a living carpet of flowers. Yellow, purple and white they blossomed, while a lark erupted into the blue, filling every hill and hedgerow with its mad cascade of joyous song.

That such a day was Sunday seemed appropriate and where most of Minister Blair's texts remained forever obscure to his congregation, the Divine Resurrection became instantly believable. To simple, frail, doubting creatures with little ecstacy to be gleaned in the harvest of this world's sufferings, spring's annual rebirth held a secret of survival already ancient long before Jesus Christ brought his promise of eternal life.

As they went to church that morning, Caitlin felt proud to be at her father's side. The Glencorrie Clan waited to greet their returning laird. And as he passed among them, many commented on his still youthful appearance. The years had scarcely touched him, an impression created by a tall slender figure and boyish flaxen hair – until a glimpse of deep haunted eyes destroyed any such illusion.

Dressed for Sunday in the fine elegance of black velvet jacket and satin knee breeches, a starched full white collar and cuffs with just a suspicion of lace, the Glencorrie plaid across his shoulder fastened with the Campbell boarshead brooch, Caitlin observed that Liam was grander than any of their neighbours, save only Dominie McKerchie's uncle, Judge Forbes, whose full periwig and wide-skirted brocade coat was causing something of a sensation in the congregation.

For his part Liam was guiltily aware that the women of his household were abominably ill-dressed according to the standards set by his life at Meggernie Castle. Petticoat, kirtle and Glencorrie plaids were respectable enough for working days but nevertheless they represented servants' costume rather than suitable adornment for the laird's close kin at Sunday kirk.

Especially Caitlin.

He was both shamed and embarrassed by her gown which he guessed rightly was one of Jean's castoffs, that the older girl had outgrown. Too short and too tight, he was fully aware that others besides himself noticed her slender calves and budding breasts. He frowned sternly in Eunice Stewart's direction. Whatever her feelings, or his own, for that matter, Caitlin was his daughter in the eyes of the world and of Fortingall in particular. As his housekeeper, Eunice was responsible in his absence for matters of wearing apparel. A poor serving wench she looked, in all but the proud way she carried her head.

Caitlin. He found himself watching her constantly, secretly, still bemused by his homecoming discovery of the child he had ignored and left three years since, without regret. She walk's like a princess, he thought amazed. Even at fourteen she has an inborn quality of dignity and grace. And others noticed it too.

'Blood will out, look at her,' said Red Alistair nudging him proudly. Liam turned with a startled look. Surely Alistair did not know? 'A true grandchild of your lovely mother,' added the old man.

How her face lit up for the old man, Liam thought enviously. Yet she must have heard all his stories a hundred times and never once wearied.

'Blood will out,' hissed Eunice, watching them. 'How can any man seeing her walk to church with us, believe her to be a Campbell?'

Ignoring the whisper, Liam said: 'You should devote more

attention to her gowns, mistress. It is not fitting to show so much limb at her age.'

'We have no monies for new gowns, sir,' said Eunice stiffly.

'Then for pity's sake, ask for some,' he said and hurried ahead, leaving her staring furiously after him. Her expression of thin-lipped anger which indicated that Caitlin would pay dearly for Liam's displeasure.

Minister Blair took pride in the length of his sermons and the ferocity of prayers in which he took good care to reproach God on certain matters that might have slipped the Divine attention. He gave due thanks for the approach of summer, for Fortingall's safe emergence from battle with a long, cruel winter, and that there had been fewer casualties than usual for him to lay to rest in the kirkyard. Along with gratitude, however, Minister Blair humbly beseeched the Almighty in His mercy to smite those who, unlike themselves, had not yet found the true religion, for no Papist, only those of the Reformed faith could expect to sit at God's right hand in Paradise.

The church which had been built three hundred years ago, smelt of damp and age. Caitlin shivered; even on the hottest day of summer, it smelt like the fresh turned earth of an open grave. Little sunlight penetrated the gloom through the arched stained-glass windows, many of which depicted the heads of saints, once revered, now despised and deposed.

By glancing sideways, she could observe several niches at different heights, which had been built into the stone walls to hold disgraceful and idolatrous images, communion vessels and holy water. This church, like many others throughout the land had been stripped of Popery, although its foundations had been blessed in the Roman Catholic faith. Caitlin wriggled uncomfortably – to enquire further even in her own heart was to tamper with the forbidden.

She watched Liam ascend the steps of the pulpit. As befitted his safe return, he was to read the Eastertide message from the Gospel of St Matthew:

' "What shall I do then with Jesus which is called Christ?" They all say unto him: "Let him be crucified." And when Pilate saw that he could prevail nothing, but that

46

rather a tumult was made, he took water and washed his hands before the multitude saying, "I am innocent of the blood of this just person: See you to it." Then he released Barabbas the robber unto them; and when he had scourged Jesus, he delivered him to be crucified.'

At those dreadful words, Caitlin sank down further on to the hard bench, in an effort to be invisible before God's wrath. She wished she could have warned Liam about the inadvisability of drawing His attention to the misdeeds of one, Pontius Pilate by name, seeing that the most infamous and accursed Roman in the Gospels had been born here in Fortingall. What further vengeance besides two plagues and two famines, would God demand of this long ago station of the Roman legion where Pilate's father had been sent on a mission of peace from Caesar Augustus to the Highland King Metallanus?

The site of the old Roman fort was still visible and Alistair had found there a Roman coin long ago. When Caitlin held it in the palm of her hand, with her eyes closed, she seemed to see neat columns of buildings, the streets with their sharp angles and flagstones arise from those few sorrowful stones that remained. The bridge the Legion had built over the river was less exposed to the elements and had endured the storms of passing centuries. Sometimes with the sun in her eyes, Caitlin wondered whether the shadowy figure of a Roman lad sitting on the parapet, swinging his short sturdy legs, full of glee as he tried to hook a fish, was Pontius Pilate. What kind of child had he been, unaware of the terrible destiny that awaited him in far-off Judea?

'And Pilate's wife said: "Hast thou nothing to do with that just man; for I have suffered many things this day in a dream because of him." ' But Pilate had not heeded her. Men in Biblical days paid even less heed to what their wives had to say, it seemed. But Caitlin was curious to know what became of Pilate and his wife and family after the crucifixion. Surely the stain of the death of the Son of God must have marred their lives for ever. She could not believe that they had ever thrust that terrible day behind them or that they had ever ceased from being watchful and afraid. By no stretch of imagination could she picture them at ease happy and laughing with their children, or living happily

47

ever after as did the people in the stories her beloved mother had told her.

'And Pilate took water and washed his hands before the multitude saying, "I am innocent of the blood of this just man ..."'

The Minister had replaced Liam in the pulpit and began his sermon by repeating the text while Caitlin looked nervously over her shoulder. In that dark shrouded corner by the church's arched doorway, she half expected to see Pontius Pilate washing his hands in the baptismal font.

The sermon seemed endless to Caitlin guiltily aware of tempting frivolous sunshine and bird-song which penetrated even the mighty thunder of the minister's sermon. The church bench was harder than usual, and she was hungry too. As the eyes from the pulpit met hers and the finger Minister Blair jabbed towards the congregation seemed for her benefit alone, she realised she had lost the thread of his discourse once again.

'Repent, ye sinners – '

Caitlin looked around cautiously, conscious of coughs and creaks. She wondered wickedly if others in the congregation besides herself found little comfort in this weekly harangue upon their sins.

'Amen. Amen.'

Only the minister seemed regretful that the two-hour long sermon was at an end. Down from his lofty pulpit, outside the church, he seemed to diminish, lose stature and power.

With dismay, Caitlin saw that they had now exchanged the gloom within the church for the gloom of an overcast sky, as if the sun offended by their disappearance had gone off to sulk behind the clouds. Even the bird-song was muted, as if they too had lost heart with the change in the weather.

Walking back through the kirkyard, Caitlin shyly took Liam's hand and led him to the grave his aching heart best remembered. Now he saw the reason for the fast-wilting posy she had carried with her. She handed it to him. Awkwardly he leaned over and placed it against the headstone while Caitlin knelt and smoothed the earth as he had often observed her smoothing the blankets on Mairi's sick-bed in the past. Now quite unself-consciously, she folded her hands in prayer.

Liam looked over his shoulder uneasily, wondering if such public kneeling, which had been rejected by the Reformed Church, was part of her inheritance from the Papist Macdonalds. Embarrassed by this show of devotion he left her and walked rapidly to where Eunice and Jean talked with neighbours. But the sight of the girl at the grave, her utter and abject desolation, struck a chord in his own withered empty heart. He also noticed how Eunice's lips had formed a thin line of disapproval as she muttered: 'That girl must come at once – we need her help in the kitchen.'

Chapter III

There was to be a homecoming break fast at the house in Fortingall, where senior members of the Clan Glencorrie would celebrate the safe return of their chief, by bringing before him matters of urgency and dissatisfaction which had arisen during his absence. Of equal import, their own curiosity would be satisfied regarding events in the rest of Glenlyon and at Meggernie Castle.

For a meal prepared at short notice, Eunice had proved her efficiency as housekeeper. While the more boisterous children, whose conduct was still unreliable, were tucked away in the large barn, their parents sat solemnly around the oak table in the kitchen: Minister Blair, Dominie McKerchir, Innkeeper Fergus and their wives, whose households had contributed extra servants, utensils and donations of food from precious stores, since frugality was the rule until harvest time.

Eunice, Jean and Caitlin were to sit down with Liam. Although Eunice's attention was constantly diverted to the behaviour of strange servants occupying her kitchen, Caitlin was delighted with the novelty of a grown-up occasion hitherto denied her. She studied the guests. Apart from Judge Forbes, who seemed grossly over-dressed in such a modest assembly, she decided that Liam was the most elegant. To which she added, the most handsome and distinguished too, in part due to his scorn of periwigs, for the Campbells were proud of their own luxuriant fair hair.

With little to be grateful for since Mairi died, Caitlin sighed for the sheer joy of this fleeting hour. With dreams and hopes no longer centred upon a vague future, the sun had re-entered her life. For the first time in all his travels, her father had considered her worthy of a homecoming gift. Did that mean he had at last forgiven her for not being a boy? She touched the miniature of Caitlin O'Rourke like a talisman.

For the first time she felt important, proud. She wanted to be noticed by the guests, not as a child but as a woman. However, the appreciative glances from the men who had greeted Liam's lass, were soon withdrawn. As always when men have been long apart, the conversation turned almost immediately to burning issues of politics.

'Is the new king well thought of, sir?' Alistair asked the Judge who smiled and said:

'He can hardly be considered in such a role, since he has been restored to his kingdom these past twenty years.'

'Mark my words, times will go ill with us until we have a king of our own in Scotland,' Alistair continued bravely. Although his Campbell father had acceeded to the Reformed Church, he had staunchly supported Mary Queen of Scots and Caitlin had often heard the story he now told: Of how his father had walked all the way to Menzies Castle to see his Queen.

'Aye, and he bragged to all who would listen that Queen Mary was a lovely and most gracious lady, tall as any man. To the end of his days he was proud to have bowed his knee before her and kissed the hem of her robe. And he loved to tell how in return, her gentle hand had touched his shoulder and her smile, which stole men's hearts and made them her slaves had bound him to her forever.'

Caitlin listened with a feeling of recognition, that among females who were frail creatures and of no significance, there were occasionally born women who yielded power over men from the first breath they drew. Was this how it began in the eyes of the Fortingall men who had ignored her in childhood but who now treated her to silent respect? Their veiled and secret glances she did not completely understand. The only comparison, oddly disquieting, was the look she had encountered on the faces of hungry tinkers suddenly offered food. Now listening to Alistair's eulogy, she wished desperately to be like Mary Queen of Scots, to be loved by all men.

'Times have changed since then,' snapped Minister Blair, 'We have ample reason to believe the signs of God's displeasure with sinful mortals. Why, only last year there were three eclipses of the sun and two of the moon.' He had thundered down from his pulpit that these were singular portents of God's wrath, heralding the end of the world and the worst of Old Testament disasters, Babylon and Jericho, Sodom and Gomorrah were all in turn given an airing and compared, not without difficulty, to quivering fearful Fortingall.

Those around the table whose secret vices had been cautioned by the minister's sermons now exchanged amused and relieved glances.

Red Alistair who did not take kindly to having his own lengthy discourses interrupted, leaned forward: 'Aye, minister, and what happened? Naught to ail men but a rarely hot summer and some fine bold storms. The only disaster, God be praised in His mercy, was that one great branch of yon yew tree out there was struck by lightning.'

'Were any hurt by its fall?' demanded the Judge.

'Only a solitary cow, your Worship.'

'There was fine meat to eat,' said Innkeeper Fergus with a grin in the direction of the discomforted minister.

'What of the king, your Worship?' Red Alistair was anxious to keep the illustrious visitor's attention to himself. 'You have met him?'

'I have bowed my knee before him. A fine figure of a man.'

'Let us hope he has a stronger – and a wiser head – on his shoulders than his father,' sniffed Minister Blair.

'I mind the day well,' mused Alistair. 'My lord Glencorrie here was born that very February day in 1649 when the old king was beheaded, so we learned later. And rumour had it that every other monarch with disgruntled subjects, trembled for his own head. I mind hearing how they urged young Charles, a lad of nineteen, to make a brave stand by placing himself at the head of loyal Irish or Scots.'

'They had no reason for fear. His tutor, the Earl of Newcastle had not overrated scholarship too highly in his pupil,' Judge Forbes explained, 'He maintained that being too studious is bad for a king, while good manners and a good seat on a horse were the only qualities that mattered. ''Be courteous and civil to everyone, the putting off of your hat and making a leg pleases more than any reward. Especially with the ladies," ' he added with a laugh that was echoed around the table.

'He certainly needed no second bidding in that direction,' said Liam drily.

The Judge nodded. 'He is a comely man.'

'Comely indeed,' snapped Minister Blair, 'but how stands he in his faith?'

'As you are aware, minister, those who now rule Scotland demanded that Charles accept their faith and swear to impose it on England and Ireland. He had scant option.' The Judge paused choosing his words carefully. 'His court at Perth was a polite prison and his coronation at Scone a mockery. He must have been sick at heart when Montrose who had been despatched to Scotland to raise a Royalist army, was betrayed to Argyll and suffered a traitor's death.'

The sudden silence alerted him to the fact that his listeners were all Campbells and he shrugged, taking up his glass. 'His flight and adventures before he reached Paris and safety are already known to you.'

'As are the details of his immoral life,' complained Minister Blair. 'His conduct is a national scandal. But the Lord has taken a Divine revenge, by giving him no legitimate issue,' he added triumphantly. 'Bastards in plenty, but no prince to follow him. As a man sows so shall he reap.'

Liam found himself painfully aware of Caitlin. Was she the reason why he had never begotten a living son? Was his childless state the result of God's vengeance upon him for murdering her father the night she was born? By rearing this alien child had he brought his enemy's curse of barrenness upon his house?

He glanced around the table. All day in church and now in his own home, he had been aware that she was the centre of all male eyes, a beauty in the making. What would his loyal Campbell neighbours, the members of his Clan, say if they knew the truth as they watched her so covetly?

He felt Eunice's eyes upon him. Did her mocking smile as she looked at Caitlin indicate that she was aware of his thoughts and fears?

As the wine glasses were replenished, Innkeeper Fergus whispered: 'The king is a man after any man's own heart.

All must envy him, whatever they say in public. Old in years but according to travellers, his ardour for new mistresses is undimmed, and apparently he is still able to please them.' He sighed, stroking his grey beard, with a bleak look in his wife's direction. Her sharp tongue and uncertain temper were not only a byword in the parish but lost the inn much custom and goodwill.

'What say you, Glencorrie?' Minister Blair demanded. Liam turned from Caitlin guiltily, fearful that the secret was out. Was that why all eyes were upon him? Stumbling he said:

'I believe the Covenanters failed because what they planned was impracticable – in the terms of humanity – '

'But not in the Lord's terms,' roared Blair.

Liam ignored the interruption. 'The cruelties inflicted by them on the population – not only soldiers, but their women and bairns slaughtered whose only fault was that they had followed their men to the battlefield, as is the custom – '

'Whores and bastards,' sneered Blair. 'I fear you have been too much in the company of Godless men.'

Such injustice was too much for Liam. He banged down his glass. 'Come, minister, could you raise your sword against women and children, even in God's name?'

Uncomfortably aware of the eyes of his pretty wife and four young daughters, Blair could only demur. 'I believe such tales are exaggerated to put the Royalists in a good light.'

Caitlin smiled. At least Liam's outspoken comment put him in a good light.

'Sir Robert? What of him, Glencorrie?' asked Judge Forbes with deceptive innocence and a timely change of subject.

Liam was reluctant to discuss Glenlyon's affairs. Through the years Sir Robert had exacted full payment from his unpaid tacksman, secretary and poor relation for taking the Glencorrie Clan under his protection. Hardly a day went by without a reminder or broad hint to Liam Campbell that he existed solely on Sir Robert's charity, his Clan dependent for their very existence and sustenance upon Glenlyon's goodwill. Close acquaintance had taxed even Liam's loyalty to his kinsman, revealing disquieting flaws in Sir Robert's character which gave cause for alarm.

Behind the genial father-husband image, Liam had not the least doubt that his kinsman's heart beat with no other function than to keep him alive. His indifference to everything and everyone beyond the gratification of his own greed and avarice was already infamous. In order to pay one pressing debtor whose patience had expired, he would saddle himself with four more. Liam watched him askance, amazed at such cupidity. It was nothing less than stealing, for he had not the slightest intention of repayment, signing bonds with cheerful indifference to their contents, so eager to get his hands upon the money.

Once he had believed that he could prevail against the weaknesses of Glenlyon's nature, but of recent times, he felt trapped, that he and his Clan were at the mercy of a madman. From the horrendous stories that awaited his return from Ulster, he now concluded that his kinsman's condition was not weakmindedness, but madness tinged with evil. However, Liam was determined to be loyal. He had no intention of betraying his secret fears to his Majesty's spy, for that he shrewdly guessed, was Judge Forbes' role, the reason for his visit, 'representing the Privy Council'.

When he shook his head and remained silent, Minister Blair who had no such reluctance to discuss their benefactor said: 'Glencorrie, your loyalty is sorely misplaced.' And to Judge Forbes: 'Sir Robert's extravagance is a byword far further than the confines of Glenlyon. It has brought ruin on his house for he has borrowed from all his wealthy Campbell kinsfolk down to any Perthshire laird or humble neighbour who will heed his plea for a temporary loan. Glenlyon is not overscrupulous about where he finds his monies,' he added in disgust. 'He has even taken to inspecting the churches, the length and breadth of the Glen for any silver that might be confiscated.'

'There was that business last year when his kinsman Grey John of Breadalbane exacted repayment by making him lead an army against the Sinclairs of Caithness,' said Dominie McKerchir. 'Not only silver was concerned, but men's lives also.'

Judge Forbes felt there was little to chose between the two Campbells, since his nephew had told him it was common knowledge that Breadalbane forced the war upon the Sinclairs with Glenlyon as scapegoat, because he coveted the Caithness lands and title. Two scoundrels in the making. He looked at Liam for confirmation.

'I was in Ulster, and only heard the sorry story when I returned.'

'Your absence was fortunate indeed,' said McKerchir. 'You were here in '74, Uncle, when his creditors banded together and took him to law.'

'Aye, and to keep them quiet, he decided to sell the fir woods of Glenlyon,' said Minister Blair, anxious to find some common ground of agreement with the illustrious visitor.

'Leased them to a group of timber merchants, Lowlanders all, headed by yon rascal John Crawford,' Red Alistair's indignation suggested that this shortcoming might have been tolerable in loyal Highland men. 'They built a sawmill, dammed the River and then their insolence extended to invading our land and our privacy with their demands. And when his tenants complained, Glenlyon shrugged the matter aside. He did not expect them to retaliate by taking matters into their own hands.' And the old man thumped his fists on the table. 'Aye, sir, we gave them a lesson. Roasted Crawford's oxen over the timber he had cut down. Tell them what happened next, lord,' he said to Liam.

Liam took up the story with reluctance. 'Sir Robert could not afford to quarrel with Crawford. Worse than that, Meggernie itself was under threat. However, I discovered a loophole in the timber agreement which put Crawford at a disadvantage. Sir Robert served them with an order to leave his land and when this was not obeyed, we rallied the tenantry – '.

'Who threatened to hang Crawford and his men if they stayed,' crowed Alistair delightedly.

'Crawford was never the calmest of men. He took an apoplexy, and died soon afterwards.' Liam did not add that Sir Robert immediately rushed into Crawford's dwelling, and ignoring both Crawford's corpse and his weeping widow, ransacked the house for all papers relating to the lease which he carried for safe keeping to Chesthill. 'We are not much better off. Crawford's successor is a Highlander,

Patrick Stewart. He arrived with armed clansmen, cut down eight thousand trees and built more dams, as well as burning down every house and crop that stood in the way of his ox wagons.'

Judge Forbes knew the story. Sir Robert had complained to the Privy Council that the salmon fishing, from which he drew most of his rents, was ruined. But his claim for thirty-five thousand pounds Scots was ludicrous. It was dismissed and he found himself threatened with 'letters of Fire and Sword' should he molest the said Stewart. Further troubled stirrings in that quarter were the reason for his investigation, thinly disguised as a family visit.

The fowls and roast meats had been eaten, and honey cakes and bannock bread. The claret wine that Liam had brought from Meggernie had given place to home brewed ale provided by the innkeeper. The guests were in no hurry to leave, and stayed around the table talking. Caitlin with no excuse to linger, had been summoned by Eunice to help with the clearing up.

But Liam had put a delaying hand on her arm. 'Where go you now?'

She curtseyed. 'I am to help Aunt Eunice. I beg to be excused, father.'

'Remain seated,' he said sharply. 'I have not excused you. Your aunt has many helpers.'

Aware of Eunice's furious expression at overhearing this statement Caitlin feared she would be made to suffer for it once her father had left. That and many other privileges would have to be accounted for in blows, punishments and angry words. But she would not let such shadows spoil her present joy. Instead of being relegated to the barn, from whence issued the noisy shouts of the children who were working off their high spirits in shrill horseplay, she had her hour of triumph. Grown up and proud, sitting by her father's side, she had seen mirrored in his and other men's eyes, that she was no longer a child. She was a woman, a woman who pleased them.

As the wax candles were lit against the growing dusk and outside the birds sang their first carol to the gloaming, she resolved never to forget to be grateful. However many bad things might happen in the future, she would remember to thank God in her prayers, for this one perfect shining day.

'Aye, sir, she is almost fifteen.'

She realised that she was the subject of a conversation between the Judge and her father as the older man considered her in the shrewd manner of one used to seeking out the deficiencies in men's characters, to appraising horseflesh, and womanflesh too. There was a hardly concealed sensuality in his heavy florid face under its monstrous periwig as he took out a lace handkerchief and touched his face delicately. 'Fifteen, you say, Glencorrie. I presume you have marriage plans for her.'

'Not as yet, sir.'

'You must not tarry over long, the lass is ripe for a husband.'

'I have been away some time, sir.' Liam reminded him.

'Now that you are returned, you must be brisk about it, lose no time. I presume there is a dowry goes with her.'

Liam suppressed his amusement and thought cynically that the girl he had newly discovered who was suddenly a woman was in the next breath to be considered overripe for marriage. Time was indeed flying at a stupendous rate.

'A dowry is part of the condition of my service with Sir Robert, for as you know, there is no income or estate to Glencorrie.'

'Quite so, quite so. But after all you are kin to his lordship. It is right and proper that he should provide.' Again the heavy-lidded eyes raked over Caitlin as the Judge sucked in his lower lip thoughtfully. 'I know of good families in Perth, with your permission I will make enquiries.'

How dare they discuss her in this way, as if she was not present, no longer a woman to be admired, loved and cherished but some domestic beast or inanimate piece of furniture considered worthy of acquisition and on sale to the highest bidder.

Caitlin's startled – and indignant – intake of breath alerted Liam. He turned and smiling slowly, eyed her in the same appraising fashion. New dread filled her. Was that the answer to the secret glances, not appreciation nor admiration but merely a shrewd, practical man's consideration of a marketable object to be traded to the highest bidder? And in that moment, she would have settled for her father's former

58

indifference and all their new closeness seemed to vanish.

'Well, Caitlin, what say you? It seems we are to find a husband for you.' His tone was jovial, his look now merely amused.

She bowed her head, hiding the mutiny in her face, knowing how useless rebellion would be, knowing that this was also the price of womanhood. The comelier a lass, the earlier the betrothal. A flower that might be illicitly plucked, she must be hustled into the safety of marriage.

'What say you, Caitlin?' repeated Liam.

Her reply was that expected of a dutiful daughter, 'As my father wishes.' Liam grinned, well-pleased by her obedience, and mercifully changed the subject.

But Caitlin's eyes pricked with tears. She felt as if her lovely day had been ruined, the memory of brief triumphant womanhood sullied for ever. Mutinously she wanted to shout that she refused to be married off, to sob and wail that she was not ready for marriage. She wanted time, years, to bask in the sweetness of undemanding girlhood, a princess dismissing suitors who did not please her. She longed to escape again into her fantasy world, tearful child in need of parent's comfort and love, rather than mistress yearning for lover's arms.

Sickened, she felt the need to breathe fresh air, to take away the sour taste left by people like Judge Forbes. While the two men were in conversation, she slid out of her seat unobserved and, avoiding Eunice who had not noticed she had left the table, she slipped outside and away from the house.

The day had eased into an evening that promised to be fair and tranquil. The hills were hung with cloud-feathered wisps hiding their summits. Caitlin sighed, breathing deeply of the pure air, glad to be free, away from the stale odours of food, wine and tobacco smoke, for the men would now be lighting their long stemmed clay pipes. Here the air was fragrant with peat-smoke and heather drifting down from beyond the Sighe Stone.

Somewhere near at hand a dog-fox barked, its cry echoing strangely in the wind-free muted silence. She looked up into a sky where the star-candles had not yet been lit against the night, a sky like jade crystal, faintly echoing the cloud

59

banners, red and gold, of the approaching sunset.

Luxuriously, she stretched her arms above her head. How good it was to escape dull politics and domestic matters – and talk of marriage, which frightened her. In the normal way she was always willing to join in girls' gossip of marriage, but not of her own – and certainly not discussed like the sale of cattle at a summer fair.

Climbing up to the Sighe Stone, she cast aside the burden of this new womanhood worn like elegant but too-tight shoes. In the more comfortable and familiar role of childhood, she sat down, chewing a blade of new grass, and pondered the events of the day. Far below she watched the Cairn na Mabh, the stone that marked the mass grave of the plague victims of three hundred years ago, stalk the evening casting its great shadow across the fields, growing monstrous and sinister in the fast fading light.

From her bedroom window Caitlin often watched the same shining arc of stars that now appeared, fall down between the hollow of the hill and disappear into the land where the Macdonalds of Ardarroch lived, bearing the sunset in their midst. That the Macdonalds should be given in proportion to their wickedness the most lovely sunsets and the brightest crop of the stars, as if beauty bloomed on corruption seemed grossly unfair, as the colour drained from the Campbell's land and with sweeping splendour vanished into the forbidden territory of their enemy, leaving Glenlyon only the grey darkness.

Such sunsets radiant in their glory, haunted her, creeping over the hills, folding them into sleep, like landscapes leading into an enchanted kingdom whose warriors slumbered awaiting the summons of a king's hunting horn from a page of history as yet unwritten.

She longed with all her soul to follow that red and golden banner, even into the very jaws of forbidden Ardarroch, which looked vastly different from high Culdares Hill. A fearsome place with a narrow pass twisting away between the hills to the Black Wood of Rannoch. Fearsome but familiar too. Familiar as a melody heard once long ago and never quite obliterated from memory. Never quite lost.

As a child, she had begged Red Alistair to take her on one of those sunset journeys. He shook his head, laughing. How

60

to tell this grave innocent lass that the sunset passed over Ardarroch and far beyond the Western Isles, to drown in the great ocean each night.

'Some day,' she had told him, 'when I am grown up, when I am strong and brave with all I have learned from you, I will make the Campbells proud of me. I will slip over those hills some sunset evening, and walk right along their sky and down into their land.'

'Do not be daring such a thing,' Alistair had said sternly, 'for they will lock you into one of their dark prisons and we will never again be seeing you in Fortingall.'

'I can take care of myself.' And now she smiled at the memory for what she had intended to do when she had reached Ardarroch, she never had the slightest idea.

At that moment, as she looked down at Fortingall, the house grew faint, remote, for the people it held with their passions and problems had no part in her destiny. As if the thread that had bound her to life within its walls had suddenly snapped. No longer concerned with childhood fantasies of glowing sunsets, the steep path before her led into a fiercer stronger land where darkness and sorrow dwelt and great, great joy. Now for the first time in her short life, she was completely unafraid of Eunice. She flexed her hands, slim and shapely despite their toil, as if within them she held invisible power.

Power. Aye, that was what she felt flowing through her life-blood. She knew from the changes in her body that needed no mirror other than men's eyes, to tell her that she was now a woman and beautiful too. She could never be royal but as if the Sighe Stone had whispered the words to her, she guessed the secret of Mary Queen of Scots and the other legendary women of history, who had bent men to their will. Womanhood, life-bringing, fearless, surged through her, bringing strength and power. Power to be used wisely and well, for its secret was love. Love all-encompassing, love taken and love given, for the more that was given, the greater its return. Was that the secret, she thought in wonder, of Christ's parables? Was that what was meant by the miracle of the loaves and the fishes?

Love was eternal power. Not love of man alone, that was wasteful, but the deeper love of life which allied her to the greatest and the smallest of all living creatures, the perfect form in every detail of each flower and blade of grass that grew, each note of bird-song that soared into the highest heaven. She rested her hands upon the earth and felt the past of every living thing that had bloomed and withered, had breathed, loved life and died, every man and woman who had passed this way and touched this ground in brief sorrow or rapturous joy. Each had left some part of themselves and that unseen army was her ally, this harvest of understanding which she had come upon unawares was her strength and power, her birth-song to a newly discovered world.

And God was everywhere.

'Caitlin. Caitlin.' But the voice was Liam's.

She ran back down the hill towards the house where already the orange flames of candles gleamed brightly in the windows against the coming night.

'Come, our guests are ready to leave and would take their farewells of you.' Liam felt her trembling, thought she was afraid. 'What is wrong, child? What has frightened you out there?'

She looked at him sadly, wishing the blessing received could be shared with him, but conscious of her aunt's shadow hovering in the doorway, said: 'It grows dark and cold, father.'

Liam watched her with almost a parent's pride as, by his side, she curtseyed low to the guests. He felt other men's approving glances rest upon her, particularly Judge Forbes. And it pleased him, for she carried herself well and proud, despite apparel that was a disgrace. Her manners were regal, a matter for amazement, considering that she had been quite untutored in manners of style. He found himself wondering what a year at Meggernie Castle would do for her.

Too excited for sleep that night, Caitlin stared at the pale square of her window until a waning moon rose above the hills and wove a gossamer pale light over the scant furnishings. Far away she heard the swish of the trees like a woman's gown in the wind that had grown with the night. From somewhere in the yew-tree's great depths, there echoed the 'Ki-kwee-kwee' of a hunting owl.

Stirring restlessly, she heard again the sounds of the house at night, sounds which were never heard during the day. Scufflings and the creak of a floorboard, as if the old stones stirred and groaned in sleep.

She was thirsty. The food had been richer, more plentiful than the frugal table of everyday at Fortingall. As discomfort grew, sleep was impossible and she decided to go downstairs and fetch water from the ewer in the kitchen.

She climbed out of bed carefully so as not to disturb the sleeping Jean, and with no need for taper or candle in cloudless moonlight, glided downstairs. Suddenly she was halted by the unexpected whisper of voices. Could it be that old Alistair who slept in the box bed was still awake?

But there below her in the kitchen, Liam and Eunice sat at the table, a solitary guttering candle between them. They were unaware of her approach and something conspiratorial in their attitudes suggested an intruder might not be welcome at that moment.

'I like not this second sight. You say there have been other instances?'

'Many,' said Eunice in triumph. Pausing for the full effect to sink in, she added: 'And we might well ask ourselves, what other traits did she bring?'

'What mean you by that, mistress?' Liam's voice was quiet. Quiet but cold.

'We Campbells do not have the second sight. You know full well – Glencorrie, where *that* came from.'

Eunice's voice dropped and Caitlin's eagerness to overhear was her undoing, her foot on the edge of the stair slipped and she stumbled forward.

'So she's been listening again, has she?' Eunice's harsh laugh was followed by the sound of Liam's chair scraping the floor as he sprang across the room.

'What are you doing here, girl? Why are you not in your bed?' he demanded angrily.

As he reached her side, Caitlin saw his expression and she cowered against the balustrade, shielding her head from the blow which never came. Her terrified face halted Liam in his tracks.

'What is it, Caitlin, what do you want, child?'

She looked up at him amazed, realising that she must have mistaken anger for weariness, for although his voice sounded tired, it was also gentle, concerned.

'I am thirsty, father. I came down for some water.'

He regarded her sternly, brows down and silent, as if considering whether she lied. How much, dear God, had she heard? Then he nodded, as if satisfied and pointed to the ewer. 'Take it and then to bed, at once.'

At his unsmiling abruptness, she moved rapidly, while Eunice watched her, hardly-veiled victory in her glance.

If only the Macdonald brat had overheard all. If only she knew the truth. And heard it from Liam's lips. Then Eunice Stewart could never be blamed. She would be safe from his wrath, her promise unbroken.

'Goodnight, Father. Goodnight, Aunt.' Eunice did not glance in her direction and Liam's back remained turned from her.

'Goodnight, child.' But his voice was kind now, as if he smiled.

Eunice Stewart too lay awake long after Liam's footsteps walked past at her door without faltering. Her ambitions now lay far beyond Liam as lover. She saw herself as his wife, Lady Glencorrie. On that she was determined, having taken it for granted ever since Mairi died. To neighbours she insisted that Liam had begged her to come and take care of his motherless daughter and to Liam himself she hinted that Caitlin wished to have her stay.

On the day she moved her possessions and her two children into the house at Fortingall, in her own mind the marriage knot had been already tied between them. Once this was secured by law and sanctified by the church, she would find a way to rid them both of Caitlin's presence.

A few searching questions revealed that Liam had no plans for remarriage, nor what she most dreaded, had he lost his heart to some young Ulsterwoman. She had little time to bask in this satisfaction, however, for at the end of the first week of his return to Fortingall, she found herself witnessing an extraordinary change in Liam's attitude to Caitlin.

Their secret alliance over the Macdonald brat was, she realised, at an end and, while she, Eunice, kept his house, washing his linen, baking his bread, a wife to him in every way but the one she craved, between the white sheets of his bed, he now spent every moment with the child he had once ignored.

Not prone to imagining, she felt that they moved in a kind of aura, there was a bloom of shining light that made the air about them dance too. It sickened her to notice how their sudden laughter diminished the years between them. At thirty-two Liam's years lay lightly upon him, a golden-haired youth still at first glance, happy, light-hearted.

Eunice's eyes narrowed as she regarded Caitlin's taut body, budding breasts against a gown which had fitted her only yesterday, but overnight was short in sleeves and skirt. She traced hands downward over her overblown body, breasts that hung like waterskins, large feet and thickly veined hands and heavy legs, features fast fading under the sagging contours and extra chins of middle age. As for her face, how could forty compete with fifteen?

Those two out there. Their laughter, their shining faces — like lovers, they were.

And Caitlin was no longer afraid of her. One day when the men were absent, she felt a desire to work off some of her ill-nature on Caitlin, regarding a matter of burnt bannocks.

She struck out fiercely and the next moment screamed, as Caitlin seized her wrist and held it painfully tight. 'Aunt Eunice, the baking is not my concern.' Her voice was calm although she did not relinquish her grip.

'Let me go, at once.'

'Only when you have listened to me for a change. You are a hateful, unjust woman and I will no longer be the victim of your spite.'

'Spite? You impudent wretch. Liam Campbell shall hear of this.'

'Hear me out, first. If you ever raise your hand to me again, I give you due warning, I shall hit you back, and hard too.'

And Eunice, released suddenly, staggered back against the chair, in time to hear smothered laughter from her ungrateful daughter Jean, sniggering in the corner and nodding her simple head approvingly.

When she ran to Liam with the story, she expected sympathy, indignation, hoped to see suitable punishment inflicted on Caitlin.

'Was she truly insolent?' Liam asked almost dreamily. 'I will speak to her about it.'

'Speak to her? That is not enough. I want her chastised – immediately.'

Liam frowned. 'If the lass was truly innocent, and you have always insisted that the baking is your province, mistress, then your chastisement of Caitlin was unfair. She had a perfect right to defend herself. So let us hear no more about it, if you please.'

And he remembered how often he had witnessed Caitlin cowering away from her step-aunt in the past. Red Alistair had also hinted at bad things done to the lass in his absence. Liam sighed. He would have felt it difficult to interfere in the matter without evidence, but now he had such from Eunice's own lips and was heartily glad that Caitlin had asserted her own rights.

For Eunice, worse was to come.

Caitlin was now to be Glencorrie's heiress. And there was that old fool Alistair nan Creach hovering by, full of simpering importance and useless advice, watching Liam teach her how to handle a pistol.

To Eunice's acid comments that the girl's proper place was in the kitchen, and that it needed a man to heir Glencorrie, Liam merely smiled indulgently: 'The title can be handed down the distaff side.'

Caitlin laughed in disbelief. 'I would like that.'

'Then you will be needing better targets than marked stones on dykes to shoot at,' shouted Red Alistair delightedly.

'Must I go to war?' she asked, looking from one to the other to see if they teased her.

'No, child. You would stay at home.' Liam put an arm about her shoulders. 'You need not worry. The clansmen would fight in your name.'

'I would forbid any to fight, if I were chief,' she said solemnly.

'But your husband will fight for you,' said Liam.

'Husband?' Caitlin's voice was shocked.

'In a year or two,' said Liam echoing the words of the neighbours who thought to comment on this new happy Glencorrie, his bonny daughter constantly at his side: 'Aye,

Glencorrie, that's a fine looking lass you have, enjoy her while you may. Any day now, some braw young man will be stealing her away from you.'

They were right, he had been betrothed to Mairi when they were fifteen years old. He would have to think about it. But not now. For the time being he would rejoice in the happiness that every day held for him with her presence. He had not felt this young in years, his marriage though happy had been tinged with sadness and anxiety over Mairi's health. How long was it since he had experienced the bouyancy of carefree youth, the feeling that he had not a care in the world, and that this newfound happiness must last for ever. Had he ever felt like this in his whole life before? And the solemnity that marked his nature vanished in a cloud of merriment for a world grown young too, where birds sang and flowers danced in sunlight. He wanted to skip and dance with them, rejoicing in his own re-birth, sure for once, that God was on his side.

One evening later in the same week, the door opened and a tall young man stood framed against the sun.

'Stephen? Stephen — ' Eunice threw down her sewing and rushed over to him.

Jean too threw herself into her brother's arms, half-laughing, half-in-tears. Amid the gabble of conversation where everyone asked questions and no one bothered to wait for answers, Stephen managed at last to explain why he was not in Aberdeen. The minister who he was to assist had died. The new minister appointed had ideas of his own, young and sturdy, he could run the parish single-handed.

'What will you do now?'

Stephen smiled. 'Await what God sends. Meanwhile, I shall help Uncle Liam, for I write a tolerable hand.'

Liam's mind had already raced ahead. Such services would be invaluable at Meggernie as he sorted out with increasing tedium, Sir Robert's muddled finances. But he discovered that he had lost Stephen's attention, drawn to a new arrival. A tall girl with long windblown black hair who had been locking up the hens for the night.

'Caitlin? Cousin, is it you?' Stephen laughed delightedly and Liam was amused to see them shake hands gravely in the cautious manner of strangers. But during the next few hours he was acutely aware that Stephen's eyes followed Caitlin, clearly astonished as he himself had been, at the transformation a two-year absence could make. And in the days ahead, Liam intercepted shy enquiring glances between the two, suggesting that each was perfectly aware of the other's thoughts and not displeased by the discovery. It brought to Liam a pang of isolation – and desolation.

Red Alistair shared in the delight of Stephen's homecoming. 'We will see a match there, lord, make no mistake. All the signs are evident, do you not see it when they are together?' His chortle of pleasure ignored Liam's irritable shrug. 'And an excellent match it would be, seeing that they are only cousins by marriage – no blood kin. A fine son, he will make you.'

Liam bore it patiently and said nothing. True, a minister was considered a great matrimonial catch, next in the hierarchy to the local gentry. And yet, and yet –

'He is a fine set up lad.'

Liam could not deny that either. Stephen had been exceeding plain as child and boy, but such ugly ducklings had a habit of surprising their elders by turning into remarkably elegant swans. There was little resemblance to his mother except about the strong jaw and nose. The indefinite sandy hair had resolved itself into the glossy brown of a chestnut, and eyes muddy in youth had also deepened to the same attractive hue. He observed with amusement how Stephen in clerical bands, briefly deputising for Minister Blair absent at a family funeral, created a considerable flutter among the females of the parish. Church-going was considerably more pleasant, and sermons less tedious, if the minister who gazed down on them was also young and handsome.

Red Alistair's match-making ideas were very soon shared by their Fortingall neighbours and the old man was amazed and a little hurt by Eunice's hostility. When she stormed off in a rage, after one of his teasing rejoinders, he murmured to Liam: 'What on earth has got into the woman? It is only right and proper, after all, youth must go to youth,' he added with a shake of his head, 'and whatever we might think or plan, whether we approve or disapprove will not make any

68

odds if they have made up their minds. Anyone can see how the lad is smitten with her.'

Liam held his peace about Eunice's behaviour. She had never accepted Caitlin. He sighed. Once they had been silent allies in their secret feelings about this alien child. And he guessed the nature of her distress. She had no desire to see her son married to one of the hated Macdonald clan.

'And what think you of this talk of a match between your nephew and her?' she asked.

Liam was aware once again that she never referred to Caitlin by name. It was 'she', 'her' or 'you', one might refer to some anonymous domestic beast.

'I have given the matter little thought, mistress. After all, it is merely an old man's romantic notion.'

Eunice's hands crashed down upon the table, as she sprang to her feet. 'If you so believe, then you are totally blind, Glencorrie.' Fighting for control, hands now clasped together, their knuckles white, she added: 'My son is besotted with her and he is twenty years old, and ripe for marriage. He has hinted as much to me – dear God, I would rather see him ... ' As violently she turned her back on Liam and stared out of the window, he did not have to ask her to complete the words.

'Come, let us not be too hasty.'

She swung round to face him again. 'Hasty, is it? If it comes to marriage, I will not stand by and see my son marry her without knowing the truth – the truth, Glencorrie. You know what I mean, *all of the truth*.' And she stormed out and left him sitting at the table, a very wretched man indeed, as he considered what the nightmare disclosure of Caitlin's birth would mean to everyone and to himself in particular.

Supposing she chose to return to her own people, as was her right. What then? In that moment his: 'God help us all' was heartfelt, as he saw the foundations of the peaceful life he had established through the years shattered, and the smouldering fued with Ardarroch sparked into blazing fury again.

Chapter IV

One afternoon, as Liam rode back from Chesthill, Caitlin rushed towards him across the field. Breathless, she pointed to the hill beyond the Sighe Stone.

'The white hare, the white hare, I have just seen her.'

The white hare was a legend. He who caught her – alive – would have good fortune and happiness for as long as he could keep her captive.

'That does not say a great deal for the good fortune and happiness of the hare,' Caitlin had said, who loved all creatures. Liam's more practical approach considered that hares, in their more mundane summer coats, were considered excellent eating, and their skins never went wrong either. He did not give a second thought to following where Caitlin led. Since capture alive depended on stalking their prey, they took no hound with them.

Before they had gone fifty yards, Liam began to suspect that the white hare was another figment of the 'lively imagination' that Eunice sneered at.

'Look, over there, beside that tree.'

And there it was. So close, he caught a glimpse of a red eye turned quizzically in their direction. For an instant the creature stood quite still, paw upraised indecisively and then it was away, bounding towards the shelter of the spinney.

Up past the Sighe Stone, across boulders, stream and ditch, they pursued it. Both were now wild with excitement, their quarry temptingly within range. The distance between them diminished to twelve feet then ten. They had it trapped. Suddenly it swerved from their outstretched hands, leaping ahead, a ghostly white shape in the gathering evening dusk.

Liam was finding it difficult to keep pace with Caitlin who

had developed a new turn of speed. Laughing, she bounded away after the hare, moth-like in the gloaming, her flying feet sending trickles of stone slithering down towards him.

He stopped, winded. 'Caitlin. It's no use, you'll never catch her now. Come back.'

Only her distant laughter and another trickle of stones came for answer. Annoyed and resentful that she, a mere girl, could leave him, a man in the prime of life and just past thirty, far behind and out of breath, he struggled after her.

They were now high up the mountain side heavy in the silence and sombre chill of rapidly approaching evening. Storm clouds hid the summit and Liam was disturbingly familiar with that oppressive silence and cold. Unless he was very much mistaken, the ominous signs indicated that they would soon be in the grip of a raging blizzard.

'Caitlin,' he called, hollowing his hands. 'Caitlin, come back.'

He listened. No answer, not even a trickle of stones. And panic seized him. He climbed sharply, scrambling upward. Hampered by shortness of breath and a stabbing pain in his side, he hesitated long enough to scan a hillside empty of all but boulders. In the grey light they assumed the sinister shapes of crouching men, watching him.

Where was the girl? Superstitious terror seized him that she might have vanished into thin air, that the spirits of the mountains, those giants of Red Alistair's legends had carried her into their stronghold to keep her prisoner there. Forty years might pass before she emerged again, according to such tales, still the lass who had vanished, to find her father a heartbroken old man of seventy.

'Cait–lin.'

Was that her voice, or an echo?

'Cait–lin.'

The echo turned into the wind's moan as the first pinpoints of icy rain dashed into his face. 'Cait–lin.'

'Here – over here.' Her voice was faint, far off, but he headed thankfully in its direction. 'Where are you?'

'Down here.' He beheld a pale face, a cloud of dark hair staring up at him from the bottom of a twenty-foot scree.

'Take care, Father.' And his heart almost stopped beating when he reached her and realised that the frail stem of a

71

protruding root she clutched lay between her and the steep gulley fifty feet below. Mercifully she was unhurt.

By the time Liam had made footholds in the scree strong enough to support them both back onto firm ground, the whole brunt of the storm had unleashed itself. The upper reaches of Glenlyon's hills had vanished under clouds like great ghost armies swirling down upon them, the rain sheets leaping upon them with arrows of icy needles. In a few moments they were drenched, unable to breathe.

Worse was to come. All familiar landmarks below them had disappeared, obliterated by heavy mist that came down from the upper corries, the limits of their world reduced to visible scree and bog cotton a man's height away.

They could go neither up nor down. They were trapped. Trapped up here until the storm lifted.

Already the first deadly chill ate into their bones. They could not stay out in the open, lest they freeze to death. They must find shelter and, as a corner of the storm twitched aside a curtain of mist, Liam thought he saw shelter.

A darker mass visible against the mountain side. An overhang of rock? As the mist closed in again, he took Caitlin's hand and dragged her in its direction. As they ran, the rain thudded into them stinging their faces, smarting their eyes. Fighting for breath, they dived gratefully beneath the rock and found themselves at the mouth of a deep cave.

'Where are we?' gasped Caitlin, wringing water from her hair.

Liam had lost all sense of direction, although in normal weather he would have sworn that he knew the glen's every twist and turn above Fortingall. Now he knew, groaning inwardly, that they could be anywhere between Culdares Hill and Alt Odhar.

'I'm c-cold,' shivered Caitlin, snuggling into his side. 'What are we going to do?'

'You know fine well what we must do, Caitlin,' he said sharply, angry with himself for allowing her headlong pursuit of the white hare to trap them in a violent summer storm. 'We must bide here in patience until the mist lifts.'

'Oh no.' Her teeth were chattering. 'Let me come inside your plaid.'

He wrapped it round her and she continued to shudder

against his side as they sat on the floor, soft under its ancient carpet of moss. Backs resting against the rock wall, they were reasonably comfortable and good humour restored, Liam hugged her shivering body to his side. As his warmth seeped into her frozen limbs, a memory, a very old memory stirred. Once long ago his warm body, his naked breast which lay under her hand, had restored her to life.

'Still cold? That better?'

'Much better. Father – I had a strange feeling there – that all this has happened before.'

'Then you must have dreamed it. I would never been so foolish, child, to let you lead me on a wild hare chase. More like one of old Alistair's legends. When I couldn't find you back there, I wondered if one of the old mountain giants had stolen you,' he added lightly, stroking back her hair.

'Would you have been sad?'

'Of course. After all my work preparing you as heiress to Glencorrie,' he laughed, knowing that the true reason, which he could never tell her, was this new found love and hope she had brought into his sterile world.

'Where are we now, do you think?' she asked.

'We must be somewhere close to the summit, judging by the weather.'

'We have travelled all that distance.' At her delight Liam bit back the words of reproach.

'But we did lose the hare. I wonder where she is now.'

Liam had forgotten the damned hare, cause of their present woeful condition. 'Safe in her burrow,' he wanted to add 'as we should have been,' instead of: 'She probably vanished into the mountainside. Like old Alistair's magic.'

'Do you really think that she was a magic hare?' And with a reversal to childhood, she added eagerly: 'Tell me about it.'

His attempt at sarcasm had been lost. She was truly a child still, wanting some fairy story, to shiver at a gory tale.

'I cannot tell you any such stories,' he said brusquely.

'Alistair will know, he's sure to know. He knows about everything.' Liam, did not reply. 'Will the mist lift soon?'

'We cannot move from here until it does.'

'Make it go away, Father. I'm hungry,' she shivered, putting her arms around his waist.

Liam grinned into the dusk. Even if he lacked Red

Alistair's legends, at least he was supposed to have magic powers over the weather. 'Are you warm now? Good. Then my advise would be try to sleep for a while.'

'Mmm,' she sounded sleepy too as she yawned. Liam closed his eyes and settled down. Better that they both slept the storm out, warmed by each other's body heat.

As he dozed, he had strange dreams. He saw Mairi and relived the sweetness they had known together. He held her close and she whispered that her death had been but a cruel dream. And he believed her. He awoke to hear her moaning – oh no, dear God – not those last hours of her life, not those to be lived all over again.

It was Caitlin who had moaned. Eyes open, thankful it was not the wraith of Mairi he held, he asked: 'What is wrong?'

'My feet, my feet. I think they are frozen.'

The plaid had slipped from around her legs. Kneeling beside her he took her feet in his hands and chafed them, rubbing them hard until she said:

'Oh, that hurts.'

'Feeling has come back, eh?' he grinned and touched her ankles and knees, frail, bird-boned, cold as ice. He rubbed them until they too warmed beneath his hands.

'More, more,' she murmured sleepily. 'I am so cold. Cold all over. Oh, that is good.'

Higher, higher ...

'Oh. Ohhh,' she squirmed under his hands thrusting her body forward.

Suddenly he stopped, horrified. His hands had reached up over her buttocks, they had slipped round the small waist and encountered sweet mounds of breasts – a woman's breasts, with nipples that responded to his touch. This was not the child he had seen bathed and dressed by Mairi. This creature under his questing, excited hands was a woman, a stranger, hauntingly beautiful and desirable. He had lived celibately since Mairi died, three long years of a heart and body in mourning which stifled all desire for any woman's comfort and love.

He heard her breathing, fast now, her small pleasurable moans. Longing, longing for her – his body hardened, yearning, aching for release. He wanted this child, this woman, who was no daughter of his. Oh, dear God, how he wanted her. And forbidden images of wild delight crammed his mind. After all, the act would not be incestuous, for she was not of his begetting. But temptation brought its own reckoning. Take her and with innocence destroyed, he would have to put at rest her terrible guilt by telling her the truth.

The truth of her birth. And no fleeting hour of pleasure could cancel an act of destruction and violation, worse than incest.

He sat up suddenly, slapped her legs, ashamed of his carnal thoughts. Heart still hammering, aware of his physical discomfort, as he lifted her to her feet and she leaned heavily against him, afraid she might also be aware of his manhood aroused he said sharply: 'Look – the mist has lifted. Quickly now, we had better go while we may.'

He could see like a cat in the dark, but what if the mist had not lifted beyond the cave? What if there were no lights visible like beacons gleaming from windows in the glen, to lead them safe home to Fortingall?

What if they were forced to return and spend the rest of the night in this dark cave? His flesh could no longer be held responsible for such temptation, and for what might happen then.

No daughter of yours, remember, no daughter of yours, whispered his demon.

As they walked a few yards beyond the cave, he breathed a sigh of relief. God had seen and understood. There was the answer to his prayers. The night was intensely cold and dark but the clouds twitched aside like a raised curtain to reveal an arch of stars. He needed no compass to find his way now, only that one guiding north star which hung above them.

'Wait, wait,' said Caitlin. 'I have dropped the pin from my shawl – it must be back there in the cave.'

The pin had been Mairi's. As she raced back up the hill, he followed her cautiously, waiting outside, wondering what new trickery his thwarted demons had in store.

'I cannot find it,' she called. 'Help me.'

The place where they had lain was still warm under his searching hands. And there was the Glencorrie pin. She took it from him with a cry of delight. There was more light now and he looked round the cave, saw that it extended further back than they had realised.

Something white lay in one corner. White and shining.

'What is it?' Caitlin asked.

'The bones of some animal, I expect.'

'Oh, do you think this was a wolf's lair?'

'Perhaps.' He went closer, blocking her view with his shoulders. The bones curled up were human.

There was a rotted plaid and the skull grinned at him cheerfully, its teeth excellent. But the dirk in the ribs indicated that the man had died by violence. Either murdered as he lay there, or having crawled into the cave to die.

'Is it a sheep?'

He swung her round and out of the cave. 'Yes, must have wandered in out of a storm. Been there for long enough, I expect.'

'Oh, the poor thing.'

Liam was disinclined for conversation and rather brusque, Caitlin thought, as they walked back down the hill, where in the safe world of Fortingall, lambs bleated and peat smoke, from comfortable turf houses, curled into a tranquil evening sky.

As they reached the Sighe Stone, Jean ran out of the square doorway of the house to greet them. Assured of Liam's safety, Eunice greeted Caitlin with a scowl. Hearing the tale of her misadventures on the scree, she silently wished that the girl had broken her neck and that Liam had returned to her alone. But Jean was overjoyed, hugging and kissing them both, and Eunice watched her daughter sourly.

Liam rode up to the cave next day. He was curious. Was this an unsolved murder, someone who had disappeared? These were troubled times, easy for a man to vanish and leave no trace. He felt impelled to return but had a superstitious dread about doing so. He had begun to pay dearly for the events of that evening, by a starved body whose dreams haunted him with the forbidden joy of fulfilment. And the face was no longer that of Mairi, but of Caitlin.

In daylight the cave was unprepossessing enough, but the skeleton was that of a young man, his teeth good, his scalp still patchily covered with black hair. Liam touched the dirk with distaste. It came away in his hands as did the rotted plaid. He carried both out to full light and saw that the dirk was Campbell in origin. The plaid, as he had suspected, was Macdonald. He sat down suddenly, the dirk in his hand could have been his own. He had one identical to it. As for the murdered man, he could have been sent across time and space, a demand for retribution, a terrible reminder of the debt that Liam Campbell one day must pay for stealing the child Ardarroch had died to protect.

Liam flung down plaid and dirk and rode from the scene, never glancing back in his panic flight, for fear that he would see the grinning skeleton leaning against the overhang of rock, or assuming flesh to avenge his murder.

As he ran to where his tethered horse waited, the ghostly pebbles showering down at his heels, became the foosteps of the man whose presence in dreams he could never escape, Caitlin's true parent.

As for Caitlin, the longings Liam had aroused in her, his closeness to her flesh aroused a deeper memory touching the moment where time itself began, a memory so distant that any attempt at reconstruction in her own mind became an intangible blur. There was fire, terror, and the great peace-calm of oblivion under the growing spread of death's cold angel wings. But Liam had dashed them aside. Gathering her to his warm breast, he had given her back to life.

For that moment of resurrection, there were no words but the desire to lose herself in him, to be utterly possessed and lost within his arms.

Confused, often fearful, she began spending more time with Stephen. Grateful for the company of a young man with whom she could find the release of hugs and kisses, she tried to convince herself that here was an accessible lover who could somehow fill that hollow ache within her, the ache of knowing that she wanted much more than that. Much more that no man save Liam could give her.

So it was that during the wedding party of Innkeeper Fergus's daughter, Liam found Stephen kissing Caitlin. Eyes closed, head thrown back, she was obviously enjoying such attentions. Minister of God or no, Stephen was still a man with a man's lusts, and Liam leaped forward and flung him to the ground.

Stephen picked himself up and ashen-faced disappeared without a word. A moment later, Eunice was demanding to know why Liam had hit her son.

'He was but kissing her. What do you expect to happen? It is time we were rid of her.' She stared at his expressionless face. 'Before God, Glencorrie, what is getting into you?'

Liam could have told her. Loneliness, lust even, the need for a lover to eradicate his obsession for that child-woman doomed for ever to regard him as father. He was fond of Stephen, but guessed from his violent reaction that any man who touched Caitlin would fill him with explosive hatred. A sobering thought indeed, that any suitor for his supposed daughter might arouse murder in his heart.

Eunice took his arm and led him back into the inn with its sounds of merrymaking to the strain of a lively jig. Candlelight and her new yellow gown became her. 'Come, do not be surly. Dance with me,' she pouted.

Eunice danced well. He was surprised to find her light-footed, despite her heavy body. Holding her close in the dance's measure, her tender smiles were for him alone and the naked desire she no longer tried to hide, proclaimed louder than words the truth he had already known when Mairi lived. She had been his for the taking at any time he had so willed.

His understanding and compassion grew in proportion to the amount of *usquebaugh* she poured into his glass, as she stared into his face with wanton eyes. He knew everything there was to know about the aching loneliness of an empty bed, night after long night, month after long month, year after endless year.

And so all things came together that night for Liam. Eunice needed no second whispered bidding to come to his bed. But dawn brought its own reckoning and he knew that for what he had received – in his own mind intended as a kindness, a mutual release for two hungry people – there was a reckoning. A price plain and unmistakeable as if it had been blazed across the bedchamber walls. And that price was marriage.

Sober now, Liam remembered little of those hours of dark passion, no more than a drunken soldier feels for a tavern

78

whore. He was vaguely aware of dissatisfaction, that Eunice lacked Mairi's warmth and tenderness as a lover. The fact remained that he was trapped. That one night of illicit love had cost him his freedom of choice, for Eunice's triumph allowed for no other interpretation than the sharing of his bed as a prelude to marriage. Liam was hers. And she would make certain that all rivals were excluded from his life.

Liam dreaded breaking the news to Caitlin.

'I have something to tell you. Your aunt Eunice – we are to marry.' After many rehearsals of the words, he was taken aback at her unemotional response. He did not realise that to her marriage meant sleeping in the same bed in the manner of young brothers and sisters, as she shared a bed with her cousin Jean.

Since Mairi died, her aunt had taken a wife's place in Fortingall. Caitlin did not consider the significance of Liam and Eunice sleeping in different rooms. To her marriage was cooking, cleaning for a man. Bearing children was something that God gave in His mysterious way, a reward to some, a curse and sorrow to others. Her main preoccupation was whether her aunt might be less of a virago with a wedding ring on her finger. That she might be kinder in Liam's absence, no longer saving her sweetness for her own children and for him.

Jean hugged her. 'Now we will be real sisters, as well as cousins. And Stephen will be your brother.'

'How will you like having a new mother?' asked Stephen sharply. In the new feelings Caitlin aroused, there was scant room for brotherly love. But since his return to Fortingall, he had observed his mother and Caitlin, even his sister, seemed ready to idolise Liam Campbell. Liam made him feel insignificant, jealous even.

'What was your father like?' asked Caitlin as he helped her feed the hens.

'A kind good man,' he said realising that such honesty betrayed his mother's version of her marriage.

'Truly? You never speak of him. Were you sorry when he died?'

Stephen nodded. 'Very sorry.' He had been ten years old when he saw his father dead in bed, who had, but a half hour earlier, joked and laughed with him in the harvest field. His mother tried to hustle him out of the bedchamber where her cousin, a handsome ruffian called Moray Campbell, was pulling a shirt over his nakedness.

'Your father came in and said he was tired, he would rest for a while. Cousin Moray had come by unexpectedly, and we were having a bite to eat, when there was a noise. We found him on the floor – dead. He had tried to get to the ewer of water, Moray lifted him on to the bed.' She had spoken breathlessly, in a series of rapid jerking sentences.

'Is that why Cousin Moray is changing his shirt, did it get wet?'

His mother nodded vigorously. 'That is so,' and she smiled, ruffling his hair, almost grateful, he thought. Later, when Cousin Moray had slipped out by the back door before shocked neighbours began to arrive, she whispered, 'I would that you do not mention Cousin Moray's visit. It is better we both forget, for it might go ill with him. He is in trouble with the law again.'

That did not surprise Stephen since Moray's dubious activities were mostly outside the law. As he grew older, the scene in the bedroom so simply explained, became oddly sinister, especially when he learned that his mother and his cousin had once been betrothed. Considering his father's flawless health and strength, had there been a fight and had Cousin Moray killed him?

'Does the marriage please you?' Caitlin was asking, staring into his thoughtful face.

'Oh Caitlin, for pity's sake, let us accept the marriage and do stop asking so many questions.' At her hurt expression, he put his arm around her, anxious now for more of the kisses she enjoyed and did not refuse. It was as well, he thought, for already determined to marry her, he had resolved to stop at kisses until they were wed.

As for Caitlin, her loving, caring father had vanished and on the rare occasions when they were alone together, she thought she detected a return to his former indifference.

Then suddenly the small cloud which threatened, vanished, to reveal the laughing loving father again. Of course he still loved her, his black moods had been merely preoccupation with matrimonial plans although she considered her step-aunt far too old for thoughts of remarriage.

Liam and Eunice were wed that Sunday, by Minister Blair in the presence of neighbours well disposed towards this long-overdue match. As they left the church, Eunice nodded to where Caitlin and Stephen wandered through the kirkyard, heads close in deep conversation, with Jean trailing behind them. 'He lusts after her.' Eunice missed. 'See how she encourages him. People have remarked upon it. She must leave Fortingall.'

Life without Caitlin so soon. Liam's eyes followed the couple bleakly. With a wife of his own to keep him safe from temptation, he had hoped to keep her at Fortingall. Now he saw a sad procession of empty years stretching ahead. Yet Eunice's suggestion was wise, the right one, but for the wrong reason. As for Stephen lusting after Caitlin, he closed his mind to such images of indecency, hoping they existed solely in his new wife's imagination.

'Well, husband, what say you?'

'She is young still for marriage.'

'A great girl, touching fifteen? Where are your eyes? Is it possible you have not observed her shape. She has outgrown two of Jean's gowns, her breasts bursting her bodice, indecent it is.'

Bursting. Indecent. Liam looked at her, how coarse she could be.

'I do not know what would have happened to your house, had you not persuaded me to marry you and take an interest in the girl's appearance and her future,' she said lightly, for both of them knew it was not true.

I know what would have happened, thought Liam, opening the door for his bride to enter, Caitlin and I would have been happy together in her childlike world of fantasy. But that was not true either. He would have wanted more than an insubstantial soul marriage with Caitlin. His dreams were still haunted by those moments in the cave together, and he knew that his love would have demanded flesh of her flesh, bone of her bone.

'You must indeed be getting old, husband,' said Eunice, briskly leading the way upstairs, 'when you no longer recognise that youth belongs to youth.'

Liam was deeply offended. He did not consider himself

81

old at thirty-two, especially when Eunice herself was touching forty. He regarded the bridal bed bleakly and with rather less anticipation of its delights than might have been expected from a new bridegroom.

For Eunice awakening from a week of less than satisfactory nights of married bliss, suffering through anguished days of her only son's infatuation for Caitlin, sickened rage threatened to engulf her. Did Liam not have eyes to see, as everyone else did, that the 'child' as he called her was now a woman and beautiful too? Eunice's mirror told her that she could not compete with such a rival. True, she was Liam's wife, he belonged to her. She had something of him that Caitlin could never hope to possess. Each night he slept at her side. And when she put out her hands and touched him, his body was beautiful and it was hers. Hers alone – but she also recognised sadly that his spirit was not. His spirit still roamed free, well beyond her possession or understanding.

If only she could be rid of Caitlin. She looked at Jean, her own daughter with distaste. At seventeen, her monthly courses of womanhood had not yet begun. A child still, despite herbs and simples recommended by sympathetic neighbours. A simpleton, whose permanently vague manner and smiling nods would disappear instantly if any dare utter criticism of her beloved Caitlin. Oh yes, her eyes could flash fire then, and tears flow too.

'That is untrue, my Caitlin would never do – or say – or think … ' And so on. Eunice had been forced to whip Jean soundly in the past for making her mother into a liar, but such punishment availed nothing. Now she knew that not only had Caitlin stolen her husband and her daughter's affections, she had stolen Stephen from her too.

As for Stephen, once he had been her ally. Encouraged by hints about his rights as his uncle's heir, he had bullied and tormented Caitlin, but the University and his Christian beliefs had changed all that. Now his handsome face burned with rosy anger at the slightest criticism of this adorable new stepsister he had discovered.

Constantly observing Liam and Caitlin, a dark seed of suspicion was sown in her mind. Affectionate glances, a lingering hand's touch – were they already guilty lovers awaiting their chance to betray her? Had that Macdonald brat wormed her way into his heart by unnatural means? Was witchcraft the answer to her power over men, she thought enviously watching a group of Fortingall lads who never gave Jean a second glance, crowding to Caitlin's side, grinning like apes, hanging upon her every word. Should she whisper her fear into Minister Blair's ear? The temptation was great.

Then a small incident occurred which changed her mind. Liam had obviously forgotten all about the hated Macdonalds and she shuddered to remember his fury when, at some minor misdemeanour, she had whispered after the retreating Caitlin: 'We know where she takes that from.'

Liam's hand had been raised against her, and lowered, just in time. 'We have only your word against my daughter.' His face was composed, his voice tightly controlled.

'*Your* daughter,' she shrieked contemptuously.

'Yes, my daughter. As far as you – and Fortingall – and the Campbells – are concerned, she is the child that Mairi bore me. Your senses must be crazed, wife,' he added with a mocking smile that held no warmth, 'To suggest that I would harbour a Macdonald of Ardarroch under my roof. It must be that you are dreaming.' But he was no longer smiling as he leaned across the table and seized her wrist. 'I would never have married you, Eunice Stewart, and I would still turn you from my door this day – aye, without one single qualm – should you so much as breath such fantasies to any living person.'

There was no mistaking the threat, which she knew he would not hesitate to carry out. She had trespassed on to forbidden territory and had come face to face with the truth she had always known in her own heart: that she could never be first in Liam's affections.

As long as Caitlin lived.

Increasingly of late, she found herself remembering how easy it had been to rid herself of her hated old husband. Alive, shouting at her, seizing Moray who was in bed with her, and the next moment still on the ground, where her blow with Moray's pistol had cracked his skull. She had been terrified by Stephen's unexpected appearance but his innocence and a few of her own tears had added validity to her story of an apoplexy, his head striking the stone hearth as he fell.

She had killed once and got away with it. Many times in Caitlin's childhood she had been tempted, deterred by the watchful presence of Alistair nan Creach. Devoted to Caitlin, he would be harder to deceive than a ten-year old boy.

On the next occasion when Caitlin accompanied him to Chesthill, Liam questioned her about Stephen: 'I prefer him now, for I did not like him much as a boy,' she said. 'He was unkind, he bullied me and pulled my hair.'

'And now?'

She shrugged. 'Now, he loves me and I can do with him whatever I wish. I can bend him to my will,' she added gently.

Liam was ill-pleased at this secret expression of a woman's power and dominance over another human creature. 'How so?'

'Oh *you* know, Stephen will do anything for me. If I asked him to run the length of Meggernie and bring me back a solitary snowdrop growing on the braes there, he would go, without a single question or a moment's hesitation.'

'Do you love him?' Liam interrupted impatiently, hardly daring to hear her answer:

'Of course I do.'

It was worse than he had imagined. His voice unsteady, he asked, 'Will you marry him then – in a year or two?'

'Marry Stephen?' Her eyes widened as if such a thought had never entered her mind. 'Oh no. That is not what you and Aunt Eunice intend for me, is it?' Her voice was agitated and amazed he beheld her eyes filling with sudden tears.

'It is not. But you said you loved him.'

Caitlin closed her eyes. 'I love Stephen, and Jean,' she explained patiently and hesitated. In strict honesty she could not add Eunice. 'I love them because they are my cousins.'

'And your father?' he demanded lightly, having learned to say the word without hauntings of that other long-dead image from Ardarroch, who lived and grew steadily each day in Caitlin's eyes and sometimes stared out at him with whispers of a reckoning still to come.

Caitlin hugged his arm. 'It is not the same kind of love at all. They do not belong to me as blood kin – as you do. If I lost them, I should survive.' She paused, looked at him critically as if examining every feature of his countenance, aware that of late some change had taken place between them, so subtle she could not find words to describe it, that would not shock or offend.

'Dearest Father,' she whispered, 'if I lost you, my heart would wither and die inside me. Oh, if you were Stephen, and possible to me as husband, then I would marry you tomorrow.'

Her words deprived him of speech. How easy it would have been, dear God, how easy she made it sound. And roughly to hide his own emotion, he said: 'That is all very well, but you are a child and when you are my age, I will be an old man. That is the law of life. No creature can hope to have parents for the full span of their own lifetime. That is why God gives us children.'

'I hope I shall have children some day.' Wistfully she added: 'Must I have a husband also?'

'Generally speaking, that is the custom.'

Caitlin sighed. Babies came with marriage, like rewards for good behaviour. Those who produced babies without marriage were treated like lepers, cast out by their families, their disgrace and humiliation stressed publicly by Minister Blair in a thundering sermon of hellfire and brimstone.

'After all you are no longer my sole responsibility. I have a wife and a family who need me too.' Even to his own ears, his words sounded cruel. God forgive me, for I lie, he said to himself, avoiding the pain in her eyes. You are the only being in this world that I worship and adore. For Eunice he felt lust and once satisfied, forgot her existence until the next time her questing hands aroused him.

Caitlin, oh Caitlin. He watched her walk away from him back to the house, saw defeat and misery in the young shoulders. He yearned to rush to her side then, take her in his arms, cradle her head against his shoulder and promise thus to hold her against all the world's disillusions.

There was only one answer to this dangerous state of emotions between them. Eunice was right. Caitlin must leave Fortingall. And soon. For her sake, for his sake – and for the many innocent people, born Glencorrie Campbells and Ardarroch Macdonalds, whose peaceful lives would be irrevocably destroyed if the truth was not buried deep and lost for ever.

Caitlin, his heart cried after her. Forgive me, forgive me.

Chapter V

There came a day no different seeming to any other. A day of swallow's flight and a cuckoo's sad call, echoing across the river as if to mourn summer's swift passage. But for Caitlin and Liam, it heralded a tide of events to change entirely the pattern they had awakened to that morning. And when nightfall came both would be travelling to their destinies unaware that they now did so by different ways.

There was a great stir and commotion outside, which sent Eunice rushing to the front door wiping her hands on her apron. When she recognised the visitor's carriage, she ran back into the kitchen shouting: 'Glencorrie, Glencorrie – come at once.'

Liam was upstairs occupied with the Fortingall accounts in the room adjacent to their bedchamber, little more than a closet which it pleased Eunice to proudly refer to as 'the Laird's study'.

Wondering what had set Eunice in such a panic, Caitlin went out to behold a large travelling carriage bearing the Glenlyon coat of arms with four horses trembling and sweating in the traces. Strapped on behind was a multitude of trunks and assorted luggage. A vision of elegance had descended and was walking up the path. His heavy velvet *justaucorps* or riding-habit reached his calves, swinging open to reveal full wide breeches, a gold-tasselled sash at his waist and large military boots with wide flaring knee flaps. A jabot, a waterfall in lace, at his neck, leather gloves with heavily embroidered cuffs and a wide-brimmed hat decorated by an ostrich plume fringe, which he doffed in Caitlin's direction, completed his travelling wear.

Even as she recognised Sir Robert Campbell, she heard Liam's footsteps hurrying across the kitchen. She sighed.

Her father did indeed look like a servant as he rushed forward in leather jerkin, plaid trews and homespun shirt.

'Robert, we bid you welcome. This is a most pleasant surprise, cousin.'

'I could not pass by without looking in to see how you used your time away from me.' Although his greeting was kindly, his words affectionate, Liam was in no doubt of the reason for his cousin's visit. His brief sojourn at Fortingall, where there was so much still to do, was over. The Glenlyon begging bowl was due for another airing.

Liam gently pushed Eunice forward. 'There are some changes, indeed. This lady is now my wife.'

As Eunice curtseyed, Sir Robert's lavish flattery concealed disappointment, at his cousin's surprising choice. Since his first long marriage at sixteen had produced only one lass, Glencorrie should wisely have made certain of an heir by taking a young wife. And he pretended not to notice that the new wife was rather too old to fill all the empty rooms of this house with bairns. The Campbells were a fertile clan and for one who was touching forty when he had wed, Sir Robert regarded his own vast and ever growing family with comfortable pride.

What did Liam see in this dowdy woman, unmoved by a dozen charming Campbell ladies from Glasgow to Stirling, Edinburgh to the borders, who had unashamedly sought his favours. 'I am not in a mood to seek a wife,' had been his reply when Sir Robert tactfully pointed out some eligible lady and whispered of her dowry.

With a regretful sigh for the advantages a wealthy marriage would bring Glencorrie – and perhaps Glenlyon's 'begging bowl', Sir Robert had become reconciled to the seemingly inevitable fact that Liam might become a crusty widower with passing time. He consoled himself that this might prove a more of a blessing in the long run, rather than a Glencorrie interested in breeding warriors for another bout of war with the Macdonalds of Ardarroch and thereby seriously interfering with his cousin's unpaid services as tacksman.

He had early recognised the benefits of Glencorrie remaining a ruin with scant hope or money for restoration, whereby Liam also continued dependent upon Glenlyon's charity. Besides, he had seen enough of war, having inherited at eight years old and at fourteen witnessed the Glen's ravage by the Keppoch Macdonalds on their way home from Montrose's wars. When his niece Sarah had married MacIan of Glencoe's younger son, Alasdair Og, he had sighed with relief. He was glad of peace, unless war could be guaranteed to accrue him personal profits.

Now as he sat back in the kitchen's one comfortable chair with a glass of claret before him, flattering everyone, he was aware from the unyielding face before him that Liam was quite unmoved by gallantries. He recalled that despite Liam's university education, his manners when he first came to Meggernie fifteen years ago, were little better than those of a serf. He had decided that his handsome young kinsman needed the acquisition of considerable polish if he wished to get on in the world and thereby further Glenlyon's cause of money-raising. With the proud but hollow name of clan chief, Liam had little then in the way of worldly charm and wit to accompany the role. But any doubts about Glencorrie accompanying him as cousin, tacksman and secretary were soon put to rest.

Sir Robert had been relieved and surprised that, far from shaming him, Liam became the target for women's romantic sighs and men's trust. And Sir Robert stood by somewhat resentful of this poor cousin's success, observing both men and women rush to do his bidding. Amazed, he saw great ladies flutter mothlike to his side, attracted by good looks and grave dignity, simply because in some deep inaccessible part, he did not notice them at all. He had doubts whether Liam availed himself of opportunities thus offered for romantic dalliance, but it was extremely useful for the man who carried the Meggernie begging bowl to inspire confidence, when it came to men – and women – digging deep into their pockets.

As for Liam, he swiftly discovered that in Edinburgh the title of clan chief held no prestige whatever. The Highlanders were regarded as brigands, cattle thieves and savages. City folk considered there was naught to choose between a Macdonald and a Campbell and were cynically amused by their barbaric customs and ancient feuds.

Caitlin was presented and as Sir Robert bowed low over

her hand, she saw again the look of brooding, heavy-lidded interest, that she often beheld in humbler men's eyes of late.

Behind their illustrious visitor, there trailed a young girl. At first glance, Caitlin wondered if she was a servant, she appeared flustered, hot and uncomfortable, but her clothes were too grand and her features unmistakeably Campbell. She looked at Sir Robert but, with his arm about Liam's shoulder deep in conversation, he seemed to have forgotten all about the other occupant of his coach and Caitlin was left to escort her.

'I am Isobel.' Her imperious tone left no doubt that Caitlin should be aware of her identity. Curtseying, Caitlin wondered, could she be a daughter? No, that was not possible since at a time when most men were grandfathers, Sir Robert's hearth was cluttered with young children and babies.

'Are you a servant?' Isobel demanded haughtily.

'No, indeed. I am Glencorrie's daughter.'

'There is no need to be sharp with me, miss. Although I beg pardon for the mistake.' Her survey of Caitlin's shabby attire clearly suggested where it might have arisen. 'I am sure that others are confused, for you look not in the least like a Campbell.'

'Have you travelled far?' asked Caitlin politely.

'From Edinburgh. And I trust it is not a great deal further to Meggernie.' Considering the girl's woeful expression, Caitlin forbore to say twenty-five miles and over very uncomfortable roads. 'I am much in need of a house of easement, too.'

Caitlin had not heard a privy so called but she led the girl upstairs to her bedroom where a commode was kept, an innovation direct from Meggernie Castle.

'I am grateful to you,' sighed Isobel and Caitlin smiled as she closed the door upon her guest. Waiting for her to emerge, Caitlin was pleased that they had such bedroom luxuries. Ordinary glensfolk performed such functions under the heavens, where and how they could best find privacy.

Sir Robert smiled as they came downstairs together.

'So that is where you are, niece. I thought you had turned tail and rushed back to Edinburgh.' When Isobel grimaced, he roared with sudden laughter, as if he had made the greatest joke.

'And what mischief are you set upon now?'

'I am to accompany Glencorrie's daughter, an it please you, uncle.'

The two girls exchanged shy glances and Eunice darted forward: 'You will sup first,' she said, her furious look in Caitlin's direction told her that later she would pay for this intrusion, this presumption.

As they sat at the table, Caitlin was proud of Liam's appearance. His modest dress was not in the least diminished by his lofty cousin. An upper servant, maybe, but his was the stronger more manly appearance. Deprive Sir Robert of his grand attire and he would present a much less noble appearance than his young cousin. Although they looked closer in age than past thirty and pressing fifty, for Sir Robert's still yellow Campbell hair was thick and youthful, his complexion was florid, a nose long and thin above a mouth red-lipped as a girl's, at once too petulant and small for his heavy chin. His eyes were heavy-lidded and half-closed, as if they drooped with sleep or the unnecessary effort of concentration. A look instantly recognised by the more worldlywise, as the permanently glazed countenance of the heavy drinker.

Sir Robert was laughing at some story of Red Alistair's. Caitlin had often wished to meet him thus, with only glimpses of him riding past the house. How bluff and genial he seemed, and yet, and yet, at this first meeting, there appeared something quite indefinable but not altogether trustful in his countenance, something evasive in his eyes which never lingered long on one person or object. Restless, shifting eyes, for ever searching. They made her think, quite wickedly, of Pontius Pilate, washing his hands at the baptismal font in the dark shadows of Fortingall Church.

How he flattered them all, she thought. Eunice fluttering, old Alistair preening himself, even her father smiled when Sir Robert said: 'In Edinburgh and Glasgow we were always taken for brothers. We are like, are we not?'

Yes, Liam was pleased and so was Red Alistair although he did not approve of Glencorrie being led along on Sir Robert's empty purse strings. He felt that his young chief was worthy of better things, and was hurt when Liam chided him about filling Caitlin's head with their ancient grievances. The past is dead, he was sternly told. Time to forget. Let the Glencorrie children grow up in peace.

Now regarding Sir Robert across the table, Red Alistair shared Caitlin's feelings that there was something unmanly, not altogether sincere about Glenlyon's yellow curls, his mouth was small and mean, his voice too high and his laughter too shrill. Despite his proven manhood in begetting so many bairns late in life, there was a kind of womanish treachery hidden by too ready smiles, a too-honeyed tongue merciless to friend and foe alike.

'This beautiful wench of yours, cousin,' Sir Robert was saying, 'she should be gracing the king's court.' Caitlin looked at him contemptuously. The man was a liar, that smooth flattery when it was obvious to anyone that such a description was inept, unearned too, for loveliness to Caitlin was something not contained in the wrappings.

She glanced at Isobel and saw that they were allies, that the girl shared her own feelings on the subject of her kinsman as she whispered: 'Let us go out for a while and you may show me your clachan, for that is all it is. I do not suppose it will take us long, but my legs are weary with sitting in my uncle's abominable coach all the way from Edinburgh, and I do not relish hours of this boorish conversation. Men have nothing to say, but expound upon matters of politics and religion. I do not understand in the least how their wives tolerate them without dying of boredom.'

As Isobel had suspected, it took little time to walk around the village of Fortingall and turf-roofed houses with peat smoke belching from their roofs caused no comment.

'Must she come with us?' Jean was walking respectfully a few paces behind Caitlin as usual smiling and nodding to herself. 'The creature is simple-minded, is she a relative?'

'She is my step-sister, and my dearest friend.'

'Oh, very well, let her remain.'

Isobel was a difficult guest to entertain. The legend of Pontius Pilate brought forth a shrug. 'I expect it is not true, perhaps even the name Pontius Pilate was common in Roman times. Besides this kirk is very cold and very dull. I should go mad worshipping here. The Cathedral of St Giles in Edinburgh is very beautiful and when one is bored with the sermon one can enjoy the ladies' gowns and bonnets, the very height of elegance they are too, it is quite a parade each Sunday morning, the event of the week.'

As they walked through the kirkyard, Caitlin pointed out Mairi Campbell's grave. 'It is exceeding ordinary for the wife of a clan chief, even an impoverished one,' Isobel said disapproving. 'My parents have a tomb, a vast mausoleum. However, you were lucky to have a mother. Mine died when I was born.'

'I am sorry.'

Isobel looked surprised. 'You need not be, for I never knew her. I had not time to have any feelings for her in the least.'

'What about your father?'

Isobel shrugged. 'Oh, I never knew him either. He was killed fighting in the Low Countries.'

'Then who has taken care of you all these years?'

'Uncle Robert is my legal guardian, but I have lived with an old aunt in Edinburgh. And I was very happy there, I can tell you. I had everything I wanted, until she died two weeks ago. It was a most unfortunate time to leave, for I had to miss a hanging, a traitor who had once served with Montrose. It was to be a great event, and my aunt's window looked out upon the Tolbooth.'

Caitlin had heard that women as well as men went to public executions and that a holy day atmosphere prevailed. She was filled with no curiosity, to witness a felon's last moments, to watch any man die would fill her with horror. What a strange creature, this Edinburgh Campbell who relished the prospect of an execution and made it sound as if her aunt had died merely to inconvenience her personally. She decided that a more cheerful topic was necessary and as they were approaching the old yew she said:

'This tree was at least a thousand years old when – when Pontius Pilate lived here. Many travellers to Scotland have declared it the oldest as well as the largest tree in the whole world. And it is still growing. Every five years its girth is measured by five of the tallest men in Glenlyon, all must be six foot tall, and with arms outstretched. Now their finger tips barely meet about its trunk. It has passed thirty feet in circumference.'

Isobel surveyed this marvel critically. 'Indeed – I will take your word for it.'

As she hurried on, Caitlin added: 'As for the forests around here, there were wild boars within Alistair nan Creach's memory, even the Black Wood of Rannoch, cannot compare to our yew tree.'

'Did your tutor tell you that?'

'Alistair told me,' Caitlin said meekly, not wishing to admit that she had no such luxury as a tutor.

'It sounds like a school lesson,' was the bored reply.

Caitlin was disappointed in her companion's lack of enthusiasm. In the tranquil procession of days and seasons which had marked the passing years of her life, the yew gave her a sense of protection. Benign and wise, watching over her childish games, beneath its boughs, with the sunlight glinting down through fresh bright green summer needles, she felt that nothing terrible – like one of Red Alistair's bloodthirsty wars – could ever happen again. But what was the use of telling Isobel, who was now staring across the field opposite the house at the solitary standing stone.

'What is that?'

'Cairn na Mabh, the Mound of Death, and marks the time when the Black Death came to Fortingall long ago. Practically everyone died then and there were too many corpses for burial in the kirkyard. Besides, folk were afraid too that the graves might be broken into by some hunting animal, since the survivors could only scratch the earth aside – none had strength to dig deep pits.'

Isobel gave a pleasurable shiver. 'And then those roving animals would have spread the sickness again.'

'The sole survivor was an old woman, too aged to fear death for herself any more. So she carried the corpses into the field on a sledge, drawn by a white horse.'

'And that great mound – are all the corpses buried under there?' asked Isobel fascinated.

'Yes, and even now the farmers take a wide berth, they are still afraid of ploughing too close, and folk have a horror of walking in its shadow.'

'I heard Uncle Robert talking about the famine years – oh,

when you were a child, I suppose – and how the caterans came down from the hills and were found dead of hunger by the wayside. Too weak they were to carry off a sheep or a goat, or even catch a hen. They were found dead by the wayside, their mouths stuffed with grass or roots. Are they buried over there too?' she added eagerly.

Caitlin had no idea where such folk were buried, to Isobel's obvious disappointment. 'I wonder if we could get a closer look at the mound?' she asked.

'If you wish,' said Caitlin reluctantly. 'But the farmers are not very pleased if we walk through their crops.'

Isobel thought this a poor excuse. 'Uncle Robert will make it up to them, I dare say.' Caitlin followed her reluctantly. However after the first muddy encounter which threatened to get worse, even Isobel's enthusiasm was daunted. Ruefully inspecting her shoes made for more delicate walking, she regarded Caitlin's sturdy brogans with distaste.

'If only I had my plattens, but they are packed. We need high-soled shoes for walking in Edinburgh streets too – they are often quite disgraceful.'

This was a new insight for Caitlin who had imagined they might be like the streets of the Roman towns she had 'seen'. Clean, with spotless gleaming pavements.

'Well, what else have you to show me?'

Caitlin indicated about the Sighe Stone. 'It is thought to have magical properties.'

Isobel dismissed this wonder scornfully. 'Just an ancient boulder. We passed by many fields containing many such stones on our journey.'

Caitlin was relieved. She had little desire to share the Fairy Stone with a disbelieving companion: 'There are the ruins of the old Roman town up there on the hillside and by the stream, a bridge they built.'

'Oh, those old Romans. They bore me.'

'Tell her about the ghosts, Caitlin,' piped up Jean, whose presence they had almost forgotten, as she trotted at their heels like a faithful dog.

'Ghosts?' Isobel sighed deeply. And Caitlin felt she had betrayed Jean, when Isobel smothered a laugh with a behind-hand whisper: 'She is a little mad, of course, anyone can see that.'

Caitlin, who could think of no defence except that she loved Jean, was silent. As they approached the house, Isobel asked: 'Have you always lived here?'

'Yes, I was born at Meggernie, but my parents came to Fortingall soon afterwards.'

'Then where is Glencorrie?'

Caitlin pointed. 'Across the hill there – up the Glen.' She remembered that 'up the Glen' was the point at which so many stories told by Mairi and Red Alistair had always ended. 'Up the Glen' was like one of them, unfinished, forbidden, out of her childhood reach. Stories of saints and repentant sinners were turned into legends but if the grown ups could supply no satisfactory ending, she was firmly told that 'up the Glen' was not for children, either.

'Is that where the Macdonalds massacred your Clan?'

'Yes.'

'Is anything left of it?'

'Just some ruined houses.'

'Have you been there?'

'Yes.'

'Would you take me?' begged Isobel, her voice an excited whisper.

'It is a long way, but we can see the glen from the hill up there.'

'Then let us go.'

'But ... '

Her protests were in vain, Isobel was already marching ahead. Caitlin saw Jean's frightened face and said: 'Go back to the house and if anyone should ask where we are, say that we walk to the Pass.'

'But – Caitlin.' It was Jean's turn to protest. 'We are not allowed.'

'I know that, Jean, but I cannot let her go alone. If anything happens to her I will be blamed. Go quickly and say we will be back shortly, but only if any ask, do you understand?'

Hurrying after Isobel, Caitlin remembered her first and last visit to Glencorrie. Long ago, lured on by Red Alistair's tales, she had decided to have a closer look, to brave the Pass which had not been used for fifteen years and whose now overgrown path was hardly visible.

The sight terrified her, corbie-haunted houses lost in huddles of crumbled stone. Worse was the tall tower. As she opened its creaking door, the corbies rose in an angry cloud above her head, their shrill cries echoing from empty rafters where a tree had long since taken root and now flourished sturdily. Around her, the pathetic burnt-out shells of pots and unrecognisable household goods were all that remained of the Glencorrie stronghold.

The church was similarly afflicted by time and storm and in the kirk yard, waist-high in grass, she could scarcely decipher the graves or find the one where her grandmother lay.

'Caitlin Campbell.'

The name was a shock to her. She had not expected it, thinking always of her as Caitlin O'Rourke.

'Caitlin Campbell.' Eeerie, terrifying to see her own name staring up at her from a gravestone, as if she had been swept into the future, and had already become a ghost. Around her, the day darkened swiftly into evening and she was suddenly aware that this dark land with its feeling of emptiness thrust out fingers of hatred. The coarse grass whispered of alien feet of those who were no kin to her.

She stood up. 'Go away – leave me alone. You are dead – dead.' But her courage availed her nothing. The answering silence was so full of menace that she ran, ran as fast as her legs could carry her back up the hill and down through the narrow pass. She needed no further punishment for disobedience than the ghosts of all the men slain that night who seemed to be tumbling after her, breathing heavily, their plaids flapping at her heels.

She told Red Alistair who approved of her bravery but still chided her, since the ruined buildings were not only the haunt of ghosts but of much livelier creatures who could do a lass more lasting harm than any spectres. And he told her about the broken secret men of the Highlands, the caterans of Macgregor's Gallows Herd.

'The Pass, aye, you're safe enough on this side, but no further, lass.' After all the Campbells of Glencorrie took their children to that dread spot to gaze down upon those fearful ruins, their first lesson in hating their enemy with all their heart and soul and might. Even the minister took good care to remind their good covenanting God of his duty to smite their idolatrous Papist enemy.

Caitlin reached Isobel's side and together they gazed down on ruined Glencorrie. The sight still shocked her, the skeletal shapes of crofts, blackened and terrible, like imploring arms stretching out into the sky and beseeching vengeance.

'How many Campbells were killed that night?' asked Isobel with a relish for the gory details of the massacre. She listened eagerly and then asked: 'And where is Ardarroch?'

'Over there.' Caitlin pointed to the hills where the sun was setting, in a blaze of glory, creeping over the hills, turning the sky into a pathway into an enchanted kingdom which she longed with all her soul to follow. Unfair, she thought again, that the wicked, cruel Macdonalds should benefit as they drained the day's bright banners from the sky.

'Do you think there is a country out there, where all the sunsets are?'

But ignoring this interesting possibility, Isobel merely shrugged and said: 'Let us go down then and look at the graves.' And at Caitlin's reluctance: 'You are not afraid of graves surely.'

'I am not.'

'Then why do you hesitate.'

'It will be dark soon and Sir Robert might be looking for you.'

At that moment the situation was saved as Jean appeared over the hill.

'You are to come at once. Sir Robert is about to depart.'

Liam had just learned that his travels were to take him well beyond Scotland where all the resources of kinship had been exploited to the full. Regretfully there were no more loans forthcoming from kin long alerted to his difficulties. 'There are in London, however, some very wealthy Campbells attached to King Charles' court.'

'Do you think it wise?' asked Liam.

'Wise, cousin, of course it is wise. Just see what you can charm out of them, that is all you have to do.' Sir Robert's voice rose in shrill indignation, as always when his wild suggestions in the fantasy realms of possible loans were questioned.

Liam regarded his flushed happy face, his optimism and

refusal to heed rational discussion indicated some derange-
ment of the mind. Worse still, Liam realised that his own
future besides that of his unfortunate Clan was now linked
to this madman's whims.

'You are to proceed to England with all possible speed for
you need no telling from me how urgently the matter of our
finances stands. I would accompany you gladly,' he added
persuasively, 'had I not to remain at Meggernie in
anticipation of my wife's confinement. So soon after the last
babe, there are difficulties expected.' Sir Robert frowned,
shaking his head sadly, as if he had played no part in
creating such a situation.

As Isobel was hustled into the carriage, she turned and
said: 'Uncle Robert, I have enjoyed Caitlin's company. She is
a strange girl, difficult I think. But may I have her to stay
with me at Meggernie?'

Sir Robert regarded her thoughtfully. She was as yet
unaware that his benevolence was occasioned only by her
obligation to him and that her intended fate was to join
Meggernie's many unpaid domestics. Thus far, he saw no
reason to suspect that she would ever amount to more than a
whining burden. The idea appealed to him. Another pair of
strong hands and under similar obligation would be useful in
nursery and kitchen.

'You would like that, niece?'

'I would indeed, Uncle.'

He patted her hand. 'Then it shall be done.'

Chapter VI

'Meggernie? Stay there, live there? I cannot, I cannot,' cried Caitlin.

'Hear me out,' Liam told her sternly. 'It is not for ever, just a kindness to Sir Robert who has been so good to us. Caitlin,' he said, silencing her further protests, 'Listen to me. This is a request I cannot refuse. Isobel has taken a liking to you.' He put his arm about her shoulders, 'She wishes you to be her companion.'

He sounded pleased despite Caitlin's misgivings that there was little in that first meeting to suggest any prospects of friendship between them.

'Besides, child, there are many advantages – '

'I do not see any,' said Caitlin recognising only that he always called her 'child' upon those awkward moments when they no longer understood each other's thoughts.

Now he indicated the kitchen with an impatient gesture. 'Do you want this for the rest of your life?' If this included Eunice, then she did not. But for her father and herself she asked nothing more. 'I have had scant chance to educate you in the ways of genteel society,' he continued. 'I am bound for England.'

'That heathen shore?'

Liam grinned. 'Aye, London, on Sir Robert's business.'

Caitlin seized his arm. 'Take me with you, please, please.'

Liam looked at her. Had she been truly his daughter, he might have considered it, but not with the certainty of shared tavern lodgings on that long journey, of bed as well as board. He shuddered. Never again, not after the temptation of the cave on the hill.

'I do not want to be genteel,' she sobbed. 'I need no such education. I can read and write and count, I would be a help to you in London.'

'No, child. My mind is made up.' His inflexible expression reminded her of less happy days. 'Besides you must be prepared to take your rightful place in the world as heiress to Glencorrie – and you cannot yet count into three figures with ease.'

'Enough to count any merks or pounds Scots that come our way, Father,' she reminded him bitterly. 'And I can ride and shoot, like a boy, you know I can.' She thrust out her chin and Liam's angry look in Red Alistair's direction said plainly: It is all your fault filling her mind with those daft stories.

The old man merely scowled at him and turned away. He did not want to lose his beloved Caitlin to Meggernie either. In that they were allies.

'You want to know all about music and painting, books and suchlike, do you not?'

'And what am I to do with such things, a lass like me?'

'Let me remind you that such qualities are valuable in making a good marriage.'

'Marriage,' she said scornfully.

'Yes, marriage, for that is what your Father in heaven – and your father on earth intend for a lass,' he retorted angrily. Mollified, he took her hands gently. 'Dear child, my chieftainship is but a hollow name until we can rebuild Glencorrie, you are aware of that. And an alliance with a wealthy family would release us from dependency upon Sir Robert. He has great influence among Campbell and other Highland gentry with marriageable sons and nephews. And he has most generously guaranteed to provide your dowry.'

'Dowry,' shouted Caitlin. 'I do not want a dowry.'

But Liam could be obstinate too, determined that she would change her mind about marriage when the proper time came. Meanwhile he made clear his refusal for further discussion by leaving her abruptly and closing the door none too gently behind him.

Caitlin was bitterly hurt by his refusal to take her to London. Bewildered, betrayed, by this unexpected turn of events, for her prayer – the miracle of a loving father – had been answered, only to be snatched from her again.

Eunice had first place in his life and others also observed that Lady Glencorrie was no longer the meek housekeeper serving her lord with downcast modest eyes. Thrusting, shrill and possessive, she made sure that Caitlin's faults were manifestly evident whenever possible.

'She is trying to be a second mother to you, Caitlin,' Liam said.

And Caitlin bit back the angry words she longed to shout at him: 'Then you should be a fly on this wall and see how she treats me in your absence.'

As for Eunice, her only regret was that she could no longer beat Caitlin since the girl bruised easily.

'We leave for Meggernie tomorrow.'

'So soon – oh, Father.'

Liam was overwhelmed by the reproachful whisper, the tears bravely unshed. But his resolve was firm. His hearthstone was sorely troubled by strife these days. He had hoped to find comfort, a docile partner in Eunice. God knew that he had not built his marriage upon false hopes that he might grow to love her as he had loved Mairi but he had expected content. Guiltily, he was aware of her disappointment for they both knew that her desperate hungry lovemaking failed to arouse the fires that had burned so brightly for his first wife. Passion was no substitute for the warmth and tenderness he sought. They were the sun without which his soul shrivelled and only in Caitlin's undemanding innocent love had he found that which his spirit craved. Had she been a servant in his house, the humblest lass in the clachan, he would never have married Eunice. In a blissful Utopia he saw himself arranging their betrothal, asking parents or guardian for her hand in marriage – marriage – a whole lifetime together.

The images of Caitlin which plagued him when Eunice clutched him to her in their marriage bed were violent, sweet but terrible, demons that refused to be cast out. The lass must be placed out of temptation's way, or he would destroy her. Aye, and remove her from Stephen too. He was relieved indeed that he had not sent the lad to Meggernie as he had intended before Sir Robert's visit. Now Stephen was to remain in Fortingall, to assist Minister Blair.

Jean wept copiously and begged to go with Caitlin.

Hugging her, Caitlin regarded him with wounded eyes. 'Can she not come, please, Father? She would be no trouble.'

102

'Stop it, this minute, Jean,' said Eunice angrily prising them apart. 'You cannot go. Someone must bide here to help me if I am to run this house without servants.'

Had she forgotten her own enthusiasm for the idea, thought Liam, consoling Caitlin with: 'It is only for a little while, child. Until I return from London. Besides Sir Robert will let you home for Hogmanay.'

Caitlin's look held reproach and desperation. It was still summer. Christmas belonged to another world unimaginable, as yet unborn. Oh, if only she had the power to turn the seasons back and relive each one of these precious days she had shared with Father.

Their leavetaking was sorrowful, Jean wept and clung to her, old Alistair dabbed at his eyes unashamedly. Now Eunice regarded Liam with great haunted eyes and the rain that had fallen during the night became an omen of tears to be shed.

As Caitlin rode pillion behind Liam, the neighbours' doors in Fortingall opened to recognise their passing. A hand raised in farewell, a smile then lost, gave her a tight feeling of panic in her chest. She did not look back and the yew tree stirred its leaves for them, shaking out branches like the arms of a sleeper suddenly awake and yawning, thought Caitlin, raising her hand and blowing it a kiss. She would miss the old yew as much as any real person. After all, she told anyone who would believe her, trees were living creatures too bound by the mysteries of their own world.

Out of sight of the clachan, the day suddenly brightened as if they had progressed into another happier world. Twisting paths that led through the glen were suddenly dappled in sunlight and Caitlin told herself that it was good to be alive and setting out upon an adventure. For she had never been further than the kitchen of Lady Glenlyon's dower house at Chesthill, sitting on a creepy stool, listening eagerly for the familiar sound of her father's spurs as he returned across the unseen polished floor that seperated servants' hall from a wealth of marvels glimpsed briefly beyond the great oak doors.

With her arms about Liam's waist and the pools among the heather reflecting back an azure sky with a sailing of high clouds, galleons on a tideless sea, she could not be unhappy for long.

Now a narrow burn looped its way through tall hedgerows thick with the curdled cream of dog roses, with every bird singing fit to break its heart with joy. Through the coiling waters silver flashed as a salmon leaped. Then, still and blue and secret again, the river was a lady's looking-glass mirroring the shadows of sunny banks.

Suddenly the landscape widened, spread out to reveal wind-frayed trees devoid of summer leaf, gaunt as sentinels on ever changing horizons. Hillsides fell away sharply as if sliced by some great sword and the pasture land was dotted by plots of land where crops grew tall and ripe for the harvest scythe. Tiny clachans, marked by peat smoke, too small and insignificant in character to bear other than their tenants' names, huddled under turf roofs or heather thatch. Beyond lay a rough wild land dotted with misshapen trees doomed never to thrust strong proud arms to the sky, strangled by the heath's roots as it stretched without end to misted hills, now blue in summer's haze. And on the far side of the river, a waterfall, a maiden's veil of white.

On and on to the rythym of Barby's hooves, through paths tortuous, made by man through the interlocking hillsides where ivy and creeper, dark and secret, held dominion. In such caverns even bird-song fell mute and the air, sinister with forebodings, whispered of ambush and dark deeds as yet unborn.

Now their hoofbeats echoed in a gully where the shivering bushes and fury of breaking twigs in their path, marked the timely departure of some forest creature more surprised than they.

'There are places here, farms and clachans,' said Liam 'which never see the sun from mid-October until mid-February.'

Out again into the dappled sunshine past Woodend where the women churning butter by their doorsteps, curtseyed and raised hands in greeting. Liam smiled and doffed his bonnet. 'Word will soon be travelling nearly as fast as ourselves, that Glencorrie is taking his lass to Meggernie Castle.'

'How can they know that?'

He laughed. 'They have sharp eyes, which have already observed Glencorrie's daughter's best gown and cloak. The bundle on Barby's panniers indicates no fleeting visit, but a long stay. Now, they reason, Glencorrie's daughter is unlike to be a servant, more like a companion. Where news is scarce, they are ready to make their own. And so are legends born.'

Past the tall grey castle of Carbhan, home of the Macgregors. Caitlin knew their story from Red Alistair. A hundred years ago they had owned Glenlyon but outlawed for their misdeeds, the glen had moved into the hands of the Campbells of Glenorchy, the second of that name famous as Red Duncan of the Hospitality.

Now they were absorbed into a bleak and alien world, whose boulders lay like some forgotten giant's playstones, cast into ridges along the valley floor. Low on Ben Lawer's steep sides a deer herd turned towards them, still and poised for instant flight, until the stag dipped his antlers and placidly continued to graze, dismissing their presence as of no consequence. His hinds promptly followed, docile but now unafraid in the wake of their lord's indifference.

On and into Camusvrachan. Caitlin knew its name well, expecting to feel benediction from this holy place. For on this spot a thousand years ago St Eonan had halted the Black Death. Bruach followed, then Innerwick, site of the annual sheep fair. Here too Glencorrie was recognised. There was a bow and a curtsey for his pretty daughter, who acknowledged their greeting, feeling rather grand.

At the Brig o'Balgie, which held tentative mastery over the river tumbling with dramatic boulders and gurgling pools, Liam dismounted and lifted Caitlin down.

'This is the halfway mark. We will rest here for a while. Are you hungry?' She was and they ate the bannocks, cheese and ale Eunice had provided for the journey. Replete, sitting with their backs resting against the ancient stones, Caitlin's eyes closed and Liam looking down on her face remembered how once long ago he had approached Meggernie by this very bridge, carrying Caitlin new born, clasped to his naked breast.

He looked at her again in wonder, certain that she had been dead that night. She would never have revived had he left her in Ardarroch. But he had carried her against his heart and the warmth of his body had given her life. Sometimes his dreams were haunted by that small questing velvet head, the mouth that had turned to his breast as her first contact with life. His face had been her first sight on earth. She was utterly his own.

He shook his head. No. No it was not true, could never be true. Too late, he had come to realise that he loved her above all living creatures. And now he cursed those lost tender days of infancy when he had wished to forget her presence. Such regret that memory was barren of the least remembrance of her winsome childhood years. Nothing, as if she had been no more than the passing song of the mavis in the tree above his head. How he wished he could relive even one day of her early life in perfect detail. For now he had only yesterday, the day on which he had discovered her. And today. But what of tomorrow?

As she stirred in sleep, protectively he put his arm around her, rested his lips upon her hair. Today and tomorrow, he vowed, she should be his. No man would ever take him from her. No man …

Her eyes sprang open and seeing him she smiled, snuggling contentedly into his shoulder.

'Are you happy, my Caitlin?' he whispered.

'I wish we could stay here for ever.'

He looked at her beloved face. Her eyes were dark pools swimming with love for him. He longed to take her in his arms, kiss her lips, not as father for daughter, but as man for his wife ordained by God, to kiss her and draw her soul and body to his own in adoration. Oh, temptation!

'I shall leave Barby for you at Meggernie, she is getting past long journeys,' he said and cut short her affectionate thanks by springing to his feet, and pushing her aside almost roughly.

Bewildered she sat behind him, wondering what had brought about his sudden coldness, his change of sunny mood as wordlessly they continued their journey. Even the scenery seemed to reflect Liam's sombre mood as fairytale gorges, ravines and waterfalls, befitting surroundings for a castle, vanished. A monotonous expanse of scrub and ragged thornwood, with only the distant flicker of roe dear amid bracken-covered braes, of curlew and snipe rising shrilly before them, indicated that they had reached the parkland of Meggernie.

Caitlin blinked in disbelief. At close range, the Castle's vast walls could have swallowed both Chesthill and Carbhan, as well as the entire population of Fortingall. Nor was Sir Robert's generosity to Glencorrie quite so impressive when she realised how he could have resettled the entire clan here in his fine castle and scarcely noticed their presence.

'Only Sir Robert and his family live here?'

'About twelve people, yes, and perhaps forty servants.'

From tales of Glenlyon, Caitlin guessed that the servants would be overcrowded, herded into one comfortless small room. Now as they rode nearer she counted twelve windows, which meant twelve rooms, one for each member of the family. Twelve souls, a number more often than not sharing one miserable turf-covered croft in Fortingall.

So this was the scene of her nativity. She felt proud but where was that twitch of familiarity she expected, following Liam across the sunlit cobbled courtyard through a side archway and up a flight of stone steps?

Opening the door, he said: 'These rooms are set aside for my personal use.' And Caitlin noted comfortable furnishings approvingly, pleased that Sir Robert had also remembered that his cousin Glencorrie was a clan chief in his own right.

A flight of wooden stairs led into the bedroom. 'This is where I was born?'

Liam nodded and put down her bundle by the window.

'Here?' She touched the bed-curtains narrowing her eyes as she tried to reconstruct the scene of her mother lying against the pillows with herself, a tiny babe, in her arms.

Liam walked over to the window, praying that she would ask him no more questions. 'When you are ready, I will take you to Lady Glenlyon.'

And conscious of his eyes watching her impatiently, she tidied her hair quickly and removed her travelling cloak. As she did so, she shivered, catching sight of his reflection in the mirror. How masked and cruel his face, how sharp his voice. Suddenly she felt as if it was a stranger – a hated stranger she had never known, never loved – whose face she beheld.

Time too was a cheat, the shadowy bed behind them

illuminated with spectral light was occupied by two people who lay, their naked limbs entwined. The woman with a cloud of long dark hair hidden by the man's body, was not her mother, although the back of her lover's head was undoubtedly Liam Campbell's.

Even as she looked they faded and were gone. A trick of sunlight? But the uneasiness of this vision remained. Who were the lovers and why had she seen them? Was the moment past or still to come?

She looked at Liam who was smiling, beloved again as he asked: 'Well, child, are you ready now? Come along, you are bonny enough to please my lady.'

For a moment she hesitated but was too embarrassed to tell him what she had seen. Besides the dreaded *taibhsearachd*, the second sight angered him, she thought warily, as he led the way swiftly across the courtyard. As they entered the Castle's main door, she sniffed the air. She was used to houses that smelt of peat fire smoke, of cooking, and of homely agreeable and the quite indefinite odours that made up each individual habitation.

This vast hall smelt like a forest, oak, pine, yew, many trees had been used in the transformation of Meggernie Castle from defensive tower built by Sir Robert's grandfather, Mad Colin Campbell, into the handsome mansion whose abundance of windows indicated clearer than any promises of men, rosy hopes for a peaceful future.

'Caitlin – Caitlin.' A smiling Isobel greeted her wearing an elaborate but too large gown of green satin its bodice sewn with tiny beads (which she learned later had replaced the costly pearls Lady Glenlyon's kinswoman had removed before handing it down). Caitlin felt honoured that Isobel had dressed as if for a grand occasion, at this hour of the day when ordinary folk worked in homespun and apron.

'Welcome to Meggernie,' said Isobel and to Liam. 'Very well, Glencorrie. You are not needed here and my uncle awaits you in the chart room.' Her tone reduced him to a servant and Caitlin could do no more than dart a helpless look in his direction as he bowed and Isobel hurried her towards the massive staircase that rose towards the lofty ceiling. From its summit they proceeded between walls hung with gilt-framed portraits.

'Are they not handsome?' demanded Isobel proudly. 'All members of my family, you know.' At Caitlin's bewildered expression, which clearly had naught to do with the paintings, she added 'What is wrong now?'

'What a strange-shaped room.'

Isobel laughed. 'How stupid you are, Caitlin Campbell. This is not a room, just a passageway from one room to another.'

A passageway, the size of a house, thought Caitlin, staring out of its large windows overlooking the courtyard. Underneath the portraits the handsome padded chairs were presumably for decoration only. Stupid she might be, but that seemed wicked in its wastefulness where some of Sir Robert's tenants were lucky to have a wooden settle and one creepy stool to sit upon.

A servant approached and Isobel asked: 'Where is my aunt?' in the special rather high voice she kept for those she considered her inferiors, as if they were also somewhat deaf or short on understanding.

'Lady Glenlyon will receive you in the drawing room, miss.' He bowed opening handsome double doors through which Caitlin beheld more marvels. In a fireplace, the size of her bedroom at Fortingall, and set between two turrets, half a tree-trunk blazed cheerfully. The vast proportions of the room were cluttered by more paintings, tapestries, rugs and elegant chairs and small tables in a dazzling array of colour. This was indeed one of Red Alistair's fairy tale halls come to light.

At her exclamation of delight, Isobel said: 'This is the drawing room.'

'The drawing room,' repeated Caitlin. 'Then where are the children?'

'Children? In the nursery, I presume. Why do you ask?'

To her timid suggestion that they might be busy with their slates in the drawing room at this time of day, Isobel put both hands to her mouth in a shriek of merriment.

'Caitlin Campbell, how can you be so ignorant? Come with me.' She marched her across the floor and opened the door into a room dominated by a gleaming table with twenty matching tall-backed chairs. Its walls were hung with tapestries, depicting the exploits of larger-than-life heroes.

About who they were, or the reason for their fierce expressions, Isobel was vague, since her education had lacked any mention of the myths of Greece.

'This is the dining room and the carpet is from Persia and very valuable,' she said impressively and as Caitlin leaped aside in alarm to avoid stepping on it. 'It is meant for walking upon,' she added scornfully.

Caitlin shook her head. Tapestries on the walls, rugs on the floor. A special room in which to eat. Then where was the kitchen?

'Kitchen? Somewhere down there. I know naught of kitchens,' was the reply.

Caitlin was soon to discover this was why food was invariably cold, travelling from distant kitchens, down lengthy corridors before it reached the table. Sensible poor folk, like those she had left in Fortingall ate their food where it was cooked, still hot from the fire.

'This is where my uncle entertains his important guests. When they are finished eating the ladies leave them and return here,' she said as they retraced their steps, 'into what is really the withdrawing room.' From a piece of furniture, prettily painted with shepherdesses, her touch brought forth notes of music. 'A virginals, which I am learning to play, a great accomplishment for young ladies and much to be admired in society.'

Again Caitlin thought of Fortingall and of Sir Robert's tenants in Glenlyon doomed to dark smoke-filled windowless hovels from birth to death, who would never in their whole lives have their souls refreshed by even a glimpse of the splendour in which their lord spent his days.

Lady Glenlyon entered attended by a bevy of small children of assorted ages. Caitlin was presented and endeavouring to answer her ladyship's questions as to her abilities as nursery-maid and seamstress, found her concentration centred upon her ladyship's splendid gown. Of deep blue satin, long-waisted and dipping to a point in front, the busked bodice thrust forward her ample bosom. For modesty's sake she wore a deep muslin collar to cover her bare shoulders. The full skirt revealed a richly embroidered petticoat. The pleated satin train that swept the floor as she walked across the room, Caitlin decided,

110

contained enough material for yet another gown.

Her hair had been coaxed into corkscrew sidecurls, known as 'confidants', heavy ringlets or 'heartbreakers', and a curled fringe. The remaining hair was adorned by pearls, lace and ribbon bows (the daily witness of such procedure led Caitlin to substitute 'tortured' for 'coaxed'). The bright yellow colour was her ladyship's own. Caitlin knew from her father that only gentlemen wore periwigs. A matter he and Sir Robert scorned personally, both proud of their abundant Campbell hair.

The small children clustered around their mother stared her out of countenance and wonder of wonders – they were similarly gowned, elaborate replicas of their parent but difficult to establish which were lads and which were lasses.

Lady Glenlyon carried a large ostrich feather fan wielded briskly to emphasise a point in conversation or to maintain discipline among her brood. It was now levelled at Caitlin who realised she was being questioned.

'I am honoured indeed to have been chosen as Isobel's companion, your ladyship,' she said, curtseying. The feathers were now flourished in a signal of dismissal.

'A moment, niece. Did you tell Master Campbell that Sir Robert awaits him in the chart room?'

Caitlin looked at Lady Glenlyon reproachfully. 'Master' was how they addressed cobbler, blacksmith or common trades folk at Fortingall. Never had she heard her father addressed other than 'my lord' or 'Glencorrie' as befitted a clan chief of the cadet gentry of the Campbells.

As Lady Glenlyon led the way down a succession of passageways lined with closed doors, the children darted ahead, screaming and fighting, a crowd of rowdy butterflies in their splendid billowing silks and satins. Occasionally her ladyship paused and called them to order, counting heads to make certain that none of her charges had strayed.

Their ways parted outside Isobel's bedchamber, plainly furnished with canopied bed, armoire, candlestand and table, an ebony framed mirror its sole decoration. A door concealed in the panelling was opened by Isobel to reveal a tiny closet, containing bed, table and tallow candle, Caitlin's room.

By the time Caitlin had stored her few possessions in the

depths of the ancient shabby chest, Isobel had vanished and only the deserted wilderness of Meggernie Castle's upper regions stretched before her.

'Isobel?' she called. An alarming echo brought disturbing visions of roaming endless passageways, peering into empty rooms until she dropped dead from exhaustion or starved to death. Ironically she decided it would be as easy to perish in this vast mansion as from exposure on the hills of Glenlyon.

Beyond the windows, drenched in afternoon sunshine, the hills beckoned, never more benign, or well-beloved. In the courtyard far below the jingle of spurs and harness alerted her. A horse was led forward which Liam Campbell prepared to mount. His departure was imminent, she realised, as he flung his plaid over his shoulder while Sir Robert's urgency indicated last-minute instructions.

'Father, Father.' He was leaving without saying farewell to her.

'Father.' As she beat her hands against the closed windows, she thought he had heard as he turned, frowning. And then with a final word, a handclasp to Sir Robert, he rode out.

'Oh, Father, take me with you, take me with you,' she sobbed. 'Do not leave me here.'

She never knew that as she ran from the room, at the gateway Liam turned and stared up at the windows hoping for a last sight of her. His heart too was saddened as her own by this abrupt parting, forced upon him by Sir Robert. 'You will merely unsettle the child with farewells. We will take good care of her, never fear.' Sir Robert was not a sentimental man, especially where the fortunes of the begging bowl were concerned.

'Isobel,' shrieked Caitlin. 'Isobel, where are you?'

To her relief at that moment Isobel poked her head out of a door whose noisy interior indicated the nursery. 'What on earth has happened?' And as Caitlin sobbed out her fears, Isobel laughed.

'Lost? Idiot. And you have been crying, have you not?' she added accusingly.

'My father – my father, he has just left,' Caitlin sobbed.

'What of it? He will return.'

'I know that. But he – I – I – was not able to bid him farewell and Godspeed.'

'What a baby you are, Caitlin Campbell, just a stupid cry-baby. Why, I have never had a father or a mother to bid farewell but you do not find me shedding tears about it.'

Caitlin was not sure where consolation lay in this oblique comfort as Isobel seized her arm and said sternly: 'Come, we are to sup now.'

Even as Caitlin considered approaching Sir Robert, he called her over and said: 'Your father has now departed upon his travels – '

'Will he be long gone, sir?'

'I know not, but be a good child and do not give us any trouble,' he continued, patting her hand in the same vague but hearty manner he reserved for his wife's pet spaniels.

On most days, only twelve persons sat to supper. The food served, however, would have provided for the entire village of Fortingall for a week. The quantity and variety never failed to astonish and shock Caitlin, since Fortingall existed on a meagre diet. Meat made a very rare appearance at poor folks' tables, harvest-time excepted, and she had been reared to dread the words: 'This is the last until next year.'

At first fascinated by meat, fish and fowl served at one meal, she was alarmed to observe dishes carried out almost untouched. Guiltily, she felt that her own participation in such waste invited Biblical retribution and she prayed that servants and their families benefited from the constant tide of leftover meats.

As for those valuable carpets, Fortingall's rushes, regularly replenished, sweet and clean, would have served Meggernie's dining room more appropriately, since pet dogs, readily admitted had discarded food carelessly thrown down to them. Caitlin decided they threatened greater damage to property than all the Glenlyon children put together. Great and small alike they piddled on the rare carpets, which were stained and foul-smelling, their owners unperturbed by such scenes of domestic carnage which they surveyed with tranquil indifference.

Lady Glenlyon and her unmarried female kin, whose exact relationship Caitlin never discovered, all dressed with pomp and competitive splendour, the older ladies satin-gowned, beribboned, sitting bolt upright in the high backed chairs as

113

if they were about to set forth for a grand ball or have their portraits painted. They might be expected, she thought, to possess one grand gown each to grace the occasions of several years before it was handed down to a less fortunate relative. Instead they owned a different gown for every day of the week and the wearing of Tuesday's attire upon a Thursday was regarded as social ruin. And even Sir Robert's 'at-home' dress rivalled any of his womenfolk for grandeur in the matter of velvet and lace.

Each evening, the ladies, heavily corseted and far from comfortable since ample meals left laces cutting into ample flesh, stampeded towards slender padded chairs of blue and red satin damask, where matching footstools were a wise provision since only those closest to the fire could entertain the forlorn hope of being tolerably warm. The day bed, plumply cushioned, and the 'sleeping chair' with its padded wings, province of Sir Robert and his lady, were alone sternly forbidden to them.

Thus firmly entrenched they sat hour upon hour, bravely bearing discomfort, scarce able to breathe without ominous creaking, playing cards or stabbing awkwardly at embroidery frames with fingers so encrusted with rings as to render the holding of a needle almost impossible.

The nursery was Caitlin's special domain. There she shared Isobel's duties, as fellow servant rather than the companion Liam had intended. She was soon pleasantly occupied dealing with the Glenlyon babies, admiring the starfish hands of the babe satin-clad in its beribboned cradle and freeing two siblings from red-faced square-mouthed fisticuffs, while a beguiling three-year-old lisped prettily, tugging at her skirts and begging to be told stories.

As summer moved to a close, Lady Glenlyon was safely delivered of another lusty lad whose father, his duty done, rode thankfully to Stirling, from whence good news had arrived of a Campbell's inheritance of a fine estate. Sir Robert prayed that, young and guileless, he might also be persuaded to divert some of these newly acquired riches in Glenlyon's direction.

October came and sprinkled the green and blue of summer with a blaze of golden glory while Caitlin celebrated her fifteenth birthday with presents from everyone. A tide of discarded gowns, which only the uncharitable would have suggested that their wearers were glad to lose, came her way.

Even Isobel, hardly ever free with emotion, kissed and hugged her and proffered a yellow satin gown, at once too short and too tight, with the cheerful advice: 'You will soon remedy that with your fine sewing.'

If only Father could be here to share her joy she thought, her prayers would indeed be answered. But the horseman who rode in next day was Sir Robert and a wave of excitement rippled their calm lives when he announced a marriage had been arranged for Isobel. Not the rich young Campbell heir, alas, but his widower uncle, even richer, and more eagerly disposed towards thoughts of matrimony, once he had sealed certain trading activities in the Low Countries. Regretfully he would be denied the pleasure of meeting his prospective bride until his return to Scotland late the following year.

'It will be a delight to have riches, my own carriage and my own servants to command.' Isobel was entranced, with no apparent misgivings concerning this prospective husband unseen.

'Should you not be acquainted with him first?' suggested Caitlin but this plea for caution was scornfully dismissed.

'What difference would that make? I have seen his portrait.'

Caitlin suspected that the miniature had been painted some considerable time ago, since it depicted as a young man the sitter who was now touching fifty. Isobel was to have a betrothal portrait for her elderly suitor, painted by an Italian artist. 'He was once employed in the Vatican,' she said in a horrified whisper. She found sitting tedious and the result a disappointment, complaining that Guido made her look exactly like her Glenlyon cousins. On the evidence presented by portraits past and present, Caitlin decided they were singularly unremarkable and that an absence of colour in eyes, eyebrows and hair must have driven the artists into fits of wild despair.

'I am aware, of course, that I am much prettier than any of them,' she pouted, begging flattery, her eager expression so like one of her aunt's pet dogs expecting a reward, that

Caitlin had not the heart to be scrupulously honest. Only one portrait in the gallery deserved acclaim, a youthful Sir Robert in black armour.

'So handsome,' sighed Isobel, 'And so lifelike. As for my aunt, her appearance is tolerable, but so pale and anxious.'

The Italian artist Guido was twenty years old. He had warm olive skin, liquid black eyes and curling hair. In halting English, he explained to Caitlin that he had come to Scotland with his uncle Bartelemo, an artist in stained glass, whose services were much in demand to replace horn windows in the fine castles of this new Scottish aristocracy, eager to let a little more sunshine into their homes. The Italian artists, engaged upon abbeys for the wealthy clergy before the Reformation, found that rich merchants and wealthy lords needed little persuasion to employ their talents at a menial's wage. Watching him at work, Caitlin had a feeling that their buildings, their stained glass and paintings would stand strong down the ages, long after their names were forgotten and even the powerful Clan Campbell was dust.

Uncle Bartelemo had died of the sweating sickness last year.

'Once I have enough money from Sir Robert, who is a generous patron, I will return to Italy.' Guido surveyed her critically. 'You are poor, but *bella, bella*,' and kissing the tips of his fingers, 'you, I paint for nothing, it will be my pleasure.'

Isobel had little respect for artistic integrity, disagreeing with Guido's insistence upon 'a true portrait' and frequently scattering his brushes angrily as she stormed out of the room, followed closely by Caitlin in the unhappy role of chaperone.

'I will not be insulted thus. He makes me look like a shrew. I know better than he does what I look like. After all he is just a common servant.'

'He is an artist,' said Caitlin in shocked tones.

'That may be so. But he is also very poor and dependent upon my uncle. As far as this house is concerned, he is just a common tradesman, carrying out duties for which he is well paid.'

December brought the first snow climbing the walls of

Meggernie to deposit white bonnets upon turret and chimney top. Upon every tree and hedgerow, frost glittered like the Yuletide sugar cakes which Sir Robert had introduced from his travels. And Caitlin found new delight in tumbling with the children in the gardens, breaking ice on the fish pond and building men of snow adorned by old bonnets and broken clay pipes.

As she did so, she played her own secret game: If the falling snow reached a certain window and melted from a certain turret by Sunday, then Father would return by the week's end. But long after the hazy buds of spring sent the grey ghosts of winter retreating high into the mountains, the courtyard remained silent. Empty of all but the hoofbeats of the Perth carter, struggling with provisions through the thaw-flooded glen and their only source of contact with an outside world lost for several months each year.

As Caitlin awaited Liam's return time was measured no longer in days or weeks but in passing seasons. Sadly she realised that her hopes of a pleasant, affectionate and undemanding companionship were not forthcoming with Isobel, whose moments of sunny friendship were notably fewer than her times of sharp temper. Her father had also been misled concerning the benefits upon which he had set so much store, while her secret hopes of learning came to naught since the children were considered too young for the services of a tutor and their education was undertaken by one of the resident, elderly female cousins who could read, write and count tolerably well.

That Caitlin was daughter and heiress of Glencorrie, and that all Campbell chiefs shared a common bond of respect and authority under their powerful Argyll and Breadalbane overlords, did not impress Isobel. That she and Caitlin were distant cousins, both poor relations and unpaid servants, she chose to ignore.

To Isobel, kin poorer than herself, without power to yield, were more despicable than servants. There were more than enough snivelling whining Campbell cousins she knew, fighting for a place in Meggernie. She had been fortunate indeed to have attracted Sir Robert's notice in Edinburgh, at a time when his resistance to a bereaved orphan who had a certain style was not at its strongest.

'Servants can be dismissed,' Sir Robert was wont to remark to his wife. 'Kin, alas, like the poor are ever with us,' he added forgetful that his rich relations at that moment might well be greeting the sight of the impoverished Glenlyon 'begging bowl' carried by his cousin Liam Campbell, with similar misgivings.

It was upon the matter of Guido that the two girls finally quarrelled. One day Isobel came in to discover Caitlin's half-finished portrait. The blaze of beauty expressed in black hair and yellow satin gown, ironically her present to Caitlin, the gentle curving mouth and dark eyes gazing at her were exquisite.

Isobel's consequent rage knew no bounds. 'How dare you waste your time like this? You forget your position in this house. My aunt shall hear of this.'

'Lady Glenlyon already knows. Guido sought her permission to paint me when I was free from duties in the nursery.' She could have pointed out that Isobel had relinquished such duties almost entirely, exerting herself as little as possible without drawing her aunt's attention to the fact.

'You forget yourself.'

'I do not. My father is Sir Robert's cousin,' she reminded her gently.

'Indeed. Is he now? Well then, it is not my fault I frequently forget the fact of distant kinship. For you do not look in the least like a Campbell, Glenlyon or Glencorrie, for that matter. And everyone remarks upon it. You do not resemble your father in the least.'

Unaware of any sinister implication, Caitlin said: 'My mother was a Campbell of Glenorchy, my father's distant cousin.'

Isobel smiled faintly. 'As are we all, it seems. The fact is hardly worth the mentioning.' She stabbed a finger at Caitlin. 'She was golden-haired?' and to Caitlin's affirmative, a triumphant: 'Then you do not resemble either of them.'

'My grandmother was Irish. She had black hair.'

'Irish.' Isobel spat it out with only a little more contempt than the hated word Macdonald she had been taught to spew.

118

'She was cousin to the Earl of Antrim.'

'Earls in Ireland, my dear Caitlin, are pure bog-Irish, hardly worth the mention in polite society. So that accounts for your black looks.' She considered Caitlin, painfully aware that all the men about the castle cast lingering glances in her direction. With her warm heart, her gentle manner, the children all loved her, sought to please her.

'Perhaps you were a changeling,' she said knowing how such words struck horror into any girl's breast. 'Or a Macdonald,' she added cruelly. This was the worst insult she could bring to bear and she saw as Caitlin paled, that the shaft had struck home. 'My uncle says your mother must have strayed into Macdonald pasture at some time,' she added with a laugh. It was untrue, Sir Robert had never said any such thing, but it had the desired effect and Caitlin burst into tears.

To say that she belonged to the hated Macdonalds who had murdered her kin, whose ill-treatment of her dear mother had contributed to her premature death. She raised her hand, and struck Isobel hard.

'I hate you for that, Isobel Campbell, and I will never forgive you, never.'

With a scream and a hand against her rapidly reddening cheek, Isobel was taken aback. That the gentle Caitlin could be roused to such anger. She realised that she had gone too far, when Caitlin's flight from the room took her straight into Sir Robert's arms. As she fled without apology, sobbing, Sir Robert who did not like his domestic peace threatened, demanded explanation.

'To call her a Macdonald. Have you taken leave of your senses, niece? Go this instant and apologise.' And cutting short her protests: 'Go,' he bellowed.

Isobel decided on all possible speed before Caitlin mentioned to Lady Glenlyon, her uncle's supposed speculations concerning the honour of Glencorrie's late wife. She would get a whipping, for certain – Clan feuds had begun on less.

'I did not mean to offend,' she said haughtily extending the uninjured cheek to be kissed.

Caitlin accepted the apology with good grace. She was sorely wounded in spirit. To be called a Macdonald –

degraded by this worst of insults, she felt as if her very soul was besmirched. She would never forget those cruel words, weary of excusing spiteful behaviour because poor Isobel, an orphan unloved by the ancient aunt in Edinburgh, had little chance or encouragement to develop a kind heart.

She would have a great deal to tell her father – if only he would return. She had completed her first year at Meggernie when a servant was sent to announce that a visitor awaited her. Believing her prayers had been answered at last, she raced downstairs to the drawing room.

Chapter VII

Her prayers had not yet been answered. It was not Liam Campbell who turned to greet her, but Stephen, whose delight as they embraced was swiftly replaced by sadness. Even before the words were spoken, his grave unsmiling manner warned her of some misfortune.

'Father, Father, he is well?' she whispered, scarcely able to frame the question for the wild hammering of her heart.

'Aye. And he promises to return soon.' He took her shoulders gently. 'But I bring sad tidings from Fortingall. Jean, our dear Jean, and old Alistair are dead, dead from the sickness that went like wildfire through the clachan. At first we thought it was the plague returned, but the symtoms are different.'

Jean and Red Alistair. Caitlin sobbed against his shoulder, all breath knocked from her body by this cruel news. Jean and old Alistair. She would never see them again, for Stephen was shaking his head, telling her they were buried a month since, while the snow still lay deep in the kirkyard beneath the yew tree at Fortingall.

'If only I could have taken care of them, they might not have died,' she sobbed, 'Why was I not told earlier?'

Stephen shook his head. 'That would have been unwise. We tried to keep isolated as much as we could. Besides it would have been unfair to bring sickness to the castle.' He put his arm about her. 'They did not linger or suffer long, not like the plague, or the sweating sickness that comes with summer heat. This was the French influence, a winter's rheum, fatal for some, but soon over. I came as soon as I could. I had to see Mother on her feet again, before I left.'

Nursing her had been an experience he would never forget, especially during her delirium where frightening

121

incantations had issued forth as if she were indeed devil-possessed. Stephen, praying, felt he did so for her immortal soul as much as her sick body. He had learned much of his strange mother during that time, much that he would never repeat to a living soul. Her hunger and lust for Liam, her hatred of Caitlin and of some mysterious infant from her muddled past who threatened her: 'the Macdonald brat. Kill her – kill her,' she had screamed in delirium.

Stephen's visit lasted two days and at the end of it he knew that he wanted Caitlin for his wife. In this new exultant mood, after leaving so much sorrow and anxiety at Fortingall, he was certain she would accept his proposal and that Liam would give his blessing. In Stephen's mind there was no impediment. The future glowed rosy and perfect. As for his mother, she would accept his choice, when she fully realised that her son's happiness lay with Caitlin Campbell.

On the eve of his return to Fortingall they returned through the dusk filled parkland which gleamed like an enchanted land. Secret and still, a full young moon silvered every tree. It changed them into insubstantial ghosts, gossamer as their disembodied footsteps bruising the dew-fresh grass before the castle. Above their heads, taper lights blazed a golden welcome in windows, with shutters still wide against the day's heat. Facing the house, a fallen tree. How conveniently placed, thought Stephen gratefully, and praising God for his goodness in preparing so admirable a setting, he sat beside Caitlin and after a moment of silence between them, he drew her into his arms. Kissing her, he found to his anxious heart's delight that her response was warm as his own. Grateful, heart-soaring, he whispered:

'Will you marry me, my dearest Caitlin?'

The pause before her anguished: 'No, no, Stephen,' reduced to ruins for him the beauty of the hour. She saw too late what she had done and tried to make amends with a sweet smile tenderly pressing his hand. But the damage was complete and irrevocable. The single word that could have sent Stephen soaring high with the angels and wrapped in the certainty of God's love and Divine will became the word that dashed him from the sky and to the very brink of earth's hell.

When he got back his breath, for he felt that he had

received a mortal wound in the region of his heart, he pleaded, still hoping for mercy: 'Why not – why not, Caitlin?'

'Because I do not love you.' The words were toneless, unemotional.

'Your kisses lie then,' he said sorrowfully, knowing the folly of argument that might drive her from him for ever, but he had passed the rubicon. On its other side lay flagellation of the spirit.

Choosing her words carefully, she said: 'I love to kiss you, because, because I do love you.' And cutting short his cry of triumph. 'Hear me out please. I love you, dear Stephen, as cousin, brother, friend, a very dear friend. I have none dearer now that you – '. Her voice broke. 'But not as a husband, never that.'

Each word she offered of friendship's devotion, now thrust her further out of his reach. It was as if she retreated visibly and he could bear it no longer, not even with his talent for self-torture. Silently he drew her to her feet, bleakly they walked towards the courtyard.

'You will not consider it? Until your father returns?'

'No, Stephen, I cannot let you hope in vain. That would be cruel indeed, for there is naught for me to consider. Perhaps I am too young for marriage yet.'

He left next morning before any were awake. He could not bear another parting from her or the gentle pity in her eyes.

There were none at Meggernie to mourn with Caitlin or even to understand her grief for the beloved old man and gentle Jean Stewart. She saved her bitter grief, her tears to shed, for when she was alone and her life returned to a pattern of days punctuated by small dramas of an occasional horseman appearing in the courtyard. But the rider who dismounted was never Liam Campbell.

Even Sir Robert was now rueful about the possibility of Glencorrie's return in time for the annual Baron's Court, the private court of jurisdiction at Meggernie which gratified his notions of grandeur. Copied from his wealthy kinsman, Campbell of Glenorchy, Liam had recognised it as a replica of the Crown Parliament, enabling Sir Robert to wield the power of life and death over his tenants.

Since Patrick Stewart had taken over Glenlyon's fir woods, there was less need for this compulsory gathering of the tenantry. Husbandry matters concerned head dykes to be repaired annually, vermin to be killed, the prohibition of peat-cutting in cornlands, the tenants' responsibility to plant trees, in view of the rate at which they were disappearing from Glenlyon, made nonsense to the crofters. The social order commanded that no shelter be given to poacher or vagabond. A wife was not permitted to drink in public unless her husband be present, and no weaver was to demand more than a firlot of meal for making a plaid.

For serious misdemeanours such as stealing from a neighbour, the punishment was banishment for a woman, hanging for a man.

'If only Glencorrie could be here,' said Sir Robert as they supped that night. 'His assistance on the finer points of legal procedure will be sorely missed.' He paused dramatically and grinned wolfishly around the table. 'Especially with a Macdonald at present occupying the guardroom.'

'A Macdonald!' shrieked the ladies. 'And in time for the Baron's Court.'

Sir Robert rubbed his hands delightedly at having provided so unexpected and pleasant a surprise. 'Is it not well timed?'

'Indeed it is! This will be a splendid occasion,' his womenfolk agreed unanimously. 'Fancy, a Macdonald!' Heads were shaken as if Sir Robert had managed to capture some rare animal.

'A cause for celebration.' And so opportune, thought Sir Robert, whose tenants were apt to forget their own grievances against their spendthrift laird when he had some special attraction to divert and mollify them.

'Will the prisoner be kept until Father returns then?' asked Caitlin, having never seen a Macdonald and curious to know what sort of hideous monster had been taken.

'Prisoner? Kept? Innocent child,' chuckled Sir Robert as he patted her hand. 'We do not keep Macdonalds prisoner. We hang them.'

'But what crime has he committed?'

'Crime? I know of no crime. But he is a Macdonald and he was found on Campbell land. That is crime enough.'

'But not for hanging,' protested Caitlin.

'That is the law. Unaltered even before my grandsire Mad Colin Campbell hanged twenty-three Macdonalds on the Braes out there,' he said proudly, his eyes searching the table for approval which was gratifyingly forthcoming. The ladies beamed upon him.

'Was he stealing?' Caitlin persisted.

'I imagine that was what he intended,' said Sir Robert, stretching out his glass to be recharged with claret.

'And a Papist too. God delivered him into our hands, one fewer to corrupt the world,' said one elderly female cousin piously, raising her eyes heavenward.

'Surely you know, sir, whether he was stealing or no?' demanded Caitlin.

Sir Robert gave her a black look, his geniality vanished as he said coldly. 'I do not care greatly for your remarks, miss. In fact, they cause deep offence.' He laid down his glass somewhat heavily, all mellow effects of a good wine and cheerful occasion threatening ruin at this inquisition. 'Are you questioning my authority, miss?' he bellowed.

Conscious of a hush around the table and of shocked female eyes riveted upon her, Caitlin replied in a firm voice: 'I do not wish to be discourteous, sir, but if a man, even a Macdonald, is to be hanged, then he must have committed some crime.'

'Must he? Damn your impudence!' And Sir Robert's fists crashed on to the table, causing violent shivering among the candles, and near disaster amid the crystal. 'Listen to me, miss, the man is a Macdonald and on my land. For that crime alone, he deserves to die. And now, miss, you may leave us. Now, directly, go! You too, niece, both of you,' he shouted, purple-faced, gesturing towards the door.

Unjustly dismissed, Isobel's pale face also blazed with righteous anger and she pinched Caitlin's arm furiously on their way upstairs. 'I do not know how you dare address my uncle in such fashion, when he has been so good to you. And now he thinks I am to blame for your impudence too, you wicked ungrateful creature,' she wailed. 'He will never forgive me, never, since it is all my fault for persuading him to have you here in the first place.'

Upon such matters as Isobel's discomfort, Caitlin showed

marked impatience and indifference. She made her escape as quickly as possible but slept little thinking of the Macdonald in the guardroom. If his only crime lay in his unfortunate birth, then this was injustice indeed.

An idea came almost unbidden, an idea that appealed greatly, the more she considered it. Perhaps she could go to the guardroom, unlock the door, and standing well back, let the creature escape, free to return to his wild Macdonald country.

Early next morning, as usual she went to the stables, where her day began by exercising Barby. Aware that kitchens and stables were a steady source of gossip inaccessible by normal means to the females of the household, she sought out the stable lad.

'This Macdonald prisoner. I trust he is firmly held and will not escape and cut all of our throats.'

Hamish grinned. 'No fear of that, miss. He is but a lad, little older than yourself.'

'So young and so wicked too.'

Hamish nodded. 'Aye, he was trespassing, when we caught him.'

'He can be hanged for that?'

'Such is the Campbell law.'

'Did he know he was breaking the law?'

Hamish gave her a pitying glance. 'All Macdonalds are born knowing that, miss. Claims it was a misty day and his horse had bolted. Lost, he came to Meggernie for help.'

Caitlin ignored his derisive tone. 'And for that he will hang?'

Frowning at this unusual interest in a creature regarded by Campbells as somewhat less than vermin, to be shut away with no more thoughts to human rights than would be given to a wild animal, Hamish said shortly: 'His story would all be lies, miss.'

'May I see him?'

The stable lad stared at her with sudden distaste. He often said to his wife that the Meggernie ladies shared unpleasantly morbid tastes in entertainment. He was surprised that this lass, so young and so gentle seeming was no different to the rest of them.

'You will get your chance tomorrow, miss. Sir Robert has

ordered the balcony yonder facing the Braes be prepared so that you ladies can get a good view of the proceedings. I cannot let you see him before that.' And looking her over with sudden insolence, he grinned. 'Besides, he would eat you alive.'

Caitlin shuddered and with all her brave resolve vanished, she returned indoors where she found the ladies in a great flutter over what to wear for the hanging, Isobel most of all.

'There is nothing here that pleases me,' she wailed, indicating the heap of garments on her bed. 'Nothing in the least suitable,' she said, stirring them irritably. 'Something pretty, but dignified and gracious too is called for. The blue satin?' She held it against her. 'Or would the green velvet be more appropriate? What think you, Caitlin? Do be helpful.' In the more pressing importance of a decision regarding gowns, Caitlin's indiscretion at the supper table had been temporarily overlooked.

A dozen times that morning, Caitlin observed Isobel at the window, wringing her hands as she observed clouds gathering on the horizon. 'All will be ruined if it rains,' she repeated, as if the event were wedding to be attended rather than hanging.

Caitlin regarding her excited face was shocked into silence. Then summoned to bring needle and thread to let out a seam or repair broken lace, she found similar scenes in other female bedchambers, her services urgently demanded for ostrich plumes and silver buckles. And upon every face, young and old alike, she saw no vestige of doubt or pity, only exultation and the delight that marked fair or festive occasion.

They had no more feelings of pity or mercy for the young man whose only crime was to be born a Macdonald, than for a captive fox to be unleashed before hounds.

'I am not going,' she told Isobel, who stared at her as if she had taken leave of her senses.

'Not going? Not going? Surely you have a suitable gown to wear, the yellow satin I gave you on your birthday would be perfect. Besides my uncle will be most offended if you do not appear – especially after your disgraceful behaviour last night. I should not be in the least surprised if he sends you packing.' At Caitlin's stony expression, Isobel added:

'Besides you do not have to go anywhere. My uncle has been most considerate in the matter of the balcony, so that we ladies can watch in comfort.' Narrowing her eyes, as if visualising the scene, she continued: 'They stand him on a cart with a rope round his neck, secured to a stout branch, and then drive the cart away. Arrhh, just like that. It is over in an instant, I believe,' she added, her voice tinged with what could only be described as regret.

'Please God, do something,' begged Caitlin in her prayers that night. 'Let the Macdonald escape. If that is not possible, send rain or mist to make the hanging invisible from the windows.'

Next morning she decided that perhaps God did not care much for Macdonalds either, since the day bloomed the very fairest of early autumn, mellow, golden and warm.

To be young and have to leave the world on such a day. And Caitlin shuddered, watching the Glenlyon ladies take their places on the balcony. Twittering happily, wielding fans, eating sweetmeats, a collection of gaily coloured doves, cooing with pleasurable anticipation.

Isobel had not been given a front seat and was greatly offended by this omission, well-suited to Caitlin's own plan of discreetly withdrawing before the grisly scene took place.

At last came the rumble of wheels.

'There he is, there he is.'

'Lift me up Caitlin, I cannot see anything,' wailed a junior Glenlyon. And with the boy in her arms, Caitlin leaned forward. Knowing from old Alistair's description that the Macdonalds were gross, bestial, nevertheless she had firmly decided that whatever the monster looked like, he did not deserve to die.

'Halt the cart, halt the cart. Let us have a look at him,' shrieked the ladies.

The horse was reined in smartly and the cart ground to a standstill so sharply that the occupant, hands tied behind his back, was thrown off-balance for a moment. And Caitlin found herself regarding a young man, of middle height, slimly built wearing a once white shirt, now sadly torn and bloodied, plaid trews and a leather jerkin. That was the first shock, for his clothes were similar in every detail to those worn everyday by her father as Glenlyon's tacksman.

128

Despite the stout rope about his neck, this was no monster she beheld.

Black-haired, white-skinned. Caitlin felt her hand creep over her own hair and skin. As if aware of her gesture the man's head turned slowly towards the balcony with 'its burden of brightly clad silken ladies. To them he bowed, deeply, mockingly. But it seemed to Caitlin that his eyes singled her out alone. And across the short distance, she felt the chill of recognition for a face undoubtedly handsome. It drove into her mind one terrible thought: Had I a brother, so would he look.

Unexpectedly the small boy in her arms burst into tears, and had to be set down wailing for his mamma. When Caitlin looked again, the cart was trundling away, the young man's back to them but his shoulders set unflinchingly as he faced the hanging tree.

At that last moment, Caitlin found she was trapped, her way of escape blocked by female bodies pressing eagerly forward. She closed her eyes, but could not close her ears, could not shut out that sudden expectant hush, followed by a resounding cheer of delight. She looked across at the Braes saw the Macdonald's legs still jerking in a death-jig. And most amazing, despite the head crooked on a neck undoubtedly broken, he lived still. He fought hard to resist death. Unable to draw her eyes away, Caitlin lived through those last few terrible moments, as if they had exchanged places and she was inside his head, suffering his agony. Was he still hoping, even now, that someone would waken him up from a terrible nightmare in which he had been caught by the Campbells and hanged?

Whatever the Macdonald's dying thoughts, the jerking legs twitched and were still, the death dance and his short life at an end.

She was angry beyond tears. Barbarous and cruel, Sir Robert and his family proved themselves worse than the Macdonalds. Suddenly she hated them all, knew she could endure no longer this life at Meggernie which she had suffered because it was her father's wish. But Stephen's visit and the dire news he brought, had released her. Her stepmother's ill-health offered the excuse she needed to return to Fortingall.

Tomorrow at first light, she would leave a note for Lady Glenlyon. Oh, to be back in her own home, where her father would surely understand her reasons when he returned. Stephen would be glad to see her. She closed her eyes, grateful for his love. Perhaps even Eunice would be kinder, glad of extra pair of hands.

She would leave Meggernie without regret. Here no one cared for her, or considered her feelings in the least. She would never be missed, except as a servant. And at that moment she hoped that she would never have to set eyes on any of them ever again.

During the night the weather changed suddenly with a violent storm. Thunder, lightning, reverberating through the hills and torrential rain, marked the end of a succession of tranquil summer-like days which had stretched far into a calendar pointing to autumn.

The courtyard was still awash when Caitlin made her way to the stables and a pale sun peered bleary-eyed as a drunken reveller from the watery sky. No one questioned her riding out earlier than usual but her path led past the hanging tree where, handsome no longer, the Macdonald corpse hung, black as a drowned rat. Upon his shoulders the corbies were already feasting on his bloated face.

'Get away, get away,' cried Caitlin. At this sudden noise they took off, raggedly swirling into the sky to roost nearby, staring reproachfully down upon this interrupter of their banquet.

Caitlin looked at them helplessly, wishing she could cut down the corpse and give it decent burial, a last defiant gesture to Glenlyon before she left.

'Dear God, forgive him and give rest to his soul.'

She rode quickly away but was halted at the first clachan. The river had overflowed its banks. As she searched for some trace of road above the flood, two horsemen she recognised as law officers headed towards her. Had she seen aught of any strangers?

'What manner of strangers?'

'A dozen or so ragged men, on stolen horses.'

'I have seen no one since I left Meggernie less than an hour since.'

Asked her destination, she told them Fortingall, and the senior officer said: 'Have a care then, miss, for these men are outlaws, caterans, most with a price on their heads. Several houses in the glen have been robbed, including the dower house at Chesthill.'

As she thanked them for their warning and prepared to ride on, the younger officer said: 'Better choose some other route, the road to Fortingall has been washed away by the storm.' By way of confirmation, in the brown water boiling below the river bank, there was the forlorn sight of a dead sheep, tree and broken henhouse floating by.

For a moment she pondered the wisdom of returning shame-faced to Meggernie. By now Lady Glenlyon would have read her note. No, better face floods than the anger and scorn of Isobel and her ladyship.

Half a mile further and Barby was up to her fetlocks, protesting, in swirling water. There was only one thing to do, climb higher above the flood waters, cross over the hills and approach Fortingall by way of ruined Glencorrie, from Culdares Hill. She would be safe too from encountering the outlaws, dregs of the mercenaries who had roamed the country since Montrose's wars more than twenty years since. The 'broken men' of Alistair's stories, ready to fight any man who would pay for their services, their ranks open to brigands and political refugees. The strict laws of Highland hospitality did not apply to Lowlanders or to any with a price on his head, ready to lift whatever took their fancy, and whoever, if the lass was comely enough.

As for Caitlin she was more afraid of ruined Glencorrie and its ghosts, than of an army of broken men. She could outride any man and was quite capable of taking care of herself in these hills.

The sun had come up, warm and splendid, so that far below her the earth steamed with clouds of vapour. The tranquil moment seemed opportune, the place perfect by a tiny stream. And so, with Barby firmly tethered to a nearby tree, she ate the meat and bread she had brought away secretly from last night's supper. It tasted good and the stream water, cool and clear, assuaged her thirst. Chewing a blade of grass she considered her future.

What was she going to do with her life in Fortingall? She

thought of the shabby stone-flagged kitchen where Eunice never gave her a moment's peace, where every simple action was a fault. Life in Fortingall was worse than this buzzing swarm of insects descending upon her face and arms. Life in Fortingall was like being beseiged by an army of shrill angry wasps.

There was an alternative. Marry Stephen. She conjured up his face when they had parted at Meggernie, his expression as he looked at her, identical to one she had observed in unguarded moments on Liam Campbell's face. A man's expression, deep and tortured, full of wordless, secret longing which she did not yet fully understand, but which made her vaguely uncomfortable.

If only Stephen had not proposed, said the words that could not be recalled but which changed forever the easy harmonious relationship between them. She could not, did not, would never, *love* Stephen well enough to be his wife, good Christian man that he was. She must love any man she hoped to marry at least as much as she loved her father. To marry a man and bear his children was a daunting prospect and despite her lifetime association with farm animals she could never quite reconcile their gross mating with ideals of human love expressed between man and woman and sanctified by the church. In marriage there must also exist tenderness, caring. Love between man and woman, as between herself and her father, must be touched with divinity, the next best thing to God's own love made incarnate.

Father she had always loved, from the first instant of her remembered life, there had been no man to take his place. Certainly not Stephen, well beloved as brother, despite those warm kisses, she greatly enjoyed. He had offered her time to think it over and meanwhile she knew that he would beseech God to guide her spirit in the right direction, open her eyes to see that this was His will for them both, the perfect marriage.

She yawned sleepily, her rest last night disturbed by nightmares over the Macdonald hanging and her decision to leave Meggernie at daybreak.

How peaceful this place she had chosen to rest. She was in no hurry to continue her journey, and although she could not tell whether the floods had subsided, far below the hills shimmered with sunlight and bird-song. Beautiful and serene, apart from the sheep, noisy beasts. Barby did not like them either and snorted irritably.

Those once pretty lambs, she thought, now shapeless woolsacks anxiously bleating. Something had disturbed them but she was too comfortable, drowning in sunshine, too lazy to turn her head. Gentle trees moved their leaves above her head, although there was no breeze and the stream had music of its own. The future no longer concerned her, it was for divine moments such as these, that God had created his Garden of Eden. And here she was, an Eve, awaiting her unknown Adam. She wished Stephen could have been here, he would have appreciated such sentiments, and understood.

The sound of stealthy footsteps had been covered by the rippling water, but Barby's indignant neigh had her eyes wide open.

Raising herself on one elbow she saw that a group of men stood between herself and the sun. A ragged dozen, with no plaids of any recognisable clan only a shabby assortment of ancient torn and dirty uniforms, bedraggled feather hats and bonnets. The villainous aspect they presented as they stared down at her identified them as the outlaws, the wanted men, the law officers had warned her about.

Scrambling to her feet, she regarded them with great dignity and politely greeted them in Gaelic, which they obviously did not understand. One of them gave a sniggered reply which was obviously indecent from the coarse merriment it aroused among his companions, as he pointed at her with a lewd gesture.

They were an unpleasant sight, but she saw no personal danger for herself in this encounter. Her possessions were not worth stealing, for she was poor as they. She heard another indignant snort as Barby strongly resisted one of the men trying to mount her.

'The mare is mine,' Caitlin said firmly. 'Leave her alone.'

They stared at her, the man whom Barby would not let on her back, cursing. His companions moved slowly forward, their action encircling her. At close quarters, they stank, ugly, unkempt, their evil grins showing blackened teeth. Still she was unafraid. Why should they harm her? If Barby

133

were stolen she would be sad and angry, Liam would be furious, but not with her, for she could not fight determined grown men to establish her rights over any animal. If there was a choice, she realised in sudden cold terror, then she must save herself.

As for that other danger, rape, no lass need fear rape upon these hills, for death would be the instant answer. Especially if one had father, brothers, and if there was no male relative, then the Clan would pronounce sentence.

But the thought made her uneasy and suddenly she felt anxious to set as much distance as possible between the outlaws and herself. Two of the men were now struggling with Barby, as for the others, she cared little for their expressions as they watched her, grinning but silent. Although the hope was forlorn that they would understand, she again spoke politely in Gaelic, pointing to Barby:

'The mare belongs to my father, Liam Campbell, chief of Glencorrie and cousin to Sir Robert Campbell of Glenlyon. It will go ill with any of you if you are found on his land. He hangs men for trespass.'

The threat meant nothing to them, for their lewd expressions remained unchanged, their eyes crawling over her like a horde of black beetles. With a shrug which she hoped indicated indifference, she turned her back on them and began to walk away. Swiftly as she dared without breaking into a run, remembering the croft she had passed a quarter-mile back. If she whistled now, perhaps Barby would break away, come to her.

The mare heard, rearing, neighing furiously, but was firmly held. The next moment she heard their yells, the sickening sound of pounding feet on the heath behind her.

The man who reached her first threw his arms around her, clutching her against him. As she struggled, the vile stench of him made her want to vomit.

'Let me go, let me go.'

She could not believe this outrage was happening to her, not even when the ground thudded up to meet her spine. Now there were faces staring down at her, amid encouraging cheers. A hand grabbed at the neck of her gown, ripping it open to the waist. Anger for her torn garment was replaced now by sheer gibbering terror as she felt hands on her legs, trying to pull them apart. Leering lewd faces made mock kissing sounds above her, while the man who had thrown her to the ground, leaped astride her pulling open his clothes, eyes gleaming, mouth dribbling in anticipation.

The stench of his unwashed body was nauseating as his obscene action, but it jolted her out of panic. She could never survive against their brutality by screaming. Screaming wasted strength and the only thing to outwit them was surprise, the unexpected. As for Clan laws of death as punishment for rape, such would mean nothing to these brutes who would vanish into the blue and leave only her broken body as evidence.

Her sudden immobility made them pause. Why wasn't she struggling any more? Most women they took, fought, screaming, cursing and still kept on weeping for mercy, on and on, right until the last man was satisfied. They enjoyed the screaming, crying part, but this lass would be an interesting new experience.

Looks were exchanged, hooting sounds of excited mirth.

'Is she asking for it? Is she willing?'

'She is mine.'

'No, she is not, I am older.'

In that moment of argument, as to who would be first to sample her charms, as they jostled one another aside, growling like wild beasts over a kill, Caitlin's mind worked rapidly. This was her chance, her only chance and she must not hesitate. All now depended on swift movement, taking them by surprise. She was young and strong, and no stranger could keep up with her, bred to these hills. She could run, leap across streams like a mountain goat.

The man grappling with Barby, pushed them aside. They let him pass respectfully. This was their leader and for a moment, Caitlin considered appealing to him, begging mercy. Then she saw the cruelty of his face.

'A virgin for your worship,' said one of the men grovelling.

So that was it, his was the *droit de seigneur*.

'Take your hands off her,' he said to the men who held her legs apart.

'We are only holding her for you, your worship.'

'I need no help from scum like you. I can manage her

135

myself. Stand back from me. Don't worry, you will all get your turn, when I have finished with her.'

'Enough left for all of us to sample, is that it?'

As the leader knelt astride her, unfastening his breeches belt, Caitlin twisted round, raised her knee savagely into his groin and as he rolled away, groaning, she made a great leap forward. The men had moved a little distance away and her swift action took them off-guard. Even as they gathered their wits, yelling in pursuit, she was away across the heather.

'Catch her, you fools! Don't let her escape.'

Shrieking, whistling, they tore after her. This was better sport than they had hoped for. They did not even run too hard, so confident that they must meet up with her on the hill's summit. She ran gracefully, swiftly but carefully choosing her terrain, for a twisted ankle could bring her down. Her feet skimmed across the heather. But where was she running? She realised that her flight had taken her into an area away from Fortingall, away from Glencorrie. Dimly she recognised that she was running to the north and west and panic flowed through her.

Had she already crossed the border into the territory of the Macdonalds? She remembered the poor hanged man, probably women met with a similar sentence. Trespass, punishable by death and she could expect as little mercy as the Macdonald had received from the Campbells. Less, considering their certain knowledge of his fate. Hanging Glencorrie's daughter would be sweet revenge.

She was trapped between two enemies. Lost indeed.

Breathless now, she glimpsed far below the gray huddle of a clachan, a tall tower. The tower was something she recognised from a remembered dream, familiar, although she had never been there. She paused. If only she could double back and find her way down to Inverar. But to try to reach the twisting road below was to waste valuable time, lose the advantage she had gained over her pursuers.

Hearing her labouring breath, her thumping heartbeat told her that the strain of this upward climb was telling on her. She was tiring, her leg muscles growing ominously heavy.

She reached a ledge, paused and discovered to her horror

that she was trapped by a great scree that lay below her. There was no way across. Behind, close now, she heard the yells of triumph. Could she reach higher ground and try again? Away to the west, a tiny white blob, half-hidden by trees. Was that Meggernie?

Oh dear God, let a miracle happen, let me reach it. But it was too far, much too far unless she could sprout wings and fly. Oh dear God, let me be changed into a bird ...

An eagle, screaming rage, rose before her, gold touching his outspread wings. She lost her balance before the threat of those murderous talons. She fell, rolled a few yards, when the leader of her pursuers, who had outrun his companions despite the pain she had inflicted on him, now reached her.

With a curse and murder in his eyes, he seized her, brought his fist down hard against the side of her head. Stunned, she was rolled over onto her back and he was on top of her. She felt his hands touching her naked flesh and somewhere far off, the howls of delight, the cries of encouragement from the watchers mingled with her own screams. She thrust hands against his chest in vain and then she ran fingernails heavily down his face, catching his eyes. She saw blood, a roar of pain as he released her. Then she rolled away and was screaming into empty air.

Falling, falling. Another man reached out to grab her, but she kept on twisting over and over, carried downwards by her own impetus. The leader, his face bloodied, leaped forward, tried again to seize her, but she slithered away, dizzily spinning over and over, down the steep mountain side.

The pebbles, dust, and soil of the scree, all rolled with her. A boulder marched towards her, large and gray and terrible. She thought she screamed again, but no one, not even God, heard her. The world was empty but for herself and her pursuers. Better to die this way, than fall into the outlaws' hands.

On and on, she rolled. Over and over, spinning into nothingness. The world was empty and she closed her eyes against the dark.

Brendan: 1683-91

Chapter VIII

Brendan Macdonald, clan chief of Ardarroch, and his visiting cousin Ruari from Glencoe had been stalking on Beann Saighde since daybreak, the great deerhound Bran loping alongside.

Over all there was an air of richness and fulfilment. In knee-high heather, blooming deep rich purple and fragrant around them, in air so clear and sharp to breathe it was like drinking wine.

At last they had reached the place appointed for the kill. This would be one of the last hunts before the October deer-rut and the Braes of Ardarroch were splashed with tawny golden hues, the copper-tinted deer grass, a piebald pony's coat thrown carelessly over a wild landscape. Already the rowans' cautionary scarlet hinted at a winter of uncommon severity.

Suddenly the rim of a vast amphitheatre loomed before them. From their vantage point near the summit of the Hill of the Arrow, they looked down watercourses, sparkling rills of glistening silver channelling the lower slopes of this natural refuge, cradled and secret. Sloping heather-clad walls were sliced neat, sharp and black by peat hags.

The scene was one of grandeur and desolation, topped by a sky whose cloudless blue held a solitary occupant; a golden eagle, its wings reverberating sunlight as it hovered and then swooped gracefully over the wide corrie and out of sight.

Brendan's hand followed its flight. 'After some quarry, a weak calf, like as not. I will wager that is the place for us too, Ruari. Come along, Bran,' and giving the signal to the

138

hunters who followed them, he started down through the heather at a leisurely jog-trot.

Ruari watched his young cousin anxiously. It was a fair distance to travel on foot although he knew the rules. Horses were noisy beasts, the thud of their hooves could alert deer a mile away and hunters scorned to use them except to carry the kill home. Besides there was not one among the thirty Ardarroch men who had started off from home that morning, who could not outrun a horse on these hills.

No man, save only their young chief Brendan. On a bad day when the cough that troubled him would have alerted any distant deer herd.

As if aware of Ruari's thoughts, Brendan paused and stretched his arms wide. 'Ruari man, is this not a great day to be alive, to savour every moment?'

Ruari considered. Bull-strong, he took being alive as a matter of course and never thought much about being grateful for it. But then cousin Brendan's life had been shaped by the misfortune of bad lungs and of long winters crouched over the fire huddled in shawls.

They ran on, effortlessly downward to where at last, still far distant, the deer grazed peacefully. Surrounded by sheer unbroken mountain walls, sparkling torrents and the bright green treachery of bogs, the hunters waited for the signal.

At last came the faint whistles of the beaters.

'Now.' Jog-trot pace changed to a quick loping stride. Calf-high brogans, made of cowhide, punched with holes, to allow seeping water to run out again, gave protection against spike of heather and scrub and carried them effortlessly across the bounder-strewn terrain.

A whistle shriller, more piercing than before and Brendan help up his hand. Again.

'Now.' Swiftly, silently, they moved down the gulley towards the skein of rocky outcrop, breaking like bare bones through the corrie. Here the beaters would drive in the scattered herd, to be picked off by their arrows.

Again the signal. 'Now, move.'

'No, wait.' A hand on Ruari's arm.

'God in heaven, what has happened to scare the beasts?'

Cursing their ill-fortune, the cousins watched the deer panic, circle, waver and bolt, round and away to the north.

'Over there, look, that's no deer.'

And where the herd had been a moment ago was a tiny female figure, fleeing across the hill, with a dozen men at her heels.

Their lost kill, their hours of patient stalking wasted, the hunters cursed the woman soundly.

'What game does she think she is playing?'

'Think you it is a game?' asked Brendan.

'Who are those men anyway?' demanded Ruari angrily. 'Have they any right to be on your land?'

Brendan shook his head. 'Tell them that. They are most likely the ones who have been thieving from us.' For weeks now there had been stories from tenants about the caterans, drifting back and forth across the hills between Ardarroch and Glenlyon, lifting cattle and stealing from crofts.

'That scum. Why do we wait, cousin, let us get at them.'

'The woman?'

Ruari laughed. 'Spare your gallant thoughts, cousin. If the caterans chose to have sport with a tinker's wench that is their business.'

'Not on my land, when they disturb my deer,' said Brendan grimly.

'Whoever she is, she is doubtless enjoying the chase as much as any. I have never met a tinker's lass who could not take good care of herself.'

'You are right. Who but such a creature would be roaming the Braes of Ardarroch. Come, Ruari, our sport lies with those devils, and quickly, before they escape us yet again.'

Used to moving stealthily, letting the scrub and boulders of the hills serve them for cover, the Macdonald hunters took the outlaws by surprise. The birdlike whistles of the beaters had been lost in their noisy pursuit of the girl. They thought the hillside was their own and the last thing they expected was the sudden silent eruption of a line of angry archers, a flurry of arrows. Painfully but not fatally wounded, two of their number fell, howling with pain and the rest beat a sharp retreat.

Watching the two men stagger to their feet and limp after them, Ruari asked: 'Shall we follow them?'

Brendan shook his head. 'They are heading into Glenlyon's territory. Let the old devil have them. Vermin to vermin, say I. I will not risk one more Macdonald life in that vile land.'

'The woman? Do you see her.'

The rocky terrain was empty of life. 'They will have gathered her up in their flight.'

'Then good riddance. She is not our responsibility.'

'Right enough, we might as well return home.'

At his side, the deerhound whimpered, sniffing the air.

'There will be no hunting for anyone this day, Bran. Every deer in the hills for twenty miles around has been alerted,' said Ruari disgustedly.

'Aye, their sport with the tinker woman has cost us a full winter larder.' Turning, Brendan saw that Bran was no longer with him. 'Bran? Where is the confounded beast?'

'I dare say he will know his own way home.' And as they turned their heads sourly in the direction of Ardarroch, Brendan heard Bran's triumphant baying.

There was another sound. It was repeated. No dog this time, but a human voice, calling for help. The Gaelic words none could refuse to obey. The sound came from below them and bending down them stared over the edge of the scree.

'The tinker's woman. The devils left her.'

'And so should we, cousin.'

But Brendan scrambling down the scree, reached her first and raised her head gently. It lolled against his arm. Her face was filthy, covered with dirt and scratches, her hair matted, grey with dust. Eyes, dark as his own, flickered open, glazed with pain and terror.

'Are you hurt?'

The face before her, and the voice, were human. The words in Gaelic, she understood. God be thanked. For the last time she opened her eyes, Caitlin had encountered a large grey hairy face with bright topaz eyes. She had assumed the creature to be one of Red Alistair's monsters who lived in these hills, and whose grisly exploits had coloured her childhood.

But the monster had not eaten her as she had been warned to expect. Instead it had licked her face with a large pink tongue. Its face far from ferocious, looked amused. Amused, after all she had suffered. She had fainted away again from sheer terror.

141

Now the face bending over her came into focus. A man. His presence could mean only one thing. The outlaws had returned for her. With her last remaining strength, she tried to fight him off, striking against his chest with feeble fists, until he grabbed them firmly.

'Do not be afraid of us. We mean no harm to you.' His voice, the familiar Gaelic, calmed her.

'Those men,' he continued. 'Are they from your clan?' He had silky black hair, white skin, framing dark eyes, full of compassion.

'No, no. They tried, they tried ... '

Her torn gown was explanation enough. She was not a robber's whore after all.

The same thought had occurred to Ruari. 'I doubt those devils stole the lass from her folk,' he whispered.

'Where is your home? We will take you there. Can you walk?' The girl did not seem to understand, dazed, scared. At his attempts to raise her to her feet, with Ruari's assistance, she fainted away again. Brendan tried chafing her torn, bleeding hands, but to no avail.

'She may be hurt,' said Ruari.

'I will carry her,' said Brendan, as their leader.

'That you will not,' said Ruari Macdonald. Half-a-head taller than the young chief of Ardarroch, he took her from his cousin's arms: 'What shall we do with her, cousin?'

'Take her back to Ardarroch, of course. Elspeth will know what to do.'

'And then?'

'Find out where she comes from.'

Ruari grinned, looking at the light burden he carried. 'Who knows, she might even be pretty once her face is washed.'

Thankfully, Caitlin opened her eyes and stretching out a hand touched pillows large and soft, linen cool and clean. A nightmare only, God be thanked. She was in her own bed at Fortingall. She did not wish to recall the hideous dream and turned on her side to sleep again. It was then that the pain made her cry out. Under the sheet, her leg was bound. Now she saw bandaged wrists under the nightshift, which was not her own. This one was new and too large for her.

142

Heart thumping she lay back against the pillows, remembering. She had fallen down the scree, the outlaws ... what had they done to her, why had they brought her here? This was no robbers' hovel. Beyond the bed curtains, a stone-walled chamber with a high window. Was it a prison? When she tried to sit up, she fell back wearily against the pillow, feeling as if every bone in her body that was not shattered had turned to melting wax.

Her movement brought forth from the shadows, a *cailleach*, so ancient and wizened, Caitlin took her to be a hundred years old. But her face, as she leaned forward was kind.

'Awake at last? Here is drink for you. There, there, it will soothe the pain, make you sleep. That was a terrible experience you had,' she added conversationally. 'My lord Brendan was telling me how they thought at first that you were dead. Aye, dead.' And she shook her head so vigorously that her huge white mutch bobbed with independent life. 'You are not to worry. You are safe with us and my lord Brendan will send word to your people.'

'Where am I? What is this place?'

The old eyebrows raised and vanished into the mutch. 'You are at Ardarroch, lass, where else? No harm will befall you here.'

But Caitlin was no longer listening.

Ardarroch. She turned away her head, wanting to say that she must leave immediately, but the draught was potent and the words refused to form themselves in the right order. She was very tired. She would sleep and then refreshed, make her plans to escape the hated Macdonalds and return to Glenlyon. It would be easy to outwit them once she was strong again.

When she next opened her eyes, it was to hear whispers nearby. The grey hairy dog stared down at her, head on side, and whimpered with almost human concern. Now the white mutch was bobbing in the direction of the two young men who had rescued her. She regarded their approach through narrowed eyes, feigning sleep.

'Quite a little beauty you have found yourself, young masters,' chortled the old woman.

'I wonder who she is?' The voice was deep and

pleasant-sounding and came from the slighter, younger man.

'Perhaps there will be a reward for her, Brendan,' said his companion.

'Aye,' said the *cailleach*, with a delighted chuckle. 'She has the look of the quality about her. No tinker lass, yon, that for sure.'

The man addressed as Brendan swore. 'Those devils, not only thieving cattle, but lasses too.'

'Vermin they are, just vermin,' sniffed the old woman dismissively and peered down into Caitlin's face, beckoning to the young men. 'She has a look of our people about her. Her colouring, that black hair, her eyes too, when she was awake.'

'She is no Macdonald of these parts, Elspeth, we would have heard if any were missing.'

'But there is something mightily familiar about her, right enough,' agreed Ruari.

'We can do nothing until she can tell us something about herself.'

'Such an ordeal, the poor lass. Just a bairn, she is.'

Caitlin, hardly daring to breathe, kept her eyes tight closed. As they walked away, she could hardly contain her indignation. How dare they! How dare they insult her by saying that she, a Glencorrie Campbell, no less, looked like *them*. She would have been less insulted had they decided she resembled this extraordinary dog who watched her intently, his paw resting on her bed and at her slightest movement, looking not only likely to lick her face all over again, but to burst into human speech.

As an experiment, she winked conspiratorially and for one dreadful moment, she was certain that the creature winked back at her and smiled. Still, it was far better to resemble this nice beast than Macdonald vermin. Although she was disappointed that the one addressed as 'my lord' and his bull-browed companion, did not have cloven hooves and a tail a-piece, as she had been led to expect from old Alistair's stories.

What would become of her when they discovered that she was a Glencorrie Campbell? She shuddered. Even Eunice's anger was gentle sweetness compared with her fate then. She might fare as badly, or worse, than with the robbers. Alistair nan Creach's tales had contained grisly torture chambers, dungeons dripping with water deep in the ground, bodies rotting in chains.

One thing for sure. She need expect no mercy, not even a safe conduct back to Fortingall, once the truth was known.

She felt tears of weakness slide from under her eyelids. No attempt would be made to rescue her since she had planned her escape from Meggernie Castle so well. Too well. They would believe her to be back home in Fortingall. Months might pass before Liam returned from London and discovered that she had left the castle and had thereupon vanished into thin air. Even if she did find someone, a friend or a bribable servant, willing to risk taking a message for her, they would never survive into Glenlyon, shot by the sentries who guarded the pass or, she thought, with a shiver, sharing the fate of the young Macdonald – hanged for trespass.

The Macdonalds would deal similarly with any attempt by Campbells to invade their territory, whatever the reason. She would not endanger Liam's life nor have on her conscience the Glencorries storming into Ardarroch with certain death awaiting them. Wisest, safest, to pretend loss of memory until she was fit enough to steal a horse and reach Glenlyon. By moving cautiously, inspecting her injuries, she knew they were not really serious, her leg very sore, was not broken.

The *cailleach* Elspeth was kind to her and asked no questions apart from an hourly enquiry upon the state of her health, and an eagerness to volunteer information that her young lord Brendan was unmarried as yet. A Macdonald Elspeth might be, but Caitlin had known no such tender nursing since her own mother died.

When at last she hobbled down the stone stairs between Brendan and Ruari, the world outside the windows was a golden glory of autumn trees and purple heather bloomed upon every hillside. The Tower of Ardarroch did not compete with Meggernie Castle for splendour. Here there was no waste, no extravagance. This male-dominated castle ruled over by Brendan Macdonald and his servants was larger, grander than the house in Fortingall, but the shabby comfort of much worn, well-loved furnishings roused memories of the home she had left.

A great fire blazed in a handsome fireplace and as they sat her in one of the two padded chairs which nestled close by, Caitlin's eyes were drawn continually towards those crackling logs, as she tried to remember ... For a scene shifted uneasily in the recesses of her mind, in that region where memory ends and dreams begin.

That evening, she supped at the long table between Brendan and Ruari, with Elspeth's good thick broth, that a body could stand a spoon in, and a pie of rabbit meat, wine and wax candles in her honour. The cousins' talk, bristled with good-natured rivalry, vying for her attention, and suddenly the mist of memory cleared.

The scene she remembered was from a recurring dream that had been with her since childhood. Of crackling logs and firelight, a table laden with food, the aroma of delicious meats. But there were no diners, the banquet was set before an empty room. And over all, a terrible silence, which in her dream she recognised as the silence of death.

She had lost entirely the thread of the conversation, certain that this was the same room, the same stone carved fireplace with its heraldic arms. Now the dream had a sequel. She was alone, cold and lost, crying and afraid, awaiting death's dark angel. But instead someone came, someone real and human, who was flesh to her flesh, bone to her bone, whose warmth brought her life instead of death.

She shivered. Did this dream foretell her own future? Was it possible that her destiny could be linked with the Tower of Ardarroch? As for Brendan Macdonald, Caitlin looked at him across the table, trying to find it in her heart to hate this man who was her enemy, but unable to find any good reason for so doing, since his kindness and his good looks were faultless.

He was smiling, raising his glass to her. How infuriating that a Macdonald could be so comely and gentle too. And so was his cousin, handsome, but thick-set, older. She was sorry to find that even the humblest Macdonald servant did not sport cloven hooves or a forked tail. In fact, grudgingly she had to admit that they were all attractive, amiable creatures, none ugly or verminous as she had been led to believe, this Devil's Kin of Ardarroch, as the Glencorries called them.

Deciding she could not take refuge for ever in lost memory, she invented a story about an orphan with no notion of her true parents. Amazing, she thought afterwards, how glibly that story had sprung to mind.

'The House of Correction in Perth, sent me as maidservant to Kinnaird Castle. The outlaws abducted me.'

As a shrug, a frightened shiver told the rest of her story, the cousins listened politely, Brendan with his hand on Bran's head. The dog also seemed to listen with an expression of mocking intelligence, when Caitlin added a colourful description of Perth, by courtesy of Meggernie and Liam Campbell who had been there often.

'So none would know what had happened to you?' asked Ruari.

'Or care either,' she added with a sigh. 'My new mistress would not worry unduly. Many servants engaged at the Martinmas Fair fail to appear.'

The young men nodded, much to her relief, since this piece of fiction had been provided by Lady Glenlyon, always grumbling about the unreliability of servants.

When Brendan and he were alone, Ruari studied his wine-glass through narrowed eyes. 'Why do you suppose she is lying about the caterans?'

'Perhaps they sprouted wings and flew from Perth.' Brendan sighed, for Ruari's suspicions confirmed his own.

'You want to believe her?' asked Ruari gently, for he had noticed the change in Brendan, a careful attendance to his appearance which had not been particularly evident before Caitlin's arrival.

Brendan shrugged. 'I have not the heart to believe that her lies are harmful. I suspect that she is shielding some one, some man, close kin, perhaps a brother.' He looked at his cousin with tragic eyes. 'I know only that I want to keep her here with me.'

'I had guessed that,' said Ruari with a sympathetic grin.

'I knew from that first time I saw her lying in my bed that she belonged there. I had never missed having a wife until then or thought much about marriage.'

'Marriage, is it? You never miss what you have never had, I am told,' said Ruari, ten years happily married and with seven children already. In the next instant he knew that this

147

was no light-hearted joke. Brendan was serious. 'You cannot mean it – show some sense, man, a passing fancy to bed a lass is altogether a different matter to a chosen bride. That takes a great deal of thought and consideration.'

'I have thought, and considered.'

'May one ask, how? Since we know naught of her. She might be anyone, any sort of creature.'

'She might indeed. But one thing is certain, whoever she chooses to pretend to be, she is a lady born. A servant? Never with those dainty hands and feet. As for coming from a House of Correction, we have both seen lasses from such places among our servants.'

Reluctantly Ruari agreed. In towns like Inverness, such refuges for orphans and vagrants were the recognised market for cheap labour, thin, under-fed, crooked bones, rat-faced.

'Besides Elspeth told me, when she undressed her, that her gown and body linen were fine, well-sewn, a lady's, unless she stole them.'

'Ah, then are we sheltering an heiress, perhaps, fleeing from a forced marriage?' demanded Ruari. 'For that is the most likely explanation, and not altogether rare, since few lasses have the courage to rebel.'

'And fewer still succeed when faced with the might of a parent's wrath, their absolute right to inflict whatever punishment they feel appropriate for disobedience,' said Brendan gloomily, who did not greatly fancy the prospect of an irate father appearing to reclaim his daughter at the altar.

What continued to surprise Ruari however, was Caitlin's resemblance to the Macdonalds of Ardarroch. The same slant of chin and eyes, the slight gap between the front teeth that was a family characteristic.

Servants who remembered Brendan's predecessor were not slow to see it either. 'The by-blow of some Macdonald cousin, mark my words,' went the whispers in the kitchen, now that the sensation of Caitlin's rescue had ceased to be the main gossip.

'If I did not know better,' said Ardarroch's tacksman to his wife,' I would wonder about cousin William, him the Campbells murdered, God rest his soul. She is like him, the very image, the way she holds her head and bites her lip. As for her smile!'

148

Elspeth said nothing, but seemed deeply troubled and Ruari hoped they could escape before she launched yet again into that terrible story he knew by heart, one Brendan was more than willing to forget.

The story of 'That Night', That Night when the hated Glencorries had ridden in and slaughtered the men of Ardarroch, including her own grandson, a lad of fourteen, body-servant to their young chief. 'Murdered, both of them. Not that Ardarroch would have wanted to live,' Elspeth sniffed, still able to raise a tear after sixteen years, to fit the lamentable occasion, 'not with his beloved young wife dead in childbed and their bairn still-born.'

One day Brendan came in to find Elspeth had Caitlin as a new and eager listener. She had reached the climax of her story, and pointing at him continued: 'That was the night I snatched you up from your bed and we ran and hid in the woods. A mercy we had a home to return to, we were more fortunate than most, for stone walls and flagstones do not burn, and the fire did not spread, thanks to my Tormud. Dying as he was from a mortal wound, he had struggled back into the tower.'

Brendan had never been sure how much of his vivid remembrance of That Night's events stemmed from his own memory or from what had been planted there by his old nurse.

'I mind it as if it were yesterday,' she said, the white mutch nodding vigorously. 'I held you in my arms and said you must not cry, whatever happened out there, you must not cry. If you made a sound, we would all die under the Campbell swords.'

That had been his first encounter with Clan murder. No wonder he had grown up hating violence, determined to love his neighbours, and stay at peace with his enemies.

'My lord was four years old,' she said to Caitlin. 'Four, and he did not shed a single tear, even though his lips bled where his teeth had clenched upon them.'

Brendan shuffled his feet uncomfortably, recalling less than the courage Elspeth boasted about, remembering that only by burying his head deep in her plaid could he thrust out the blood-thirsty Campbell battle cries, mingled with the screams of wounded and dying.

149

Elspeth's taste for gory detail was unabated: 'We found young Lord Ardarroch dirked in the doorway of the courtyard, Lady Ardarroch in the solar, her new born babe in her arms, both of them dead.' Dabbing at her eyes, she continued: 'We buried them together. I laid them out with my own hands, my lovely young mistress and the babe that never breathed, and my Tormud, who died in my arms.'

As Elspeth wept again at that sorry memory, for Caitlin too, the scene came uncannily to life. The roaring flames, the fire in the great hall, again that table set for a banquet never to be enjoyed. And the man with the torch in his hand. The man from her dream. The man now had a face. The face of her beloved father, Liam Campbell of Glencorrie.

The death of Ardarroch's chief had left no direct heir. Brendan was his second cousin, a Glencoe Macdonald visiting with his widowed mother, in attendance for the birth of Ardarroch's heir. As all males in direct line had perished under the Campbell swords that night. Alasdair Macdonald, chief of Clan Iain Abrach and known as MacIan of Glencoe, had supported the survivors (in like manner as Sir Robert Campbell had supported Glencorrie) until Brendan became chief on his eighteenth birthday, four years past.

Since Brendan's mother had remarried during his childhood, Elspeth had stayed with him, nurse, almost mother too, and always in a constant state of anxiety over his health. Despite his early bravery, she recognised that here was no warrior breed, a frail bairn to whom winter chills still brought back the deep cough to rack his slim bones and keep them all awake at nights.

Elspeth shrewdly recognised the need for an heir, and that soon. Her young lord must marry and beget children while he still had time, for time was not on his side. He would never make old bones and she could not be taking care of him for ever, making certain that he was not careless about damp clothes and wet feet. She was an old woman and Brendan the last of several generations of Macdonalds she had been fated to outlive and lay in their grave clothes.

'As for that bonny new face we have with us,' she told her cronies, 'It puts new heart into an old body to see the way she has brought a rare sparkle to my lord's eyes and the sunshine back into all our lives,' right enough,' she added.

And Caitlin could have told Elspeth that she was not at all the same lass whom Ruari had carried into the Tower. Ruari, eternally restless indoors, ill-at-ease unless he could be riding the hills, hunting in all weathers. Handsome strong Ruari whom Caitlin hardly noticed, so busy secretly watching Brendan from her window.

Brendan. Not only did he combine physical beauty and gentleness of spirit, but he was cultured, witty and she realised she had never before met any young man who so attracted her. At Meggernie or Fortingall, the talk among young and old concentrated on practical farming matters or politics. In his home, Liam seemed always preoccupied with Sir Robert's troubles, while Stephen talked to her of God and marriage, and love, in that order.

Now each day as he rode out with Bran loping alongside, Caitlin knew that she loved her rescuer, Ardarroch. The monstrosity of such realisation took the breath from her body, made her turn from the window, lean back against the wall and close her eyes in weak despair. By blood her enemy, Brendan Macdonald could never be lover, or chosen husband.

He was also of a different faith. Educated in Paris at a Roman Catholic seminary, he spoke and read many languages as well as his native Gaelic. On stormy days, scolded by Elspeth for venturing to put his nose out of doors, Brendan was content to stay by the fire and read to Caitlin from the works of an Englishman called William Shakespeare, who had visited Scotland from distant London in the reign of James the Sixth. There were other tales new to her, of the Ancient Greeks and how they had sailed to the Western Isles of Scotland. And again from Brendan's lips, Red Alistair's legends of the old kings of Ireland and beautiful, tragic Deirdre of the Sorrows.

About to embark upon the story of Pontius Pilate in Fortingall, Caitlin hesitated, and received that tender but questioning look. 'Ministers at the House of Correction talked about them, of Roman legions in Perthshire,' she said hastily.

Brendan's education had been paid for by an elderly Macdonald uncle who married a wealthy French princess. A childless widower for many years, he had made Brendan sole heir to his fortune, which had been used well to improve conditions for the handful of tenants who survived the Campbell slaughter. After putting them into rebuilt crofts, he had repaired the Tower, filling it not only with the necessities of furnishing, but also with glass and silver, following the example set by chiefs who like himself, weary of Clan wars, wished to explore the great cities of Europe, far beyond Scotland's shore.

Meggernie Castle was on the tip of Caitlin's tongue. God be thanked, she stopped in time and awkwardly substituted Kinnaird, with the words: 'Or so I have been told.' She felt the colour rising in her face. She must be careful.

'For an orphan, she has learning, too. Unusual, is it not?' said Ruari to Brendan later.

'Is it truly learning, or is she a good listener who asks intelligent questions?' said Brendan shrewdly.

As for Caitlin, all thoughts of escape had been laid aside long since. That part of her life, her quest for knowledge, starved in Fortingall and Meggernie, was being fed at last. She was on the threshold of a new world, happy to linger where Brendan Macdonald held the key. Her only anxiety was for her father's grief. He must know by now of her disappearance. If only she could put his mind at rest, let him know that she was alive and well, and if only she dare add, happy.

And so the day came when Ruari went home to Glencoe taking with him sharp comment and unwanted advice. Alone together they walked in the moonlit garden, listening to the rutting deer bellow and roar as they fought for supremacy, for possession of their hinds. The eerie echoes of battle reverberated through the hills and made other animals restless. An owl hooted forlornly above the stables and far away a vixen's lovelorn keening was answered by a dog fox's sharp staccato bark.

Brendan stopped walking. He took Caitlin in his arms, and whispered: 'I love you.'

Caitlin who had kissed him back with passion and eagerness, now pushed him aside. 'You would not talk of love to me, if you knew, if you knew all,' she wept, and was appalled to remember the many lies she had told. So many, she would not know where to begin to unravel the fantasy she had woven about her life for his benefit.

But Brendan put a finger to her lips: 'I care little for what happened in the days before we met. They do not concern me, and really, dearest Caitlin, I do not wish to know about the past. Can we not pretend that life began for you, as it did for me, the day I found you on the hill, or rather, Bran here, found you for me?' he said, smiling at the dog who seemed to watch them proudly with a match-maker's gleam of satisfaction.

'I love you.'

'And I love you too.' She could not deny her heart. She believed that she loved him more than anyone on earth, after her father, Liam Campbell. Now she realised why Stephen's kisses had not been enough. He had never aroused bodily yearnings in her for more than kisses. At last she was beginning to understand the full meaning of love between man and maid. She was one standing on the brink of a tremendous discovery where all the legendary lovers beckoned to her, whispering that there was a place for Brendan and herself in their glorious ranks.

As they kissed, Bran stood close, protectively by them, so that they felt his quivering excitement.

'You are pleased too, Bran. You love her.'

The grey curling tail wagged delightedly and, as Caitlin patted his head, he seemed to regard her with the same adoring eyes as Brendan.

'What a strange creature he is,' she said. 'It is as if he understands everything we say and do.'

'As a matter of fact, he does. He has more than animal intelligence. All he lacks is the power of speech.' And Bran regarded his master in solemn approval of this eulogy before turning to Caitlin, his expression eager, as if awaiting her confirmation.

'Did you know that Deirdre possessed a dog just like him in Glen Etive long ago?' Brendan continued. 'There has always been a Bran here at Ardarroch.'

She laughed as Bran nuzzled her hand briefly before returning to his master's side. There was a great bond between man and dog, inseparable companions, and sometimes she thought the dog shared uncanny perception of what went on in human minds. Especially in her own.

That oddly disconcerting way of listening to her head on side, eyes narrowed as if in deep concentration.

'His story goes back hundreds of years. Always he appears to be the same dog in every detail as the first who came to Ardarroch. When he is growing old, he grows restless, refuses to eat and seems to be listening, waiting. Then he disappears into the hills of Glencoe, the Vale of Dogs. There is a pack of deerhounds there just like him, rarely seen, whom none have tamed. Time passes and just when the whole household has agreed that this time he has gone for good, he is back again, as if he had never left us, a new young Bran, yet with all the same characteristics, recognising me, responding to my commands. It is very weird. Come, I have something to show you.'

With an arm about her shoulders, and Bran trotting eagerly ahead, he led the way to the gallery above the stone staircase. At the portrait of a man and a boy in Highland dress, with Ardarroch's tower behind them, he stopped.

'See?' The boy's hand rested on the head of a grey deerhound, who was Bran in every detail, down to the white flash on his forehead. 'The boy? Why, that is my late cousin, William of Ardarroch, from whom I inherited. William was ten years old when this was painted.'

Brendan turned to Caitlin, conscious of a sudden change of mood: 'What is wrong?'

'Nothing is wrong. I am just thinking about your remarkable Bran.'

Brendan put his arm about her shoulders and felt her shiver. 'Come to the fire. You are chilled.'

Caitlin looking into the flames, wondered why should a boy's face staring gravely at her from a painting seem familiar as her own hand resting on Bran's head? And why should she feel certain that somewhere lost beyond the bounds of memory, this boy was a missing fragment of her own life?

As they rode together almost daily in the hills of Ardarroch, another piece of the puzzle fell into place for Brendan. Seeing her expertly handle one of his mettlesome mares confirmed suspicions that no orphan or kitchen wench could have ridden so well. Utterly fearless, she had been bred to ride and understand horses.

With Bran loping alongside, Caitlin lost all sense of time.

Like one under a spell of enchantment, each day carried her further from Fortingall and the past and more into love with Brendan. Her heart beat wildly at his approach and whatever the weather outside, his presence brought sunshine and warmth. When he touched her, even by accident, her stomach became detached and floated as if she fell from a great height.

The symptoms of her malady were unmistakeable – and incurable. She was imprisoned, without chains, by her growing love for a Macdonald. A Macdonald of Ardarroch. And fourth cousin to the young man Sir Robert Campbell had hanged for trespass, he told her bitterly.

She felt as if a great hammer thudded against her chest. What future could the future hold for her, a Campbell of Glencorrie, with the blood, the dying curses of generations for ever between them?

When the day came that their love demanded greater consummation than gentle kisses or caresses by candlelight, Brendan whispered: 'Marry me, Caitlin.' She knew then she must go. Go and save Brendan from the disillusion that her betrayal would bring, turning his love for her into loathing. She must be far away when he learned the bitter truth, far away in Fortingall before winter came to the glens and held her here, a willing prisoner. And she spared a thought for her father, and for the lies she must tell. Liam Campbell must never know that she had betrayed her clan by losing her heart to his Macdonald enemy.

She made her plans well, weeping as she realised how foolproof they were. Each Quarter Day Brendan dealt with his tenants grievances, hearing petitions and punishing offenders, in much the same fashion as the Baron's Court operated at Meggernie. While he was so involved, Caitlin would be over the hills and back in Glenlyon long before her flight was discovered.

Forbidden to accompany his master, Bran followed Caitlin to the stables. He watched her every move with intense interest, a worried frown signifying an almost uncanny perception of what she intended. Locking him into one of the stalls and ignoring his shrill barks of protest, she rode out. But not until several miles lay between herself and the Tower, did she feel certain that when she next looked down,

Bran would not be loping alongside her.

Although the day was bright and clear, the air felt ominously cold and by the time she was over the Braes of Ardarroch, the landscape had paled as if its colours were being drained away. At the shoulder of high Beann Saighde, Hill of the Arrow, she dismounted. Somewhere near here Brendan and Ruari had found her, mere weeks ago, but a lifetime in love's terms. And now Brendan was swiftly moving into the past, as the glen of Ardarroch had vanished too as if it had never existed.

Walking the mare who reacted nervously to mist and this uncertain terrain, her intention was to reach the summit and then send the animal back with the letter for Brendan tucked into the saddle. Already she felt as if the words were engraved upon her heart for ever: 'Do not follow. I am returning to my people. My gratitude for your many kindnesses, which are not lost upon me nor forgotten, but I can never be your wife.'

How cold and heartless such words sounded. But she had no gift for conveying the heartbreak behind all that simple message implied: They were never to meet again.

Indecisively she hovered. Was it easier and faster to travel through the pass, for the dangerous mountain route offered disappearance without trace into the Campbell lands? Or should she go down into Glenlyon by daylight making her tracks easy for the keen-sighted Macdonald sentinels. Weary, as if she had climbed for several hours, she had lost count of time for the sun's position in the sky was obliterated by mist and heavy cloud. At last the slope before her flattened out. Half a mile further and she guessed from the small avalanche of pebbles following her footsteps, that the descent had begun. She had crossed the summit.

She hesitated, staring into the mist. She would go to Meggernie first. Liam Campbell would be either there or at Fortingall. She would be safe from Brendan Macdonald. Never could, or would, he follow her down into Glenlyon. She decided to tell her father as little as possible about him, beyond stressing the kindness of her Ardarroch rescuers.

She thrust the note into the saddle, slapped the mare's rump with the command: 'Home.' Nothing loathe, the animal trotted rapidly back down the track. Caitlin listened to the sound of the hooves until only the silence remained. A silence complete, enveloping and oddly threatening, as she scrambled blindly down the deer track, barely visible to anyone who did not know these hills.

After what seemed like mile upon mile of tortuous slow descent, she became aware that she was no longer alone.

She stopped, listened, her scalp prickling with the certainty of being followed. In this fine air sounds carried over great distances. And yet there was no definable sound, only that faint stirring of the mist …

As if someone ran through it, phantom-like.

The sound was beyond the range of human ears, still in the realm where beasts alone recognise the hunter's stealthy approach. But Caitlin was aware with every sense screaming in silent terror, that she was being pursued. At some distance still, but patiently stalked.

Who were they?

The caterans again? No one could save her now from their merciless attack. Not even herself, for she was wearied beyond fast movement, unequal to this further exertion. While she kept moving all was well, but when she paused, she became aware of throbbing pain in her injured leg muscle.

Almost certain that she had now reached the approaches to Glenlyon, stiffly she began to jog-trot through the heather. Once, stumbling with weariness, her good leg folded beneath her. Sickened by this new savage pain, she lay curled up like a hunted creature in the damp heather, amazed that faced by so much danger, her emotions still held a place for physical exhaustion.

As she lay she tried to martial her thoughts into coherence, make a firm plan. She must not give in to the instinct for panic flight without direction, that her every sense demanded. As if in encouragement, the mist twitched up a corner to reveal the outline of a loch far below. Was it Daimh or Giorra? Both lay only a few miles from Meggernie Castle.

She rose wearily. Tired, tired to death and stumbling, drawing in great gulps of air, she stopped and listened. Around her the atmosphere held a new sensation that told her, the pursuit was gaining on her.

Was there a shadowy movement behind those thin veils of mist, or were her senses, her fears bewitching her?

She lifted her face, felt no breeze stirring. No movement of air, no trembling of the plants on the heath.

At that moment the mists parted. Heart-stopping, she thought the grey shape bounding towards her was wolf. Then with a mixture of joy and terror, she recognised the long curling tail, the familiar shape ...

'Bran!'

He ran to her, licking her face and she sank down sobbing, her arms about his neck, too weak to walk another step.

But Bran was not alone. Again the mist parted and there was Brendan riding towards her, leading her mare. Dismounting, he gathered her into his arms.

'Dearest Caitlin, I thought I had lost you.' His black hair felt like silk against her face, his cheek soft and warm. She kissed him again and again, weeping.

'Why did you run away from me? Why? Answer me, Caitlin, for pity's sake.'

She looked at him mutely. Where, how, could she begin to tell him and she took from under the saddle the note.

Grim-faced, without a word, he read it. 'Come, we will return to Ardarroch.'

'No. Our ways part here.'

'Do not be foolish, Caitlin. This mist is but the prelude to a storm. Soon it will be nightfall and then we will all be lost on Beann Saighde.'

'Nightfall?'

'Of course. And it was morning when you left.'

'So long ago.'

Curtly he replied: 'You cannot stay out here on the mountain and you certainly cannot descend in safety, not anywhere, without a guide in such weather. Caitlin,' he said sternly cutting short her protests, 'Explanations will keep until later and I promise to listen patiently, once we are safe home. Now we must hasten. There is little time to lose.'

As they rode back, the storm broke above their heads with the sharp needles of hail stinging their faces, turning Bran's coat white with melting ice. Conversation was impossible in such conditions, as choking, gasping for breath, they passed through the eye of the storm.

Caitlin, who had been inventing, and immediately discarding some very unconvincing reasons for her dramatic departure, had never believed she could be so thankful to see the Tower of Ardarroch. In her bedchamber, warm and welcoming, Elspeth poured steaming water into a large tub before a cheerful fire:

'Out of those wet clothes and into this with you, lass, or you will be taking a fever.' Calm as if Caitlin had just returned from an afternoon's ride, she smiled with not one hint of reproach for the anxiety my lord Brendan had suffered.

When she was bathed, dressed again in woollen gown and petticoat, with Elspeth drying her hair, the door opened to admit Brendan. Dismissing the old nurse, he studied Caitlin grimly.

'I want the truth, if you please, no more lies between us. Do you hear, no more lies, Caitlin Campbell.'

Caitlin Campbell. So he knew.

'Yes, I have know, or guessed rightly, it seems, that you were from Glenlyon. A serving wench indeed! With such manners and fine speech? But you do try, Caitlin, you lie very convincingly, although I suppose that comes as second nature to a Campbell. God knows they have plenty of practice,' he added with a bitter laugh. Next moment he seized her hands and said contritely: 'That was unforgivable of me, dearest Caitlin.'

'I tried to tell you many times ... ' she began.

As if she had not interrupted, Brendan continued: 'There was so much that did not fit your story. And always I came back to our first meeting on the hill, and to this,' he added lifting a strand of black hair and letting it run through his fingers. 'This hair, those lovely eyes and white skin. Your appearance gave the lie to my suspicions that you were of that, that hated Clan. You are like us, like the Celtic people of the Highlands.'

'My grandmother was Irish, the Earl of Antrim's cousin,' she said proudly.

He smiled at last. 'That accounts for the difference. So, Caitlin, what are we to do now? Nothing had changed for me since the last time we sat here together by this fire and held hands. I still adore you.'

159

She looked at him amazed. 'You mean, that you do not mind, about, about – '

He shrugged. 'I cannot say that I am overjoyed. I would much rather you had been what you pretended, a poor orphan. Anything but a Campbell. However, Campbell you are and you cannot help your birth, any more than I can help mine. Since this disagreeable fact has no power to stop me loving you, I shall just have to get used to the idea. I do love you, my Caitlin,' he whispered, his voice humble, deep with suppressed longing.

She kissed his hands and held them to her cheek. 'And I love you. I only ran away, to spare you the grief of knowing the truth.'

Wordlessly holding her to his heart, it was some time before he continued: 'My dearest, what are we to do? There will be hell to pay among the Macdonalds, and the Campbells too, when they hear. But I can face them if you are willing to do the same. I have always spoken out plainly that our survival depends upon us living peacefully together.'

'We have said the very same words.'

'So that is why Ardarroch has been untroubled by Campbells these past sixteen years? Ah, Caitlin, we have the answer in our hands. A marriage alliance, there is no better, lasting way to secure peace. After all enemies can marry. Glenlyon's niece Sarah is married to my cousin Alasdair Og MacIan in Glencoe. Theirs is a good example.'

Caitlin avoided the joy and hope in his eyes. 'I am not of Glenlyon,' she said miserably. 'I am of Glencorrie.'

His lips whitened. Oh dear God, what a hideous coincidence. He pressed her stricken face hard against his shoulder. She could hear his heart beating in the silence as they clung together. This must end it all. After this shattering revelation, there was no future possible for them.

'Glencorrie and Ardarroch,' he said as if the words were being broken out of him. 'Sweet Mother of Jesus, we have both slaughtered each other's kin. We carry the deepest, blackest of hatred, worse by far than Glencoe and Glenlyon.'

Caitlin pulled her arms free of him and said: 'You see how impossible it is, my darling, and why I was right. We must part.'

'I see nothing of the kind. All the more reason for putting the past behind us, for peace guaranteed by our marriage alliance. Because I, an Ardarroch Macdonald love you, a Glencorrie Campbell more than the whole world. Our love makes nonsense of hatred. Even if you were the Prince of Hell's daughter, I should still want you for my wife. What have you to say to that?' he demanded triumphantly.

Caitlin's kisses were his answer. He held her tightly. 'You will marry me?' When she did not reply immediately, he continued: 'I shall, of course, require your father's permission.'

Her lips seemed too stiff and painful to frame the dread words: 'My father is Liam Campbell, chief of Glencorrie.'

Brendan released her so savagely, she staggered back hearing only his sharp intake of breath, the curse he stifled.

'The Prince of Hell's daughter? Oh, I knew that would change your mind, Brendan Macdonald of Ardarroch.'

Recovering, he took her hands. 'Foolish girl. It does not make me love you the less, but it does introduce some complications. Will he give his consent, think you?'

Caitlin laughed. 'I can settle that doubt immediately. Never. His father and grandfather, besides other close kin died at the hands of your Clan. And my mother brought me into the world prematurely because of her rough handling by your Clan. She was an invalid for the rest of her short life. Oh, Brendan Macdonald, harbour no hope in your beloved head that Liam Campbell will give his consent to our marriage. There is only one answer he can give. No, *never*,' she sobbed.

'I do not believe that. Stop crying and listen to me, Caitlin. He is chief of his clan as I am of mine. We have both sworn to fight no more, to put the past behind us. So if there is to be a future for Ardarroch and Glencorrie, we must be united, like the Glencoe Macdonalds and the Glenlyon Campbells, by marriage. Dearest, if I can forgive, so then can, must, Liam Campbell.'

'Perhaps I should go to him, explain.'

'No,' said Brendan firmly. 'What if he refused to give his consent and let you return to me? What if I never saw you again?'

God only knew what form Liam Campbell's anger and

vengeance might take, thought Brendan privately. Erring daughters or sisters had been locked away in the turret rooms of castles and slowly starved to death by fathers and brothers rather than allow them to bring disgrace on the family name, by betraying their Clan by marrying some unsuitable lover or hated enemy. 'I have a better idea. We will write to him.'

'A letter? But how can we deliver it?'

'Through Sarah Macdonald at Glencoe to her uncle Campbell Glenlyon. It will take a little time but we will bide in patience.'

The story of Caitlin's flight from Meggernie, her pursuit by the outlaws and Brendan's rescue took many hours to compose and many quills were re-sharpened before they were satisfied it was the best their joint efforts could accomplish. Even then they both guessed their letter would not move the heart of Liam Campbell. The only tears it would bring to Glencorrie's eyes, would be tears of rage, Brendan thought grimly.

A messenger was despatched as they prepared for the arrival of Brendan's mother, to act as chaperone until the priest made his spring progress from Glencoe to celebrate the Easter Mass and solemnised their wedding.

But there was one further impediment which both had chosen to ignore in their greater anxiety over Liam's approval.

Caitlin belonged to the Reformed Faith.

When she first came to Ardarroch, the images of Christ crucified and the light burning before the Sacred Heart had filled her with superstitious dread. But living in the house, loving Brendan, had soothed her fears of Calvinistic hellfire awaiting her immortal soul.

'It is one God and one Jesus Christ we both worship,' she told Brendan. 'Only the rituals are different.'

Brendan kissed her. 'If only all men saw it your way, most of the world's wars would never have taken place.'

The long wait began, as both Liam's blessing and Lady Frances Appin failed to arrive. Her plan to meet her son's chosen bride had ended with a riding mischance. A consequent soaking, had brought about a return of the lung congestion Brendan had inherited from her. No cause for anxiety, his stepfather Sir Hector's letter was reassuring, but she had been forbidden to travel before spring.

Glistening December snow filled the garden, the hills were blanketed in silence for even the roaring of the stags, that ancient drama of survival, had subsided and and was heard no more. But snug inside the Tower, beseiged by cold winter's blizzards outside, the preparations for Ardarroch's wedding began. In a flurry of activity and excitement, no female hands were to be seen idle, lacking their piece of sewing. The corridors echoed to the skirl of practising bagpipes as appropriate wedding music was composed. The *seannachie* burnt candles late into the night, preparing his ballad, to celebrate this first peaceful meeting between Ardarrochs and Glencorries for centuries.

A great occasion. It would go down in the Clan history.

Chapter IX

Brendan had his own secret reasons for wanting the marriage to take place without delay. He feared the coming of winter as some men fear the devil, sharing his Clan's unsaid pessimism that before many years were over his head, one more illness of the lungs would carry him away into eternity. He loved life, he did not want to die, but if God so willed, then he must leave his beloved Caitlin with an unsullied reputation and provision for her future. As his widow, she would be secure in Ardarroch as her home, however Liam Campbell chose to regard their marriage.

He would never have suggested handfasting. That was Caitlin's idea.

'The only sensible solution for humble glensfolk, when lovers are forced to live together under one roof before they marry.' She put her arms around his neck, her face radiant. 'We could be handfasted tomorrow. All we need is to declare before witnesses that we take each other as man and wife. Such marriages are legal under Scottish law.'

'In the heretical religion, maybe,' said Brendan gloomily, 'but not in the Roman Catholic Church. Lacking the Holy Sacrament and a Nuptial Mass hints at immorality and would be swiftly declared null and void by the Pope.' Drawing her face to his shoulder, with a sigh, he whispered. 'This is what you want, truly?'

Listening to the fast beat of his heart, Caitlin smiled. 'More than anything else in the world, my darling, to be yours now, and for always.'

The next day being a Sunday, the household was summoned to the tiny chapel. There, with gentle snowflakes drifting past the window, Brendan and Caitlin knelt by the altar and before the tenants and servants of Ardarroch, in calm firm voices, declared themselves man and wife: 'In the sight of God and this congregation.' Many heads were shaken, for although gentle Caitlin was well-beloved, there were older Macdonalds present who could not forget the old bitterness.

'Had it not been for those devils of Glencorries, God damn their black souls, my man and my lad might still be with us this day.'

Blessing the pair with a kiss, Elspeth remembered her dead grandson and wiped away a tear. Her conscience troubled her sorely these days. She wished there was someone in whom she could confide her terrible suspicions.

When Caitlin went to Brendan's bed that night, he pulled back the sheets, touching the pillows and once she climbed in beside him, earnestly wished to know if she would be warm enough.

'Your feet, my love, are they not cold? Can I get you anything? Are you quite comfortable now? Will you sleep – '

Brendan had never asked so many questions at such speed and Caitlin realised with compassion that he was more nervous than she as they both sat upright against the pillows, hand-in-hand, but far apart. Their only activity was to stare into each other's faces from time to time as if fearful that a complete stranger had suddenly appeared in the bed.

Caitlin saw with apprehension and disappointment that the event she had awaited with such longing was unlikely to take place. Brendan who was never at a loss for words with her, was now tongue-tied with embarrassment. She laid her head against his shoulder. He stroked her hair with a hand not quite steady. Motionless, they leaned back against the pillows, staring into the darkness beyond the bed curtains to where Bran rested head on paws in the firelight.

'Kiss me,' whispered Caitlin.

But handfasted Brendan's kisses were considerably lacking in the ardour of suitor Brendan's who had so merrily, light-heartedly clasped her to his heart on every occasion when they were alone together.

Caitlin however, responded with such passion and eagerness, that the pillows went all awry as they slipped in the deeper realms of the bed. Such kisses, she thought delightedly, a prelude to more delights as deep within her, desire kindled.

'Brendan,' she whispered and guided his hands to her body. She felt his convulsive shudder, but movement was hampered between them by their voluminous night garments.

Caitlin knew what she wanted. To be naked in his arms, truly loved, truly possessed. With my body, I thee worship.

Brendan paused. 'I am afraid of hurting you, my dearest. Besides, Bran is watching us. I cannot, not with him.'

They looked over to where Bran was indeed watching them, his heavy browed expression so shocked and disapproving that the next moment, they were convulsed with merriment.

'He will have to sleep outside tonight.'

'Oh no, Brendan.'

'Oh, yes, Caitlin,' said Brendan and Bran seemed to understand that too as he was led out with great dignity.

Brendan came back to bed and took Caitlin firmly in his arms. 'May we continue, my darling.'

'Please do, my darling, oh please do – '

And so for a little while, the world outside the Tower's walls became blurred and unreal. Caitlin was anxious to believe that this was how all lovers dwelt, in an enchanted land. Brendan's lovemaking was considerate and tender, arousing delightful sensations of harmony rather than ecstacy. Here were none of the great stirrings of emotion she had expected in submission, abandoning her body to the man she loved. Nothing to suggest that deprived of consummation, distraught lovers might be driven to madness, murder of a rival, bodily decline and the ultimate despair of taking their own lives.

As she lay in Brendan's undemanding arms, while an inquisitive moon borrowed through a gap in the bed curtains, and Bran returned to his place at the fireside, Brendan often talked of his summers spent in France and Italy. As Caitlin applauded his courage in travelling over such vast distances and returning unscathed, he smiled. His health was never better than in sunshine and tranquil weather.

Caitlin was to remember this shortly afterwards when an

unexpected soaking on the hills brought a return of his fever. At his first bout of coughing, Elspeth raised the alarm, urging servants to replenish fires all day, while instructing Caitlin in the art of concocting soothing potions from herbs.

As his fever increased, Caitlin cradled him to her, no longer as lover but as she would have held a sick child or pup. The attack passed quicker than usual with fewer complications, and the household breathed freely again.

Elspeth sighed with relief. 'The Blessed Virgin sends miracles to those sustained by love. Now that my lord Brendan has a mistress, perhaps all will be well with him.'

Caitlin was more scared than she ever admitted, for she had never before encountered such a raging fever. He seemed so close to death. Death, dear God, she had lost Jean and Alistair nan Creach, to that land where all sunsets began and birdsong never ended. If she should lose Brendan too.

When he was sufficiently recovered to talk wistfully of a January once spent in Italian sunshine, Caitlin, suddenly brave enough to dare any journey at his side, said: 'Could we not go there?'

'Leave Ardarroch, you mean?'

'If that will keep you well.'

He shook his head. 'Never, Caitlin, never. Here my first duty lies and duty is stronger than life to me. Taking my ease in the sun, that would never do, I would be for ever haunted by what I had left here, my people and *their* needs.'

As soon as he was able to leave his bed, he had his horse saddled and, muffled against the needle-sharp winds, he toured the glen, with his tacksman, visiting sick tenants, noting croft repairs and discussing spring crops to be planted. Caitlin recognised in this dedication, as in so many aspects of Brendan's character, a similarity to her father. Here were two men so alike they should have been friends instead of hereditary enemies.

Liam Campbell, like herself, was fiercely strong. A soaking meant nothing to him. Wrapped in his plaid he could sleep outdoors in any weather and Caitlin suspected that he could fight the very hills themselves. But Brendan was frail, despite his noble attempts, his ruses to conceal this grievous shortcoming for a Clan chief. When she begged him to remain indoors, only then did they ever come close to quarrelling. Sternly reprimanded she was also reminded that Glen matters would not wait and who, might he ask, was to take care of his tenants if he shirked his duty?

Caitlin bit back the obvious statement. That in the event of his death, Ruari Macdonald from Glencoe would inherit, but how would *she* survive if he insisted on killing himself and leaving her a widow who had never been a bride?

Lady Frances Appin arrived with the priest from Glencoe as the first snowdrops dappled the glen. Emerging from her retinue of servants in the gentle balm of sunlight, she embraced her son. Caitlin took an immediate liking to the smiling youthful woman, slim and vivacious, with a look of Brendan in fine dark eyes, now regarding her curiously. She was unaware that the appearance which had once started Ardarroch whispering, now had Brendan's mother questioning that same chord of familiarity.

As she walked through the Tower later, Lady Frances paused triumphantly before the picture of her late cousin, William of Ardarroch. 'Of course, that is who the girl reminds me of. How exceeding strange.'

Curious to hear more of her origins, when at last she succeeded in getting her son alone, she learned that Caitlin had been born prematurely at Meggernie Castle on the night of the Ardarroch raid.

'A weird coincidence, indeed.' She repeated this extraordinary story to Elspeth and said: 'If I did not know better, I would be willing to swear that she was Cousin William's offspring. I am amazed that you have not seen the resemblance.'

She was astonished to see Elspeth thereupon burst into tears. Burying her head in her apron, the old nurse sobbed out a long overdue confession, which she said she had been saving for her ladyship's arrival, hoping against hope that her own suspicions were not confirmed. 'I did not know where to turn, my lady, who to tell, I had no wish to distress Mistress Caitlin, nor my lord Brendan.'

'Then you had better tell me,' said Lady Frances patiently, expecting some titbit of servants' gossip. Elspeth's story, however, not only shocked her but removed her last doubts about Caitlin's true identity.

She found Brendan alone in the stables. His reaction to Elspeth's confession was first amazement, then delight. Hugging his mother, he said: 'So this is why Glencorrie has ignored our letter. And this puts an end to my guilty feelings about marrying Caitlin without *his* consent,' he added grimly.

Caitlin was in the kitchen assisting with the final preparations for the wedding feast when Brendan and his mother appeared and led her upstairs where Elspeth awaited them, her normally cheerful face a study in tragedy.

'There is something I want you to hear, dearest,' said Brendan. 'Tell her, Elspeth.'

Caitlin listened, polite but bewildered. She knew Elspeth's story of 'That Night' word for word. Why was this tale being repeated now, at the request of Brendan, and his mother, if her constant prompting of the old nurse could be judged as significant?

'Afterwards, tell Mistress Caitlin what happened when you returned to the Tower from the wood.'

Elspeth shook her head and said in a trembling voice. 'We buried my Lord Ardarroch and his lady together.'

Caitlin looked from Brendan to his mother. She knew all this already. There was nothing new here.

'And the babe?' prompted Lady Frances, for Elspeth's story always ended: with the babe in her arms. 'Tell Mistress Caitlin about the babe, Elspeth.'

The old woman burst into tears and covered her face with her apron. 'I lied, mistress, I have always lied. There was no babe, dead or alive, lying beside my lady when we came back that night. I told a lie because I did not know what else to say. As God is my witness, the bairn never breathed. I was midwife, mistress, I have delivered generations of bairns. And everyone had grief enough to bear,' she said heavily. 'My grandson died in my arms that night, God rest his soul, but in his last breath he whispered that he had seen one of those Glencorrie devils with the babe in his hands. And who would steal a dead babe unless for some devil's purpose?' she added with a shudder. 'The thought has haunted me all these years – oh, terrible, terrible, worse even than the killings,' she wept.

Lady Frances took her hand. 'I was present the birth,

moments before the Campbells raided. Her labour was long, difficult, over several days. The babe was born dead, that I would swear. Alas, I have much experience in the matter,' she added regarding Brendan sadly, 'brothers and sisters for you, who never breathed.' To Elspeth, she said gently: 'Tell her what you think happened that night.'

'I believe you are my poor lady's babe, Mistress Caitlin. Whoever set fire to the Tower, his conscience overcame his black Campbell heart. He could not leave a live child to burn, so he snatched you up and carried you away to Glenlyon with him. You are the image of the late Lord Ardarroch. A body just has to look at the painting in the gallery to ken that.'

'That is true, my dear, I noticed it immediately,' said Lady Frances.

But Caitlin was no longer listening. Had she not always known, from her earliest days that there was something strange and unnatural about her birth? Now overheard fragments of conversation between her Campbell parents slipped into place. Doubtful looks exchanged, reluctance to talk about the past. 'Suppose she ever learns the truth? You know where she gets that from – ' The words would choke off when she appeared and she had tried to pretend that they discussed some grown-up matter unrelated to herself.

But the truth of Elspeth's words lay in her own recognition of an atmosphere of familiarity and tragedy when she first stepped into the hall, the deserted banquet and the dream image of a man running through the flames. And that man, she knew now for certain, was Liam Campbell.

She had been happy in Ardarroch, reluctant to leave, not only because she loved Brendan but because she had come home. Home to her own. Her mysterious affinity with the Macdonalds was explained: Her blood, her bones, the very seed of her creation knew and remembered.

She could only guess at the truth behind the events of that night she was born. As Elspeth suggested, Liam had thought she was alive and, for his own reasons, pray God they were humanity, carried her to Meggernie, where she had been substituted for his wife's stillborn child. Mairi's history of subsequent miscarriages somehow confirmed that the healthy child Caitlin did not belong to that same pattern.

But Eunice had always known and hated her for it.

As for Liam, her beloved father, worshipped above all but God himself, not only was he unrelated to her by blood, but he was also her hereditary enemy. Liam Campbell had murdered in cold blood, her real father, cousin to Brendan Macdonald, the man to whom she was now handfasted and whose wife she would be when they exchanged their vows before the priest tomorrow.

As the enormity of it all closed upon her, she put her hand to her mouth and gave a scream of such mortal agony, it was as if the knife that had murdered her real father had risen from a rusty grave and been plunged into her own heart.

Brendan rushed to her side and gathered her into his arms, while his mother, with a sad shake of her head, ushered Elspeth out and left them.

'Dearest – you had to be told. It is glad tidings indeed for me.'

'Glad tidings, this horror!'

'Aye, for me, to know that my wife is not a Campbell but of my own kin.'

Caitlin shook her head, hurt by such insensitivity. Could he not understand her reaction to the years of betrayal, of misplaced love and deceit that had bound her to the Campbells of Glencorrie? A lifetime could not be dismissed in a few moments, just because the truth had been revealed. 'Leave me, leave me for a little. I must think.'

Brendan sighed, lifted her chin and said. 'If this has changed your love for me. If you wish to return to Glencorrie, then I will understand. We are not legally bound until tomorrow.'

She looked at him. Dear saintly Brendan, there were few like him in this world, always ready to forgive their enemies. Now that she knew the truth, Liam's silence became obvious. From Ardarroch, he had known she was bound to learn the truth sooner or later.

She would never see him again. Never. His guilt would keep him away from her, but how could she hope to remove all traces of his name, his adored image from her heart? But if she were tempted to think of him with kindness ever again, she must also remember that his lack of a father's love toward her in childhood had good reason. Not as she and

Red Alistair had pretended, because she was not the son and heir he yearned for, but because he was afraid. Afraid that she, child of his murdered enemy, would one day stumble upon the truth. The image of her Macdonald father, they told her. How Liam's guilty conscience must have cried out each time he looked upon her face.

She found Brendan in their bedchamber, staring disconsolately out of the window. He turned to regard her sadly and she flung herself into his arms. Kissing him again and again she said: 'Dearest, you are my lover, my husband, and now my cousin too, it seems,' she added shyly. 'Nothing is changed between us except that I am now a Macdonald heart and soul, and that other name and the devil who bears it shall never be mentioned between us again. For me, Liam Campbell of Glencorrie is dead. I am wholly yours.'

'You must not harden your heart against him,' said Brendan sternly, 'remember always that he did his duty as a father to you, the alien child within his house. I cannot believe that such a man is evil.'

Caitlin wanted to cry out, loyally protest that she hated Liam Campbell, for murdering her father and destroying Ardarroch. But she could not. It was a lie. Elspeth and Lady Frances were right. She had been born dead. How could she ever hate Liam, whose body had warmed her and breathed life into the cold wings of death.

Brendan, holding her close, knew that his own personal dream remained unaltered by Elspeth's revelation. He still believed that with Caitlin as his wife, the ancient bitterness between Ardarroch and Glencorrie would be laid to rest for ever. As for Liam Campbell, whatever his motives for stealing an apparently dead babe to take to his own wife, he had treated Caitlin honourably, with a parent's care. Such a man could never be *his* enemy. Whatever their differences, they must be united in the love of Caitlin, dear to both their hearts.

He longed to stretch out the hand of friendship and kinship across the miles that separated them and, that night, dreamed of Liam Campbell. And how he came smiling, all forgiveness, to be present at their marriage.

Liam Campbell did come to Caitlin's wedding. To change

Brendan's dream into a nightmare few present would ever forget.

Liam had returned to Fortingall shortly before Christmas.

Jean and Alistair were dead. Obliged for decency's sake to spend a couple of nights with his wife, he longed to escape from the house, desolate and ominous without Alistair nan Creach who had cherished him all his life with more of a true father's love than Peter Campbell had ever possessed.

But even mourning could be thrust aside by clinging to the joyous thought of Caitlin waiting for him at Meggernie. Riding out with a lover's eagerness, he could not believe she was not there.

Sir Robert, more anxious to learn of Liam's success with the begging bowl was a little impatient. 'She left for Fortingall. When? I cannot remember exactly. Oh, some time after the Baron's Court, I believe. She was worried by her stepmother's illness, quite naturally.'

Liam was no longer listening: 'I must find her.'

'In due course you shall, I am sure,' said Sir Robert soothingly. 'Wait, Glencorrie, we have urgent matters to attend.'

He spoke to empty air. Liam had departed as rapidly as he had arrived. Shocked and dazed, he proceeded to comb each hill and clachan between Meggernie and Fortingall. Refusing to believe that Caitlin was dead, each dawn he set out certain that she would appear when he least expected it. The reason for her disappearance would have some simple explanation. Then, as time went by, even his daily optimism gave him the lie, and his search became a frantic bid for some clue to her disappearance.

Eventually his exhaustive enquiries brought forth the two law officers who remembered meeting the lass on the day of the flood. Telling him how they had warned her against the journey, they shook their heads sadly. And he saw written in their faces his own worst fears. She must be dead.

Caitlin dead. He could not, would not believe that she could have died without him knowing, without some thread snapping in his own heart too. Grief added to his despair a kind of frenzied madness. When the letter came from Ardarroch, he was too far spent in emotions to feel the full measure of relief that she still lived. Impossible that she could love Ardarroch and wish to marry him. Caitlin was his unhappy prisoner, forced by God only knew what indignities, to write the letter.

'It may be part of some trick to get us to Ardarroch,' he told a less-than-attentive Sir Robert. Reduced to penury by his extravagance, Glenlyon's irresponsible behaviour had become a matter of honour to the Clan Campbell. Humiliated, he was made to sign letters of guidance at the dictation of Argyll and Breadalbane. In such circumstances he was only moderatedly concerned about the fate of Glencorrie's daughter. However, never one to neglect any opportunity that could be turned to his own advantage, the idea of providing Liam with a small army to accompany him to Ardarroch and bring back Caitlin, created the possibility of an interesting diversion. Such an outburst of chivalry might not be ill-timed and might well serve to stifle the grumbles of his tenants and reinstate his own tarnished shabby honour.

In Fortingall, Eunice was enraged by Liam's decision. Had she not always warned him about the Macdonald brat's ingratitude, her bad blood that would out? Protestations fell on deaf ears. Even when Liam was in the house, which was rare, he was no longer with her, his spirit far away as he paced the floor or stared for hours out of the kitchen window. Eunice saw in his stricken countenance what she had always known. He had never loved her. If she had fallen dead at his feet, she could not have prevented him going after Caitlin.

As for Liam, his mind was made up. As soon as the snows cleared, he would go across the hills into Ardarroch, kill Brendan Macdonald, rescue Caitlin and bring her back to Fortingall. Back to him, where she belonged.

In Ardarroch the wedding day dawned fair. The sun-shot treachery of March weather now held promise of spring, with corbies raucously nest-building in the sycamores' topmost branches and every tree flushed with rising sap and thickening buds, soon to burst into leaf of appropriately bridal green.

The rarely used chapel adjoining the burial ground of the

Macdonalds witnessed a scene of unusual activity. The stained glass windows threw their bright painted banners over ancient grey flagstones. The altar draped with exquisite lace, the sacramental vessels provided by Brendan's travels in Catholic italy and France, while the chapel's gloomier corners blossomed under banks of massed spring flowers and garlands to decorate the image of holy saints and the Blessed Virgin.

Centuries older than the Tower, dedicated to St Eonan, ironically the same saint who had halted the plague in hated Glenlyon, the chapel's atmosphere conjured up images of earlier gods, the spirits of these ancient hills and the glen itself. In the days of Ardarroch's greatness, it had been allowed to fall into ruinous neglect when a resident priest had more requirements of comfort than those early fathers who had not shuddered away from celebrating early Mass in outdoor chapels, draughty and damp in summer and in winter, snow and ice bound.

At least the entire Ardarroch clan could be accommodated, Brendan thought ruefully. A small celebration since the coffers would not stretch to entertaining his kin from Glencoe, for whoever invited the Chief of Glencoe must expect a hundred retainers to wine and dine, to carouse far into the night with him. Such was the law of hospitality of the Highlands.

While he kept a watchful eye on the outside preparations, the Tower witnessed the final touches in kitchen, hall and bedchamber, where Lady Frances helped Caitlin dress for her wedding. And Elspeth wiped away a sentimental tear for the bonny bride in the white silk gown with its pearl-sewn bodice.

For Caitlin over all hung the shadow of unreality that she and Brendan were to be married, their nuptials so effortlessly accomplished despite the heavy forbodings in her heart. If only Liam Campbell had forgiven her. That would have been her crowning joy.

Brendan was waiting for her at the foot of the stairs. How could she be afraid of anything ever again with him at her side, not only lover, comforter but friend too. He tucked her arm into his and amid gold banners of broom blazing on every hill slope, bird-song from every bough, they walked the short distance. In the garden's sheltered corners late snowdrops nodded among the daffodils and the warm sunshine added a welcome.

As they entered the candle-lit chapel, Caitlin saw that every tenant fit to walk or be carried, was present. In the loving and now familiar faces smiling upon her progress down the aisle, there was not one heart empty of a blessing for the pair.

The service conducted in Latin increased Caitlin's feeling of unreality. She found her attention constantly diverted and realised with a shock that she was missing her own wedding. She would never be able to recall it in great detail to tell their children. It was not until Father O'Donnell joined their hands and solemnised those same vows they had made in Gaelic at their handfasting, that she knew she was truly Brendan's wife at last.

During the Nuptial Mass, Caitlin looked shyly at him, kneeling so solemnly at her side. Would this exchange of vows, her now official status as Lady Ardarroch, unleash strange new emotions that she told herself, the uncertainties of handfasting had held in check? Their love was gentle undemanding, devotion mixed with admiration, but so lacking in passionate ecstacy as to be in keeping with a couple long-wed who had endured the test of time. Where was the all-consuming rapture she awaited with the giving of herself, heart and body to the man she loved?

Desperately she tried to thrust out the wickedness of such carnal thoughts at this sacred hour, with the priest's hand on her head and the congregation genuflecting as they echoed the benediction: 'Amen. Amen.'

Coughs and stirrings told her that the wedding ceremony was over. She looked at Brendan who smiled and squeezed her hand. His proud expression said: You are my wife now, and forever.

A sound of creaking as the old door swung open, admitting sunshine and bird-song. A new whispering behind them as if a swarm of bees had been released. Another sound, the ring of spurs on stone.

Even before Caitlin turned, she knew that Liam Campbell had come at last. Still holding Brendan's hand, she looked at him with adoration, wearing the sun like a crown upon his golden head. How beautiful he was, there was no man in the entire world his equal, she thought proud that he had come to her wedding after all.

Liam covered the distance to the altar in a few short paces.

At her side, Brendan stepped forward smiling. He too was relieved at Liam's presence. 'Welcome, sir. We bid you welcome.'

Seeing them together for the first time, Caitlin saw how tall Liam was by comparison. Tall, all-powerful. As if he could have broken her slender bridegroom in his two hands.

'You are in time to give us your blessing, sir,' said Brendan, his arm about Caitlin's shoulders. He could feel her trembling and his steady pressure assured her all was well.

'My blessing?' And Liam looked into Caitlin's eyes for the first time. So beautiful in her wedding gown. The white of purity, of lilies. He longed to stretch out his hand, touch her, but no, that would come later. The priest stepped forward, nervous but smiling.

'My blessing, is that what you want?' Liam laughed harshly. 'No blessing, but my curse, that I will give you. Aye, and willingly.' He held up his hand. 'I call upon God in this place to curse the Macdonald who has betrayed my daughter. Curse you – may a shroud be upon you.'

The Gaelic words thundered out, brought a horrified gasp, a series of genuflections from the congregation. Father O'Donnell snatched up the cross from the altar, flourished it before Liam's face.

'Sir, I urge you to take back such blasphemy, in God's name, in His house. This woman, your daughter, is now Ardarroch's wife.'

'His bride she may be, but his wife, never.' So saying Liam stretched out his hand to Caitlin. She went to his side willingly, her one thought to reason with him.

Misunderstanding her eagerness, he held her with one arm against his side.

'No, no.' To Brendan's horrified eyes, it appeared that the sword Liam withdrew, was to be plunged into Caitlin's breast. He rushed forward, withdrawing the dirk from his brogan and realising that he was the only armed man present, with a ceremonial weapon.

It was Caitlin's turn to scream a warning to Brendan. Even

fully armed he could never have stood a chance against Liam. But still holding her, Liam pointed his sword at Brendan's heart.

'No, no.' Even as she screamed again and tried to deflect the blade, Brendan staggered back, uttered a cry and fell at her feet. Still watching the rose of blood grow across the white cambric of his doublet she struggled fiercely as Liam lifted her, dragged her bodily, out of the chapel.

At that moment the shocked congregation sprang into urgent, shouting life and while women screamed in terror, their men rushed to the door where they found Glencorrie's retreat covered by armed Campbell men. By the altar, Lady Frances and the priest knelt at Brendan's side.

As Liam reached the tethered horses, Brendan's clansmen were halted helpless before the Campbell drawn swords, stunned by the sight of Glencorrie, grim-faced, sword in hand and Ardarroch's bride firmly held, her face white as her wedding gown.

Brendan appeared leaning on Lady Frances, a bloodied hand to his side. At the sight of him Caitlin cried out, fighting to be free of Liam's restraining arms.

'Let me go to him, please, let me go to him.'

Liam's grip tightened. 'Listen to me, Macdonald of Ardarroch. You took this woman as your wife without a father's consent. The marriage ceremony is therefore null and void. I take her back to where she belongs. Be thankful that more than your own blood is not required of you, that your Clan is spared.'

'Do you think we will let you get away with this?'

'Whether you do or not is for you to decide. Your insolent letter talked of peace between us. Be that as it may. The men you see here are but a fragment of Glenlyon's army who have come with me. All Glencorrie and Glenlyon's fighting men,' he pointed to the hill, 'are there, waiting for my signal. If I fail to return, if any delay our peaceful departure, then two hundred armed men will descend upon Ardarroch and raze it to the ground as your hated family once did to Glencorrie. This time there will be no survivors, no women or children, we will wipe the name of Ardarroch from the face of Scotland.' He paused. 'The choice is yours. This woman, or your Clan.'

Before Brendan could reply, Caitlin said in a firm voice. 'There is no choice. Listen to me, both of you. I will have no man's blood on my conscience.' And to Liam: 'I will return with you, if that is your wish, but first I must speak with my husband.'

'He is not your husband,' whispered Liam grimly, ''that he will never be.'

This was no time to argue and Caitlin said wearily: 'Then let me speak to the man who saved my life a second time, as you did long ago.'

When Liam frowned, she continued: 'Brendan Macdonald snatched me from rape and certain death at the hands of the caterans, as you once snatched me, a helpless infant from this Tower which you had set on fire.'

The blood suffused Liam's face. So she knew. She knew.

At last the moment he had dreaded had come to pass. But did Ardarroch also know? If so, then the Campbells lost most of their bargaining power.

He released her and she ran to Brendan's side, who led her a little away but still within Liam's sight.

'You are hurt. Oh my darling!'

'This is but a scratch, it is not deep. You are not to worry about me, there are more important matters – '

'Nothing is more important than you are to me.'

'Does he mean what he is saying?'

'About Glenlyon men waiting to fall on Ardarroch. Have no doubt he means that.'

'What are we to do?'

'Dearest love, you must let me go with him peacefully. There is no other way. And I promise you I will persuade him to leave Ardarroch in peace.'

He shook his head, sadly. 'He will take you from me.'

'Have you no faith in me, my darling? No man can take me away from you. Especially Glencorrie, who is not my father. That is our strongest weapon.'

'Why do we not use it now? Tell everyone – '

'Here, at this moment, you mean? Announce the truth to these men, these old enemies, longing for just such an excuse to fall upon each other. Oh Brendan, Brendan, such a slaughter there would be. How much of Ardarroch would survive against two hundred armed Campbells?'

It was true. What evidence did they have for Caitlin's abduction in infancy? A frightened *cailleach*'s tale when everyone in Glenlyon knew that Mairi Campbell was Caitlin's mother, her dark looks inherited from her Irish grandmother.

'Who would ever believe that a Glencorrie would take a hated Macdonald brat and rear it as his own?' she whispered.

Caitlin was right. And in a court of law, Liam Campbell would be regarded as her father. Real or foster, he would have legal rights and she was in default, having eloped and married without his consent.

'He will take you from me. I know it,' Brendan repeated miserably.

'My dearest, nothing, nothing, in this world will keep us apart. When I explain everything to him, how you saved my life, how much I love you, he will let me return. I know. He cannot refuse, he cannot love me and refuse what I want most in all the world.' She kissed his cheek: 'Besides he cannot marry me to anyone else, I am no longer a maid, remember, I belong to you.'

'What if he refuses to be convinced?'

'I do not know what will happen then.' She shrugged, her eyes on the grim-faced horsemen. 'I will escape, somehow, never fear.'

'Better than that, I will come for you.'

'That you must do, even if blood be shed,' she said desperately. 'Come for me.'

'Aye, and Glencoe will help, they have long awaited a chance to settle with these hated Campbells.'

'You must give me time, for pity's sake do nothing on impulse, nothing to bring war between us.'

'I will give you a week.'

'Promise.'

'I promise.' He held her close. 'I love you, Caitlin, my wife.'

Lingering, she kissed his lips. 'I will come back, never fear.'

Watching that lovers' embrace was agony for Liam. Then Caitlin was at his side.

'I will come with you, but will you not give me time?'

Liam regarded the Ardarroch men, silent but dangerous. This was no time to waste. 'No.'

'Only to get suitable clothes, my horse,' she pleaded.

'No. Here is my plaid, a Campbell plaid which you were once proud to wear,' he said bitterly, throwing it over her wedding finery. 'And I have a horse for you too. Have I not always thought of everything?' And so saying, he threw her none too gently on to its back and gave the order to move out.

Never was man so glad to put the dust of Ardarroch behind him. He had not set foot in this accursed glen since the day he carried Caitlin out inside his plaid, naked against his breast. He remembered that velvet downy head, the questing mouth that sought her dead mother's breast.

What had he done? And what was next, his demon mocked him? Now that you have her captive, do you intend to lock her in a tower room for the rest of her life if she will not stay with you willingly?

Liam's held her horse's leading rein. They rode fast and without any words until they entered Glenlyon. Once, looking over her shoulder she saw that their journey which had begun with twenty men, was now accompanied by a small army. Its presence made her shiver. Liam had not lied.

Where the road led to Meggernie, they parted company from the Glencorrie's men, some of whom she recognised, friends and neighbours from Fortingall. But evading her eyes, they were Liam's, she saw, loyal to a man to their chief.

She spoke to him for the first time since leaving Ardarroch. 'Why do we not go to Fortingall?'

He shook his head, eyes averted. The blood draining from her face, she saw the great grey walls of Meggernie Castle towering above them. So that was the plan. There was no place in the house in Fortingall to keep a prisoner. Easier to put her into one of the old dungeons here. Until she changed her mind.

'Sir Robert is absent for Isobel's wedding. I am in charge here,' said Liam, helping her to dismount. As he led the way into his apartments she remembered, a scared girl going as companion to Isobel Campbell, believing Meggernie to be her birthplace, Glencorrie to be her father. A girl troubled by a vision of ghostly lovers, one of whom she recognised.

181

'You will be comfortable here,' he said awkwardly.

'So I am not to be a prisoner?'

'A prisoner?' He made it sound as if such an idea had never occurred to him. 'Of course you are not a prisoner.' His smile was gentle, wanting to reassure her. 'You will have servants to wait on you. And then we will return to Eunice at Fortingall.' To her questioning look, he added hastily: 'When you see the folly of this ridiculous marriage.' He tried to speak calmly, without emotion, throwing his gloves on to the table.

'And what if I refuse?'

Liam could think of no answer, aware only of the joy in his heart that he had her here at last and alone with him, the rest of the world far away. Trembling, he was aware that she had grown more beautiful, more fulfilled, and his months of tortured suspense had made him love her with a wild abandon and passion that had lost all semblance of sanity. Had she asked him, he could have told her in infinite detail, all about a love that defies death, a love of the kind that she had never experienced, would never experience in a lifetime with Ardarroch.

'If I do not agree, will you put me to the sword as you did my rightful father when you stole me from Ardarroch, and carried me back here to substitute for your wife's stillborn child.' How cool and unafraid her voice despite her fast-beating heart. She would not show fear, not to Liam Campbell of all men.

'What nonsense is this they have been telling you? You were born here in this room.' His voice was surprisingly light to his own ears. He even managed a smile.

'You are not my father, Liam Campbell. You stole me from the Macdonalds. Anyway, you cannot keep me here. I belong to my husband now.'

'Husband?' He laughed out loud.

'Aye, husband.'

'Did he tell you this fantasy about a babe and a burning tower? Is that how he wooed you?' He wanted to be good-humoured now, keep a bantering mocking tone.

'No. A *cailleach* who was midwife to my real mother, not Mairi Campbell, she told me.' Caitlin could not restrain her tears, for the woman she loved and trusted as her mother been party to Liam's deception.

'She loved you, Caitlin, she loved you as her own.'

'And I loved her. I loved *you*.'

'Caitlin.' As he said her name he knew he had won and his hands were strong, warm upon her shoulders. To his surprise she twisted away from him.

'You cannot keep me here – you have no right,' she said coldly.

'I have every right.'

'Then how will you do so, against my will? Lock me in a room and starve me to death, or put me to the sword, as you did my father?' she reminded him.

'Caitlin, Caitlin.' He held up his hands as if to thrust away that terrible memory. 'It is true I killed him, but face-to-face, him or me. And I have been punished, believe me. Through you, and your likeness, he has never ceased to haunt me. That was why I could never love you as a child. I was afraid of you, afraid.'

'Why should I believe you? You would tell any lies to stop me going back to Ardarroch.'

'Caitlin, I cannot beg forgiveness. I would not know where to begin. But since that night I found you, I have tried, dear God, how hard I have tried, to expiate the guilt. Since I came back from Ulster I have loved you with all my heart and soul.' Humbly he whispered: 'With more, so much more than any parent's love.'

She knew it was true. His grip on her hands tightened. A lover's hands, whose warmth went all the way to her heart. She pushed them aside.

'Today has cancelled out our debt of love.' The words felt as if they had been torn from her.

'Only death can do that, Caitlin. You are my joy and my life. In this world, there is no one but you. What I did at Ardarroch long ago, was an act of war. Christ's blood, they had slaughtered us, I was carried on a wave of revenge. But I have kept the oath I made that night, I will never again shed any man's blood.'

'And what of my husband's blood?'

He winced at the word. 'I had no intention of hurting him, it would have been my fist had he not come at me with a dirk. Caitlin, you know I could have killed him, easily, had I wished.'

183

She knew it was true as he continued: 'A fine bridegroom you have chosen. Closer by blood to you than I am,' he said bitterly.

'He is not my bridegroom,' she said softly. 'He is my husband. We were handfasted last winter.' And if she wanted revenge, she had it now: Had she driven a knife into his heart, she could not have wished for better effect.

'Handfasted,' he repeated. He leaned against the table, a broken man in need of strength. 'So that's the way of it, you run to the arms of the first bonny man who beckons to you,' he said bitterly.

Her heart ached for his defeat, as she reminded him: 'You were the one who urged me to take a husband.'

'You do not know why?'

She shook her head. 'No.'

'You cannot guess?'

'No.'

He took a deep breath before replying. 'I love you. I have been in torment loving you, wanting you. Do not mistake me.' He leaned across the short distance between them and seized her arm, his face anguished, as he added: 'Not as your father but as your lover. No man can ever love you as I do. I have been mad for love of you, I thought marrying Eunice might cure me, but it only made me want you more. All this time, dreading that you would find out the truth and at the same time, longing that you should be told – the truth, that would release us both.' He no longer touched her, but felt light-headed, free, as if the terrible burden he carried had been shed at last.

How silent the room had become, as if outside its walls all time had ceased and the two of them were new born into a strange and frightening world. A world that offered its terrible forbidden beauty. They need only stretch out their hands. It waited, theirs for the taking. Neither of them moved, standing apart, frozen into the stillness lurking with its thousand blind eyes around them.

'Caitlin, say it. For God's sake say that you love me and that you forgive me.'

'I love you, Liam,' she said simply. 'I have always loved you. When we are apart you live in my heart, waking, sleeping. I think you must have taken possession of my soul when you carried me from the fire.' She looked up at him and whispered. 'You were the first earthly creature my eyes ever beheld.'

'If you told *him* all this, Caitlin, he might not have wanted to marry you. Dear God Almighty, what had he to offer you to compare with our love?'

'If you had told me the truth, I would never have been any man's woman but yours,' she said sorrowfully.

'Now that you know, will you leave this bridegroom of yours and come to me?'

She shrugged. 'Have you not forgotten Eunice?'

He sighed heavily. 'Would that I could.'

Fleetingly, they glimpsed in each other's eyes that small miracle called infinite possibilities. Brendan and Eunice existed, but belonged to some other world and time, their existence remote, they were more unsubstantial than the wreaths their breaths made in the still air of the cold unused room.

Liam seized her hands. 'Come with me, come with me, my darling.'

'Where, where?' she whispered, wanting to believe that Liam had the power to make the dream come true.

'Anywhere, as long as you are with me. Ulster, the Colonies, or to the Devil himself if he will have us.'

Caitlin shuddered. 'You do not know what you are saying –'

Liam's hands dropped to his side. 'And you would say anything, promise the world to save Ardarroch from fire and sword,' he said bitterly. 'You will not leave him for me, for the life we could have together?'

She shook her head. 'He is my husband, and you have a wife.'

'Eunice? That is over.'

And suddenly the moment they had shared had turned flat, soured. Fighting to keep it alive before the unity was lost for ever, she said: 'I would say, and do, anything to keep your love,' she whispered. 'But I cannot desert Brendan. I gave him my word I would return. But that does not mean I lied to you.'

'Is that so?' His tone was idle but he knew it was true. The story was all there written in her face, the story of her love

185

for him, the only difference was that the child's face had vanished, and the face of a woman had taken its place, a beautiful woman he longed to possess. 'I may not allow you to go back to him. I might after all keep you here as my prisoner.'

His tone was light, mocking, not to be taken seriously and she smiled crookedly: 'I think I have been your prisoner all my life, Liam Campbell.'

'Even now as another man's wife.' And when she did not answer. 'So how do you intend to prove your love for me.'

She bowed her head. 'Whatever is your will.' And then raising her eyes to his. 'Whatever you will, as long as you allow me to return to Ardarroch and keep your word, never to harm him or his Clan.'

He considered her, his manner suddenly remote and detached, for he could not find the words to frame what his heart demanded, the need his aching body and his blood thundered.

'I will make a bargain with you, Caitlin. Keep your side of it, and I will not lay one finger on Ardarroch or your precious husband.'

She looked up at him, joyous, triumphant. 'Whatever you wish, I will do it.'

Gently he removed her plaid and stretching out his hands undid the laces that held in check this yearning of flesh for flesh. Then holding her, even before their lips found each other, she was already his, had always been his, and in that moment of ecstasy, she knew that the ghostly lovers she had once seen were themselves.

Chapter X

Each passing hour away from Caitlin brought new anguish to Brendan as Elspeth dressed the sword thrust, painful but not serious, she assured him. Forced to lie inert against his pillows, far greater was his agony over what might be happening to Caitlin. With the truth about her birth revealed, Glencorrie had nothing further to lose. He had fostered his enemy's child who had disobeyed his will. If she refused annulment, for she was no longer a maid to be married off as he willed, with his bargaining power as guardian at an end, he might exact a terrible revenge.

Meanwhile, the hotheads amongst his clansmen surrounded him, urging, in no uncertain terms, to break his word to Glencorrie.

Brendan shook his head. 'Glencorrie could have killed me. I know that. And most of Ardarroch, if we had opposed. Besides he has Lady Ardarroch, you will do nothing to endanger her – nothing – do you understand?'

Unable to understand his stubborn reluctance to let them take immediate action, dark looks from his clansmen hinted that his behaviour in such an emergency, was what they had always feared. Books and learning, building a library and a garden. What sort of pursuits were those for a Clan chief, whose business should be war?

Aye, a warrior chief was what they needed. Like William, his late cousin, the last of the true Ardarroch line. Had a Campbell snatched his bride from the altar, he would have been in Glenlyon by now, tearing it apart with his bare hands.

'This would not have happened, had Ruari Macdonald been our laird either,' they whispered.

As for Brendan, he could no longer bear the accusing looks in his household that called him coward. 'Very well, arm the men, tell them we leave at first light,' and to himself, he added: 'And may God have mercy on our souls and upon my poor Caitlin.'

During that night, however, the 'scratch' Glencorrie had inflicted on him became infected. At first light Elspeth found him in the grip of a burning fever.

'We could go alone,' said his men.

'And if he dies, what then? If only Ruari were here.' But the priest who had scuttled hastily back to Glencoe, had not yet had time to raise the alarm. Even if MacIan were disposed to rally an army to bring back Ardarroch's wife. Of late, he too had been living peacefully among his neighbours and to commit his Clan to war over Caitlin's abduction was a big step to take.

Heads were shaken. There was nothing they could do but wait, their loyalty to Brendan Macdonald absolute until he died. They were his to a man, grumble as they may.

Elspeth and Lady Frances whispered at his bedside. 'Most men take far worse hurt and never flinch,' said his mother, bathing his forehead.

'But it was never so with my lord, from childhood his cuts turned foul, infection and then fever followed. What a constitution for Macdonald of Ardarroch,' groaned Elspeth, remembering scarred arms, legs and faces of his clansmen, proud token of battles and skirmishes that she had dressed through the years. She knew fine well that there was mutinous talk among the Ardarroch men furious at their sensitive peace-at-all-price chieftain..

Fate, however, took a hand. Later that morning, the door suddenly opened and Caitlin stood there.

Brendan blinked. Had his longing for her brought back the fever again? But there was nothing spectral about the girl who ran towards him still wearing her wedding gown, crumpled and travel-stained. Sobbing, she took him in her arms.

'Dearest, dearest Brendan, how is it with you?' She touched the bandage. 'Does it hurt, my darling?' Kissing him, she cradled him to her breast. Stroking his damp forehead, she felt the fever heat.

'It is nothing. It will pass.' He tried to sit up straight and look strong for her. 'But I was determined that we were coming to Glenlyon to get you, this very day,' he said proudly.

'Even after your promise to wait six days?' she reminded him.

He clutched her hands, kissed them. 'No man could abide by such a promise, you know that. I was certain I would never see you again. How did you persuade him?' Her face paled suddenly and he realised that she was trembling. 'He did release you of his own free will?' Wordless, she nodded. 'Then all is well, we are forgiven.'

Caitlin's eyes brimmed with tears. How could she ever tell this good kind man so full of generosity towards his enemy, the price that she had paid, aye and so willingly paid, for peace in their time at Ardarroch, for his life and for their future together? How was she to go on living with him and the conscience that she now possessed, the body and heart of her that now belonged to Liam Campbell. Already every sense she possessed betrayed her with yearning, stirred rapturous demands that would not be silenced and could never, never again be satisfied, except by one beloved man.

Dear God, teach me, show me, how am I to live again?

'You are tired, my darling,' said Brendan gently. 'A long ride back from Fortingall.'

'It is, it is,' she said holding desperately to this logical excuse for the distress she could no longer hide from him. She buried her face in the pillow as he stroked her hair, said soothingly.

'We can talk about it later.' A somewhat crooked smile, as he added with a sigh: 'When we both feel stronger.'

'I came only from Meggernie,' she said carefully, '*he*' – never again could she use the word Father in her relationship to Liam Campbell – 'he is in charge there, while Sir Robert is absent.'

'Meggernie is still a long distance,' he said. 'Come, lie down here, ' he patted the bed. 'Beside me, and we will both sleep.'

Unworthily Caitlin was glad of the respite his fever provided. Hating herself for such thoughts she realised that had he tried to make love to her, she would have rushed out of the Tower and ridden out of Ardarroch, back across the hills and into Liam Campbell's arms. 'Take me, take me

189

back,' she would have sobbed despite their solemn vow never to meet again. Had he refused, then she would have taken her own life, plunged into the loch or down some ravine. For now she too had discovered the full and terrible meaning of a love that one would gladly die for.

She lay motionless on the bed beside the man who was her husband and in the most complete silence of her life, tried to find her way back to the reality of tomorrow. This man who loved her was Brendan and not Liam. Each time he held her in his arms, would she be for ever doomed to remember that other time, that other lover?

Had Liam taken her by force, she could have stormed and wept, hated him as Ardarroch's enemy and hers. Now with her victory, she knew that she had always, would always, love him. He was part of her life and her being, the air she breathed, the ground she walked upon. There was not a dream in her life of which he was not the centre. So had it been all her life, and now more than ever, she would never cease to search for him, in every stranger hoping for some glimpse that would be like homecoming.

Perhaps by the time Brendan was strong enough to be a lover again, she would be stronger too, she thought in weak desperation, as he drew the deer-skin rug about her tenderly and talked to her gently, holding her hand, as might loving father to little hurt child. Bewildered, she had beheld husband turned father, father turned lover.

But somewhere that day between uneasy sleep and nightmare awakening, the law of Caitlin's survival took command. No matter how much her heart died within her, in this, the springtime of her marriage, she must steel herself to accept Brendan as her husband. As with some incurable disease, she must learn to live with body's anguish, that this was not the all-consuming passion of Liam Campbell. For Brendan's sake, this dear kind man to whom she owed much, she must strive with every sinew to make their marriage happy. With his love to sustain her she would build a fortress against the past, a fortress strong enough to allow no secret stain of guilt to invade, and mar the peaceful fabric of their lives together. Her reward was Brendan's happiness.

So Caitlin awoke one day to discover that although storm and tempest still raged in her own heart, the tempest was

190

secret and the sharp edge of agony dulled in a harmonious marriage that, like good baking, depended upon the smooth blending of two people's personalities, their wishes and desires. And only in the quiet darkness of the night did her soul cry out for that other love, love forbidden and lost forever: Oh, Liam, why, why?

Visiting Brendan's tenants, there was evidence in plenty of similarities between Ardarroch and Glencorrie. Traditions, superstitions, the food they ate, the clothes they wore, their language, all were identical. The ancient festivals of Beltain and Samhain, the visit to summer shieling in the hills, with households and animals. Each home bound by the same law of hospitality sacred to Macdonald and Campbell alike, their only difference, religion.

'But with so much in common,' Caitlin protested, 'they should be living side by side in perfect harmony, growing strong together, united by a common purpose in life.'

Brendan shared her feelings. 'Some day, long after we are dust perhaps knowledge and tolerance, aye, and travel too, might bring all Clans together as brothers. Think of it, Caitlin, a time when even Macdonalds and Campbells can trespass into each other's land, without being hanged.'

Caitlin shivered, remembering that but for the Macdonald hanged at Meggernie, she might have never taken flight, never found either Ardarroch or the truth about her birth. How good each day at Brendan's side, how distant and remote the past of Fortingall and Eunice's small cruelties. As with the shutters closed against the night, Brendan read to her as she sewed, here in Ardarroch everyone ran to serve her, to attend to her every comfort and whim. Brendan allowed her to spend little time in the kitchen, where any domestic disturbance was soothed by Elspeth and its cause rarely reached her ears.

Cocooned in this web of kindness in the world that Brendan Macdonald had created for her, there were neither heights nor depths nor dangerous edges in sharing her life with a man who, had he not been husband then would have been dearest brother, closest friend. Their life together was a smooth plateau of peaceful serenity, along which they walked, and at the end of each day drew the curtains, loved and slept.

Lady Frances had long since returned home when summer smiled on Ardarroch. In a garden now unrecognisable as the one Caitlin first entered six months earlier, bird-calls echoed from tree to tree, from dawn until dusk. Resurrected under the beauty of blossom, delicate rainbow hues blended on ever-changing hills, and the wild-heather perfume blew sweetly across the Braes of Ardarroch.

Walking with Brendan in his walled garden amid the quiet grandeur of knot beds full of pinks and heartsease, where smooth lawns bordered by tall clipped hedges surrounded a paved arbour, and solemn statues guarded a rustic seat which invited contemplation, Caitlin sighed happily. A sense of well-being enveloped all her days, serene as the white briar roses nodding sleepily against the sun-warmed Tower walls, her heart light as the mavis in the mulberry tree, whose song seemed to issue from the very heart of Ardarroch itself. She had good reason for gratitude. Even her thirst for knowledge was being satisfied by Brendan's many books, the ever-increasing load of volumes brought by the carter from Glasgow and Edinburgh to add to the library, housed in what had once been the solar of Ardarroch.

Always ready to explain, a patient teacher, Brendan was in his turn fascinated by the legends of Fortingall, its yew tree and Pontius Pilate. A devout Catholic, his conversations and attitudes to life, his forgiveness and tolerance constantly reminded Caitlin of Stephen. Brendan was delighted. A man not only Campbell-reared but of a different faith who shared his own fundamental beliefs. 'I hope one day we shall meet. We will enjoy tearing the world to pieces and putting it together again to our hearts' desire.'

Caitlin visited her husband's kin in Glencoe that summer. After the gentle loveliness of Glenlyon and the fertile valley of Ardarroch with its undulating hills, the pass which led into Glencoe was fearful in its steep and unequal desolation, a nightmare landscape from an abandoned world, a dark sinister Biblical land in imminent dread of the Lord's displeasure.

With Brendan and herself leading, Bran keeping pace alongside, the household of Ardarroch straggled behind. Before them lay a deep and gloomy chasm formed by the

192

northern range of hills, shooting upwards like the fingers of a giant's hands, its numerous torrents a series of unlikely bridal veils, swaying above the wild waters of Cona.

Brendan pointed. 'These hills, Aonach Eagach, are the Caves of the Feinn. According to legend here three thousand of Fionn's warriors sleep. Their breathing is the wind and one day, they will arise at the call of Fionn's hunting horn. The entrance to the cave is lost to man, guarded night and day by the deerhounds of Bran.'

Caitlin could well believe Brendan's story. She would not have been in the least surprised had a supernatural army erupted, tumbling out of those hills and sending their snow-capped summits, echoing with ancient war cries, the clash of steel.

Through this narrow pass, a small green line snaked and vanished. Brendan pointed, 'There lies our road.'

Road, thought Caitlin, it is hardly more than a sheeptrack, as she looked back with concern at the cavalcade from Ardarroch, some of them no longer young and obviously feeling the strain of this upward climb with their heavily laden ponies.

Tortuously they ascended into the steep corries. The horses bred for the hills of Ardarroch, cared little for these fierce mountains closing in upon them. Normally sure-footed, they stumbled as secret sharp projections of rocks suddenly thrust forth from deer grass as if to trip the unwary. Other hazards lurked in the bleached skeletons of ancient trees mingling with the moss and heather.

Brendan gave the signal to dismount. 'The beasts are a little put out.'

'I can see that,' said Caitlin grimly, as she took the leading rein and dragged her unwilling mount up a particularly appalling slope, where heavy rainfall had washed away the whisper of a path.

The horses quivered wide-eyed with fear, their nostrils dilated. Caitlin shivered, for their terror communicated itself to her. Such fear seemed out of proportion, in sympathy with the spirit of the place, rather than the difficult terrain.

Bran felt it too. Normally joyous, questing, he stayed very close. With her hand on his collar, she felt his hackles rise and he gave her a look of almost human alarm, which might have been comical had it not registered as sheer terror of the unknown.

High above them, vast curls of mist wreathed the mountain peak. There the ravens circled, splitting the silent air with their croaking, Sabbatical witches around a great cauldron, as they feasted upon some dead beast's carcase. Golden, majestic, a solitary eagle hovered, unmoving, watching their progress.

Brendan gave her a helping hand. With every sense she possessed alerted to danger, she clung gratefully to his human warmth.

'This is a fearful place,' she whispered.

'There is none other like it.'

'I am thankful for that.'

Brendan smiled proudly. 'Look back the way we have come.'

Caitlin's glance did not linger. 'Impressive it is, like the gateway to hell,' she added with a shudder.

Brendan laughed delightedly. 'Aye. The Devil's Staircase, so it is called.'

The rugged heights above them now added oppression to threatening gloom as they waited for the other members of the household. When all were assembled and Brendan assured that they were of good heart and ready to proceed, he led the way along the path ahead.

At his side, Caitlin shivered, observing how the chill around them intensified as they were stalked by sheer walls of rock that might have supported the fortress of Red Alistair's giants of legend. Even to an imagination reared on folk lore and fable, the scene was daunting. The summits of two ranges, jagged and broken, assumed fantastic shapes of domes and battlemented walls, of lofty pinnacles and spires lost in huge mountain fastnesses. Mighty eminences of rock, grotesque statues perched precariously and threatened to topple and crush the unwary travellers. Encircling them, the mountains, interwoven with fissures, created an impression of colossal rocks piled at random one upon another, the playthings of malicious giants flung pell-mell across the earth.

Even the noonday brightness of midsummer could not soften the mighty range of Buchaille Etive Mor and Buchaille Etive Beag.

'The Great and Little Herdsmen of Etive,' said Brendan.

Caitlin regarded them silently before asking: 'What kind of beasts might have earned them their name?'

'The famous black cattle of the Macdonalds, of course. Cattle that roamed here centuries ago. Long before the bastard son of Angus Og of Islay fought side-by-side with the Bruce at Bannockburn and was given title to this land as Clan Iain Abrach. My uncle, MacIan of Glencoe is his direct descendant.'

Caitlin was surprised to find Brendan, normally sensitive to his surroundings, unaffected by the desolation that struck a prenatural chill into her heart. A chill, like the foretaste of doom. Only Bran, and the horses, seemed aware of the terror that lurked everywhere, unseen, while Brendan cheerfully rallied his household. When they had again briefly rested, he pointed: 'There lies our road.'

A path through the upraised fingers of a giant's hand, hardly less daunting than the Devil's Staircase, lay before them. A hand, thought Caitlin grimly, quite capable of coming suddenly to life and closing its clenched fist on the tiny group of travellers who descended the long gully. No fantasy was beyond belief in this fearful place whose snow-patched summits gleamed blue-white under summer sunshine.

'It never melts from one winter to the next,' Brendan explained. 'There are places in these mountains where sunlight never penetrates, places so secret and hidden that, since time began, they have never felt the foot of man.'

Caitlin shuddered. Man's presence was as insignificant in this alien world, as the maddened clouds of insects they rode through, brushed aside and immediately forgot. As for the remote and tiny houses occasionally visible, they made no more impact upon this vast stage than a solitary raindrop from a thundercloud. She had to remind herself that this fearsome aspect belonged to the balm of gentle summer. What horrors must lurk when winter storms relentlessly closed in upon these hills and passes.

They had left Ardarroch at first light but it was already dusk when they sighted their journey's end and looked down on to Achnacone, the Field of the Dogs.

Bran's interest suddenly stirred. He ran a few paces ahead

now, panting eagerly.

Brendan laughed. 'Down there, his ancestors, the legendary deerhounds of Fionn once roamed freely, before the advent of mortals made them take to the hills. Here they now breed in the mountain fastness, living on the deer they can bring down.'

Looking upwards, Caitlin could image the mist full of the grey shadows of dogs, watching them impassively. A wild hound pack, a far cry from their gentle Bran.

'They are still there somewhere,' Brendan continued. 'I dare say Bran knows the way.' And Bran wagged his tail and seemed to smile. 'He knows, for that is the path he will follow some day when the time comes for him to leave man and return to his ancestors, those Brans who through the centuries have faithfully served us at Ardarroch.' He sighed sadly. 'At least he knows the place of destiny even, I think, sometimes, the secret of death itself.'

Caitlin regarded him sharply wishing he had not spoken of death. For death gave the name to all she felt around them. Death in the ravens' cry, and the darkening sunset, purple, scarlet and gold, moving like a tapestry caught by a sudden draught upon the Tower's walls. How childishly she had regarded such moments from Fortingall, resentful that the Macdonalds held a key to the magic sunset land. Now she knew where all the sunsets go on for ever, eternal in their beauty and majesty. Where time itself ends and only mortals die.

As the colours deepened and darkness threw veils of obscurity about the landscape, the air was full of other sounds. The sigh of the wind was a harp-like moan stirring the treetops.

'Fionn's warriors?' she whispered to Brendan and he smiled as the voice of a solitary raven sent forth its ominous comment on the day's events.

'You will see more ravens and eagles here than in Ardarroch,' said Brendan.

'Or anywhere else,' replied Caitlin with a shudder, for the whirr and rush of their wings sweeping through the air, their gliding movement suggested dark angels returning home.

Then, from the depths of that eerie wind, whispered her own name.

'Caitlin.'

She looked at Brendan. He seemed far ahead now beyond her reach, walking as if he glided above the ground, a gentle glow shimmering about him. She took a sharp breath. The Shroud of Death. A moment later she blinked and it was gone. Had she ever seen it at all?

'Caitlin.'

But Brendan had not called her. The voice was unmistakeably that of Liam Campbell. Liam Campbell who haunted her dreams and her waking hours, a living spectre who refused to be banished, who refused to release her from the thraldom of love. What was he trying to tell her? To warn her that this was the place appointed for her own destiny?

'See, over there, that's Carnoch.' Brendan, a warm living Brendan, was at her side. 'They are expecting us. Look.' And, as one by one, torches pierced the gloom, they cantered swiftly down over the greensward and there, in the courtyard of his dark tower, a giant of a man waited to welcome them.

Alasdair Macdonald of Glencoe, twelfth chief of Clan Iain Abrach, descended from Conn of the Hundred Battles, High King of Ireland and from Colla, Prince of the Isles, also known in the splendour of his youth as Red MacIan.

At first glance, Caitlin thought he could have doubled for Alistair nan Creach. Now the famous mane of red hair, the sight of which had struck terror into the hearts of his enemies, was snow-white. Dark eyes, a falcon's beak of a nose and like Red Alistair, a man belonging to legend. Men of their calibre were more than mortal she thought, with her small hand lost in that mighty grip of welcome, that fist more at home over a sword blade. Such men belonged to the same heroic pages of history as Fionn, whose warriors slept back there among those fierce dark hills.

As for MacIan's sons, his heir John and Alasdair Og, tall, handsome men, in the normal way they would have seemed exceptional, but here they were overshadowed, scaled down by the presence of such a father.

Lady Glencoe came forward and embraced the weary travellers. At first glance, in the dim light, she seemed little more than a girl, a small doll-like creature whom MacIan could have crushed between his two hands. Elegant and dainty, with tiny feet and hands, not at all the kind of mate Caitlin would have envisaged for Glencoe, or as mother to his two strapping sons, Their daughter, married to a Keppoch cousin, favoured her gentle mother.

The outside structure of the Tower of Glencoe was reminiscent of the home they had left, but its interior suggested nothing other than the transient resting-place of warriors between battles. The hall, lofty and spacious, its crude stone walls six feet thick, reluctantly allowed light to pass through sombre loopholes of horn-filled windows. A rush strewn floor supported rough tables and benches, its walls hung with faded, tattered banners, armour, martial weapons and trophies of the chase. Well-rusted steel caps perched on branching deer antlers, shields and corslets, suspended from bulls' horns that formed pegs between chinks in the stones.

The whole onslaught on the senses was a tapestry of barbaric male splendour and Lady Glencoe leading them up the twisting stone stairs to their bedroom apparently felt that apology was necessary: 'Our house at Glen Muidhe would be more to your taste, Lady Ardarroch. This is such a barracks.' She shuddered delicately. 'I can do nothing with it, but Glen Muidhe,' she sighed. 'It is so elegant. You must come and visit us there. We have real window-glass, you know.'

Caitlin smiled, suspecting that MacIan's lady's determined effort to grace her home with a woman's touches was continually thwarted by her warlike menfolk.

'That's a fine beast you have there,' their hostess continued, as Bran somewhat cautiously submitted to having his head fondled, his ears and teeth looked at, 'We breed deerhounds, but if MacIan notices this one, you will be lucky to take him back to Ardarroch with you. I have rarely seen a finer specimen. Does he not go to the stables with the other animals?'

Bran darted a look of agonised appeal at his master. Brendan smiled. 'No, Lady Glencoe, he stays with us.'

Lady Glencoe shook her head restraining some comment on such extraordinary behaviour towards a four-legged beast. 'I suppose it will be all right here at Carnoch. Of course, things will be different once we move to Glen Muidhe.'

At supper in the great hall, Lady Glencoe seated Caitlin with her back to the fire that roared up the chimney. 'There is a footstool for you, my dear. At Glen Muidhe, we have rugs on the floors,' she added loudly, with a reproachful glance quite lost upon her husband, beaming genially upon their guests.

Whatever the Tower lacked in elegance was compensated by the warmth of MacIan's hospitality and Brendan, far from sober, was thrust bodily into his bedchamber that night. Caitlin helped him undress and crawl into bed, watched over by an anxious Bran, who seemed perturbed by the effects of inebriation on humans in general and on his beloved master in particular.

Caitlin smiled. He tried very hard, poor dear Brendan, it was not his fault that his drinking was not on the scale of heroes. And blowing out the candle, she gathered him into her arms.

Next morning, Brendan's headache was at least of heroic proportions. Groaning, slit-eyed against the light, withstanding Bran's cheerful greeting, he insisted that fresh air was the only cure.

After break fast, MacIan, enviably spry, considering his years and the night's mighty carouse, had their horses saddled and Brendan took Caitlin on the long promised visit to Glen Etive.

Her first sombre impressions of Glencoe vanished in the magnificence of an uninterrupted view along the Bay of Oban to Lismore where gnarled fingers of water thrust into dark shapes of land seperating them from mountains and the faint shapes of islands lay like basking whales upon a glittering sea. Over to the south east brooded Ben Cruachan, patched with red gulleys, and fretted by woods, its countless streams gushing crystal in the morning sunlight.

Glen Etive's associations with the legend of Deirdre of the Shadows, led Caitlin to expect strange magic. As they rode down the valley, the land gleamed bright with emerald field and gentle pasture. And there beside Loch Etive, Caitlin saw reflected every kind of Highland scenery, strath and vale, mountain torrents tucked away in ravines, spewing out waterfalls or cascading towards a gentle river. Sometimes the greenness around them took on the quality of a fairy glade, the water music producing an eerie effect that deepened the mysterious gloom.

Over all, there lurked a feeling of expectancy. Here some enchantment awaited upon the hour. With the right circumstances and the right people all that lurked behind the thin veil of time would become visible, possible. Bran seemed aware of it. Normally he stayed close to their horses, unimpressed by the human reaction of delight or displeasure to whatever the scenery offered. But here, he loped ahead, baying a joyous greeting.

'Chasing shadows, look at him,' said Brendan. Had he discovered that other deerhound, and was Deirdre the lingering shade he met again with such delight?

'In such a place it was not hard to imagine the passion of Deirdre for Naishu and their tragic doomed lives,' said Brendan with his uncanny gift for interpreting his wife's thoughts, as he called Bran to heel.

Caitlin shivered. Tragic doomed love was something she knew all too recently and had no wish to remember. She looked at Brendan's happy, unclouded face, so well-beloved. Leaning over she took his hand, wordlessly held it against her cheek.

It would break her heart to bring him sorrow.

'Race you back to the tower?'

'I love you.'

'And I love you.'

And her moment of guilt as the face of Liam Campbell looked into her heart was over, as back at the Tower she was declared loser and swept from her horse and into her husband's arms. Laughing, breathless, they ran indoors hand in hand.

As day succeeded sunny day and even summer seemed to hold its breath, Caitlin found constant pleasure and fellowship with Brendan's kin, with MacIan and Lady Glencoe and their family so ready to love her.

There was an added celebration before they left when Caitlin shyly announced what she had suspected for some time. They were charmed and delighted that the new Lady Ardarroch, cousin Brendan's bride of less than a year, was with child.

With many promises of future visits, they returned to Ardarroch to summer's end and harvest time, and watched the saffron mellow autumn harden into the steely grip of winter. Of events in the world beyond Ardarroch, they remained happily ignorant unless a rare visitor brought gossip. Such visitors were warmly welcomed, eagerly listened to and then happily relinquished as the cocoon of Ardarroch engulfed them again and the waiting-time for the birth continued. As the year drew to its close, both became more preoccupied by their own secret fears, which they would not have willingly shared with anyone, least of all with each other.

'A son,' said Brendan, laying his hands gently over Caitlin's abdomen. Not until he had felt the first fluttering bird-like movements of the child, did he fully believe in that other life growing steadily inside her. 'A son,' he repeated loudly, 'who will one day have Ardarroch.'

'Who can be certain? Perhaps a daughter ... '

'I can be certain,' said Brendan firmly. 'We breed sons here, it is nature's way of keeping a supply of warriors.'

He looked so solemn, Caitlin touched his cheek, whispered, 'Are you glad?'

He did not answer at first, afraid that this child might come between them, destroy the delicate love-fabric of their life together, the pattern they had so painstakenly, patiently woven. He was bewildered too that this wife of his grew daily more beautiful, afraid that such beauty was an affront to the fates who seize just such an opportunity to destroy her.

As for Caitlin, the latter days of pregnancy were merely burdensome. Weary of her heavy body, her restricted freedom, she had long ago worn out emotions of secret dread about the nightmare events the birth of her child might unleash. She knew only that the child was restless too for his constant nocturnal movements disturbed her rest.

The New Year of 1684 dawned unusually mild but January was almost at an end before a path was cleared of snow in Brendan's garden. This, at Lady Ardarroch's insistence, sighed the servants, so that she might enjoy some daily exercise, so near her time too.

Caitlin had ridden in the hills each day as long as she dared, which was longer than Brendan approved. Now she felt trapped. A prisoner, even though the cords were of silk, for Brendan and Elspeth, eternally vigilant, seldom let her out of their sight, so precious and delicate had she become. Giving them the slip became a game with her, a game in which she recaptured an almost childish glee.

Oh, it was so good to be out here alone. If only the babe would come, in whose existence she still found belief almost impossible. Would she ever be free of this clumsy burden? And she thought with apprehension and compassion of women in Fortingall who spent twenty years in almost constant child-bearing. Was this her own beginning of the thraldom of womanhood?

If only she could escape, escape before it was too late, she thought wildly. Even the hills around her seemed watchful, silent sentinels in a dead world.

Suddenly she screamed out loud. Her body was seized in a steel grip and giant teeth clenched down upon her spine. The agony was so unexpected, so unlike any kind of pain she had been led to expect, that she slid to the ground and lay there gasping, all the breath knocked out of her body.

Again the steel clamp of agony shuddered through her as the beast of pain bit deeper, deeper. This time, it was too great to bear and stay alive.

The blackness of blessed oblivion was penetrated by intense cold. Shivering, she lifted her head. What was she doing here, lying on a little path in the arbour, concealed from the Tower, with the smell of dead leaves pungent around her? She struggled to rise, on trembling legs, clutching at the stone seat for support.

She looked at the Tower. Dear God, how far away it seemed. How could she possibly reach it before the next onslaught of pain, already slowly building up inside her. Was the child to be born out here in Brendan's garden on a winter's afternoon?

'Dear God, dear God, help me,' she screamed as another wave of pain thudded into her.

Crouched on the path, afraid to move, she heard hurrying footsteps. And there was Brendan. Sobbing she clung to him. There were others now making a great fuss – Elspeth issuing orders – as they got her somehow into the Tower and upstairs to her bedchamber.

Now the pains that she had thought unbearable an hour

earlier in the garden seemed mild by comparison as her body was torn apart. How could anyone endure this agony and continue to live?

Just when she had prayed to die and thought her prayer had been answered, there was Elspeth smiling, dangling a crumpled red object that moved feebly but was hardly recognisable as human, apart from its faint mewing cry.

'A fine son you have, my lady. And my lord Brendan is waiting to see you.'

Hours later it seemed to Caitlin, she opened her eyes to Brendan beaming delightedly upon the swathed bundle rocked in his arms.

'The image of my lady, he is,' said Elspeth proudly. 'Hair colour apart, but never fear, it will turn black, come a year or two.'

'Let me see him, please.' She was conscious of Brendan watching her. Did he notice her anxiety, the hand that trembled as she touched the downy golden head and how closely she stared into blue unfocussed eyes?

The celebrations were considerable. Even Elspeth laid aside her own secret fears different indeed from those of her master and mistress and rejoiced. No weakling-born like his father, to be cosseted every day of his life, this Ardarroch heir was lusty and strong from the moment he uttered his first cry.

'William Macdonald.' So Brendan insisted that the child be named, for Caitlin's real father and their common Macdonald grandfather, although Caitlin would have preferred some other name.

William thrived. Spring came, painted the world for summer's glory and brought Caitlin a new joy in living. She could not bear to stay indoors and ignoring Elspeth's protests insisted upon taking William into the sun each day. With bird-song in the branches above her head, the reassuring sound nearby of Bran panting for shade from the sun's heat and William kicking lustily in the safe warm world bordered by his cradle, at her side, this was a time to close one's eyes, hold one's breath, to marvel and adore. What had she done to deserve such a good life, with Brendan and William and the love that surrounded her? Her heart overflowed with thanksgiving.

When William was a year old, he was carried to Glencoe to make the acquaintance of his grandmother, Lady Frances, visiting with her husband, Sir Hector. The heir to Ardarroch remained obstinately golden-haired, but his eyes were a strange amber colour, remarked upon as a fleeting curiosity. Like his hair, they too would darken as he grew older. Good-natured, serene and ready with winning smiles, he enslaved them all, and they were eager to declare him the most beautiful baby they had ever seen.

There were visitors other than themselves, a Macdonald lawyer recently returned from London, eager to report momentous events from that distant country where, they learned, history had moved on apace. A few months earlier, in February 1685, King Charles had died.

'As a king, he is no great loss to Scotland.'

'Or to the Highlands,' said MacIan.

Lawyer Macdonald shook his head. 'That is true, cousin. I well remember his crowning at Scone, how he shied away from this cold forbidding northern kingdom of his.' There were pitying smiles from around the table as he continued: 'He maintained that it was full of treachery, its subjects unruly, especially those who inhabited the Highlands and could be safely dismissed, in his opinion and that of his statesmen, as little better than savages.'

He raised his glass to his host MacIan, who found these remarks extremely diverting. 'Aye, Glencoe, His Majesty frequently pronounced any news that came from the direction of Scotland, was unlikely to be good news.'

'And he was right, by God,' roared MacIan, proud indeed of having been a thorn in the side of the king of England.

'I will say one thing in his favour,' said his cousin. 'He managed during his long reign to skate very carefully over the perilous surface of religious controversy. It pleased those of us who follow the true religion that he secured the succession of his Catholic brother James, Duke of York. A strange thing I remember at his coronation, in the spring, it was. They could not make the crown stay on his head. However firmly they fixed it, it appeared ever in danger of toppling. This was remembered as significant when young Monmouth, the king's first and best loved bastard,' he explained, 'declared himself his father's true heir and king at Taunton.'

Few who listened, or few Highlanders for that matter, could have defined the exact location of Taunton or of Somerset, thought Lawyer Macdonald, as he continued: 'Some more ambitious Scottish nobles having ascertained whether the meeting place could be reached with advantage, considered raising their clans and following the Duke of Argyll's example by siding with Monmouth against the old enemy England. But before their plans were hatched, Monmouth was defeated and with Argyll executed.'

As Caitlin listened, she realised that none would feel his loss more sorely than Sir Robert Campbell of Glenlyon. Argyll had always been good for a loan. She wondered how Liam Campbell had taken this news.

Oh, Liam, Liam, where are you this night as I break bread with your enemies in Glencoe? What are your fortunes, my beloved, my lost, lost love?

At home again in Ardarroch, matters of national importance in England were of less concern than whether Brendan's new formal garden would survive the particularly dry summer that following year.

For Caitlin, the life-building continued. Emerging from the babyhood's cocoon, William drifted from her side to Brendan's, and he began to explore the amazing wide world beyond his nursery. Watching them together, she knew Brendan was entirely happy, lost in his blissful enduring love for his wife, his clever young son.

But outside the Tower, Elspeth could have told him of anxious speculation among his tenants. Was William to be the only son? For only sons had been the curse of Ardarroch in the past. And what was ado with Lady Ardarroch, young, strong and healthy, in not providing a string of sons to her laird when she had shown such promise by being prompt indeed with that first one.

William was five years old when with a sigh of joy and relief the glensfolk heard that Lady Ardarroch was with child at last and in July 1689 a daughter was born.

From the moment of her birth Kirsty Macdonald was nothing but Brendan's child, from her dark eyes to her strong little chin, the black hair which would one day be like her parents.

One glance was enough for Ardarroch to decide that this daughter would do well enough, as they took her to their hearts and forgave nature's chronic oversight in not providing another son. Undoubtedly such omissions would be rectified in time.

Brendan and Caitlin had shared in their tenants' secret misgivings and, holding Kirsty in her arms, Caitlin wondered what magic had brought about this lovely answer to all her fears? Nothing had changed in Ardarroch, in the routine of their lives together, nor in their lovemaking now accepted as a pleasant comfortable expression of marital devotion. What magic then had conceived the miracle of a child that ordinary September night? Did the stars tilt at a different angle, did the sun lean over in a special way, or the mellow autumn light bring the hills a step nearer? As Brendan touched the downy head at Caitlin's breast, he thanked the Holy Mother, Queen of Heaven, for hearing his prayers and setting the seed that brought the miracle home to Ardarroch.

Love for Kirsty was burned deeply into Brendan's heart long before her birth, which was an easy one. To his delighted eyes, she seemed at first sight a miniature Caitlin, yawning sleepily, stretching out starfish hands. He lifted her gently, a protective hand holding that tiny head, so insecure on its frail stalk. Suddenly she became alive, alert, arms and legs thrusting in all directions, and her first gesture to this world and this father was to wring her hands and croon like a *cailleach* over her spinning wheel.

To Brendan that moment of their first meeting felt like his own rebirth, certain that nothing in his life would ever be prosaic or ordinary again after the wonder that was his daughter.

When she cried, he had just to hold her, kiss her and those threshing arms would fold together neat as angel's wings. With a little sigh, calm serenity replaced the raging storms, a tiny enigmatic smile proclaimed to all the world that he was her hero and her slave.

Yet in those early days he trembled for her survival, refusing to be consoled by Elspeth's vast experience or Caitlin's reassurances. Forever bending over her cradle and finding her still, he had to lay an ear against her breast to satisfy himself that she still breathed. Each lament from her sounded the knell of doom in his heart. Observing an old woman's death in keening cry and toothless wail, he obstinately refused to recognise that practical needs of feeding and clean fresh linen had brought about this holocaust of grief and saw himself carrying his angel, his treasure to the kirkyard come Sunday.

Watching her thrive each day, at last convinced by his womenfolk's amusement that his daily despair was needless, he allowed himself to be persuaded that she would survive after all. Soon all their lives were filled by her helpless rock-strong frailty, so that even her silences held them bound like ancient slaves to a tyrant.

Brendan's daughter. His very own. He wanted to be with her every waking moment, and would have carried her with him when he went out riding to visit his tenants had not Elspeth and Caitlin sternly set their faces against such a preposterous suggestion. They allowed him, however, to carry her into the arbour and there introduce her to the birds, the trees swaying above her head, the flower he placed reverently in her hands, to be ruthless crushed in tiny fingers or thrust between ever hopeful, ever hungry, but still woefully empty gums.

Caitlin watching them both felt proud and happy to be thus relegated to second place in Brendan's life. Here at last he had something that was his very own, as she would never be. As William could never be. He was proud of and still loved William but between them caution was growing, the slight reserve that often exists between a son and his father.

There was no such reserve with Kirsty. Relieved, Caitlin had more time to spend with her son. William who had never shown jealousy towards this cloud of storm and sunshine which had overwhelmed his home, regarded his family's new obsession with gentle tenderness and toleration beyond his years.

William's feelings seemed to be shared by Bran. When Kirsty was old enough, shrieking for entertainment, he would take her for rides on his back while William trotted alongside ready to pick her up, and dry her tears, should she fall.

Caitlin had certain qualms when she looked upon her son, whose hair remained an obstinate dull gold unchanged by the passing years, and explained away by Elspeth on the grounds of his mother having lived too long in that accursed Campbell country. She was relieved that Brendan preoccupied with Kirsty, observed only that his intelligent, high spirited son, thankfully strong, had inherited his own partiality for knowledge as he rushed to Caitlin to report some profound announcement William had made that day, William being now allowed to ride pillion with his father, on his daily visits to the glen.

As some facet of conversation was repeated, Brendan said proudly: 'I believe we shall have a scholar for our next laird, my dearest. When I go, I will be able to relinquish Ardarroch with good heart, knowing that William will continue the traditions I have established. You must promise me, you will see to it that he goes to the University.'

Brendan's statements, cheerful and casual, made Caitlin consider him with anxiety. Increasingly of late, he referred to a future when he would be no longer with them. Caitlin grieved secretly for the change she saw in him and knew that she was not alone. As if in confirmation of her own fears, she observed others watching Brendan with anxiety and foreboding, whispering how each fever robbed him of the dregs of fast-fading youth, leaving him stoop-shouldered, grey-faced and of how each passing winter aged him ten years. Now even in the mildest weather, caught by an unexpected storm, one good soaking and he would run a fever for two weeks and keep them awake with his coughing for another four.

When Brendan was well, Ardarroch relaxed and smiled again. There were visits to and from Glencoe to show off Kirsty, and even as far as Appin to visit Lady Frances who, like her son, was plagued by weak lungs. In poor health that spring, she was recovering.

To Ardarroch the seasons came and went sweeping blossom from bough, bringing bird-song and flowers and ripening fields. Harvest home then the frozen death of winter again.

Caitlin guessed the glensfolk's whispers, for with few exceptions, the transience of mortal life was no surprise. She wanted to forbid such speculations. As if, by ignoring Brendan's sudden deterioration this last year, by pretending that he was well and strong that he had her whole heart and she had never loved any but him, she could change God's divine plan. If only some of her own strength and will to live could be drained into him. She could not bear to think of a world in which there was no Brendan Macdonald, for now the Shroud of Death she had seen on that first visit to Glencoe rarely left him. Alone walking in the garden, it shimmered, turning a still living man into his own spectre.

Miserably in the sleepless hours as he coughed at her side, she tortured herself with guilty thoughts that if Brendan died, then it was all her own fault, retribution for the lie that she had lived with him and for the son he adored.

Perhaps the greatest agony of all was to see him so recklessly happy with Kirsty. That he was doomed never to see her as girl much less as woman, broke Caitlin's heart.

'I am so happy, my dearest, so grateful to you, my Kirsty here, and of course, our dear William. The three of you have brought me more happiness than many poor folk have known in a whole lifetime.'

Kissing him, her heart cried out bitterly that he was only thirty while Elspeth, plump and indestructible at past eighty, muttered comforting platitudes about creaking gates that last the longest and assured her that there were glensfolk, just like my lord Brendan, who had bad chests but lived to a full old age.

'Accidents and wars apart, we live long here in Ardarroch,' she said proudly but could not hold back her tears. Glencoe's physician whom she had brought into the world, 'happened' to be riding to Ardarroch with Father O'Donnell. Brendan was spitting blood, they told her. He could die at any time.

'Shall I tell my lady?' she sobbed.

Andrew MacDonald looked out of the window. In the garden, Brendan carried Kirsty in his arms, swinging her high in the air to shrieks of delighted mirth, while Caitlin gazed at them so lovingly, William and the dog Bran running alongside. That scene of devoted doomed family life was to haunt him forever.

'No, Elspeth. Keep it to yourself, if you please. Let them be happy while they may. Your master knows and has made arrangements with Glencoe. Father O'Donnell is to remain here, to rededicate the chapel for daily use and to tutor young William.'

Father O'Donnell took her hands. 'Ardarroch most earnestly desires that the main purpose of my visit is kept secret. To be with him, at the end.'

Kirsty's second birthday in June 1691 was to be celebrated by a feast for the tenants in the Tower's gardens. There her father was to unveil a special gift, kept secret with considerable difficulty.

Brendan had long been preparing a flower plot in the formal garden, with Kirsty's name and birthdate inside a heart. Each day as the time drew nearer he watched with excitement and increasing anxiety the flowers calculated to blossom all together, making sure they showed firm intention of being in full and radiant bloom on Kirsty's special day.

Despite a sudden unseasonable drop in the summer temperature, a chill wind blowing grey from the hills, he insisted upon superintending the gardeners as they worked on the final stages of preparation. As he put the proud finishing touches upon his masterpiece, the clouds opened in a downpour, complete with hailstones.

Frantic at this hideous desecration of Kirsty's gift, he rushed into the kitchen, ransacking cupboards for covers to protect the plot, angrily pushing aside Elspeth who pleaded with him to at least put some cover over his own cambric shirt.

Elspeth's remonstrances were of no avail. Caitlin was absent with both children on a visit to the tacksman's wife who had given birth to twins. There they remained until the storm was over by which time Brendan, back inside the Tower, was soaked to the skin.

'I told him, my lady, but he would not listen to me,' wailed Elspeth when by evening Brendan was coughing, breathless. Fevered, he insisted that Kirsty's party was not to be cancelled, she was to have her gift. That was the important part, the other festivities could proceed without him.

Caitlin, assisted by the Ardarroch household, managed to steer fifty glensfolk through that fearful day. Kirsty alternately sulked and howled for her absent Papa, the guests were fed, amused by games, sent thankfully homeward clutching small gifts of sweetmeats, while inside the dark Tower, Brendan received the Last Sacrament.

For three days and three nights following, he fought to stay alive. Caitlin was distraught, betrayed, since every tenant in the glen, every person in Ardarroch but herself, it seemed, had been aware of the reason for Father O'Donnell's extended visit.

Refusing to be parted from his master, Bran gazed upon the still form in the bed, hour after hour, raising his head in softly-whimpered distress that was almost human.

Brendan stroked his head, trying in vain to comfort him. 'All right, Bran. I hear you. Time to go, is that it?' he whispered and smiled wanly over Bran's head at Caitlin who had never left his side. 'Time to go, my dearest.'

'No,' said Caitlin, clutching his hand, bone-thin, his face fever-wasted. 'No, my darling. You have recovered other times.'

As if Bran understood the words, he began to whine again.

The weird *coronach* unnerved Caitlin. Bran always knew. Impatiently she said: 'Be quiet, be quiet. Is he disturbing you, my darling. Shall I send him out?' she added desperately.

'No. Let him stay with me.'

Caitlin hid her face in the pillow as she knelt by his side. She wanted to be brave for his sake, but tears spilled over.

'Do not leave me. Stay with me, please stay. And there's Kirsty too.'

'Kirsty. How is my darling?'

'Would you like to see her? Shall I get Elspeth to bring her?'

Brendan shook his head. 'Later. When we have talked.'

'Save your strength. We will have plenty of time for talking when you are well again.'

'Not this time, my dearest. Not this time. Better to go like this, while we are happy. We have been happy, have we not? I have been a good husband?'

'Oh, my dearest, the best, the best in the whole world.'

Brendan looked towards the window smiling, as if some vision he saw there pleased him. 'So few couples can boast of a perfect life together, never a harsh word, not one quarrel, how many could say that?' he asked. 'All these past years with you at my side have been like living some fairy tale. Every day, I have expected to wake up and find that it was all a dream, that you had gone.'

Now you will never have to wake up and know the truth, the truth about your adored wife, and your son. The words came unbidden into Caitlin's heart. The truth which would have destroyed your happiness for ever. The moment she had feared most would not now come to pass. Her son was safe.

She had lived a lie, enjoyed the happiness that was not hers for what she had done to him. Now at this last moment, she could not bear it.

Brendan, forgive me.

As if she had uttered the words he smiled. 'And there is no need for forgiveness between us. As for the boy there,' he

211

whispered, looking towards William who had just entered and was consoling the distraught Bran, 'William, bring your sister to me.' As the door closed behind him, Brendan turned to Caitlin: 'William has always been my son, as you were once his father's daughter.'

There was a pause before Caitlin whispered: 'So you knew, all these years, and yet you have never said a word against him.'

'I knew, I think, from the moment he was born,' he said sadly, 'Knew that what you did was to save Ardarroch from Glencorrie. There is no greater love, no greater sacrifice for any woman.'

Oh God forgive me, thought Caitlin, it was no sacrifice. If only it had been rape, if he had taken me by force, then perhaps I could have lived with my guilt.

'I have loved you the more for it, my dearest,' whispered Brendan, 'and each time I look at William, I remember that as once Liam Campbell loved you, raised you, a Macdonald child of his sworn enemy, as his own flesh and blood, so too could I love this lad as my own. In this way, the blood debt between our Clans was cancelled out. Some day, Caitlin, when I am gone, perhaps that debt will be settled in full and for ever. Believe me, had he been my own son – our son – I could not have loved him better. William –'

He came to the bedside, followed by Elspeth weeping with Kirsty curled sleeping in her arms. William knelt, took his hand. 'Father, dearest Father, how is it with you?'

'Not good, my son, not good. But I command you to love your mother, take good care of her. My Kirsty?' 'No, no, do not wake her. I do not wish her to see me thus. Rather she remember the living father who loved her, than the dead one.' Turning to William again, he said: 'Promise me you will take good care of your sister and of your people out there. You are Macdonald of Ardarroch now.'

William brushed aside his tears, straightened his shoulders, 'Yes, Father, you have my promise.'

'Off you go, Elspeth too. Your mother will be with you directly.' When they were alone, he whispered: 'How cold it is, my darling.' Despite the heat of a summer's day, his hands were icy. As Caitlin murmured about replenishing the fire, he said: 'No, I do not want to lose you, not now, not even for a moment. But I am rather tired. I would like to sleep, knowing you were with me. I want to know that you are near.'

'I will never leave you.' As she said the words, she knew another ghost had been laid, the fear of a choice never now to be made.

'Have you another kiss for me then?' he asked with the teasing, radiant smile so familiar, when he had ridden in at day's end.

'Of course, my darling.'

But his lips too were ice, as he murmured: 'I love you, my Caitlin, remember how I love you.'

'And I love you.'

He clung to her hand in a room grown cold, where the fire's gleam was an illusion. No man-made fire could penetrate such chill thought Caitlin, where the shadows in a bright summer's afternoon were cast by the hovering of death's dark angel. In that moment she seemed to hear the beating of his wings.

Lifting her head, she cried out: 'Leave him, leave him, please.' Throwing her arms across him she whispered: 'Oh, Brendan, Brendan, please stay.' Vainly, she kissed his cold lips, as if to bring back the warmth of life. His eyes flickered open as if he was surprised, well pleased. He smiled once and, with a small sigh, was gone.

And even as she called his name, she knew that he was at peace, his earthly struggles ended. From his face the grey lines of pain, the fever-hollows had gone, his face suffused with returned youth mocked the flesh that was already clay.

She was aware of Bran at her side now, no longer howling. Dogs never cried, but those strange human eyes, were shedding tears. He nuzzled her cheek and then laid his head upon his master's outstretched hand with a sound like weeping.

Caitlin put her arms around his neck and together they shared the bitter grief of Brendan's passing.

Chapter XI

Caitlin was unprepared for the desolation of widowhood. Although she had known that she must outlive Brendan, she now saw how readily the human heart deceives itself. She had never truly believed that Brendan would die, or imagined the reality of life without him. Deprived of his cheerful companionship, the empty pillow where once his head had rested, his comforting arms and undemanding tenderness and humour, their long conversations, she missed most of all the small incidents which had strung together like beads on a necklace, a multitude of blissful, contented days.

Daily she listened for the sound of his footsteps on the courtyard's cobbles, whistling as he went to saddle his horse. And then for the welcome ring of his booted spurs as he climbed the stone staircase, weary at the day's ending. Thus the inescapable tokens of her bereavement became not the moment of laying Brendan in his grave, but the everyday events which she had taken for granted.

William and Kirsty seemed to draw away from her, unused to this sad-faced, black-veiled figure. Kirsty's tears were hardest to bear as she asked where Papa was, why had he not taken her with him. And when was he coming back to her?

Caitlin's description of heaven and where Papa awaited among the angels, was no consolation. Kirsty who had been her father's angel on earth added childish jealousy to despair. Although William nodded solemnly and seemed to understand, Kirsty screamed: 'I do not believe you, Papa would never leave me, for *them*,' she ended with a baleful glance heavenwards, to those whom her disgust might concern.

Brendan's wish had been that Caitlin hold Ardarroch in

William's name until he came of age, by double right of marriage and inheritance, as William Macdonald's daughter, with MacIan of Glencoe to act as adviser and guide on legal matters. Had Brendan known this would be the best cure for grief, she wondered, ever more absorbed in running this small estate, aided by the tacksman.

Sometimes in those early days, she dreamed that Brendan still lived. She would drift into a room and there he was, sitting by the fire and explaining that his death had been a mistake.

The happiness built on the fragility of a sad heart's longing was shattered by an awakening, almost more than she could bear. Other dreams came to haunt and taunt her. Desires, secret, long suppressed and denied.

For Liam Campbell.

While Brendan lived, she had successfully banished such yearnings, but without her husband at her side, with no man to love in that empty bed, her dreams overflowed with haunting fragments of the past. Liam came to her, violent, passionate, and tender too. And she ran blindly, joyously to him, held close as the barriers of flesh dissolved melted between them, as once for a few hours, their love had stopped the clocks of time and reality had ceased to exist.

There were darker unhappy dreams, when she awoke in the darkness, hearing Liam's voice, crying out to her as he had on that night when they had made love. Her part of the bargain complete, he knew that the promise must be kept. She must be allowed to go free.

'I love you, oh, Caitlin, I love you. Stay with me.'

She could not. Love must be denied and body's longing. Now over and over, he came to her. Always the same words: 'Stay with me.'

Time and again, she heard his voice, no longer confined to the night, but in the whisper of trees stirred by a freshening wind, or in the hush when bird-song is suddenly stilled. And when summer breeze changed to autumn storm, it was the ghost of her still living lover's ghost and not her dead husband who came to haunt her.

On such days she would go through the day, pale and lost, answering questions with a vague frown, too preoccupied to recognise those who were alive and needed her: William's sums remained unchecked, Elspeth's wails over some culinary disaster went unheeded, Kirsty's grazed knee and tears, received only a perfunctory kiss while Caitlin, certain the dream was a portent, watched for a door that must open and bring Liam Campbell, striding into her life again. Reality became the passing shadow, the entirety of her true world, Liam Campbell.

Where was he at this moment? Why did he not come to her as those dreams promised? A frightened echo: Did he still live?

Brendan's garden lay desolate, its paths deserted under the melancholy of a mid-November day when the Reverend Stephen Stewart-Campbell Glencorrie, Minister of Fortingall, rode into Ardarroch. His cloth gained him instant admission, and the word that he carried news for Lady Ardarroch's ears, to whom he was kin. He was asked very civilly to wait while an enquiry was made whether her ladyship was at home that day.

She was and would receive him.

Although the Tower's exterior was grey and somewhat forbidding, the entrance hall and furnishings were finer than he had anticipated, many were reminiscent of Meggernie, but chosen he realised by an owner who brought discernment from his European travels, whereas Sir Robert had brought only money.

Caitlin ran downstairs to greet him; his grave expression, this unexpected visit. There could be only one reason. Her ashen lips framed one soundless word: 'Liam.'

Heart hammering, clutching the balustrade for support she heard him say: 'I thought you would wish to know,' a pause, 'my mother, alas, she is dead ... '

But Liam still lived. Overwhelmed with relief, Caitlin scarcely heeded the details of Eunice's sudden illness and death, as in the drawing room with the door closed, she embraced Stephen warmly. The bewildered widow vanished in the compassionate girl he remembered.

Behind the sombre dress, the black veils and starched cap, he saw that she was beautiful. More beautiful than ever as wife, mother, and widow. His heart ached with envy for the man who was now dead but had known her love. Oh for those missing years, to have shared his own sterile life with her, to have had her bear his children.

'Only a very short visit,' he explained, banishing his carnal thoughts, 'To beg passage across the lands of Ardarroch on a short cut to the north – '

Intended as a mere courtesy visit to offer condolences on her bereavement and bring news of his own, within moments of meeting Caitlin Macdonald, he was amazed to know that he still loved her, had always loved her and was in danger of so doing for the rest of his days.

'You have chosen inclement weather,' she said, looking at the rain which now streamed down the windows, spitting against the bright burning logs. 'You must stay, Stephen dear, I insist, you can spare us one night,' she added wistfully.

Delighted he accepted: 'If that will be no trouble.'

Assuring him that it would be a pleasure, she added: 'You have not supped? Neither have I.'

They sat at either end of the long polished table with its sconce of wax candles, kept for special guests, the great fire behind them and the grey dog before it. An unnerving dog, thought Stephen, eyeing it cautiously. He had few happy experiences of canines, especially large ones, which he soon learned had scant reverence for men of God on their pastoral visits. As for this dog, the size of a pony with a long curly tail, some trick of the candlelight gave it the appearance of listening intently to every word of their conversation.

In a quiet unemotional voice Caitlin talked of Brendan's death. Her calm surprised him and he commended her sensible attitude.

She smiled. 'Harvest home and winter again. Ardarroch has gone but little changes in the glen. With or without him, life must go on, for all of us. We grieve, but we will survive.' Suddenly, wishing to divert the conversation from painful subjects, she said: 'So you have been to London at last. Is it such a very foreign land – I have always imagined it as a different world entirely?'

Stephen smiled. 'It is a world seething with intrigue, especially in Royal circles.'

She learned that her anxiety over her childless years after William's birth had been shared by no less than a personage than the Queen of England.

217

'Early in '88 she suddenly became pregnant. There were those who regarded this,' Stephen paused delicately, 'as more to do with padding and the folly of wishful thinking than the wish to deceive the realm. When in June a son was born, his birth was so contested and controversial that he has already become infamous as the "warming-pan" babe, smuggled, rumour has it, into the palace by the Queen's sympathisers. A few weeks after his birth a group of statesmen invited William of Orange, his kin by marriage, to come to England and bring an army with him, to add force to his investigations regarding the legitimate claim of this new Prince of Wales to his title.

'They had a long wait. He landed in November, but by early December had gained sufficient support to have poor Queen Mary Beatrice fleeing for her life with the infant prince to France, closely followed by the king. Our king-in-exile, he is being called by the group who have rallied round him at the court of St Germain – mostly English Tories, Irish Catholics and Highlanders, like old Alistair had he lived.'

Caitlin smiled sadly. 'My dear old Alistair,' I miss him still.' With a sigh, she added: 'His great loyal heart would always beat faster at the name of poor ill-fated Mary of Scotland, great-grandmother of this King James.'

Stephen nodded and continued: 'Two years ago, in the spring, he set about winning back his kingdom, but when he landed in Ireland he found Protector William and the English forces ready for him. In Scotland the Duke of Gordon held Edinburgh Castle in King James' name and when the castle fell to the Orangeists, Viscount Dundee raised the Clans and that July at Killiecrankie, he won the day, the 17th it was, for the king. You look surprised?'

'That was the day our little daughter, Kirsty, was born.'

'Did you know aught of the battle?' Stephen asked.

'A rumour only, a long time afterwards, by way of Glencoe or the Inverness carter as is the way here at Ardarroch. We have few knowledgeable visitors, I am afraid. However, we did hear that, when Dundee was mortally wounded, the Clan Donald finding themselves leaderless, quit the field.'

She avoided adding what she knew so well. The

218

Macdonalds of Glencoe and Keppoch had marched homewards through the Campbell lands of Breadalbane, then through Glenlyon which they stripped bare from Fortingall to the southern wall of Rannoch moor. She had heard MacIan boast that they found little opposition in Glenlyon, the women scarce home from the sheiling, the men dispersed busy with harvests, unarmed and taken by surprise. In their absence the Macdonalds pillaged and burned their houses, drove off more than a thousand head of cattle, horses, sheep and goats. From the cottages they took everything that could be carried.

'You know of the raid?'

A sharp nod, the hasty question: 'What of Fortingall?'

'A black day for us, but worse for Sir Robert, with eight thousand pounds Scots in goods stolen. They did not spare Chesthill either, stripped of livestock, furnishings, everything movable.'

Caitlin remembered how she used to sit on a creepy stool in the kitchen of Chesthill awaiting her father, absorbed and overawed by the imagined splendours that lay beyond the servants' quarters.

Stephen shook his head. 'The raid on Glenlyon was the last word in Glenlyon's saga of ruin. After Argyll, his benevolent kinsman died in Monmouth's rebellion, Sir Robert conveniently forgot that order for the "restraint and guidance of his house" and was merrily signing bonds. Breadalbane who was responsible for his debts, was extremely angry and demanded instant repayment, or prison. Glenlyon's loyal tenants rallied and most generously offered half their cattle to save him. He refused and nothing was left to him but to sell Glenlyon to the Murrays of Atholl. He keeps Chesthill, for what it is now worth. The dowerland is Lady Glenlyon's, for her lifetime.'

'I am sorry for Sir Robert, although I am not surprised, for I was always alarmed by the extravagance of his life at Meggernie. Now that I have Ardarroch to run, I know how frugal one must be.'

Stephen sighed. 'A lesson Sir Robert never learned. He went from bad to worse, and somewhat deranged, for that is the only possible excuse for his action, he raised a force of the ragged broken men of Argyll and led these despicable

219

soldiers of fortune on a raid into Strathfillan, with a game of tit-for-tat in mind, hoping to bring home enough cattle to pay off some of his more pressing creditors. Breadalbane could hardly believe his ears. Certain now that his cousin had gone stark raving mad, he told everyone: "He ought to be sent to Bedlam, I wish we had chambered him years ago. When I set eyes upon him, he is an object of compassion but when he is out of sight, I could wish he had never been born."

'The saga does not end there, alas. Last winter, Sir Robert almost starved and when he failed to repay a loan from Glenlyon's new owner, Murray had him outlawed. Had it not been for his son-in-law who honoured the debt he would have been jailed. At this stage he decided to take the alternative way out.'

At Caitlin's startled expression, for she had never considered Sir Robert as a man of such courage, Stephen smiled. 'No, not by shooting out his brains because it now sounds, to anyone who ever had dealings with him, extremely doubtful if he had any brains in the first place ... '

'What has the foolish man done now?'

'Joined Argyll's regiment as Captain of Foot, at eight shillings a day.'

There was a pause before Caitlin asked: 'How does this effect Fortingall?'

'Oh, Murray is prepared to be merciful and do his best for us as long as we do not take any undue liberties.'

Another silence. Then in a voice that strived to be firm, Caitlin asked: 'What of Glencorrie, Stephen. What news of him?'

Stephen noted that this was her first direct reference to Liam Campbell. He thought such omission strange. Did she not even retain curiosity about the father who had disowned her when she married Brendan Macdonald? Had she wiped out the past like once cleaning a slate with a wet rag?

'Oh, did you not know?' he said. 'He accepted a commission in the Argylls too. Went with his cousin, gallant man. When we tried to persuade him against such folly, you know how determined he can be, he told us he no longer saw himself in the role of secretary, tacksman or poor kin, but more in the nature of keeper and nurse to this poor madman.'

'Sir Robert has always been his own worst enemy,' said

Caitlin, remembering Liam's words: He is a prey to his sorry nature which will never let him rest content. It is up to me to do the best I can to keep him from such excesses.

'So Glencorrie, the man of peace, has now turned soldier. Who would have thought it?'

'Without Glenlyon any longer, your father,' Caitlin started at the word, 'your father had to keep himself and my mother from starving. He was, I fear, too readily persuaded for Sir Robert had never been slow in reminding him that without his charity, Glencorrie would have perished long since. I expect Argyll was so delighted to see his mad kinsman in Liam Campbell's sensible hands, that he granted him the rank of Lieutenant.'

Stephen paused and looked at her for a moment before adding: 'Before he left, he bequested Glencorrie to me, or what precious few tenants remain, in the hope they might prosper under Murray's care.'

Caitlin was silent, her eyes on the firelight. Her voice was little more than a whisper: 'Have you seen him since?'

'Aye, at my mother's funeral.'

She realised she had almost forgotten the second purpose of her visit. Guiltily she said: 'Oh Stephen, I am so sorry … '

Before she could say more, the door opened and a boy entered, followed by the grey dog.

'This is my son William.'

'Eight in January, did you say,' Stephen laughed, for the boy who bowed gravely over his hand was tall, well grown for his age. 'And he favours the Campbells in his looks.'

Caitlin's hand tightened imperceptibly on the wine glass, her smile had vanished.

'That was tactless of me,' whispered Stephen as head bent she offered the lad a sweetmeat. 'I realise such reminders are painful for your father behaved abominably to both yourself and your husband.'

The silver dish clattered back on to the table as Caitlin held up a dismissive hand. 'No matter, Stephen, no matter.' The next moment there was a smile of welcome and open arms for the little girl who rushed in accompanied by an ancient nurse.

'And this is Kirsty, she is two.'

Stephen beamed upon the exquisite small replica of

Caitlin solemnly bobbing a curtsey before him.

The children went to bed reluctantly. There were fewer visitors now with winter's approach.

'We leave for Glencoe immediately, for a family wedding, another Campbell marrying with a Macdonald this time Sarah's young sister niece to Sir Robert,' she added smiling. 'We are preparing our departure, two more days and we should have missed seeing you.'

'When do you return?'

'Not before the spring. Glencoe has persuaded us to winter with them. Ardarroch is costly to run, I am learning that very quickly, since it has become my responsibility. The Tower is very old, built in the days when chieftains were powerful warriors with many bairns, servants and clansmen. It is difficult to keep warm, the roof leaks, repairs are constantly needed. Until William is of age, we must maintain it for him, but we cannot afford the winters, with a storm of servants to wait upon one woman and two children, especially when those servants have cosy homes of their own. Besides in Glencoe, the children have many Macdonald cousins.' She sighed. 'It is good for them. After all you have been telling me about the outside world, I realise how lonely and isolated we are here in Ardarroch.'

Times were harder that she cared to admit. Brendan had been a philanthropist who never turned a beggar from his door, or his back upon a worthwhile charity. She could save money by spending six months of each year at Glen Muidhe, put it aside for William's education and for his inheritance. And the cheerful society of her kin at Glencoe would ease her own loneliness too.

'The Macdonalds of Ardarroch resemble the Campbells of Glencorrie in so many ways. They are no longer strong enough to exist in their own right, or by raids on other men's properties. It is time we joined forces with stronger branches of our Clans, like Glencoe. I should not mind staying in Glencoe until William is of age and MacIan himself has promised to come and help me move house.'

Stephen's eyebrows raised. 'That seems a most unwarlike role for Glencoe. His enemies will be surprised.'

Caitlin smiled. 'He is a reformed character now that he has promised to sign the treaty with the English Government.

With the King of England's protection, he sees a new way of life and he plans to extend his Tower at Carnoch, turn it from fortress into peaceful mansion.'

'As I have noticed many other chiefs are doing. It is a good healthy sign that we may, God willing, have peace in our time. So you intend a long stay at Glencoe?'

'I am uncertain. We will see what winter brings before we decide to abandon Ardarroch.' She sighed. 'Pray God that his fortune may be improved by then with a wife's dowry, a long life and children to help restore our clan to its former glory.'

'At least the lad looks strong and healthy.'

There was the slightest of questioning pauses, before Caitlin said: 'Your mother always wished you to have Glencorrie. I am glad it came to you in her lifetime – it was always her dearest wish.'

'She had scant time to enjoy that pleasure.'

'I was to ask you earlier, how did it happen?'

'After your father went to the military she took a congestion of the lungs, and she never fully recovered.'

He spared Caitlin the scenes of anger and tears with which she had sought to persuade Liam not to leave her for the Argylls. Before the end, plagued with ancient wrongs, devils of hatred seemed to possess her. Hatred of this girl before him; her absence had not sweetened her stepmother's opinion of her. Her ravings were dreadful, her confidential whisperings worse: 'Kill her, kill her.' Such words belonged to some fiendish nightmare, evil as the postules of fever. He preferred the silent withdrawn stranger mother to the screaming virago delirium brought, hating Caitlin, loving, nay, worshipping Liam Campbell. Such love seemed terrible to Stephen, unnatural in his own mother who was near fifty and had been married for many years.

Dutifully, earnestly, he prayed and sought God's pardon: Thou knowest, Lord, that in her latter days, an evil spirit possessed her.

'Have you no thought to marry, now that you are alone?'

'There was a girl, two years past, a minister's daughter in Perth.' He shook his head. There had been no love on his side nor he suspected on hers. Neither affection nor kisses were exchanged but her father was eager for the match and brought her to Fortingall on a visit that summer. Eunice Campbell, already fatally ill was deranged with fury as Alison entered the house and he realised with horror that in the dim light she had mistaken her for Caitlin. They were not unalike in colour and height. Perhaps that was why he had briefly wanted her. Eunice's jealousy, and her language, were so appalling that both father and daughter went scurrying back to Perth, murmuring to sympathetic friends about 'Wild Highlanders – so uncivilised'.

'Well?' said Caitlin, awaiting his answer.

He smiled crookedly. 'She decided she would be better off without me.'

As he prepared for bed that night Stephen remembered gentle, pious Alison, whom he could not ask to share his life while his terrible mother lived. And now that she was dead he had no desire to reopen the subject of marriage. For by a miracle, the following morning as he looked out of his window to be greeted by a robin's triumphant song and a merry stream tumbling down from the hillside to fold itself into a pool of sunshine, he realised that the burden of his mother had dropped from his shoulders. Like Greatheart in *Pilgrim's Progress*, he was free. And part of the true miracle was that his beloved Caitlin was also free.

Even the two children charmed him. That thoughtful unsmiling boy – Stephen frowned, there was something that troubled him about William. No matter, no matter, the lass was an enchantress in the making. And Stephen, never slow to dream, felt no qualms about starting life with a ready made family, another man's bairns. If God so willed, since both Caitlin and he were young, there would be other bairns, his and hers, in due time.

As they strolled next morning in Brendan's withered garden, she talked of the Glencoe wedding, and of their possible return to Ardarroch.

Was it his imagination or did she sound less confident than last night?

'To tell the truth,' she continued, 'I love my own home dearly. On days like this Ardarroch is pure heaven and I hate the idea of leaving it until next spring.'

The two children ran ahead playing with a coloured ball. Stephen kicked it back to them and they shouted with glee,

224

at the sight of this solemn black-garbed gentleman in his Geneva bands, who had stepped out of character to behave in a young and frivolous manner they understood. It was not at all the way for a priest, as he laughed too, slapping his thighs.

Yes, he was sure they liked him. That God had willed his timely arrival and promised him a blessing. And by the stone Cupid in the sheltered arbour he stopped and took Caitlin's hands. She looked at him smiling, pleased by this friendly impulse.

'There is no need to go to Glencoe. Come back to Fortingall.'

'No. No.' Even before he had finished speaking, her hands were free and outstretched palms forward, as if to push the subject away.

'Hear me out – '

'No. *This* is my home.'

He realised he had mismanaged it, that she had no idea what he was asking her. 'I am asking you to relinquish your home in Ardarroch and to take another – come to Fortingall, as my wife, Caitlin, as my wife.'

'No. No!' Seeing his hurt expression, she was sorry, realising how ungracious she sounded. But her lips had gone dry. The idea horrified her that she might unexpectedly meet Liam again. Even the thought of him, the mention of his name, made her heart thud so loud she was sure Stephen could hear it and would be aware of her guilt. If this was but the name what would his real presence bring?

'Oh Stephen,' she saw his wounded look and hastened to repair the damage, as best she could. 'You are a dear, kind, good man. I know you have my best interests at heart. I am honoured, flattered.' She smiled, her composure regained. Her voice had ceased to tremble. 'But I cannot marry you, I cannot.'

'Why ever not? We have known each other practically all our lives, we do not have the laborious business of those who marry, much in love but with slight acquaintance.'

She regarded him sadly. What did he know of love and its ecstacies, its bitter grief? 'I think always of you as my brother,' she whispered.

'But there is no blood tie between us. Besides I have not

thought of you as my sister in many years.'

There was a pause before she replied, as if searching for the right words not to offend him. 'I do not love you. Respect and admiration, yes, these I have. But not love. I could never love you, never as ... husband.'

As she spoke the rain began and she looked up at him with its chill foreboding in her face. But she was glad of the rain too, for it offered the chance of escape, and they gathered up the children, hurried towards the stables nearby. Under cover, shaking the raindrops from her hair, he watched her inflexible profile, waiting for her to qualify her rejection of him.

'Will not you even consider my proposal?' he asked as his horse was led out.

With hands neatly folded, eyes downcast, she shook her head. He sighed deeply, hurt and bewildered, but with neither invitation nor excuse left to tarry, he had no alternative but to continue his journey.

He walked his horse towards the Tower and on the step, the two children ran forward and ranged themselves on either side of their mother. The grey dog stood firmly in front of her, wagging its tail. From these positions they seemed unassailable as they regarded him solemnly and proud too, as if they knew his intentions and approved their mother's rejection.

'God be with you,' he said.

'And with you.' She was smiling now, the dangerous moment past. In the relief of parting, she could afford to be generous for his perfunctory duty kiss, the brush of lips against cold cheek was that of a gentle undemanding brother.

Then her son bowed over his hand, her daughter curtseyed winsomely. All three held up their hands in farewell but when he reached the gate and turned, they had disappeared inside the Tower. The doorway was empty.

He was halfway to his destination across the hills, when he realised what had eluded him. It was something about the boy. And everything evasive turned familiar, his solemn face, his habit of gnawing his lower lip. Stephen had entirely dismissed from his mind his mother's ravings as the fever devoured her, her attempts to sully this woman he loved and, he feared, was doomed to love for evermore.

Now against his will, he found himself pondering a matter that the cesspool had stirred. It concerned Caitlin and his stepfather. His mother told him, in what appeared to be a moment of lucidity from her ravings, to mark well that Caitlin had been fostered by Liam and Mairi. Liam Campbell was not Caitlin's father.

'They were always in love,' she said, 'He could not keep his hands off her, that is why he married me. For their whole relationship, even in the girl's childhood was loathsome, filthy and indecent, and she encouraged him.'

Stephen rode on but the boy's face refused to be dismissed from his mind. No man who had lived in Fortingall through the years could fail to see his extraordinary likeness to Liam Campbell. And for Stephen that was the death of his love, as he cursed himself for all those wasted years, years of worshipping a girl he had kept pedestal-high above frail mortals. For her he would have gone to the world's end and never looked back, had she commanded. And now he saw himself betrayed, as she had betrayed Brendan Macdonald. She had loved neither of them. For Caitlin there had been only one secret, forbidden love.

And the proof was written in the face of Liam Campbell's son, William Macdonald of Ardarroch.

In Glencoe, Caitlin heard only one conversation among the Macdonald wedding guests.

'Have you taken the oath yet?'

'I have not seen you since Achallader.'

The sensational topic was rascally Breadalbane's scheme, that the English Government should make it worth the while of the Highland chiefs to submit and live in peace.

'You know full well that the fellow is naught but a Campbell rascal. Do not be imagining such ideas were for love of his fellow Highlanders,' MacIan shook his head. 'Naught but avarice, with a ready eye to how he could most profit from others' misfortunes.'

'Aye, a crafty devil, right enough, with the subtlety of an attorney and the barbarity of a Lowland cateran. Yon Sinclair business, how he got his Caithness earldom, was enough to sicken any decent man.'

'No wonder the English scheme was so popular among the traitors who rule over us.'

'Especially the Highland traitors,' said MacIan in disgust. 'Each hoping to be chosen as intermediary for the pickings that would accrue to him.'

'Both inside and outside the law, eh?'

'Like yourself and the lifting of Breadalbane's cows,' chuckled Coll of Keppoch. 'Have you submitted yet, Glencoe?'

'Not I,' said MacIan proudly. 'William of Orange is naught to me, he will never be my king. The words of an oath to him would stick in my throat, as long as there is hope for Jamie, our true king.'

'What news is there from St Germain?'

MacIan shook his head. 'None.' Every day that dawned he waited for the messenger that would render his oath unnecessary, the message that would have him leaping to arms summoning his warriors who had waited so long for this glorious opportunity to restore their rightful king to his throne.

'He should have been on his way by now,' whispered Coll of Keppoch. 'If he does not come soon, MacIan, we have no alternative but to take the oath.'

'Maybe you can submit to Ian Glas, but not I. Not after this summer. He insulted me – damnation man, you know, the Achallader truce was a disaster.'

'We know that the pair of you almost came to blows,' said Macdonald of Achtriochan.

'Just about, man. Just about. Such a fuss and what a memory the man has. After all, Killiecrankie was two years ago. And since when has lifting cattle not been considered lawful booty for a warrior returning home?'

'True enough,' said Keppoch. 'How else is a man supposed to feed his starving bairns all winter when he has been away fighting for a true cause?'

'You must take the oath, Father,' Alistair Og kept doggedly reminding MacIan. 'Time is running out, we are into November, a few weeks more and the year will be ended, January 1 1692 will soon be on us.'

'My brother is right, Father,' said John. 'We have already had one extension from October 1.'

'You must go, Father, Breadalbane is your enemy, you are playing into his hands, he has a long memory.'

'I can just see him,' said John grimly, 'praying that you are too proud and that will give him the chance he has been waiting for all these years.'

'What sort of chance would that be?'

'The chance to destroy Glencoe.'

MacIan chuckled, slapping his thigh. 'You worry unnecessarily, the pair of you fussing like auld hen-wives. It will take a better man than Breadalbane or any Campbell to destroy Glencoe. Although we are small in numbers, we have no traitors among us. The blood you both bear is noble and without taint of cowardice, descended from Angus Og who sheltered good king Robert the Bruce in his castle at Dunaverty. And by race and religion we remain true to the Stuarts as our lawful kings.'

The brothers exchanged wry glances. They needed no reminder.

There was a ghost awaiting Caitlin at the wedding of Macdonald of Achtriochan's son. She had forgotten until she held the hand of the bride's mother, Davina, that her sister, Sarah, wife to Alasdair Og, was also Liam's second cousin. Their first meeting sent Caitlin's heart hammering.

By one of those totally inexplicable family resemblances, Davina was the image of Liam Campbell.

Caitlin found herself looking into remembered eyes, seeing the familiar curl of Liam's mouth through Davina's smile, the tilt of Liam's eyebrows and curve of chin in Davina's head thrown back in her sudden, devastatingly familiar laughter.

The family celebrations lasted a week and by the end of that time the unnerving likeness had half of the wedding guests mistaking William for Davina's son, with Caitlin standing aside, in trembling anticipation of denouncement by her Macdonald kin. She felt certain that her mother-in-law regarded her strangely and considered her grandson's appearance with a frowning question she was too polite to put into words.

The ghost of Liam Campbell brought its own retribution, the dreams from long ago, suppressed during Brendan's lifetime, would no longer be denied and she found herself reliving Liam's bargain. The two days they had shared together in Meggernie.

In dreams she touched his flesh again, that first loving full of anger, tears and wonder. Married love was for her a tender demonstration, worthy, dedicated and rather solemn, in which she presumed Brendan received the satisfaction of knowing that she belonged to him, while part of her had remained a detached observer, aware of clocks ticking, a crying child, moonlight and chilly sheets.

Gratification she had never known, possession that is the destruction and absorption of self, far beyond a pleasant sensation which usually ceased just as the dark rose of desire deep inside her began to awaken and unfold its frail petals.

Liam's loving had demanded all her senses. He spared nothing, flesh to flesh, bone to bone, two bodies that folded into each other neat as an angel's wings, two bodies made to be one with every sense alert, eyes, mouth, and hands. She had never known that caresses held such areas of delight, to entice, to enslave, to enjoy the pleasure of a man's body. And as the petals inside her grew strong and drew him again and again into the secret depths of her being, pleasure became ecstacy, and ecstacy of one soul lost within another.

'Caitlin, Caitlin.' There were no words to describe Liam's wonder for this miracle. One naked flesh, one naked being he had warmed into life, carried against his heart on the cruel day of her birth. He had lost her, found her again. Given new life and warmth, she was indivisible with his flesh, lost within him for ever.

Afterwards she had looked at his head on the pillow beside her. The hair, tarnished gold now, she traced with one finger and a sculptor's delight in every feature of this new found love. The strong planes of firm mouth, wide lips and jawline, the eyes where the green and brown mingled, a winter landscape in exquisite miniature. The fan of black eyelashes oddly boyish and vulnerable under dark wings of eyebrows, a strange contrast to that golden head.

Eyelids shot open, lips parted and uttered only one whispered word: 'Caitlin,' as he drew her down to him again.

Still one being, Adam before God created Eve from his

side, they drifted back towards a shore of peace, to sleep and love again. But the fire that consumed them would not yet be turned to ashes, their love would not tolerate separation, they had given it life and now it knew hunger and thirst, made demands that were swift and urgent. Burning fiercely, such ecstacy was not to be tamed or made kind by everyday matters of food to be eaten or Liam's grudging hours spent in the chart room.

'Six days we have,' she whispered.

'Six nights, my love, too short for all our lost years.'

But fate willed otherwise. They were denied even those few days out of a lifetime they had promised each other. A messenger rode in with word that Sir Robert lodged in Perth that night. The documents he thrust into Liam's hands required copying and made ready for Sir Robert's signature on return.

They faced each other, neither willing to pretend to be brave or speak of a heart that would not be broken by this cruel parting. They made love for the last time, clung to one another knowing that now only the dark was theirs. Dawn's first light where sunlight and bird-song brought mortals comfort and hope, to them gave only the heart ripped wide-open in the agony of parting. Each had already died that solitary death upon a far distant shore. Dead to one another, how they conducted their private mourning concerned not only themselves, but those with whom they must spend their future years: Brendan and Eunice. They hovered on time's periphery, names unspoken, faces withheld, as befitted phantoms without a place in this world created by lovers, who alone made the laws and neither God nor the Devil ruled over them. The Liam and Caitlin who lived from this day forward would never again be the two who had built their own Paradise, who had loved and killed innocence.

'Stay with me, stay with me,' he whispered. 'We will go to Ulster to my mother's people. No one will look for us there. A new life – together, my Caitlin.'

'Dearest, dearest, do not ask me,' she sobbed against his heart. 'Do not ask me, when I gave my word.'

When it would be so easy to break it, she thought, knowing she had only to say, I will stay with you, for the course of her whole life to be changed, intermingled with his until one of them was dead. Knowing that whatever her vows to Brendan, this man would call across the earth and she would hear him and follow wherever his destiny lay. But knowing also that the price she would gladly give was not only her own soul but the remaining years of Brendan Macdonald's short life. Brendan whose image was already wilting, spectral, unformed, but nevertheless was the man to whom she owed the promise unbroken and all the happiness she could give him. She would rather face her own lingering death, the years that stretched ahead without Liam, than destroy the man to whom she owed more than she could ever repay.

Liam did not speak to her again. He seemed to sleep but when she awakened at daybreak, his pillow was empty. She called his name but there was no answer. Dressing hastily, she ran to the door, hoping to find it locked, herself a prisoner. Oh, how gladly at this moment, her will could be destroyed. Her every sense called to an unseen Liam: Come, take me back to you. Keep me with you for ever.

But the door sprang open to her touch and she ran downstairs and out into the sun-drenched courtyard with its chorus of bird-song. Her horse stood ready saddled for her. But Liam Campbell had remained invisible and made no attempt to stop her riding out of Meggernie and back across the hill to Ardarroch, out of his life for ever.

The dog Bran who had treated her with polite affection during Brendan's lifetime was now her shadow, following her everywhere, watching over her with those strange compelling and often unnerving human eyes. Her moods he could interpret, for when she was sad, he would lay his shaggy head with a sigh upon her knee. When she was pleased he seemed to smile and it made her shiver as if Brendan's spirit had entered his dog. Sometimes she wondered if he also influenced her decisions. Clouded with uncertainty, she had but to look into his eyes and her mind seemed to clear. His devotion touched her deeply. Fearing that he might pine for Brendan, now she realised that lasting grief, as humans suffered, had no place in his emotions. Perhaps he was in possession of a greater truth and knew the

232

secrets that awaited beyond the gates of death.

'I will give you a bonny price for him,' said Lady Glencoe, whose home had not yet acquired the elegance which demanded banishment of hounds to the stables and the acquisition of lap-dogs, pretty little spaniels that King Charles had made popular, for the ladies. 'Let him bide here when you go back to Ardarroch. I have some handsome bitches need whelping.'

'I would be willing, but I doubt whether he would stay.'

Her ladyship's eyebrows raised in disapproval. 'And how is that?' Beasts were beasts, they did as they were bid.

Caitlin took a deep breath. 'Brendan told me that Bran remains loyal to whoever is Ardarroch. He would follow us home.'

'You really think so.' Lady Glencoe was obviously offended by her reluctance to be parted from a mere dog. 'Excellent stud, he would be, too. We have been trying to introduce new blood from the wild pack. But it is not easy to obtain pups, and they are hard to train, quite savage with the other dogs too. And once they are old enough, alas, they return to the wild, away to the hills again at the first opportunity.' Turning her attention to Bran, she asked: 'How old is he?' examining eyes, ears and teeth with a practised hand. This Bran permitted and when at last she released him murmuring, 'Fine beast, fine beast,' he shook himself wearily and flopped down out of range, with a reproachful look to Caitlin as if he understood every word. 'How did you leave Elspeth?' Lady Glencoe asked.

'Sad. Disappointed not to come with us, for the first time insisting that someone must stay and take care of Ardarroch in our absense. Truth is, she has been failing sadly over this past year. Her joints are woefully crippled, hard enough for her to climb the stairs without making this journey across the hills to Glencoe. She gets very muddled in her mind sometimes.'

'Dear Elspeth, she must be a ripe old age now.'

'Well past eighty, she thinks, but is not quite sure which year she was born.'

'People took little heed of such things in the old days, unless you had an inheritance to gain, or were noble. With priests coming once a year to the glens to baptise, marry and

233

say prayers for the dead, if one's parents could not read or write, or were incomers to the parish, mistakes could be made.'

As November slid into December, Caitlin realised that for the first time in her life she no longer looked for a future. Each day was enough, to sit on the rug with Kirsty curled in her lap, with Bran and William inseparable by her side. Enough to feel the warm fire on her face, to exist with food to eat, a roof above her head, and the air to breathe. Enough at the moment, to be alive to gather strength knowing that this was a last lingering on the smooth plateau that had been her former life in Ardarroch. One day soon she would need to be alert and strong when that plateau came to an abrupt end. A chasm yawned before her while unheeding, Lady Glencoe prattled excitedly of MacIan's promise to take her to Glasgow in the spring.

'For the sole purpose of purchasing gee-gaws, for Carnoch, if you please. He now feels that Glen Muidhe might not be grand enough with peaceful days of entertaining ahead. After all I have done here, too,' she wailed. 'My dear, men are impossible. But oh, I so long for spring,' she added with a contented sigh.

Spring. What was spring to Caitlin, as around her the year died? An easy death for once. Not under the cruelty of bitter wind and snow, but a mere draining of colour from hill and glen. Where was spring? She had no faith in its coming. Like Ardarroch it seemed already part of her past. Would she ever return to what had been her beloved home? It was as though some stranger dwelt inside her, mouthing glib words of enthusiastic response to Lady Frances' decision to accompany them to Ardarroch, while Sir Hector attended to business which must take him from Appin most of the summer.

Summer? Even harder to imagine than spring. As remote to plan six months ahead as sixty years, and as impossible to believe in. With Brendan it had been different, there had always seemed to be a future, despite his ill-health. Was it the shock of losing him that had shaken her made her feel like one condemned to die?

Today, tomorrow, next month even, but when she tried to reach out to next year, she found a path leading nowhere, a road without landmarks upon which she could hook a future, a road that ended in a precipice, from which she shielded her eyes, afraid to look across and see what lay on the other side.

'You are young, you will remarry some day,' said Lady Glencoe comfortingly, thinking her quiet sadness meant that she was still grieving for Brendan. 'Perhaps you might come to Glasgow with us in the spring. I would welcome your opinion on what we might purchase for the house. Your experience of Meggernie would be so useful.' Such were Lady Glencoe's personal reasons for wishing MacIan to take the oath. Where her sons' urgent entreaties failed, Lady Glencoe's simple strategy succeeded.

'The old days of chivalry are over, my dear, we are both too old for them. Stand no longer on pride, but make certain sure that our boys and their bairns have never again to lift a sword against any man.' With a sigh and a pretty shake of her curls, she added wistfully: 'I shall not rest easy in my bed at nights until yon business at Inveraray is settled, my dearest, and we have the letter of the King's peace safe in our hands. That is my heart's desire. Will you do this for me, my darling?'

Raising her hand to his lips, he bowed. 'For you, my dove, anything. I will leave next week. You have my word.'

Liam: 1691-92

Chapter XII

The fort at Inverlochy was fast acquiring a reputation as one to be avoided at all costs. Seeing that the best of the King's regiments had been sent to Flanders, the enemy was considered a more agreeable prospect than the fort which had been renamed for William of Orange.

At his desk in the quarters he shared with Captain Sir Robert Campbell of the Argylls, Lieutenant Liam Campbell stared reproachfully at the peat fire. Already he had learned to treat its behaviour with respect and to interpret the miserable fact that when it burned badly, the wind was coming from the north west bringing the prospect of bad weather. A sudden gust of melancholy blue smoke belched forth making him cough and his eyes smart.

The consoling bristle of arms on the wall was an uneasy reminder that the imminent watches of the night were fraught with dangers for the unwary. But strongly fortified with its pallisaded wall, any real trouble might more readily come from within where conditions for a thousand men were appalling. Too much cold and too little food were calculated to undermine any soldier's morale. They were also short of ammunition and the state of their uniforms and boots was deplorable.

Despite the deer skins covering the floor, his own feet in their stout military boots felt numbed, his fingers stiff with cold, and the upturned collar of his greatcoat offered little protection against the draughts that seeped in everywhere. Blowing upon his fingers to restore the circulation he tried to ignore the gale which spotted the tiny windows with snow and was now loud enough to muffle the tramp, tramp of the duty sentry pacing outside the door.

'29 December 1691.' He added the date to one more urgent requisition for supplies, thankful that this doleful year was almost over and with the earnest prayer that 1692 would be more hopeful than this less-than-inviting present. Eunice's death and Sir Robert's financial ruin had broken his last link with Fortingall. He thought sadly of his Clan. They were his lost children and, the last of the Glencorrie Campbells, he had witnessed the death of a way of life that had followed his Clan since the days of King Robert the Bruce.

He shrugged aside what threatened to be a succession of woeful pictures, aware of the stack of papers to be dealt with in his new position as temporary aide to Colonel Hill, an old man, veteran from Cromwell's wars who commanded this fort which General Monk built to bridle the wild Highland men. The Colonel was apt, after a few drams in the evenings, to wax sentimental about the good old days, when the natives (as he called them) were friendly. It was his proud boast that he had hunted and fished with all of them.

'Prudent to keep them well-disposed. If events on the Continent should go against us then French ships off Scotland's coast might be ready to invade. There are plenty of Jacobite leaders lurking about, ready and willing to go over to the Frenchies and stand for the man they consider their rightful king. As for his lawful Majesty, King William, he is a good monarch and a fine soldier. But I ask you, Lieutenant, straight from the Irish campaign and presently engaged in a life and death struggle in Flanders, how can he be expected to have time or thought to spare for the affairs of his remote northern kingdom. It is not as if he had ever visited Scotland, he knows it only by reputation.'

'And a very bad reputation at that,' said Sir Robert Campbell primly, who had just come in.

A year has passed since Hill had received orders to summon and disarm the clans and compel an oath of submission at sword point. He had protested at the insanity of such an order, but with no option than to do as he was bid, found that what he called 'the middle sort of people', Locheil, Keppoch, Clanranald, MacLeans and Macintoshes, the men of Appin and Glencoe were in the humour to agree.

Sleat and Glengarry remained aloof, the latter going so far as to busy himself significantly with the refortification of his tower.

The order was rescinded when word arrived of Breadalbane's proposed mediations and a conference was held in his castle of Achallader in the summer. The chiefs rallied, with a hundred pipers and all and, to the accompaniment of atrocious weather without and a veneer of harmony within, a truce was signed to last until October 1. Later it was disclosed that the wily Breadalbane, with true Campbell caution had firmly planted a foot in either camp. If the hoped for Jacobite Rising took place, then King Jamie could count on *his* support with a thousand armed men behind him.

On August 27 a proclamation was issued at Edinburgh pardoning and indemnifying all the Clans who had been in arms against the Government, provided that, before the first day of January 1692 they took the oath of allegiance before a sheriff or sheriff-depute. Liam had observed of late the arrival of a disquietingly large number of 'sealed and secret orders' from England. The suppressed excitement of consultations behind closed doors between high ranking officers, hinted that there was something new in the bitter wind blowing around Inverlochy and that the Highlanders' ancient enemy, the Lowland Scots, were also deeply involved.

The Campbells were for King William. This fact troubled Liam who retained the Highlander's ancient loyalty to a King of Scotland. The ex-laird of Glenlyon, Sir Robert Campbell had no such niceties of devotion, always ready and more than willing, even anxious, to sell himself and his sword to the highest bidder. And being a Campbell he had chosen the winning side again, a trick most Campbells managed to achieve, Liam thought cynically, having been singularly unsuccessful in following the remarkable examples set by senior members of his Clan.

He was now ticking fewer names off his list. Locheil, Glengarry, Keppoch, Appin had not sworn. Neither had Glencoe and – that name most accursed to him – Macdonald of Ardarroch, was also missing.

Reading over his shoulder, Hill swore. 'Why the devil do

they delay? The best news anyone could give me at this moment was to know that every chief in the Highlands was posting to Inveraray or Inverness to take their oath of submission. You did not think to find me a partisan of the Highlanders, did you Lieutenant?' He grinned, showing bad teeth which sorely troubled him; a courageous soldier he lacked the bravery to face extraction by the company's surgeon. 'I am for them. They are the best natural material for soldiers God ever gave us.'

'Does that not make them a peril to the State, sir?'

Again Hill grinned, and shook a finger at him. 'Aye, but it might also make them a shining buckler, heroes in the making, some day. A good class of folk they are, friendly, well-mannered. And they speak an English tongue that a body can understand, when they speak it at all, like educated men, not like yon whiggamores of Angus's regiment.'

At Liam's suppressed smile, he added: 'I tend to forget that you speak their heathen language, Lieutenant.'

'I had to learn English, just like a foreign language, sir.'

'Is that right? Well, well, it does ye credit.'

Turning aside, Hill read through General Mackay's latest 'sealed' order: If the Clans failed to meet the date fixed for their surrender, the command was 'to rouse them out of the nation as the bane thereof'. The hint was obvious. What was not finally made peaceful by force might be permanently silenced by grimmer methods. The word 'extirpation' filled him with horror. Even if the great Clans survived, what of their weaker septs, those called the 'cadet gentry'?

Hill shook the letter violently as if he could shake off its offensive language, which smacked of Breadalbane's candid threats of 'mauling them in the long cold nights'. He had long since decided that the worst enemy of any Highlander was another Highlander. There had always been bad blood between Campbells and Macdonalds, itching for some excuse to get at each other's throats, Breadalbane and Glencoe, the ringleaders, dragging the lesser septs of their Clans behind them.

Take Captain Robert Campbell of Glenlyon, and his cousin, Lieutenant Campbell here, neither had any cause to love the Macdonalds. With an old soldier's shrewd instinct for an honest man, Hill recognised in this quiet man with the steadfast eyes, this promising secretary who wrote a splendid hand, that here was a man he could rely on, trust with his life if necessary.

He shook his head. A bad business. Sir Robert had whispered that the Lieutenant's only child had been abducted, raped and forcibly married to Macdonald of Ardarroch's young scoundrel of a chief. Aye, there was much that no decent man could ever readily forgive and forget.

It was dark when an orderly entered with a lamp and saluting Liam announced: 'MacIan of Glencoe is here, sir.' He grinned and added in English, 'A penitent seeking mercy.'

Liam remained seated and regretted it instantly when the orderly ushered in a man of astonishing stature and presence. It was as if the legends of Fionn and his warriors had come to life. Liam himself was but an inch short of six feet but Alasdair Macdonald, twelfth chief of Clan Iain Abrach, stood five inches short of seven. It was the breadth of his massive shoulders that made his height impressive and a mane of white hair, thick and curly, which fell to his shoulders, two great moustachios like a bull's horns. His warrior stance struck strange kinship in Liam's mind to the legends of the Viking sea lords.

Nearly seventy years old his back was ramrod straight, his step sprightly as a man half his years, in his bonnet, a bunch of faded heather, the Macdonald badge. Dressed in dark plaid trews, the broad leather belt at his waist with a brace of pistols and a dirk, at his side a sheathed sword. The elegance of fine buff leather coat and boots suggested origins as spoils of war from some affluent enemy. They were certainly better, thought Liam, than the local cobbler's brogans, worn for convenience and comfort rather than style.

He looked up and found himself staring into large eyes, dark and wild, eyes that were painfully familiar, for such eyes had haunted him from the courtyard of Ardarroch for quarter of a century. Other eyes, too, that exact shape and colour but in form milder, gentle as a doe's, were seared deep into his dreams. Eyes that his soul still cried out for, as the flower craves sunshine and the parched earth rain.

240

Leading the way into Hill's office, he remembered that Caitlin's mother-in-law was sister to this giant.

'MacIan of Glencoe, sir. Come to take the oath.'

Hill stopped writing and sprang to his feet. As the two men shook hands and slapped each other on the back in the manner of old friends, Liam's eyebrows raised somewhat.

'It has been all of thirty years, MacIan.'

'Would that the circumstances were happier,' said MacIan gravely.

Hill shook his head. 'You've been over long in deciding to swear the oath. And what the devil are you doing here, anyway? It is Inveraray you should be, not Inverlochy.'

'But you, my old friend, are Governor here.'

'I know *that*, MacIan, but I am the wrong man for your purpose.'

'How so?'

'I am a soldier,' Hill explained patiently, 'And the law states clearly that the oath of submission must be made before a civil officer.' Hill's impatient rejoiner hinted that his role of commander should include powers as civil magistrate under this new regime.

'I do not understand this difference,' said MacIan doggedly. 'Months back you received my kinsman Macdonald of Achtriochtan.'

'Correct. I received him into the King's peace and gave him written protection. But I warned him that he had not fulfilled the law, that he must go to Inveraray to make his submission complete. I thought you understood that,' he added heavily, 'since last May you agreed to go to Argyll, aye, with your kinsfolk of Appin too.'

MacIan's lips tightened. 'Things have changed since last May. Since then I have no cause for liking the name Campbell. I was insulted at Achallader though I went in peace and good faith. Breadalbane and myself came to hard words.'

Hill smiled. 'I understand that you ran off his cows.'

So everyone knew. 'Where is the fault in taking a few cows in a lawful act of war compared with the killing of the redcoats in battle, for which your Government now offers pardon,' said MacIan. 'Besides no Macdonald has ever wronged his neighbours as the fox of Breadalbane has, by

241

wearing a false smile and stealing from them, not by running off a few beasts, but by tricking them with words written on a parchment, stealing the land from under them, their ancestral glens ... '

'I know all that, MacIan, and I agree, it is a brutal stupid business this eternal warring between Campbell and Macdonald. Do not tell me that it was this Breadalbane business that brought you here in defiance of the order?'

The huge shoulders before him straightened, the chin proudly lifted. 'I am a warrior. A warrior submits only to one of equal rank.'

Hill shook his head sadly. 'Such days of chivalry are over for us, MacIan and, anyway, the Government doesn't share your sentiments about the sanctity of warriors, only in making short work of what it considers Highland rabble, cattle thieves and murderers – ' He cut short MacIan's angry protest. 'Listen to me. There remain but two days left in December. And when January 1 dawns, the period of mercy will close. There will be no reopening for late comers, let me assure you of that, MacIan.' His fists thumped the table top as he stared into the proud face above him and he seemed to have forgotten Liam's presence as he pleaded, 'Could you not see where your stubbornness leads you, man? That your enemies are waiting just such a chance to destroy you?'

MacIan looked at him sullenly and again Hill shook his head. 'I cannot receive you into King William's peace, MacIan, it is Inveraray for you, and you have two days left to get there.' Staring out of the window, he added, 'And I do not envy you or any man that journey in such weather. There are some good tidings though, your old enemy Argyll is absent at present and Sir Colin Campbell of Ardkinglass is sheriff-depute.'

MacIan gave a relieved smile. 'An honest man, or as honest as a Campbell can ever be.'

'Ardkinglass is a personal friend, I will give you a letter for him.' He motioned towards Liam. 'Lieutenant Campbell here will write at my dictation.'

As Liam prepared pen and paper, MacIan said: 'There is one other matter, Colonel. I am also to offer Ardarroch's submission.'

'Ardarroch? Why cannot he take his own to Inveraray?'

242

'Because he died this summer. His Clan is under my protection until his heir is of age.'

Neither were aware that on the other side of the table Liam Campbell's face had paled visibly. His hands shook so violently he had to lay down the pen. Macdonald of Ardarroch dead. Here was the long-awaited vengeance. He longed to ask in what manner did he die?

'He leaves a widow,' said MacIan.

A widow. Caitlin.

Caitlin free.

Oh, my love, my dearest love. He looked towards the window, so like a prison. If only he were free, free of this accursed place, free to run to Ardarroch, free to take her in his arms.

'Why are you not writing, Lieutenant?'

'If you would please repeat that last sentence, sir.'

'Do pay attention, man,' said the Colonel.

MacIan was induced to stay and sup with the Colonel, to leave at dawn. And later, hearing their voices and occasional shouts of mirth as he played cards with Sir Robert in the adjoining room, Liam would have given much to be present, eager for details of Ardarroch's death.

Sir Robert had been tactfully excused from the supper table and was in a vile temper at the thought of his old enemy Glencoe being hospitably received and in such jovial mood. Although the stakes were slight, he lost heavily and went grumpily to bed.

On the other side of the room Liam also slept ill that night and, when MacIan prepared to leave at first light, he had firmly resolved to declare himself and beg news of Caitlin, beg MacIan to send a message, a loving message to her.

He found Colonel Hill in great coat and nightcap seeing MacIan off in a wind that had set icily and a heavy snowfall. The Colonel shivered in sympathy as MacIan prepared to mount his shelty attended by his four running ghillies.

Turning to bid his host farewell he caught sight of Liam in the doorway. 'For your good offices, Lieutenant Campbell, my thanks.' Liam rushed forward and seized the chief's hands. The words were all there, ready formed: For God's sake give me news of Caitlin Macdonald. I am Glencorrie. But he could not say them. The old man must know of his alleged ill-treatment of his nephew's wife. Catching a glimpse of Hill's astonished and somewhat disapproving countenance, Liam's powers of speech suddenly failed him.

'The Colonel tells me you are from Glenlyon,' said MacIan as he put both his strong hands over Liam's, and searched his face. 'And none the worse for that, I swear, for you have the look of an honest man. God be with you, Lieutenant.'

'And with you, sir, and with you.'

As the little party disappeared into the driving snow, Hill considered Campbell's impulsive behaviour amazing and quite out of character for a man who had his emotions under tight control.

'Let us hope that both God and Ardkinglass will show mercy, for in all truth, if he survives the journey he will be a week late,' he said as Liam followed him inside and the snow rapidly obliterated all trace of the departed travellers.

Lady Glencoe's delight in playing hostess to her large family and many friends at Glen Muidhe's Yuletide feast was somewhat marred by the continued absence of her lord. She did her best. There was food in plenty but the Hogmanay celebration, that time of glorious inebriation among the clansmen, was but a poor shadow of its normal self in MacIan's absence. Anxieties were carefully hidden for the sake of the grandchildren, grand-nephews and nieces, all of whom received Yuletide gifts and were encouraged to be merry.

Raising their glasses to the New Year, Lady Glencoe said cheerfully, 'To our new days of peace, with the protection of the English King. Here's to His Majesty, we have much to thank him for.'

'No more fighting, ever, Grandmother?' piped up Alasdair Og's lad in a voice of gloom.

Lady Glencoe laughed and ruffled his hair. 'Only with these, lad,' she said, picking up one of his wooden redcoat soldiers. 'The rest of us are looking forward mightily to a peaceful ripe old age and dying in our own beds.'

By the time the New Year was into its second week, Lady Glencoe was at the window a hundred times a day as if her anxious presence there might help speed the traveller home.

244

'Where is the darling man? What has happened to delay him? He should have been home days ago by my calculations.'

Caitlin, helping her assemble the treasures they had brought from Carnoch for the comfort of Yuletide guests, silently shared the alarm of the household that MacIan had perished on his fearful journey.

Even a tearful Lady Glencoe had given up hope when on the twelfth day of January, the party of foot runners with MacIan in their midst, were sighted. The old man was almost frozen to his shelty's back. While Lady Glencoe hugged and kissed him, mad with joy, Caitlin fled to the kitchen, alerting servants to the need for copious tubs of hot water, fresh linen and food for the exhausted men.

An hour later, with a dram in his hand, MacIan beamed upon his anxious family. His mission had been successful. Jubilation followed. This was now a festive occasion indeed. When the table was cleared of food that evening, the candles replenished and the glasses recharged, the *seannachie* took second place to MacIan himself, who held the listeners' rapt attention.

He spoke of Colonel Hill, his old friend at Inverlochy, of Captain Thomas Drummond, Tayside neighbour and crony of Breadalbane who had delayed him for one precious day: 'With Lowland ill-manners, hateful to a true Gael, who would at least use his enemy like a gentleman before he dirked him,' MacIan added piously. 'By the time we reached Taynuilt and I sank into my hired bed, the New Year had begun, the time for submission was at an end. Next day we set forth again. The abominable weather continued to hamper our journey, as we struggled up the Pass of Brander beside a swollen river in search of a safe crossing-place.

'Had it not been for our loyal ghillies here, who can run five, or six miles to the hour and could guide a man anywhere,' he explained to Caitlin, 'I would have perished many times over. Aye, it would have wrung all your gentle hearts, ladies, to see the brave lads running, bent double, their bonnets dragged over their faces, wet kilts plastered, freezing about their bare thighs, purple with cold. But even they fared better than I on my shelty, my very bones were frozen and no amount of plaid could keep that fearsome weather at bay. We were slowed to less than one mile in an hour, almost a standstill for the lads. I leave it to your imaginations the joy with which we had our first glimpse of Inveraray next morning.'

Lady Glencoe took his hand and held it against her face. She was crying. Caitlin found her own eyes brimming at the devotion of this old couple who had seen many years together and were still much in love. A love about which they were mercilessly teased by the family.

'The turtle doves are cooing again.' But there was no scorn only tenderness, and a tinge of envy.

Caitlin frowned, wondering had Brendan lived, would they have seen the years through so happily engrossed in each other?

'My troubles were not over,' MacIan continued. 'I was two days late and Ardkinglass, the sheriff-depute whom Colonel Hill had beseeched to look kindly upon my petition was visiting his family, his return delayed by the storm. Inveraray is no place for the betterment of health or spirits of a body wearing the Macdonald plaid, especially to the drunken Hogmanay revellers. The sight of MacIan would have been a red rag to a large number of very angry bulls,' he added grimly.

'Three days I had to skulk in a quiet hostelry knowing that if the sheriff had a mind to stand by the letter of the law, my estates were forfeit, and yours, my dear lad,' he said, touching William's uncaring head, as he brought a new chessboard over for his great-uncle MacIan to admire. 'Later, lad, we will have a game later.'

Caitlin put her arm about her son. Ardarroch meant nothing to him yet, not as much as a sweetmeat or a new pony or a warm bed. Let it bide in the shadows of the future for a long time yet, dear God, leave its heir protected by the magic of childhood from the sorrows and betrayals of an adult world.

'You cannot imagine my relief when on the fifth day of January, I found Sir Colin awaiting me in his office. A fine man, as Colonel Hill promised, whose patriotism extended to all the Highlands not just the confines of his own Campbell clan. However, matters were as I had feared. He had not the power to extend the period of submission laid down in the

King's proclamation. I pleaded with him, not for my sake only, but for you, my people, all of you dear to me beneath my protection, here in Glencoe and over yonder in Ardarroch.' In the sudden silence, he dashed his hand across his eyes and his voice was dropped low. 'I, MacIan of Glencoe, begged him, begged a Campbell on my knees, and weeping too, not to let this misfortune, befall my people. Let me take the oath, I said, and every man of my clan and Ardarroch shall do likewise. If any refuse, I swear, I will personally turn him over to the authorities for prisonment or to be impressed for the Flanders war.' At his side, Lady Glencoe sobbed. 'There, there, my treasure, it is all right.'

She smiled at him and kissed his cheek, running her hands through his thick white hair as if they were alone. 'Who could resist you, my darling?' she whispered.

Hugging her to his side, smiling, he was a youth again. 'Ardkinglass thereupon promised to send my submission with a letter beseeching the Council in Edinburgh to be merciful, to take into account my fruitless journey to Inverlochy, the terrible weather and Drummond's accursed delay, at the same time warning me that he could not guarantee that his action would not be declared null and void. In my presence he wrote to Colonel Hill asking him to afford MacIan of Glencoe and those under his guardianship, including Ardarroch, interim protection,' he added proudly. 'The Colonel is my friend, so we can sleep soundly in our beds, that for sure. There is no further cause for alarm.'

The tension over, everyone relaxed and MacIan his troubles at an end, a happy and contented man in the midst of his family, held high his glass in the toast: 'A Happy New Year to all of us. Never again need we fear the English king or the Campbells. For Ardkinglass is a powerful friend, second only to Breadalbane in rank. He will see to it that the peace is kept, for that is his own earnest desire. As for Campbells, the world seems to overflow with them. At Inverlochy I was tripping over them at every turn.' He sighed. 'Perhaps I am growing soft with age, for they seem not as fierce or untrustworthy as when my blood was hot and young and my sword eager. I like not Campbell of Glenlyon but his cousin, Hill's aide, is a reasonable fellow.'

Caitlin's head raised sharply from her sewing.

'The Colonel thinks highly of him.' He laughed. 'He even ran out into the snow as I was leaving, clutched my hand and wished me Godspeed. Changed days indeed! Never would I think to get so fair a speeding from a Campbell, more like a bullet in my back.'

'Glenlyon's cousin, did you say, Uncle?' Caitlin whispered.

'That is so.' MacIan rubbed his chin and looked at her, frowning. 'Why did I not remember? With so much on my mind, I had forgotten that you once lived under Glenlyon's roof at Meggernie. This Campbell is a tall man, about forty, fair-haired, broad of cheek and brow. Somewhat silent, but I had a feeling that he was honest and well-disposed. Perhaps you knew him, lass?'

Alasdair Og interrupted with a question regarding the oath and Caitlin's face was hidden, as William came over to bid her goodnight. Holding him close she looked into the child's face that promised one day to mirror MacIan's description of Lieutenant Liam Campbell, late of Glencorrie.

Oh, Liam, Liam, my dearest, dearest love.

MacIan's first official action was to summon a gathering of his cadet gentry, Macdonald of Achtriochtan, Achnahon and the tacksman of Inverrigan. He requested that Caitlin represent Ardarroch and that William also be present as hereditary chief of his Clan.

He told them of his promise to Sir Colin. 'You and all the males of our Clan must proceed at once to Inveraray and take the oaths as soon as the weather slackens.' To anxious looks and more anxious questions, MacIan said: 'Mark well, the kindness of my reception by a Campbell must be honoured. No more forays into other folks' glens this winter, even if our larders are empty, and our bellies too. The word of MacIan has been given, it will be kept. You understand me?'

Afterwards, MacIan came over and put his hand on William's head. 'How much of that will you remember, my young chief?'

'All of it, sir. And I give you my promise to be good, and not to be any trouble to you or your household. It is the promise of Macdonald of Ardarroch, and here is my hand on it.' MacIan took his oustretched hand and shook it solemnly and then with a great shout of laughter swung him up into the air and gave him a great bear-like hug.

Serious again, he said to Caitlin: 'Take good care of that son of yours, mistress. We will all have reason to be proud of him some day.'

She found herself blinking back the tears. At eight years old he combined childish exuberance with grave concentration and reasoning. William said little but his kind heart, his thoughtful behaviour were beyond his years.

'Brendan's dearest wish was that he should go to the University.'

'Then send the lad if he has a mind for it. We will need chiefs with brain instead of brawn for the peaceful times ahead.'

Lady Glencoe listening to them, smiled, glad that she was no longer young and had only MacIan to care for, a task which absorbed her completely. She had accomplished her sole ambition to love and serve her family. Seeing their sons grown with children of their own was her life's fulfilment. She was well content. Each stitch she sewed, each thread she span was with proud and loving thoughts of her menfolk. In her eyes they could do no wrong.

As if he read her thoughts, MacIan came and kissed her downbent head. 'Dreaming again, my dove?' She held out her hand and he cradled it tight against his chest. Married couples who complained that love grew stale or even died outright, shocked and pained her, for she loved MacIan more with each passing year. Her heart still ached for him when they were parted for even one day, just as it had long ago when both were young.

'See, it snows again,' he said. 'At this rate we will not be on our own again until April.' Since his return the weather had worsened. The glen was closed, cut off from the rest of the world and as the snow drifted and levelled the spaces between the hills and the corries, what had been waterfalls now hung like a giant's silver arrows, glistening in sunlight.

Lady Glencoe was thankful for the extra beds carted over from Carnoch for the Yuletide guests, seeing that their sons and families could no longer return to their own homes a quarter-mile away. As for the children, they all slept together in one big room and made no complaint of overcrowding. Children, especially those two Ardarroch bairns, seemed to thrive on company.

But that January weather had surprises in store and the month ebbed with a season so mild that all the song birds in the glen believed spring had come. Overnight, snow was transformed into wild torrents of water and a succession of soft mild days revealed bleached, sodden fields and miniature lochs, mirroring a bland blue sky. There was an old Gaelic saying for such weather: 'When the Badger turns in his winter sleep and dreams of the spring.'

Now assured of Government protection and peace with their neighbours, glensfolk turned their minds to the age-old demands of the four seasons and considered profitable crops.

Caitlin settled thankfully into Glen Muidhe where she joined the women as they set about weaving, making dyes of kelp, heather and lichens for the wool they had spun. Hunting was easy in such weather and empty larders were replenished with deer or the wild fowl enticed back by mild weather to feed on the sea loch.

Days were short and when torches were thrust into the walls, by rushlights' gleam and peat fires singing with birch twigs, the snug family gathering was occasion for content. The ladies sewed, the men smoked their long pipes while the *seannachie* retold the old legends, many of which Alistair nan Creach had related to Caitlin in Fortingall. Sometimes the legends made MacIan drop off to sleep and snore deeply with his head on his chest.

At such a sign, Lady Glencoe would tactfully call upon the piper to play and at MacIan's request the great glorious battle songs, rattled the peaceful rafters of Glen Muidhe. There were other evenings when she laid aside her sewing and played the *clarsach*, bringing the harp's gentle melancholy to the scene.

On one such occasion, after a small family supper, Lady Glencoe thought to have her fortune told. Among the ladies, the talk had drifted to spey-wives and omens, while Caitlin who knew much, remained silent and contributed nothing.

'We must have Peg Brodie up, Mother,' said daughter-in-law Sarah excitedly. 'She has the *taibhsearachd*. By good fortune, she came with me tonight since Alasdair Og is away at Carnoch. She has told our household some mightily astonishing things.'

The company listened politely to details of births and deaths and weddings accurately foretold, but as the same rules apply to other peoples' fortunes as to other peoples' love affairs, and sustained interest depends upon personal experience, Lady Glencoe suggested that the maid be summoned to demonstrate her powers.

'Merely to entertain us, of course,' she added hastily. 'However, if she has glad tidings, then we will believe her.'

'Implicitly, Mother,' was the laughing reply.

Caitlin, who rarely had 'visions' any more and had to learn to suppress those that threatened, expected the spey wife to be a *cailleach*, back-bent and sinister. When at last the door opened, the woman who bobbed a curtsey was young, stout, and rosy-faced.

Such a mild appearance belied any glittering-eyed prophecies of doom as Peg Brodie, modestly dismissing her 'powers', shyly claimed an ability to 'read the hands and foretell weddings.' This threw the unmarried ladies into a considerable flutter of coy glances. However, the spey-wife's intention was towards the older ladies who waited patiently and as she regarded them, Caitlin was aware that Mistress Brodie was suddenly ill-at-ease. It was as if a faint chill, felt only by herself, touched the group by the fire. And Bran felt it too. He raised his muzzle from the deerskin rug and stared hard at the spey-wife. A moment later he was on his feet, a menacing rumble deep in his throat and Caitlin felt his hackles rise starkly under her hand. Peg Brodie's nervous glance in Caitlin's direction as she attempted to quiet Bran, indicated that she also knew and recognised the room's changed atmosphere.

'What on earth is ado with him? Is he needing out?' demanded Lady Glencoe. 'Put him out, for mercy's sake, if he is going to be a nuisance.' She had not forgotten nor forgiven Bran's superiority in the matter of her favourite deerhound bitch, whom he had declined to serve. Caitlin Macdonald made far too much of the beast, treating him more like child than dog.

Obedient to Caitlin's soothing command, Bran quietened,

but not without an imploring look. It begged her – but for what?

Lady Glencoe sniffed. 'Now perhaps we can proceed.'

One by one the ladies held out their hands. Their cries of amazement told of the accuracy of the spey-wife's knowledge of their pasts. Caitlin felt her fears diminishing. It could be that Mistress Brodie was a clever fraud, for in the Macdonald kitchen, she had ample opportunity to sift through servants' gossip. Most gentle folk live their lives in the belief that maids and serving men are deaf, dumb and blind, thought Caitlin. They would be shocked and angered by the gales of mirth their behaviour provoked in the servants' hall.

She noted that past and present offered no difficulty. The words rattled glibly, descriptions of former houses, parents, children dead or gone abroad.

'And what of the future? This summer? Next year?' Ah, the future. That brought a darkness to the woman's brow.

'You will have great-grandchildren, my lady. Your bonny curls will grow white.' This was inoffensive foretelling, thought Caitlin. Most of the ladies might have guessed that for themselves.

When she came to Lady Glencoe, after delivering a convincing recital of past events, Caitlin observed a moment's trembling indecision, a sudden deafness to her ladyship's eager questions regarding the future: 'What lies ahead for the two of us?'

Mistress Brodie's face was hidden in apparent concentration on the beringed hand she held.

'She wishes only to know whether I will allow her to remain in Glen Muidhe and buy her all those gew-gaws she wants to furnish the place,' chuckled MacIan, who had just entered and was listening with rapt amusement, and a sceptical expression.

'Hush!' said Lady Glencoe, with a fond glance in his direction. 'Be serious!' As he walked over to the fire, she whispered to Mistress Brodie, her eyes dreamy: 'The happy years we have shared? Tell me – will *they* continue?'

Head lowered, voice gentle and sad, came the reply: 'Aye, yer leddyship – for the rest of your life.'

'Excellent, my dear, excellent. *That* is all I wished to know.'

Seeing his wife's delight, MacIan came forward and held

252

out his great palm to the spey-wife: 'And what do you see for me, mistress?'

Immediately she gabbled of his great and glorious past and MacIan laughed: 'Spare my blushes, mistress. Besides any maid or serving man connected with Glencoe would know such things about me,' he added shrewdly.

She smiled and thrust back his hand rather sharply. 'That is true.'

MacIan seemed disappointed. 'Have you nothing of an exciting nature to tell me? No events to liven the dull days ahead for an old warrior?'

'You have had a great and happy life, my lord. You will breathe your last in your own bed under this very roof, and your lady,' she paused, evading Lady Glencoe's eyes. 'Your lady will be with you, and she will go with you. You will not be alone,' she added awkwardly.

The turtle doves as their family called them, were content. They held hands, asking no greater boon of God's mercy than that they should live and die together.

'Our thanks, Mistress Brodie, we are happy to believe you.'

As the spey-wife prepared to depart MacIan pressed a golden piece into her hand. 'For your trouble, mistress.' Then Lady Glencoe said: 'Not so fast, husband, the good lady has missed one of our number.' She thrust Caitlin forward.

It was a moment Caitlin had hoped to avoid – her past revealed – as for her future ...

She felt that the woman too approached reluctantly and made no attempt to take her hand. Eyes closed, she stood stiffly before her and whispered: 'Macdonald born, Campbell bred, a Campbell dead.'

Those nearest looked at Caitlin with interest. They knew the extraordinary story of her abduction from Ardarroch on her wedding day by Liam Campbell of Glencorrie and of how she had escaped and returned to her husband. They also knew that through her parents, murdered by Glencorrie, she was hereditary clan chief of Ardarroch doubly by birth and by marriage. Caitlin's heart thudded painfully but she told herself not to be foolish, such facts had doubtless spread from servants' gossip.

Mistress Brodie's eyelids sprung wide-open as if she had been asleep. She looked around the room until she saw William playing backgammon with his great-uncle MacIan.

'Guard your son well, mistress, he who is both Macdonald and Campbell – guard him well.' And blinking her eyes rapidly, with a polite curtsey, she turned to leave.

'A moment, if you please,' protested Lady Glencoe. 'Is that *all* you are going to tell her?'

The woman turned and jabbed a finger toward Caitlin: 'She *knows*, let her look in her own heart. She has the gift too, if she will use it.'

As the door closed behind Peg Brodie, the ladies compared fortunes. Had she told them true?

'Most of them are frauds,' said the ones who had been told things from their past that they would have preferred forgotten.

Caitlin said nothing. She watched William talking to Bran on the rug before the fire. As if conscious of her regard, two faces, dog and boy, turned to her and it seemed that both wore an identical smile.

Caitlin excused herself earlier than usual. The *seanna-chie*'s stories had fallen suddenly flat after the spey-wife's fortunes. And Caitlin noticed that the room was cold now, despite the fire roaring up the chimney. She recognised these ominous symptoms, of a chill which goes deeper than the surface and touches the soul. She was full of forebodings. Something was wrong.

Bran was restless that night too, she heard him change position many times, and once he whined in his sleep as if afflicted by a nightmare. Her dreams, forgotten upon waking, left only their sense of unease, connected with the spey-wife, for she was certain sure that Peg Brodie knew much more than she was prepared to reveal. The past and the present had been based on facts however she came by them. Why did the future make her hesitate? What was to happen to all of them that was so terrible she was afraid to reveal it?

Caitlin could understand the woman's dilemma. MacIan would be furious at having his womenfolk terrorised, his hospitality abused by some madwoman's prophecies. Bring a tear to his dear lady's eye, have her upset and the spey-wife would have been trudging out of Glencoe that night and seeking new employment.

Caitlin considered MacIan, delighted to know that near seventy, God would be good and let him die in his own bed. Could that mean only one thing, peace for the rest of his life, for himself, his lady and his Clan? He had been overjoyed to seize upon the spey-wife's words as proof positive that the Macdonalds of Glencoe were safe under the hard-wrung 'letter of protection'. But Caitlin's doubts for the future, the unhappy dreams she could never quite remember upon waking, continued.

Chapter XIII

On Monday, the first day of February, Glencoe received word that a body of soldiers was approaching by the shore road from Ballachulish. It was a fine day, cold but bright and the word 'redcoats', spread as fast as horses could gallop, had every Macdonald who possessed sword or musket scratching about for a place to hide it, in peat stack, roof thatch or beneath the babe in its cradle. Government protection meant forfeiture of arms but try telling a Lowland soldier that a man's food depended on catching game or bringing down a deer.

John Macdonald, as MacIan's elder son, with twenty men at his side waited at the foot of the glen to discover what brought these armed men. His stomach muscles tightened with distaste at the sight of one hundred and twenty redcoats of Argyll's regiment, with Glenlyon in the lead. Many years had passed since their last meeting and John's first glance said that time had been good to Robert Campbell. His figure was still excellent, the long thin face, hooked nose and florid good looks marred by a mean mouth, tight-lipped and petulant. John noted that he still wore his own hair, luxuriant as ever and not sorely troubled by silver threads among the gold, which was remarkable since a quick reckoning gave him sixty years.

At first sight a man in his prime, handsome with regal bearing, at closer quarters John observed eyes slightly out of focus, the glazed expression of a man who loves the bottle and is always on the lookout for the next drink. There was also a shiftiness in manner, an avoidance of John Macdonald's eyes. With notable charity, John put down this shortcoming to a confrontation between Macdonald and Campbell with a long list of grievances to be settled. A matter to be conducted with caution on both sides, two wild dogs sniffing at each other before an exchange of canine civilities.

Sir Robert's hearty manner jarred as embracing him, he asked for his niece and nephew 'Sandy' and their bairns. It put John on edge, remembering that his father did not like or trust Glenlyon either.

''Twas an ill day for Appin when he took old Glenlyon's widow to wife,' MacIan was wont to remark.

Now he observed all time's ravages on the countenance of the man before him: gambling, drinking and living too well had etched marks which the first dandified impression could not conceal. Aye, Sir Robert had gambled away Glenlyon and sold it to Murray of Atholl and with it had gone Glencorrie too, all over a hand of cards, no doubt. When Breadalbane refused him more money, he had gone for a soldier in Argyll's regiment, driven there not by loyalty to King William but by the desperate measure of poverty, glad to take a Captain's commission on eight shillings a day.

What love could he have for Glencoe, John thought, noting with distrust this greeting of effusive insincerity, especially when Campbell of Glenlyon had more reasons than most to loathe the name of Macdonald of Glencoe. Had not their raid, returning home from Killiecrankie, given the *coup de grâce* to his dwindling fortunes?

Now he was explaining apologetically that his men were to be quartered in Glencoe. 'No wish of mine, cousin, but a humble soldier must obey orders,' he said patting his greatcoat pocket. 'It is Invergarry that is our main interest, we have unfinished business there, but the weather was against us and our Colonel gave the order to desist meantime.' He sighed deeply, looking at the sky as if in confirmation.

John thought: That's a lie to begin with – the weather is unseasonably good for February, as Glenlyon continued:

'The fort at Inverlochy is so packed full of soldiers, there was no room for my lads. What with one thing and another – there's the pesky matter of this cess and hearth money we are to collect,' he shook his head sadly and confided: 'We poor Highlanders always have to bear the brunt of any new taxes that the Government in London dream up. Anyway, the Colonel said we must march forth to Glencoe and here remain awaiting our further orders.'

At John's rather perturbed appraisal of the mass of men behind their Captain, Glenlyon grinned. 'You will hardly notice our presence, cousin. We seek only bed and bite and sup, and 'tis but for a week or two. I will see that they behave themselves, you have my word on it,' he said, laying a hand on John's shoulder, and smiling close into his face. 'After all we are friends and kinsmen, are we not?'

His regard would have passed for honest sincerity in most men and John looked at the green Campbell plaid buckled about his wasit. Perhaps his suspicions were unjustified. It was true, Campbell was a fellow Highlander, and a kinsman. So there was nothing for it but to bid him welcome with good grace and a bow: 'You and your lads are welcome, Glenlyon, welcome to whatever Glencoe has to offer. There is little enough at this time of year, you will appreciate but it is yours to command.'

'I always heard you were a reasonable man, John Macdonald, and I was right,' came the smooth reply, as he signalled to the officer who rode a little behind them. 'This is my aide, Lieutenant Liam Campbell, late of Glencorrie.'

As the man came forward and shook hands with John, the latter frowned: 'Have we not met before?' he asked quickly.

'I think that highly unlikely.' The answer polite but unsmiling.

'Glencorrie is my cousin,' Sir Robert explained and in an aside 'His daughter married Macdonald of Ardarroch.' With a comradely arm about John's shoulders, he continued: 'All told this will be quite a gathering of the family. Glencorrie here is a good man to have around, do not be deceived by his quiet exterior.'

A good man to have around, eh? So this was the notorious Campbell who had twice abducted Caitlin Macdonald, first as babe and then as bride of Ardarroch. It was a shocking story and John suddenly remembered Caitlin and her two children all-unsuspecting in Glen Muidhe. She must be warned. His father would not want any excuse for bad blood between Campbell and Macdonald. And Caitlin's story was precisely the kind that perpetrated Clan wars into the seventh generation.

MacIan received the newcomers with the dignity of a Highland gentleman who was also a powerful chieftain. He had given his word to keep the peace and made clear his intention of letting bygones be bygones by drowning the past troubles between their Clans in several drams of *aqua vitae*.

He had decided that the men should be billeted in cottages up and down the glen. Carnoch at present empty would make a convenient billet and the officers should be given a choice of more select dwellings with the cadet gentry: Achnacon, Inverrigan and Achtriochtan.

Glenlyon chose Inverrigan. 'I have no wish to put you to any inconvenience, MacIan. But my greatest desire is to be with my ain folk. The Lord knows we have much news to exchange,' he added sentimentally. 'And Lieutenant John Lindsay too, he is Lady Glenlyon's kinsman, as I said, a happy family gathering.'

The glen was heavy with the tramp of men and horses, and loud voices shouting orders as billeting instructions were read. A great deal of sorting out, directing, getting lost and arguing took place, but the arrangements were completed with reasonable good humour.

Glenlyon and Liam Campbell dined with MacIan and his sons at Carnoch that evening. There was venison fresh killed on the table and mutton and salt beef from the cellars at Glen Muidhe. Oat cakes and, Glenlyon licked his lips in anticipation, best brandy from France. The Argyll regiment had brought little with them for their stay, the Macdonalds soon learned, but French claret and *aqua vitae*. Worried frowns were hospitably concealed. These were hardly the stores for a hungry regiment in a glen crippled by winter's dearth.

Glenlyon sat back and unbuckled his belt. 'A splendid feast indeed, Glencoe, and we are grateful to you. You have no idea what it does to a man with a sensitive palate, nothing but kale soup and bannocks, at the fort,' he added with a delicate shudder, pretending ignorance of his own presence at MacIan's visit to Inverlochy when he had prudently remained out of sight at Hill's anxious insistence. He sighed, happily. 'This is different class, is it not, Glencorrie?'

Liam Campbell merely nodded. He had spoken little

during the meal and had eaten less. All appetite had been killed for him when his host MacIan had given him a reproachful look and mentioned that Caitlin Macdonald of Ardarroch and her two children had been living in Glencoe. Liam could get little further information to his satisfaction for mention of her name brought consequent embarrassment to his host, who now knew the sorry details of her early life from John, and was suspecting that his earlier good opinion of Glencorrie at Inverlochy had been sorely misplaced.

'She is not here now,' he said hurriedly. 'She left earlier today.' And he closed his lips firmly upon the subject.

Liam wondered how to press MacIan further for information concerning her whereabouts, and when she would be returning. He had a hazy idea that he might visit her, beg her forgiveness. Had she known he was coming and was that why she had taken flight? he thought anxiously and then he remembered the vow they had made long ago. Did her absence indicate that she too remembered and wished to keep her side of the bargain, never to meet him again?

As they left Carnoch he said to MacIan: 'Please present my compliments to Lady Ardarroch.'

'I know naught of her plans, she may not even return,' snapped his host. Liam lay awake that night torn between relief and disappointment, that their paths might not cross during the regiment's brief sojourn, before moving to Glengarry.

Better for the anguish in his heart, he told himself, that those old fires remained subdued. Better for a heart that felt her presence everywhere in MacIan's house. As if he had entered a room that she had vacated but the moment before. If her unseen presence could wreak havoc with his emotions what of the reality of that lovely face, that endearing smile, those warm arms? He shut off such torturing thoughts. The past was over, reawakening it served no good purpose for either of them. As for a future, he could not bear to contemplate what lay ahead, except that he hated every moment of this dreary army life.

Before they retired for the night, MacIan and his sons had a final dram together. MacIan was in jubilant mood. The evening had gone well. 'I am well pleased by this peaceful

260

state of affairs. Who would have thought a day might dawn when we would sit down at the table yonder with two Campbells?' he chuckled.

'You have changed your opinion, sir, if I might remind you, 'twas only of recent date that you held no high opinion of Glenlyon, you have long told us he was not a man to be trusted.'

'Ach, perhaps I was wrong. And indeed I hope so. After all the man has known terrible trouble, losing his estate and so forth. Maybe being a soldier has reformed him, given him a sense of duty and purpose.'

John said nothing. He felt his father's outlook was somewhat naive. He had qualms and doubts, despite the man's surface geniality, despite his protestations of kinship and constant repetitions about this splendid family gathering. There was something false about Glenlyon, something that rang a note sour as a cracked bell.

Alasdair Og was agreeing with him, warning their father: 'I find your faith touching, and I wish I could share it with you. But for my money Glenlyon never came to Glencoe for the good of any Macdonald. True, at front, he is fine and couthy and well-met. But does it go more than skin-deep?'

MacIan shook his head, disappointed in his sons. Why could they not recognise that the bad old days were gone? Glenlyon was now an ally in their new peace. Would they never cease harking back to the past with its hatred and distrust? 'Whatever your feelings, I trust you will conceal them from our guests,' he said sternly. 'For guest he is, and must be treated to every courtesy. Besides you can sleep easy John, and you too, Alasdair, for we are now doubly secure. Not only do we have the Government's word, and their letter of protection in our pocket, but these men who are our guests have eaten our salt. You should need no reminding from me that no Highlander would let harm come to his hosts in such circumstances, more so when we are blood kin. The law that binds Macdonald and Campbell is the Highland law now.' He drained his glass and asked, 'What thought you of yon Glencorrie?'

'A man who keeps his own counsel,' said John.

'He said little enough to let anyone gather any notion of his thoughts, except for questions about Caitlin. He got no help from me there,' laughed MacIan.

'Like our cousin Glenlyon he plays his cards close to his chest,' said Alasdair Og.

MacIan nodded. Campbells were an enigma. He was glad John had warned him of Glencorrie's presence and that Caitlin and the children had been despatched to Great-Aunt Honor's house, two miles beyond Glen Muidhe. He had explained to her that the redcoats were to be billeted in the glen, and that the officers would regularly be eating at Glen Muidhe. Lady Glencoe, of course, must stay and perform her duties as hostess. He omitted to mention that her foster-father would be among those officers and so Caitlin missed meeting him by less than an hour.

'I think it is wiser not to mention his presence at all,' he told John, who agreed.

'With good fortune their paths will never cross,' said Alasdair Og.

But good fortune was the last thing Fate had in store for Glencoe.

During the first week of February life settled back into normality again among MacIan's Clan and the soldiers billeted on them. Although such billets left little space, with three soldiers to one house, cramped into one room, and five in another, whatever the feelings of these families about such an invasion, the law of hospitality demanded they give their guests the best of whatever they had. There was no holding back, or putting aside, even if that meant depriving their own children. As for the soldiers they had little to complain about; there was kippered salmon and deer meat, lavish by comparison with the meagre rations in Inverlochy and in almost every home in the evenings, there hung upon a peg a redcoat and a Campbell boarshead bonnet.

Sergeant Barker, red-faced and fierce-tempered had chosen the home of Macdonald of Achnacone, MacIan's senior tacksman. There was something indefinably brutal about this Lowlander, thought Liam, with his slate-coloured eyes, his killer's face, something even his toughest men feared. They never questioned his commands and the largest party of redcoats tramped smartly behind him, through the routine of soldiery which continued with regular drills early each day. The Macdonalds soon became used to the sight of the redcoats marching up and down with their coat-skirts swinging, the butts of their muskets slapped against their thighs and the sergeant shouting orders, trying to smarten up his lads. Mothers in Glencoe considered that they had cause to bless the soldiers, for lads whose dreams were now filled with the heroics of going for a soldier were no longer tardy in rising each morn, and even their sisters could daydream over the romantic possibilities of a handsome soldier billeted on their family.

As the first reveille beaten by the drummer at Inverrigan echoed through the Glen, picked up by another at Carnoch, another at Achtrichtan, the children shivering in the bright wine-clear air watched the drill ground around each township grow suddenly alive with colour. Many a small boy imitated with a tree branch as musket, the English commands: 'Poise your firelocks ... shoulder your firelocks.' Many another lad dreamed that this particular hazel branch on his shoulder was a pike and remembering the order: 'Pikemen – take heed – advance your pikes – charge your pikes ...,' gave battle to the nearest boulder in his path.

Apart from deep snow on the mountain tops at two thousand feet and the snow-filled passes where it would remain until spring, the weather remained mild on the floor of the Glen and the soldiers passed the afternoons running and wrestling, watched by wistful, eager lads, counting the years that must pass before they could be fighting men. And when the soldiers called to them with a cheeky invitation to take part, there was more than one Macdonald lad who became his hero's devoted slave.

'Do you know what Alexander Brown was telling me?' a father would be told by his son at their evening meal, while in a neighbour's house, a wee lad hardly tall enough to see over the table, gazed devotedly at and imitated every gesture of their own billetee who had made him a carved wooden sword that afternoon.

Up the road through the glen, the redcoats heard rumours that the officers were being regally entertained by the family of MacIan and his sons, but the men had no call for complaint. Many were far from home, and although they were mostly Highlanders, there was a sprinkling of

Lowlanders from Edinburgh and Fife way. Such men were surprised indeed at the warmth of welcome they received from people they had been led to believe were little better than wild painted savages, cattle thieves, rapists and murderers. And although these Lowlanders could not understand a word of the Gaelic that was being spoken around them, they recognised in soft voices, kindness when it was offered. They enjoyed the friendly competition of races on the hillsides and the *clach-neart*, the game of putting the stone.

In the evening the glensfolk had their own activities. Stories were told, ballads were sung, but not one word was uttered by a Macdonald which would wound a Campbell's pride. Instead they talked of the heroes of their folklore and sang of the forgotten wars of other men, of the Frenchies and of long-lost Scottish kings. Such matters as took place beyond the borders of Scotland could not offend, since whatever happened in that distant place London could not deeply affect any of their lives. And although the soldiers wore her colours, there was a shared bond of mockery, head-shaking and eye-raising, against their common, more ancient enemy England.

Most evenings the pipers were called upon to play for the guests, not on the modest *feadan* or chanter, but the full-bodied *piobaireachd*, the full set of pipes, by a player who was a master at his art. Again the airs were chosen with tact and consideration for the guests. No wild tribal rants to stir uncomfortable memories of feuds between Clan Donald and Clan Campbell, instead the piper would gallantly strike up a tune from Argyll or Campbell country to remind the soldiers of their homes. More often the tunes were those that even the Lowlanders could recognise: *A Kiss of the King's Hand*, *The Macrae's March* or a heart-touching ballad for a soldier's lost lass.

Fortified by warmth and hospitality, the redcoats found that they fitted agreeably into the glen. Glad indeed they were to take each day as it dawned, knowing only that they had been fortunate indeed to pause here in order to Glengarry. The snug little homes with their peat fires were a considerable improvement on the cold, foul garrison at Inverlochy. All things considered Glencoe, with its kindly folk was not at all a bad billet to winter in and many a young man found his hostess struck a chord of remembrance of his own mother, while another began to eye the pretty daughter of the house and a snatched kiss awakened important matters such as courtship and even ultimate marriage. Aye, come to think on it, there were worse places in which a man might settle down and spend the rest of his life. So the magic of the place, older than time itself, gathered them into its fold.

Among their officers and the MacIans, pleasures of a more sophisticated nature were being enjoyed. Dinner parties with cards and wine were frequent between the Glen Muidhe home of the chief and his two sons. The food and talk were good and many a night Liam Campbell had to support his Captain all the way home to the tacksman's house at Inverrigan.

Occasionally Sir Robert took his kinsman to task on the subject of enjoyment. 'You do not drink a great deal, do you?'

Liam smiled. 'Only as much as I can comfortably carry. Someone has to be fit to find the way home,' he added cheerfully.

Glenlyon's scowl anticipated insult: 'Is that a fact? And what was with you, stepping out of the card game so early, sitting around casting dour glances on us all?' he snarled.

'Cousin, I cannot afford to lose high stakes on cards, you know that better than any man. I have not even an estate to my name that can be mortgaged.'

'Ach, is that all? Then I will give you a bag of Scots merks to play with.'

Liam groaned. 'Which I cannot accept.'

'Why not?'

'The reason is that you cannot afford to be generous with me either.' Liam did not add the obvious: Or with any man.

What had got into Sir Robert, gambling for high stakes, as high as MacIan and his sons would go? Their hosts were prudent men and much to Glenlyon's annoyance also stepped out of the game when they saw that their guest was losing heavily, which put him into an ill humour.

'MacIan is not a rich man, he cannot afford to be a gambler. He cannot afford to be bankrupt.'

'Why not? Glencoe will not be troubling him much longer, one way or t'other,' said Sir Robert tipsily. 'He might as well enjoy life while he has the chance.'

Liam looked at him sharply. 'He's good for many a year yet, he's an old man, but strong as a horse.'

Sir Robert grinned archly. 'So think you? Ah well, ah well! But that's not the way of it at all. There is many a strong man, aye and young too, who meets a sudden end, at the point of a sword.' He stopped suddenly sobered by Liam's intent expression.

'What do you mean by that? Do you intend him some harm?' Liam demanded.

Sir Robert focussed unsteady eyes on him. 'Course not, nothing further from my mind, kinsman, and all that sort of thing. Why would I be harming him. Go to sleep, cousin, your brain is raddled.' And so saying he turned on his pallet bed and began to snore heavily.

Liam Campbell, wide awake, stared at the ceiling. Ever since the day they arrived in Glencoe he had felt that Glenlyon was concealing something from him. He was often shifty and evasive and Liam thought it strange that he was no longer given charge of confidential orders. These Sir Robert read and locked away immediately. In fact, apart from the trifling routine matters of everyday, Liam no longer served as secretary, his activities as aide diminished to carrying orders to the sergeants and acceptances of dinner invitations to MacIan and his sons.

He was worried. Glencoe was en route billeting for Glengarry. Strange, thought Liam uneasily, that Sir Robert was idling. Understandable in foul weather, but the roads were clear of snow, there was nothing to stop the Argylls from marching out tomorrow. Why did Sir Robert hesitate?

Sleepless, Liam realised that his normal capacity for observation had been blunted by his anxieties over Caitlin. He had been consumed with the anxiety of possibly meeting her unexpectedly walking through the glen. What would he say to her – and she to him? What kind of further agony would this reunion bring about for him?

He sat up in bed. Caitlin! If there was danger ahead, if Glenlyon's secret orders held the diabolical 'extirpation' which had once been under discussion at Inverlochy as 'mauling the MacIans in the long cold nights', then Caitlin and her children too would be under threat of death.

Caitlin, dear God. He knew that she was in Glencoe, Sir Robert had the information from his niece Sarah, but only a vague 'up beyond Glen Muidhe somewhere'.

Would she be safe there? How could he get a message to her? He would go and ask Alasdair Og's wife for directions tomorrow. But on that tomorrow, Friday February 12 the weather changed suddenly. The blue skies and mild sunshine were exchanged for a north-east wind which shrilled through the gullies of Aonach Eagach. The glensfolk knew the signs. They told their soldier guests: 'Wrap up well for there will be snow before evening and by tomorrow the corries will be flat with the braes.'

Liam was kept too busy by Sir Robert that day to carry out his plan of searching out Caitlin, and under his own roof Alasdair Og was having problems. He had never much liked his wife's uncle and was now wondering whether his sensitivity to that gentleman's behaviour was being influenced by Sarah's nightmares. During the last week she had taken to waking him crying out, imploring him not to trust her uncle Glenlyon. Alasdair had discovered her examining their secret store of firearms and plotting an escape route from the house for themselves and their children should the redcoats fall upon them.

'What nonsense is this, wife?' he roared at her. For God's dear sake, the redcoats have broken bread with us all. The Clan have made them welcome, the oath of hospitality is between us. Besides, they would not dare harm us, we are Glenlyon's kin.'

Despite his reassuring words, he found himself watching closely that Friday forenoon for any changes in behaviour among Argyll's men. He saw there was no drilling and a route march had been substituted by Sergeant Barber with half the company swinging past Carnoch and along the Ballachulish road. Later he surprised Glenlyon in deep conversation with his other kinsman, Lieutenant John Lindsay who, with Ensign John Lundie, was quartered at Carnoch. Alasdair had no liking for the two sullen Lowland officers who kept their own counsel and whose tight-lipped faces suggested secrets they shared with none. Now as he rode through the village he saw Sergeant Barber whispering earnestly to a huddle of soldiers, gathered close around him. At the sight of Alasdair Og, they dispersed in an abrupt manner he could only consider as conspiratorial if not outright guilty. The sergeant nodded coldly, evading his greeting.

As he rode on, Alasdair was relieved to notice a group of redcoats taking their usual daily exercise in the meadow. But they were less exuberant than usual, they seemed quarrelsome among themselves. Perhaps he was imagining things and it was merely the biting cold wind which affected tempers.

As he sat down at his table that evening with the shutters closed against the night, Sarah bolted the door and stood with her back to it. She called into the kitchen and the servant's grandchild, a nine-year-old lad, entered.

'Tell the master, Hamish, tell him what you've just told me.'

'I was watching the soldiers at the meadow this afternoon, there is one of them who has been kind to me, he has a wee son my own age at home in Argyll, he came over to me and I asked him why he was not taking part. He sighed and said he was not in the humour for games today, and as I was leaving for home, he said: "A moment, lad. There is something I have to tell to yon stone over there – and you might as well listen, so pay attention." I followed him as he asked and then he did a strange thing, he slapped the boulder with his hand and addressed it, not in English but in Gaelic: "Grey stone of the glen, great is your right to be here. Yet if you but knew what will happen this night, you would be up and away." '

'Are you sure that is what he said?'

'Yes, Master. He asked me to repeat it word for word and said I was a good lad, and to remember it well.'

'What was this man's name?'

'Campbell, Corporal Archibald Campbell.'

Campbells warning Macdonalds. Alasdair felt a sudden chill.

'I told you, I told you,' said Sarah, after the lad had returned to the kitchen. 'Glenlyon means our death.'

Alasdair had little appetite as he struggled through the meal before him. 'A redcoat makes a daft speech, just to impress a child, with his oratory. Nothing is going to happen.'

Sarah threw her plaid round her shoulders. 'Nothing *might* happen, but I have a duty to our kinsfolk. I am away to tell Hamish's tale to John.'

Alasdair shrugged. There was no reasoning with the woman once she got the bit between her teeth. She had still not returned when he prepared to brave the snow for Inverrigan's house where Glenlyon had summoned them all, as his guests, to play a hand at cards that evening.

John was there before him and whispered: 'I left Sarah at home, she was ranting away, as full of dire prophecies as an auld spey-wife,' he looked over towards his host. 'And her Glenlyon's niece, too. I told her it was unthinkable.'

'That was my advice! Think nothing more of it, John. Just a bairn's havers!'

John nodded. 'Nevertheless I think we should be vigilant.'

After his initial distrust John had been friendly disposed towards Glenlyon. Now Alasdair regarded the man carefully as he stood by the fireplace, glass in hand. Glenlyon was in exuberant spirits. Never had he seen his countenance more flushed nor heard his laughter so hearty. Every man was his friend, slapping them on the back, telling bawdy stories. Their number was increased by the dour company of Lindsay and Lundie. Watchful, unsmiling, they seemed able to withstand their Captain's attempts at ribaldry. As did Liam Campbell, who was chided several times by Glenlyon for a lack of attention to the cards he was playing.

At seven of the clock, Glenlyon stood up and brought the game to an abrupt end. He had lost heavily but amazingly this did not seem to perturb him. He was in the sweetest of tempers, complimenting his guests and flattering his hostess.

Normally the evening included supper, for the officers and any who cared to make a night of it, but Glenlyon sighed regretfully. 'I have received news which means more paperwork before bedtime,' and with a doleful shake of his head. 'There is more trouble stirring up Glengarry's way and I am afraid this pleasant little interlude with our family is nearing its end. We are expecting orders to take to the road again. We go with an ill heart, I can tell you.'

He sped them on with firm handshakes and further

gallantries. It was now Liam's turn to watch his superior officer. He had not yet been told of any orders regarding Glengarry and considered this highly unusual. He noticed that Sir Robert although he was still sober, gave an impression of having drink taken. He carried the uncertain eye and high laughter which characterised his bouts of insobriety.

Closing the door on the last of the visitors, Liam followed him into the room he used as office.

'What is this about fresh orders?' he asked.

Glenlyon sniggered and threw down a paper before him. 'That is from Major Robert Duncanson at Ballachulish this morning. Read it for yourself.'

You are hereby ordered to fall upon the rabble, the Macdonalds of Glencoe, and to put all to the sword under seventy. You are to have a special care that the old fox and his cubs do not escape your hands. You are to secure all the avenues, that no man escape. This you are to put into execution at five of the clock precisely. And by that time, or very shortly after it, I will strive to be at you with a stronger party. If I do not come to you at five, you are not to tarry for me but to fall on. This is by the King's special commands for the good and safety of the country, that these miscreants be cut off root and branch. See that this be put in execution without fear or favour. Else you may expect to be dealt with as one not true to King nor country, nor a man fit to carry a commission in the King's service. Expecting you will not fail in the fulfilling thereof, as you love yourself.

Liam threw down the paper with an angry exclamation: So the truth of those manoeuvres from Inverlochy against Glengarry was out at last! Colonel Hill was under orders from London and the Master of Stair and Livingstone! Hamilton had sent a special runner to Ballachulish.

'There's a packet of copies of the orders all down the line – here, if you can trouble to read through them. Right from the King himself,' and Sir Robert went on: 'This is the plan. The trap is set. We seal the escape routes on the southern flanks with our regiment. Duncanson with three hundred soldiers will then move up to Invercoe at the mouth of the glen to stop the way out to Loch Leven. And Hamilton with another four hundred will be there from Fort William, over the Devil's Staircase to close the passes to the south and east.' He shrugged. 'We need not expect any trouble. It seems an easy enough task. But the timing is vital. Hamilton cannot be with us until seven of the clock. At least two hours after the action has begun and now Duncanson tells us in yon letter that *he* might be late. *Late* – God's teeth! – all depends on us closing the gate of the trap together. I am afraid it all rests with us, the success of this night's work,' he added, considering an ill-drawn map of Glencoe. 'Of course we have them by our weight of numbers, but I would have been happier to have had Duncanson and Hamilton nearer. What say you, cousin, have you any gems of advice to offer?'

'What is it you ask? My advice to assist with the slaughter of five hundred men, women and children by a thousand armed men. As you say yourself, it sounds easy enough to murder innocent folk who have given us their food to eat and their roofs to shelter under, folk who trust us.'

Sir Robert treated his outburst good-humouredly. 'Come now, Glencorrie, it is not as bad as all that. After all, they are no more innocent than those you and your Clan slaughtered in Ardarroch.'

Liam banged his fist on the table and glared at Glenlyon. 'Ardarroch and Glencorrie were sworn enemies, they expected no quarter from each other. We had not broken bread together, we had not sat at their table assuring them that we came in peace.'

'Well, there is nothing either you or I can do about the King's orders, cousin,' said Sir Robert testily. 'We must obey them, that is what soldiers are for! Our commissions and careers depend upon implicit obedience and if you are in any doubt I would advise you to pay particular attention to the last sentence in Duncanson's order. No need to blame *me*, man, I am not responsible. we are here merely as soldiers – and soldiers frequently have to carry out orders that are distasteful to them personally.'

Liam stood up. 'Not only distasteful, but against all humanity.'

'Well, please yourself how you look at it, Glencorrie. You

will have to lay aside all such finer feelings until the business is done, I am afraid.'

'No, that I cannot do,' said Liam. 'I swore before God after the Ardarroch raid, twenty-five years ago, that I was finished with killing. You knew that and when you persuaded me to join the regiment you said there would be little fighting, unless I wanted it. I believed you, fool that I was.'

He paused but Glenlyon said nothing. 'Do you not understand what this means? You are not asking me to kill in battle against a common enemy, but to slaughter innocent women and children – like defenceless cattle.'

Sir Robert regarded his cousin calmly. 'That was quite a speech.' And as he rolled up the map: 'I hope you are not intending to mutiny just when your services are most needed, and your loyalty to your regiment,' he added coldly. 'To say nothing of your loyalty and gratitude to me for all I have done for you and your Clan throughout the years.'

'If you expect me to repay that debt of gratitude by shedding the blood of MacIan and his clan, then all I can say is that you, Glenlyon, are no kin of mine. Your very niece is Alasdair Macdonald's wife, are you going to slit Sarah's throat too?'

Sir Robert wriggled his shoulders uncomfortably. 'If I have to, yes, if she gets in the way of my duty,' he added virtuously.

'You mean if you cannot get some underling to do it for you?' said Liam grimly. The orders indicated that Hamilton himself feared that Glenlyon's sojourn among the Macdonalds might have blunted his sense of purpose. 'It has been well thought out, this scheme to annihilate the Macdonalds.' And again remembering words like 'maul them in the long cold nights', he knew that Sir Robert had been fully aware of the orders for some time.

'You knew what our intention was before we left Inverlochy?'

Sir Robert shrugged. 'Yes, I did. It is all there,' he unlocked a chest and threw down a packet of papers: 'Read them for yourself if you do not believe me.'

'I believe you.'

'Read them, man, for God's sake, and take that mutinous look off your face.'

Sickened, revolted by the cold blooded plans that had been withheld from him until now, until it was too late, Liam realised that Duncanson had but four miles to travel with his regiment in the winter dawn to reach the glen from Ballachulish. Hamilton moving through the night from Inverlochy by way of Kinlochleven and the Devil's Staircase would come down on the upper end. A detachment of Argylls at Island Stalker would block escape through Appin. The Master of Stair was watching the Perthshire roads, while Breadalbane waited in the Glenorchy passes.

Liam Campbell was a man torn by loyalties. His first had always been to Sir Robert, his chief and his cousin. His whole life had once been ruled and motivated by hatred for the Clan Donald but the new turns of events seemed an offence against all that human beings held decent, even animals had loyalty to their kin. It was one thing to dedicate one's life to leaving less Macdonalds alive in the world, one thing to ride and kill a sworn enemy in battle. There was glory in that and honour too for a soldier. But to break bread with them, to sit at their table drinking *aqua vitae* and playing cards, to smile and put an arm around shoulders in drunken camaraderie, to greet their women folk with false smiles and gallantry, *that* was a vastly different matter. This deed was to break the bond most sacred to the Highlander. In a land where all was scarce, where survival depended upon sharing shelter and food, these were given with honour. To accept such hospitality was the unspoken bond of truce and friendship, to be accepted, trusted as a friend, defended as kin with one's own life, if need arose. And then to dirk one's host, as the order proclaimed, was to Liam Campbell a descent into the earlier bloodier and more disgraceful pages of the Highlands' unsavoury history.

'Letters of fire and sword', 'All houses burned', 'None to be spared nor the Government troubled with prisoners – ' The words leaped up at him.

This was indeed murder on a grand scale. Even if any survived, how could they reach safety, presuming that safety existed, in such appalling conditions of weather, as now ruled Glencoe?

Oh dear God, he must find her, warn her.

Caitlin? Where was she?

He stood up and buttoned his great coat.

'What is it now, Glencorrie? Where are you going?' demanded Sir Robert, imagining that his Lieutenant had been subdued by the wording of the documents.

'I wish to be excused from duty, sir.'

'Excused from duty! Are you mad, man?'

Liam shook his head, wishing indeed that he could feign madness as the easy way out. 'No, sir, it is simply that I cannot be party to brutal murder.'

'You cannot be party, *you*!' Sir Robert's face turned livid. 'You know what *you* are doing, you are deserting, *deserting* in the face of the enemy!'

Liam permitted himself a dry smile. 'I would have hardly imagined from the orders that anything as noble as a glimpse of their faces was intended.'

'Do not be presuming to tell me *my* orders, Glencorrie! I could have you court-martialled for this. Shot! You know that, do you not?'

'One life, among many, sir. I am sure that would make little difference to you, if I got in the way of your duty.'

Sir Robert leaned forward threatening. 'Do not give me your insolence, Lieutenant!' Suddenly he bowed his head. He was silent for a moment and then he looked up with a pleading smile. 'Liam, man,' he said softly, 'we have been good friends and good kinsmen all these long years. Remember all the fine times we have had together in Glasgow and Perth, here, there and everywhere. Do you not see that I have no option in the matter, I am as helpless as yourself, I must obey orders.'

'And what about your kinswomen, your niece, her young children who are also your kin? Have you forgotten them?'

'I have forgotten nothing.' He regarded him coldly now, thoughtfully, head on side. 'So that is the way of it? Well, my fine mannie, I shall make certain sure that you are kept locked up until this action is over.' He thumped the table top angrily. 'Dammit I have had more than enough of your insubordination. Sentries!' he shouted. The door opened and the two men on duty, stared in.

'Place Lieutenant Liam Campbell under close arrest.'

They exchanged bewildered glances.

'But sir, where?'

'Dammit, that is *your* business! You call yourselves soldiers!'

The men exchanged glances and somewhat cautiously laid hands on Liam's arms. He did not resist.

'Where shall we put him, Captain?' asked the less timid of the two.

'The barn, the barn outside, that will do. It has no window and a stout door. Bind him, gag him, but do it quickly, we do not want Inverrigan alerted.' As they prepared to leave, he said: 'Liam Campbell of Glencorrie, I charge you with disobeying orders. You are under arrest and you will be confined to quarters until the, er, action is over. You will then be conveyed hence to Inverlochy to stand trial for refusal to obey the King's orders.'

Liam's expression did not change. He continued to regard Glenlyon with contempt.

'Get him out of my sight! What are you waiting for?'

As the sentries marched him solemnly out to the barn, one said: 'I am sorry, sir, I do not know what all this is about?'

'Then you had better know, Captain Campbell intends that you shall murder the inhabitants of Glencoe this night.'

'What, *us*?' came the protesting wail.

'You!'

'Lock him up, for Christ's sake! We are not supposed to talk to prisoners, ye ken that fine,' said his companion.'

There was nothing with which to bind their prisoner but a straw rope used to lead the cows. They pushed a rag over his mouth and cursing tried to fasten the rope, flinging him face downward on the floor. He heard the bar slam home on the outside of the door, but it took him less than a minute to free himself from their inexpert bonds. He did not want to alert them by banging on the door for release. If he called for help, Glenlyon would hear him long before the tacksman's house could be aroused.

Cursing that Inverrigan was at the bend of the glen and away from the main part of the village, he knew that he had to escape and somehow raise the alarm. His eyes now used to the darkness, he inspected his surroundings. There was no window. Climbing a ladder to the hay loft he discovered a blink of starlight through a loose plank. Disarmed by the sentries, he used his booted foot against the next plank.

Rotted, it broke easily. Fortunately for him the tacksman was not a careful householder. There was a drop of ten feet to the ground, his fall broken by the peat stack. He was free and, with his cloak wrapped well around him to conceal the redcoat uniform, he was running for the main township of Carnoch.

Where to start? He might as well begin with the first croft and warn the inhabitants, get them to spread the word. Maybe some of them even knew Caitlin Macdonald and where she was staying. One of the sergeants opened the door. Liam had a story ready. As the man saluted smartly, he explained that he was here to countermand the instructions given earlier that day by Captain Campbell. As he spoke he counted four lads sprawled dolefully around the table, now they crowded to the door, asking what was wrong. They were clearly puzzled, but one smiled.

'I am glad indeed, sir, such a deed would have gone ill against my nature,' he whispered. 'Campbell that I am, with no love for Macdonalds, but these folk have been good to us, not even kin could have been kinder.'

'Hold your whisht, McPhail,' said the sergeant with a doubtful look. 'I ought to have a written order, sir.'

'We did not have time for such niceties, to call up and write an official order for everyone at this hour. Do you not understand, sergeant, this is an emergency, there has been a mistake and you must take my word for it, if you do not, heads will roll, that I can assure you.'

The sergeant saluted. 'Very well, sir!'

Liam sighed with relief. 'Captain Campbell further instructs that each man is to be responsible for alerting all other billets nearby of this countermanded order! You take the township over yonder, split up your men accordingly.'

The men were already buckling on coats as he ran to the next house. The old woman who came at last to his summons was clearly deaf, and annoyed. 'Water is it, ye want? Aye, aye, worrying a body at this time of night! But ye shall have some water. Come away in, come away.'

But Liam was gone. His next cottage produced an old man who swore at him for disturbing his sleep. 'There are none of your soldiers here, get ye gone.'

At his next stop he was greeted by soldiers supping

276

quietly with their hosts. He asked one to come outside and told him of the new orders. The lad was clearly delighted and as he looked beyond him into the room and saw the pretty lass in the firelight darting coy looks in the lad's direction, he understood why.

'Warn the others, take the road across there.'

There was little music in the glen tonight, he thought. No pipers, and the glensfolk seemed to have retired earlier than usual. It was now snowing heavily. His progress was damnably slow and it would be impossible to arouse everyone who was sleeping without drawing undue attention to himself. Then he would be in trouble especially if his escape had been discovered.

How much time had he lost already? In a few hours Glenlyon would give the signal and the slaughter would begin. But he was no nearer finding Caitlin. Desperately he tried the inn. The innkeeper came sullenly, grumbling, to answer his call.

'There will be trouble tonight, for the Macdonalds, from the redcoats,' he whispered. 'If you have any billeted on you, get yourselves and your family away before it is too late.'

The man gave him an astonished glance and closed the door. Liam was heading for the next cottage when he heard other voices, the inn door reopened and a redcoat sergeant rushed out.

'There he is, over there! Seize him!' Useless to run. That would not only suggest guilt but would also invite a bullet in his back. Calmly he stood his ground as the soldiers grabbed his arms.

'Unhand me instantly! I am Lieutenant Campbell!'

His captors' grip tightened as the sergeant approached. 'So it is you who has been spreading these false rumours,' and he hissed: 'Traitor!'

'They are not false rumours, they are changed orders from Captain Campbell himself.'

The man grinned. 'Are they now? Well, you come back inside with us if you please, and we will talk about that.'

Aware of lurking danger, Liam followed him into the empty taproom. Dismissing the two soldiers, the sergeant said 'I have heard about you, Lieutenant Campbell, from none other than the Captain himself. He warned us not five minutes ago that you had escaped and might make trouble.'

'What are you going to do? Shoot me, a Campbell like yourself, as well as the Macdonalds.'

The man looked at the musket he carried. It must not be fired prematurely for such was the agreed signal. In the instant of indecision Liam sprang at him, the man swerved off-balance but a moment later brought the butt of the musket heavily down on Liam's head.

The two redcoats looked in. 'Is he dead then?'

Blood formed a pool on the floor where Liam lay still.

'Like enough. Skull split open,' he added, with a vicious kick at Liam's ribs. 'He isn't moving anyway.'

'Shall we dirk him, to make sure?'

The sergeant considered. 'No, he is an officer and the Captain ordered that he was to be taken alive, to be made an example of. It is Argyll's business and not ours. We had better get busy, it is almost time. Listen – '

A shot nearby.

The signal? It was too early. Some damned fool of an eager recruit! 'Find that man, and put him on a charge,' yelled the sergeant and they raced out banging the door on the still figure of Lieutenant Campbell.

Alasdair Og knew he was going to get little sleep that night, plagued by Sarah and her gloomy speculations. She lay rigidly alert at his side, demanding: 'What was that? What was that now?' at the slightest noise. Alasdair Og groaned. There was noise a-plenty outside as the storm raged round the roof and caught at a loose board somewhere in the direction of the barn.

'Are you awake, husband,' Sarah whispered. 'The *Bean Nighe* has been seen, many times of late, at the falls of Coe.'

'A ghostly washerwoman,' said Alasdair grimly. 'I suppose that other washerwoman Peg Brodie dreamed up *that* story.'

'Others swore it was true. And the shroud she washes is spotted with blood. Death is coming to the glen.'

Alasdair closed his eyes. At that moment his first choice would be Peg Brodie. He could have strangled her for all this nonsense put into the heads of impressionable women.

'And Janet hears the keening woman, the *Caoineag*, and

Janet does not have the second sight,' Sarah added triumphantly.

'Look, wife, it is nearly dawn and not one wink of sleep have I had this night. Go to sleep. I will listen in the morning.' Turning his back on her, he resolved that Glencoe would have one less inhabitant tomorrow night, that for sure. First thing, he would be down into that kitchen and send Peg Brodie packing.

'There was another thing, husband. Do you not remember, for you were there yourself? When we were visiting your father, some of the cows broke out of the byre and ran up the lane, terrified. It was a sign. Otherwise, what scared them?'

'God in Heaven, woman, how should I know what scared the stupid beasts. A visiting fox, like as not.'

'Aye, husband, a fox called Glenlyon.'

'Glenlyon is your uncle,' he said sternly. 'Have you no respect for kinship?' Before he could say more, Sarah clutched his arm.

'Listen – listen.' And springing out of bed, she rushed over to the window. 'I thought it was marching, the clank of muskets.' Dramatically she turned to him. 'Come and see for yourself, husband. There are soldiers down there.'

Alasdair stared over her shoulder. Through the driving snow, he saw the glimmer of redcoats, not idle sentinels, but formed into marching ranks – with other figures moving among them. He tried to clean the glass for a better view.

What he beheld looked remarkably like officers giving instructions.

Without another word he dressed hastily, seized his plaid. Sarah watched him, hands on hips. 'Now, do you believe me?'

'This could be just an exercise.'

'Exercise, before dawn?'

'Well, they are preparing to leave us.'

Sarah snorted disbelief. 'Where are you going? To inspect them?'

Ignoring the taunt, he said: 'I am going over to brother John. And you, wife, rouse the children, no cause for alarm, but best be prepared.'

He ran through the snow taking care to be unobserved

and in John's house, found his brother awake and vigilant by the window.

'Sarah would give me no peace,' he began apologetically. 'She has never trusted her uncle.'

'There is remarkable activity about the glen this night,' and has been for the past days,' interrupted John. 'Too many for guard duty.'

'I passed by some of them on my way here. And sentinels do not stand in ranks with fixed bayonets, like these men.'

'Perhaps there is no cause for alarm. On such a night as this perhaps Glenlyon has regard for the men's comfort and is doubling the watch,' said John.

'In ranks of twenty men, brother?'

John sighed. He had never liked or trusted Glenlyon from the first moment he set eyes upon him, but he had tried to be just. 'I think we should have a word with Father about this.' And before he left the house, he went upstairs roused his sleeping wife and told her to be alert. 'There might be trouble this night.'

'Trouble, what kind of trouble?'

'Do not be asking questions, wife, just do as I say.'

MacIan's front door was unlocked. Only Lowlanders locked their doors and only Lowland soldiers ever tapped upon them and waited politely to be invited inside. As they went upstairs they guessed that MacIan would be ill-pleased at being awakened at this hour.

Closing the bedroom door softly so as not to wake their mother, he stood with them at the top of the staircase. 'Trouble? From our own kinsman, Glenlyon?' He was amazed at their suspicions, and in a voice of reprimand which both knew too well to deny, he thundered: 'Need I remind you that the sacred bond of hospitality unites us? This is no Lowland rabble, no cateran scum you are questioning, but the honourable word of a Highland gentleman,' he repeated, 'And that is what Glenlyon is. Never you forget it.'

Looking at their doubtful faces, he realised sadly that the old standards of chivalry were slipping, even in his own lads. A pity, a pity. With a shake of his head and a suppressed yawn, he put a hand on both their shoulders. 'I am for bed and I would advise you both to do the same. We will all laugh about this come daylight.'

The brothers parted outside and made for home, where John found his wife was asleep and the children in bed beside her. Certain that sleep was beyond him this night, he decided to resume his vigil by the window. Even through the snow, the fire outside the sentinel's post illuminated much activity from redcoats with shining muskets.

John stood up. There was only one way to put at rest his fears for his family's safety, and that was to go across to Inverrigan. Wrapping his plaid tight about him, his bonnet pulled down well over his eyes he stumbled through the drifting snow, cursing himself as he went for a fool. But as he approached Inverrigan, he was amazed at the activity for four in the morning when they could not march before full light in such weather. Everywhere he looked there were torches, lights burning in windows, soldiers with fixed bayonets watching him.

He went inside, glad of the sudden warmth. No one stopped him entering the ground-floor room used by Glenlyon. Through the smoke of the peat-fire, intermingling with the acrid smell of priming powder, he saw Captain Campbell, talking earnestly to men he recognised as officers but from the far end of the glen. All of them were vigorously priming pistols and muskets as they talked, as if the matter was of great urgency.

The conversation died abruptly in a series of nudges. Glenlyon raised his head and strode forward, grasping him by the hand.

'Ah, John. But you are an early riser this day,' he said smoothly. 'Have you come to wish us Godspeed? As you can see we are all deuced busy. A soldier's life.' Smiling, he raised his eyes in mock-tragic despair. Patting John's arm, he added: 'But it is always good to see you, cousin, whatever the hour.'

John ignored the effusive greeting. 'Why so much activity so early, and why do you prepare arms? Is it not just a route march to Glengarry?'

Glenlyon shook his head, led him aside. 'Ah, John, we must not be too simple, we are told to expect trouble in that quarter.'

'I came to see Inverrigan.'

'Inverrigan, eh? He went out to visit a sick tenant, oh, before midnight, did he not, lads?' he called to the group by the fire. A wild flurry of heads, shaken eagerly, greeted this remark. With a friendly arm about John's shoulders, he ushered him towards the door. 'Glengarry awaits,' he sighed. 'I doubt it will not be peaceful like our little stay here with all our dear kinsmen.' Looking steadily into John's face as if he read in that sober expression the real reason for this visit, he stood back in shocked surprise. 'John, John, cousin, you surely do not think we intend Glencoe some ill? Glencoe!' his voice broke. 'Is that what you think, John Macdonald?'

John's eyes, nervously evading his, gave all the answer he required. 'Man, man, if such were my orders do you think I would have given no warning, to my own dear niece Sarah, and your brother?'

From Glenlyon's own lips the protest was believable. It was true what his father MacIan had said. No Highlandman would ever murder a woman of his family. Ashamed of his base suspicions, John shook his head, and clasped Glenlyon's hand so willingly outstretched.

'Godspeed.'

'And you, cousin. Sleep well.'

Glenlyon went back into the room whistling cheerfully. He kicked the door closed behind him and with it the smile wiped clean from his face. 'Inverrigan? Is he close held.'

The officer Drummond grinned. 'Trussed like a hen, through there in the byre.'

'None from this household escaped? You are certain sure?'

'No, sir. All eight, all accounted for. Bound and gagged and awaiting your orders.'

Glenlyon nodded. 'Good lads, we are almost ready.'

MacIan, returning to bed after his son's visit, fell into a heavy slumber. He was awakened by a servant:

'Lieutenant Lindsay is here to see you.'

'It is not yet daybreak. Whatever brings the man at this hour?'

'He says to tell you that the soldiers are heading for Glengarry immediately and he wishes to thank you for your hospitality personally.'

MacIan needed no other reason. He scrambled out of bed. Whatever the hour, hospitality must be ready for the departing guest. 'I will be down directly. See you to it, that he gets a dram in his hand while he waits, Fergus.'

'What is it?' whispered Lady Glencoe fully awake at his side. 'What is the hour?'

'Get you dressed, my love. It is early but our guests are leaving. They must be seen on their way with proper courtesy.'

MacIan had his back to the door pulling on his trews and was not aware of Lindsay entering. His wife's shocked and annoyed exclamation: 'We will be with you directly, Lieutenant,' was the last sound he heard on earth. As life ended for him in a thundering explosion which shattered the back of his head and ruined the proud face she had loved.

The room was full of soldiers with bayonets at the ready. As MacIan fell face downwards across the bed, another pistol shot thudded into his back. Lady Glencoe screamed and threw herself across his body.

'No, no, do not kill him. Do not kill him!'

She looked round but Lindsay, his grim execution accomplished had disappeared. Instead there was now laughter all around her, the nightmare laughter of fiends. She had no doubt that her beloved MacIan was beyond help for there was blood everywhere. But her boys, she must escape, warn her boys.

'Let me go, let me go. This instant.'

But the voice whose commands had always been readily and eagerly obeyed, was now the object of some mirth.

'This instant eh? You are not going out in your nightgown, me leddy. Nay, we will see to that. The proper dress for yer leddyship,' they mimicked and one stepped forward, ripping the gown from her body, in one savage downward movement. As it slipped to the floor, she watched its folds gather around her ankles. Then without word or cry, head bowed, modestly she covered her nakedness with hands and arms, and the tears spilled over from her eyes.

'Her hands. Gawd, man, look at them rings.'

'They are for me.'

'Away with you, they are mine.'

'Mine.'

They stank of sweat as they fell upon her. She was too old for rape, besides they were under orders, and had no time for such frivolities. But those damned rings, those they would have. They seized her hands, pulled at the rings, but they would not come off. They tugged and dragged, but to no avail.

'There is one sure way. Bite them off.'

She offered no further resistance. At that first cruel gnawing of flesh, she screamed once only and then mercifully fainted.

The sound of musket fire aroused John Macdonald, who had slept badly. He sprang to the window and saw twenty redcoat soldiers marching towards his house with fixed bayonets. Within moments, he had his family and household out by the back door, the front bolted and barred hoping this ruse would delay the soldiers.

He heard the door break open when they were halfway up the hill, heading west towards Meall Mor. There they met Alasdair Og and Sarah, who embraced them weeping.

Their uneasy slumbers had been roused by a servant who had heard shots coming from the direction of John's house. ' "It is no time for you to be sleeping when they are killing your brother at the door." Those were his words. Oh, brother, brother, we thought never to see you again. We thought you were all murdered.'

What of their parents? The same terrible thought was in all their minds as they climbed the hill, two families carrying children too small to walk. Once they stopped and listened. There was shooting from Inverrigan and then from Achnacon. They exchanged ominous looks as flames brightened the greyness of the storm closing in behind them.

Back at Inverrigan, on the stroke of five o'clock, Glenlyon gave the order to proceed with the execution of his host, the tacksman Macdonald and his family. They were shot one by one, including the female members of the household who had served Glenlyon and Liam Campbell, who had baked their bread, tended their fires, made their beds and washed their linen. A soldier searching through Macdonald's pockets silently held out a piece of paper for his Captain to see. The letter of protection signed by Colonel Hill.

Other members of the family from houses near at hand

were quickly despatched. A lad of twenty who had served Glenlyon and with whom he had many friendly exchanges was brought before him. Weeping unashamedly, the lad pleaded for his life. Glenlyon frowned. He would have liked to allow the lad to go free.

At that moment, Major Drummond rode up and demanded to know what was delaying the execution. As the men hesitated, Drummond drew his pistol and shot the boy through the head. The lad's brother, aged thirteen, was led out. He threw himself down before Glenlyon, clutching at his knees.

'Spare me, sir, spare me. I will do anything, go anywhere, anything you ask, if only you let me live.'

Again Glenlyon hesitated. Again Drummond drew his pistol and the boy was shot in the head, where he knelt.

Glenlyon seemed to come out of a dream. He responded to orders, but moved in a bewildered fashion. It had never been his intention to be personally involved in the bloodbath and to have victims pistolled at his feet as they begged for mercy. He saw a woman, with a child of four in her arms, both shot before his eyes.

At Achnacon, downstream from Inverrigan, Sergeant Barber surrounded the house and burst in with his men. Five Macdonalds were killed instantly in the musket fire at close quarters. Four others lay wounded. Among the dead was Achnacon's brother, Macdonald of Achtriochtan, who also carried in his pocket Colonel Hill's letter of protection.

Achnacon, who had been Barber's host, was one of the wounded. He asked to be carried outside to die.

Barber agreed cheerfully. 'Since I have eaten your meat, I will do you this last favour. Right gladly I will kill you outside.'

As Barber's men closed in on Achnacon, thrusting their muskets towards his face, in one quick movement he hurled his plaid over their heads and charged through their midst, making his escape into the darkness. As their shots passed harmlessly over his head, the three other wounded Macdonalds made good their escape by the back door.

It was the sound of a piper, playing a lament, that crept through the raw edges of Liam's agony. He was cold and uncomfortable, so cold. He groaned, hugging his sides to keep warm. What was the man about? Here he was with a colossal hangover *and* a blasted piper. He stirred unwillingly, imagining for a moment that he was back in the tavern at Fortingall suffering from the effects of too liberal Hogmanay.

He closed his eyes firmly, trying to shut out the cold, the pipes' wailing, determined to get back to sleep again. Even his bad dreams were better than coming to terms with the day quite so early.

Above the pipes, he heard, a new sound. Shouts, screams.

He tried to sit up and the effort was agony. He touched his head. His hair was matted, a contusion bigger than two hens eggs made him cry out and withdraw his hand quickly. It was wet, sticky with fresh blood.

Eyes fully open now, he remembered that he had been struck over the head with a musket and that thereupon Glencoe and all its troubles had dissolved.

Glencoe? How long had he been unconscious?

And that piper! Now he recognised what he played: the *Cruinneachadh*, the 'gathering of the clans' that was also the warning lament!

The struggle to rise made him vomit, and had the blood pouring down the side of his face from his split scalp. He felt like death, his head a heavy ugly stone resting upon too weak shoulders. Heaving himself to the door, he was grateful to find it unlocked. He took in great gulps of air, but his legs refused to obey him any further. Knees buckling, he struggled to rise again and forced himself to stagger down the road like a drunken man, one foot dragged after the other, each painful step, each jolting movement brought fresh shafts of agony and more bleeding from his skull.

All too soon there was a different kind of agony. There had been a fresh fall of snow during the early hours of the morning, but by first light it was tinged with red, the red of blood. Soon he was among the dead. It was as if a pack of wild animals had fallen upon the glensfolk under cover of darkness. There were bodies sprawled everywhere and the open doors of houses told him that their occupants were either fled or lay crumpled and still beyond any help from him.

He must reach MacIan's house. He never knew how he found strength to reach Glen Muidhe. His blurred senses told him he had reached it for he was among the carnage again. Once he staggered, fell and fainted. When he came back to consciousness, he thought bewildered that he was back at Ardarroch and there was the burning tower, with Caitlin's face at the window.

Caitlin!

There were flames everywhere. He was outside Glen Muidhe. MacIan's house was not ablaze and he knew a moment's hope. He ran inside but halfway up the stairs, he stopped, confused. Where was he? Was this the tower at Ardarroch, had time run backwards? He knew from the ugly painful sore where his head should have been, that it had not. The Liam Campbell of that far off time had been young, courageous, fully armed. This Liam Campbell was past forty, unarmed and like to die.

Through an open door, he saw MacIan. The chief of Glencoe was sprawled across a bed in his nightshirt, with a bullet hole in his back and another in his head. He was dead, and Liam half-ran, half-fell down the stairs. The rest of the family? Where were they?

There were bodies all round him but none moved. Yes, *there* was a sound. It came from the bloodied naked body of a woman! He took off his cloak and covered her. Suddenly her eyes flickered open.

Horrified, Liam hardly recognised the elegant dainty little woman who had once graced MacIan's table and entertained the officers of Argyll's regiment with wit and charm, her songs on the *clarsach*. 'Lady Glencoe, who, who has done this to you?'

Her lips moved but no sound came and as he cradled her into the cloak, he saw that the hands he had never seen without jewels, the love tokens MacIan had brought her through the years, were now stripped bare, bare to the bone, bloody shreds of flesh showed how the soldiers had torn, or more like, bitten the rings from her fingers.

Eyes open, she looked at him: 'Liam Campbell, you too! Kill me and put an end to it. Kill me!'

'My lady, I am no party to this night's work. I have tried to warn your people, but Glenlyon had me arrested.' Her

287

eyes closed again. Liam could not leave her here in the snow for another soldier to find and murder. 'I will get you to safety,' he whispered.

The effort of trying to stand and lift the dead-weight of her in his arms made him stagger and his knees buckled under him. Again he tried. Blood from his head trickled on to her naked chest.

'No, lad, no. You are hurt too. Besides I do not wish to leave – him,' she smiled suddenly towards the house she had loved so well. 'We must be together, you know, always together, now, most of all.'

At least there would be shelter inside. She would be safe there.

'Let me take you to him.' Did she know what she would find? – dear God!

'I will be obliged to you, sir,' she whispered, with a gallant return to the graceful speech, so tragically inept in these terrible circumstances.

Tottering, clinging together, Liam managed to get her indoors. It seemed to have taken a long time and he stared up the long flight of stairs. He dared not attempt to carry her in case they both fell down.

'I will manage fine from here,' she said, supporting herself against the balustrade.

'Lady Glencoe, you know *he* is – is – '

'I know, lad. And I will join him directly. But you go now – go and rescue your child.'

His child?

'Your Caitlin, she is a mile from here at Gleann-leac-na-muidhe, with an old aunt of ours. Up the glen there,' he could hardly hear her voice was so faint. 'Go to her, go.'

She sank down on the stairs and he left her there. He could not stay. There was no comfort he could give to one whose life was thus ending in the house where her happiness had begun.

Anguish for Caitlin lent new strength and as he struggled along the path between the hills almost blinded by snow, he closed eyes and heart to pity for the scene of murder, for a mother and babe in her arms both shot, a young boy, a child's hand cut from its body, pathetically curled in the snow.

288

After a few hundred yards there was only the white purity of snow around him. He prayed that he was heading in the right direction. Suddenly he heard a horse's hooves drumming behind him. He crouched down beside a boulder, praying that the rider was not a Campbell officer. But the horse was riderless. It belonged to the regiment by its trappings and had run off during the killing, perhaps scared by the noise.

It came to his whistle obediently enough and he struggled on to its back, although the effort of trotting suggested that his head might split into two halves at any moment.

Caitlin –

Now it was fully light. He looked back down the slope and saw the burning houses, tiny squares, smoking, glowing against the snow.

At last there was a grey stone house. Leading the horse, he knocked at the door.

'Caitlin Macdonald? Caitlin Macdonald? Are you there? Caitlin? Caitlin, it is Liam!'

A scuffle from inside, then silence. Oh dear God, was he too late?

'Caitlin, if that is yourself, please open the door. I mean you no harm. For pity's sake, open the door!' He rattled the latch and the scurrying turned into stealthy footsteps.

'Caitlin, Caitlin.'

A hoarse whisper: 'Who is that?'

'It is Caitlin's father. Is she with you?' There was no reply. 'There is no need to open the door if you do not believe me, just tell me, is she safe?'

The door was unbarred cautiously and an old woman stared out at him. She gave a stifled cry when she saw the redcoat uniform and was about to bang the door in his face. He thrust his boot in the opening and said, 'I am Caitlin's father, Campbell of Glencorrie, for God's sake believe me, help me, I am not your enemy.'

'She took the bairns up yonder, heading for Dalness, hours since. The dog is with her, he will look after them. I could not go, I am not to leave my bed.' She was racked by sudden coughing. A clawlike hand extended, seized his arm. 'Do not let them kill me, sir, please save me from them.'

'I do not think they will get this far, *cailleach*. You will be

289

safe enough. Just stay inside and keep your door locked – and pray!'

As he reached the edge of the wood, it was fully light. He rode up to a small rise, reined in and looked back and down on Glencoe. Burning houses still, smoke rising, all else was mercifully blotted from view.

Throughout the night the atrocities had continued and by the time Major Duncanson arrived on the scene, Glenlyon's men had completed their slaughter and were driving great herds of cattle, horses, goats and sheep down the track from the townships. On every handcart they could find was loot taken from the houses before firing them.

Duncanson had completed his guarding of the shore road and mouth of the glen. Hamilton however had not managed the encircling movement from the east by bringing his men over the Devil's Staircase, defeated by a twenty-mile march in darkness through a driving blizzard. Long overdue, it was almost midday when they struggled down the track at Altnafeadh. Ordered to let none escape, they killed a bemused eighty-year-old man, despite the fact he was past the 'killing age'.

Duncanson's men were angry and frustrated, they had failed to stop the escape routes south and west and when the two officers met in the centre of the glen, they realised their 'rooting out' had failed.

True the 'old fox' had been killed, but his two cubs had escaped with their wives and families, and most of their Clan. The total corpses amounted to thirty-eight.

Thirty-eight. King William would not be pleased, for this was less than one-tenth of the Clan Iain Abrach they had been ordered to put to the sword.

'The soldiers are delighted with their booty.' But Glenlyon soon discovered his mistake in mentioning this consoling fact to Duncanson.

'A cattle raid was not the reason why the soldiers were sent to Glencoe under your command, Captain Campbell.'

As the Macdonalds, the appalling weather had aided their escape despite the Master of Stairs' quaint notion that no Highlander could survive for long in harsh winter weather. The severity of the weather, the lack of visibility had cloaked their flight and hampered their pursuers.

In hidden corries on the slopes, groups of survivors gathered and made their way out of Glencoe by the southern passes, towards Appin country, and through Glen Muidhe, two escape routes which had been considered impassable and were therefore unguarded.

Considering the fearful journey and the condition of the half-naked travellers, it was a miracle that any survived. Among the wounded, the old and the very young there were casualties who died of exposure that night in those cruel winter hills.

Lady Glencoe was one of them. She had been found still alive and carried by other escaping clansmen to join her sons. She lived just long enough to tell them of their father's murder and of how Lieutenant Liam Campbell had tried to warn the glen at the risk of his own life.

He had gone in search of his daughter, Caitlin. And in almost her last breath, Lady Glencoe whispered:

'I pray to God that he will not be too late.'

Chapter XIV

Caitlin's offer to stay at Glen Muidhe while the soldiers were
billeted there had been firmly rejected by Lady Glencoe: 'We
will need your rooms, my dear. We have servants aplenty.
Besides, soldiers are well used to taking care of themselves.'

'Which regiment are these redcoats?' asked Caitlin with
sudden hope that if they were from Inverlochy, then Liam
Campbell might be with them. Could she face meeting him
again, after all their vows which her tortured dreams refused
to accept?

Lady Glencoe frowned looking out of the window. 'Er, not
from these parts, the Borders, I think. Yes, that is so, I
distinctly remember John mentioning they were a Lowland
regiment,' she lied, with a bright smile, MacIan having
instructed her to keep Caitlin in strict ignorance of
Glencorrie's presence. He wanted no excuse for any more
feuds breaking out between Macdonalds and Campbells in
his glen.

'Get her away, and as fast as you can,' he had told his
wife, who did just that aided by one of MacIan's fast runners
sent with a note to old Honor Macdonald who bided a mile
away at Gleann-leac-na-muidhe. Caitlin and the children
were to stay with her. On no account were they to be allowed
to return to Glen Muidhe until the redcoats had left the glen.
'Use any excuse, but keep her with you.'

Honor Macdonald was Brendan's great-aunt. Touching
eighty, she had been far from well after a winter attack of
bronchitis. Staying at Glen Muidhe over Yuletide, a passing
acquaintance based on short visits from Caitlin and the two
children, had blossomed into the stronger bonds which often
bind the young to the very old. Thoroughly mystified by her
niece, Lady Glencoe's note, she was delighted to see Caitlin

again, especially as the children liked the old house perched on the hillside. As for Caitlin, she blamed her own sadness on the melancholy approach of February 12, on which day Brendan would have been thirty-two years old.

That morning, the old lady awoke with a sore chest and elected to stay in bed bolstered by pillows and cosseted by Caitlin. William fell and grazed his knee, Kirsty showed alarming signs of a slight fever. Both children were disagreeable, and even Bran refused to settle. There was something wrong with everyone, thought Caitlin, as Bran cried constantly and rushed back and forward to the door. But when Caitlin opened it, he merely ran a few yards down the path. There he stopped, listened eagerly and then with an almost human shrug returned to the house, only to repeat the performance within the hour.

That night Bran would give her no peace. As soon as she slept, his paws touched her awake, as if a human hand seized her shoulder.

'Oh do stop pestering me, Bran,' she cried. 'What do you want *now*?' After the fourth time he had awakened her, she led him firmly into the kitchen and closed the door. 'Stay here, then.' She returned to bed and fell into a troubled sleep, to sit bolt upright when a noise outside alerted her. What she thought she heard was a musket volley. Grudgingly she arose to a grey dawn outside. In the kitchen Bran excitedly growled at the locked door. She opened it and he rushed out to the edge of the road down to Glen Muidhe, running back and forward to her whining. Were those more shots? Sounds travelled far in the mountains' still air, for the snow had momentarily abated. Seizing a plaid, she followed Bran as he led the way to a place where they could look down on the distant Glen Muidhe and far beyond to Glencoe itself.

'Oh Bran, Bran,' she whispered and put her arms around him. What she saw below left in no doubt what Bran had known. Smoke was spiralling up from tiny houses, the people scurrying insects. But some were spots of red — redcoats. Another musket volley, and then like a merciful curtain the snow began to fall again. Seizing the children from their beds she went in to Great-Aunt Honor and awakened her.

'I thought I heard something. But I am staying where I

am,' said the old lady. 'No soldier is going to bother about me. Besides it might be just drilling they are having.'

'Drilling! At this hour!'

'Ach, soldiers do odd things, especially yon redcoats. But I am biding in my warm bed. Do you think I want my death of cold? How long do you think I would last tracking about in the snow?' she grumbled, as another bout of coughing seized her. But she had lived through many acts of treachery between the clans in her long years and her advice was sound.

'You do as you think best, for your children's sake, lass. Maybe they will not get this far. Take what food you need. Go to the cave halfway up the mountain side, if you can still reach it in the snow.'

Caitlin knew the cave, a favourite walk with the children.

'You can shelter there until the alarm is over. They will not find you. But if they come here and ask I will say that I am alone in the house.' As she held out her arms and embraced Caitlin, she said: 'I will bolt and bar the door after you. Take care, my dear. I will keep a lamp burning in the window. If it goes out you will know that the soldiers have been,' she added grimly.

Caitlin set off with Bran loping at her side and Kirsty, well-muffled against the cold, clasped in the plaid fastened about her waist. William carried in a bundle their few provisions.

'Are the soldiers coming after us?' he asked.

She could not lie to him. 'Maybe.'

'Why?'

'They are Campbell soldiers and they do not like the Macdonalds.'

'Why?'

'Because we are their enemies.'

William said nothing until they reached the cave. With Kirsty snuggled into the crook of his arm, he said: 'You heard all that, little sister. We are in great danger and you must be good and brave and not breathe a word or cry. You must not cry out,' he added severely, 'whatever happens.'

Kirsty gave her mother a choking, frightened look. 'Why not, Mama?'

'Because it is a game we are playing of hiding, hiding from

the soldiers, that is why,' said William.

In the cave, there was naught to do but huddle together for warmth and wait for the hours to pass as the snow-storm waxed and waned. Bran occasionally stared out, but eventually he lay down head on paws. Then suddenly he stood up growling, coat bristling.

'Listen – listen,' said Caitlin.

It was no redcoat but a young lad wearing the Macdonald plaid. She recognised him as one of the MacIan servants from Carnoch. He led three bairns, two smaller than himself on the back of a shelty. As he walked he was weeping, dashing the tears from his eyes.

When Caitlin came out of the cave he ran over to her. 'Oh mistress, mistress, you will never guess what those vile Campbells have done, they have murdered our chief MacIan and all his servants in their house down there,' he pointed to Glen Muidhe, 'All the way from the village there are bodies everywhere. Those soldiers were not for Glengarry at all, they were meant to murder us, just biding their time. If some of the redcoats had not turned against their officers, all of us would be dead. One of their own officers would not carry out the orders and tried to warn us. They killed him too, left him in a pool of his own blood. It is awful mistress, awful. What are we to do?'

A strange cold feeling stole over Caitlin, a dread she hardly dare frame into words. 'This officer,' she whispered, 'What was he like?'

'Oh, a Campbell too. He came to the Tower and sat with the officers, kin to Glenlyon he was and fair like him.'

'He is dead, you say?' Had she uttered those terrible final words out loud?

'Aye, mistress. They bashed his head in. I saw him lying near the inn.'

She told herself the lad could be wrong, that Glenlyon might have other kin. Would she not have felt it herself, his deathblow? And then trembling she remembered the dreams, the warning dreams, that invisible glass barrier between herself and Liam, that was death! She could not go to pieces now, keening like the Highland women at a wake. She had to survive, for her children. Crying would come later.

'We are going over the hill yonder,' said the lad in answer to her question. 'My uncle is tacksman at Dalness.'

'We will come with you.'

The lad regarded her doubtfully. 'If you like, mistress, but you will need to keep up with us. We cannot delay, we may be followed. They are putting everyone to the sword, sparing none old or young. There are a lot of young ones, just like us back there, lying in the snow, pistolled. The redcoats are slaughtering them like cattle. I have these, of course, to protect us.' He patted two pistols perilously stuck into his breeches belt beneath the plaid, trying to sound like a man, ashamed of his tears.

'Where did you get them?' she asked.

He sniffed. 'Took them off a dead man.'

'Do you know how to use them?'

He bit his lip, shook his head.

'I know how to use them, give me one and I will show you. Did you remember the powder horn?'

'Aye, and the shots.' He handed it to her without argument and she loaded the pistol and showed him how to fire it.

'Now, can you remember that, are you sure?'

The lad frowned but said he would try.

'Use it well, then. It is primed ready for firing.'

As he turned to leave he ran back with the other pistol, the remaining shot and powder horn. 'You have these, mistress. For you and your bairns. I would never be able to fire and re-load a second time.'

She put an arm round his shoulder. He was very young, only a year or two older than William and she was teaching him how to kill a man. Her gentle action threatened a return of his tears. 'I must away, mistress, God keep you.'

'And you, lad.'

'I think we should move too, Mother,' said William, watching the children hurrying away. 'I think we are in more danger if we stay in the cave here. Besides it gives us something to do, to keep warm.'

'Kirsty cold,' whispered the child.

As they walked Caitlin found the tears slowing her up, blinding her so that twice she stumbled and fell. MacIan and his family dead. Liam – oh could it be Liam? – dead. She remembered the chill at her heart. She told herself even without the dreams and her forebodings for days past she would have known the moment he died.

They soon lost sight of the children, who had looked back a few times, but were hidden by the falling snow. She put Kirsty on Bran's back, but her bare legs were chafed, her little hands soon numbed and William was too tired to hang on to her.

At last Caitlin saw a faint dark overhang of rock. This was no cave but just a vantage point from where they could see anyone approaching for about thirty yards down the steep path they had climbed. The children were tired. They must rest. If they could keep out of sight until darkness and then travel on. She had a pistol now, and one shot to defend herself and her children. It would be useless against a regiment but might keep a solitary redcoat at bay.

She wished they had not left the shelter of the cave. It was horribly cold on this exposed side of the hill. The children huddled inside her plaid, ate some of the food they had brought. She could eat nothing herself. She felt as if she would never be hungry again. Examining the pistol she thought of the years since she had handled one and she tried to remember all that Liam had taught her, to shoot straight, like a man.

The snow drifted on and off, fierce showers, blotting out the landscape. They could not sit here inert all day, they would freeze to death. They must find shelter, she was even considering returning back down the path to the cave, if she met any redcoats she could claim the protection and mercy of her 'cousin' Glenlyon, but the words would stick in her throat. Besides she might get no chance to argue, she wore the Macdonald plaid and the soldiers already drunk on blood, if they found her first, even her children present, would not spare her from their lusts – oh dear God, help us.

At her side Bran rose, growled deep in his throat. There was no mistaking his warning. She stared through the driving snow down the pass. There was a bulky shadow approaching, a horseman. He was travelling slowly, staring from side to side, obviously tracking any prints that remained in the falling snow.

A soldier. Her heart sank as she caught a glimpse of the

redcoat, the boarshead bonnet pulled well down over his eyes. The worst had happened. They were being followed and their tracks led right underneath this crag. And where there was one soldier there would be many more.

William slapped a hand into hers and held it tightly. At her other side Kirsty who had been dozing, wakened and began to whimper.

'Hush,' said William. 'Hush!'

But it was too late. The man stopped, listened. Caitlin clasped her hand over Kirsty's mouth. Where there were cries there were now snuffles, as the child felt she was being smothered. The man came closer, the horse walking easily. Caitlin's mouth was dry. There was no sign of anyone behind him in the pass. Perhaps there was still time to escape. If she killed him, his horse would be useful. She looked towards the distant mountain pass above them. If only she and the children could reach it. Could they? She could never run that fast in deep snow carrying Kirsty. But perhaps William could. He watched her levelling the pistol in the direction of the approaching rider.

'Listen, my darling. If the soldier does not fall at once, if he comes on at us, you are to run, run for your life, up the mountain pass there and you are not to stop or look back, but run, run, do you hear?'

'But, Mother, Mother.' His voice was a sob.

'You are to do as you are told. Bran here, he will look after us. He will deal with the soldiers, but you must escape. You *must* get back to Ardarroch. Catch up with those children ahead of us. Their uncle, the tacksman will look after you, oh promise me, promise me, my darling.'

'I cannot, I cannot leave you, and what about Kirsty?'

Kirsty looked at them, bewildered but unafraid. Was this all a game in her childish mind? Caitlin pushed her out of sight. 'Stay there, darling.' Her baby, what could she do with her baby?

'She must stay with me, her legs are too small to run. But you must do as I say.'

She must save one of her children. If William were to reach safety, Kirsty must die in her mother's arms.

If only she could see clearly through the driving snow, for the rider was closer now, well within range and still studying their tracks. 'Hush!' she said, for he stopped and listened. Voices travelled for some distance in this clear air. He must have heard them.

'Promise me, William, you will do as I say.'

'I promise, but oh Mother, Mother!' His voice broke, and he clung to her side.

The horse was moving again, slowly, cautiously. Let him come close enough, dear God, let him come close enough for that one shot to kill!

'Faced with death, you will have but one chance. No time to reload. You must make one bullet reach its mark.' She seemed to hear Liam's words across the years.

The redcoat moved into range. She could not wait any longer. Raising the gun she fired. The horse whinnied, reared, and the man rolled off its back into the snow. He lay still. The horse unhurt, bolted back down the path.

They might survive with his horse. 'Bran, bring him.' She pointed and Bran leaped away. Should she go and inspect the redcoat? Was the man really dead? He was very still. She listened. That shot would have echoed, like a blast of gunpowder through the hills. If he had comrades, they would come at once to find out what had happened. She was safe no longer.

She snatched up Kirsty now crying in terror. 'We must find another place, William.'

'You shot him, Mother, you killed him.'

'I know, but we must get over the mountain before dark. Hurry.'

'But where, where?'

'There is maybe a wood where we can shelter for a while.'

'But there will be wolves and wildcats.'

'Bran will keep them at bay.' And there was Bran, with the horse trotting obediently in front of him. Caitlin soothed the beast, patted its nose and noticed, with distaste, the blood on its mane, from the rider. 'Up you go!' She put William on the horse's back with Kirsty in front of him and prepared to lead the animal. 'Bran – '

But Bran had loped away. He was sniffing over the dead man.

'Bran, come.'

She could delay no longer, although it would have been

prudent to search the corpse. But she could not. And turning her back on the ugly scene, she trudged up the steep path.

Suddenly she thought she heard a cry: 'Caitlin – Caitlin.'

She stopped. There it was again.

'Caitlin!' The voice was weak, far off, but it was Liam Campbell.

'Liam!' Liam had come to her rescue. But where was he? There was no one. Only the huddled redcoat in the snow, the man she had killed.

Oh dear God, Liam –

She ran back to where he lay, his bonnet beside him, his face bloody, his fair hair matted with the red stream that poured from his head.

'Oh Liam, Liam – '

She tried to lift him in her arms, and his eyes flickered open.

'Liam, oh Liam, I am sorry, I did not know – '

'You did not hit me, but if that pistol had been in better prime you would have done.' He touched her arm. 'Oh Caitlin, my dearest, is it really you, I am not dreaming or dead? It *is* you! I was in time, your children?'

'Yes, yes, we're safe. But, your poor head!'

He winced as she touched it. 'That was the result of an argument with a musket butt, from a Campbell soldier I hasten to add, who did not like my suggestion that we should warn MacIan and his people.' Tearing her petticoat into strips to bind his head, she began to cry.

'A boy and his brother and sisters told me – they fled this way. I might have guessed, it was you that warned them.'

With considerable effort Liam tried to stand up. He groaned,' I think my ankle is broken too. Damnation! This was not my lucky day, imprisoned for desertion, my brains bashed in – and now this!'

'Can you walk?'

'No, but I can ride. We had best be out of this trap before nightfall. I could try and get you and the children back to the Macdonalds, some must still be alive, probably heading towards Appin.'

'No.'

He looked at her. 'It is all very noble of you, Liam Campbell, but you know and I know that for you to go back

300

is certain death. You will be either shot by any lurking Macdonalds who are around or by the Argyll soldiers as a deserter.'

Liam groaned. 'Well, as long as I am shot *properly* this time I do not really mind. I care little for little bits of me being broken and bloody like this. I am sore all over and I ache like the very devil. Well, have you a better plan?'

'We will head for Dalness and hope that we do not encounter any redcoats.'

'True, if there had been a detachment of soldiers coming up this way, they would have been here by now.' He tried to remember those cursed orders. Had this area been included in the trap that was to be closed by the encircling movement?

She helped him back into the saddle, with Kirsty in front and William behind him. Their journey was painfully slow through that white wilderness of lost paths in which only Liam's sense of direction kept them going. Caitlin trudged alongside, refusing to exchange places with him. Soon they felt as if their clothes were freezing on them and although neither of the children uttered a word of complaint, Caitlin and Liam knew that unless they found shelter as the next blizzard began, they would never survive a night in the open.

Liam put his hand on Kirsty's head and smiled down at Caitlin. 'You have a brave wee lass and a son to be proud of this night.'

Caitlin smiled into the snow and said nothing.

Suddenly Bran began to bark excitedly and ran along a small gully to the left.

'I think we had better follow him. He always knows best,' said Caitlin.

'A very remarkable dog indeed,' said Liam approvingly, as they saw huddled under a crag, a tiny cottage little more than a shepherd's hut. It was occupied, for at the sound of their approach an old woman came to the door. Incredibly old, she seemed beyond age or even surprise, she welcomed them inside without question, and saw the horse bestowed in the shelter of the crag with a blanket and a nosebag of hay. As she listened to their story, she went briskly about building the peat fire into a steady blaze, with no more than a shake of the head or an occasional comment, as if massacres happened everyday.

Finally she settled the two children before the warm glow and thrust bowls of soup into their eager hands. 'Aye, that's good mutton broth – one of my brax sheep,' she whispered to Caitlin 'died in the lambing, but it was good meat. That is the last – but God will provide the next meal,' she added when Caitlin looked guiltily at their empty plates.' And now to attend to you, sir,' she said to Liam who had sunk into a chair, head lolling on his chest, almost unconscious from loss of blood and exhaustion.

The *cailleach* produced an ewer of water, linen and unguents. 'We have to be prepared for anything up here.'

He winced as she bathed his scalp. 'Fortunate that you have a thick skull, sir, or you'd be dead as mutton this night.'

Caitlin helped her remove Liam's boots. He was almost asleep until then.

'That leg of yours,' she shook her head. 'You will not be rushing up any mountains on that for a while,' she said producing more binding. 'No, it is not broken, but the muscle is badly torn.' She told them that she was a Macdonald tenant and she cursed the Campbells to all eternity, for their wickedness. She gave a hard look at Liam's redcoat and boarshead bonnet as she did so and Caitlin whispered that he had given his plaid to a dying woman and that the soldier's coat went with the regimental horse which they had found wandering. The woman seemed satisfied and looked fondly at the little group about the fire before taking up her plaid.

'I have to tend my sheep. There is but one bed, in the wall there, but it was aye big enough for my man and our two bairns. I would advise you and your good man to rest there, my lady, that way all four of you will keep warm. I will fetch more fuel if I can find it.' She drew Caitlin aside. 'That man of yours is like to take a fever, I do not care for the looks of him one bit, you had better keep his body warm, that blow could give him brain fever. Besides he has lost a lot of blood. I will give you a hand into the bed with him.'

The woman was strong for her size and when the door closed behind her, Caitlin sat down beside Liam, suddenly embarrassed by this unforeseen situation.

'She presumed that we were man and wife with our two children.'

'Why did you not tell her the truth?' he whispered.

Caitlin shrugged. 'She would not want to know that this was a Campbell she was sheltering under her roof.'

'Mama, I am cold,' said Kirsty shivering and burrowing her head into her mother's shawl.

'Into bed with you then, you too, William.' She thought the boy was going to refuse for during the conversation she had noticed him looking long and often at Liam as if he was about to make some profound observation and then thought better of it. Now he crawled into bed obediently and put his arms around his sister, keeping as much distance between Liam and themselves as possible.

Caitlin's heart ached as she looked down at Liam. His eyes closed, he had grown old, his face grey and drawn with pain. She realised that while she and the children might have survived the night without shelter, without the old woman's mercy, Liam would have died. His eyes flickered open. When he saw the children lying beside him, he struggled to sit.

'I will sit by the fire. You and the children may have the bed. I insist. 'Caitlin cut short his protests.

'This is no time for delicacy, Liam Campbell, our survival depends on warmth, as the *cailleach* said. The only kind we have left is that of our own bodies. You as a soldier should know that.'

Liam nodded absently, too weak to argue but as he sank back against the straw pillow, he summoned the ghost of a grin. 'At least your virtue will be in no danger, Caitlin Macdonald – I assure you I am in no condition to take advantage of you this night.'

Pretending she did not hear, Caitlin said: 'Move over to the back of the bed, if you can. The children will sleep between us and I will sleep at the front. It will be a tight fit but we will be snug, especially if Bran sleeps across our feet. Up, Bran!'

Exhausted but warm, they slept. At last Caitlin heard the old shepherdess return with sticks and her grumbling attempts to rekindle the fire. Bran moved restlessly and whined.

Caitlin poked her head out of the bed and greeted the old woman. 'The dog wants to go out, if you please.'

The woman held open the door. 'Off you go, Master Dog.'

Caitlin closed the curtain and sank back on to the heather filled matress as if it had been made of down from angels' wings. She thought she slept for a long time. Then there were voices. The soldiers? With considerable relief she recognised the *cailleach* talking to Bran, laughing and praising him. She looked out and Bran came to her, tail wagging.

The woman held up two rabbits. 'We will not starve, my lady, this dog of yours is a miracle, finding two fat rabbits in this weather.' Bran looked from one to the other, showing his teeth in that pleased almost human smile. 'A rare dog you have there, he seems to know every word a body says,' said the shepherdess.

Restored by sleep, the children leaped out of bed and disturbed Liam who opened his eyes to smells of cooking. He made a sudden movement which he instantly regretted. His brains felt as if they had been stirred with a stick, as if he would never again find the way back to coherent thoughts. This was how madmen suffered.

Then he saw the dark head on the pillow beside him.

Caitlin. His heart sang for joy. He had found her at last. Smiling, content to have her near, he closed his eyes and drifted back into calm slumber. A little while later, Caitlin awoke as if from a nightmare, but turning she looked down upon the face of Liam Campbell who she had never expected to see again upon this earth. She saw that he was aged by past years and present sufferings, her beloved and her enemy. Her best and her worst. Her life and her death too, her heart whispered, for had she killed him her own life would have been over back there on the hills above Glencoe.

As if conscious of her eyes, he stirred and smiled up at her. He stretched out a hand, she took it and even as his clasp tightened, his eyes closed and he slept again, falling back into that strange fevered world where all things are possible.

The shepherdess announced that the rabbit stew was ready. 'Come away, bairns, eat now. And you too, Master

Dog, you shall have a goodly plate for it is thanks to you we do not go hungry this day.' She added delightedly. When Caitlin came forward she handed her a plate and said: 'There are turnips in the stew and bannocks to eat it with. What about your man, my lady, will he eat now?'

'He sleeps.'

'Aye, best thing for him, leave him that way. His poor head has been somewhat addled. He must rest for a day or two and sleep is the best mending for him.'

Liam did not waken that day, the only sound from the bed was when he cried out in his sleep. Caitlin and the children were glad to sit by the fire and play guessing games or tell each other legends and sing ballads of the past. Would Glencoe and its terrible story one day be added to the *seannachie*'s tales, she wondered, with Campbell going down in Scotland's history as a name accursed? But not all Campbells were bad, there were men like Liam and others doubtless too in the regiment who had refused to carry out their officers' orders.

On the second day, Liam sat up and announced that he was hungry. Had he been dreaming or did he smell rabbit stew? The shepherdess came and went and advised them to go through Glen Etive to Alasdair Macdonald of Dalness. They soon learned the reason that the soldiers had not come this way or included him in their plans; Macdonald was under the protection of Campbell of Inverawe. 'There is a small township and you will be safe there until you can get back to your own people. I must make haste to the sheep. God keep you all, keep you in his mercy together, for I have rarely seen a neater family.'

The eyes in that ancient face were topaz-bright, ageless, thought Caitlin again. It was as if a young person hid behind the folds of wrinkled skin and stared out at them, imprisoned by the years.

'And you have a son to be proud of, sir,' she said to Liam, who stared at William as William stared back at him, intently surveying this Campbell who was his hereditary enemy.

The shepherdess patted William's head. 'Aye, aye, the image of your father, you are, young sir. Be good to your parents, lad, do you hear? Take good care of them both on the way ahead, and your little sister too. Just a mile along the road and you will be safe in Glen Etive.' She smiled and was gone.

Liam and Caitlin inspected the basket of food she had generously left by stripping bare her meagre larder. They decided to replace most of the food, save a few rabbit pieces for the children who were playing in the sunshine at the door, while Bran, joined in the game tail-wagging joyously.

'If only this were home, journey's end and we could stay for ever,' said Caitlin, leaning her head against Liam's shoulder.

He held her for a moment and then asked: 'Was it true what she said?'

'What who said?'

'The *cailleach*, about William?'

Caitlin sprang free of his arms and became very absorbed in gathering their possessions together. He seized her hands. 'Put those down and answer me. Is it true?'

'Is what true?'

'About William. He is my son. You need not look at me like that. I have the evidence of my own eyes.' He sank into the chair and buried his face in his hands. 'Oh dear God, that I wronged you so, and that you have had to carry that secret all these years,' he whispered and his eyes were filled with tears when he looked up at her. 'I ruined your life, Caitlin, dishonoured you, stole from you the love that was another man's. Can you ever forgive me?'

Caitlin knelt beside him and put her arms around him. 'I kept my side of the bargain, we both did, for you spared Ardarroch and left us in peace. Besides I did not know when we, when we, loved each other, I did not know until the child was born and grown that he was yours and not Brendan Macdonald's.'

'What of your husband? Did he treat you cruelly?'

'As you would have done?' she asked quickly.

'Aye, if the child had been another man's. As any husband would have done.' He would never have been able to forgive Caitlin had the situation been reversed.

Caitlin smiled. 'Brendan never even mentioned that William *looked* like a Campbell, not even when Kirsty was born, in his own image. For the family's sake he accepted that William's colouring was because of *my* living so long in Glenlyon.'

'Why did he call him William, or was that your idea?' he added gently.

'The English version of Liam?' She shook her head. 'No, it was not my choice, but he insisted as it was my father's name. Such irony, was it not? He could not have known then how appropriately my child was named. Not until William was past babyhood did he grow more like you each day.'

'He did not guess?'

'He did more, he knew! On the night he died, I suddenly could not bear the barrier between us. He had been a good and perfect husband, kind, considerate, loving in every way,' she pretended not to notice how Liam winced at this eulogy. 'I could not let him die without forgiveness for the great wrong I had done him, to believe that the woman he had loved was without a blemish, that I had never been any man's but his. And so I told him, at least I began to stumble out the words and he put his hand to my lips and said he had always known from William's earliest days that he was not his son, and that he was the child of Liam Campbell. He also guessed that William was the result of the bargain I had made with you to save Ardarroch. He praised what I had done, said that a child was God's will.'

No more was said, as the children entered and the light showed that day had past forenoon. They must reach Dalness before nightfall or Liam would perish, for sure, with another night in these hills. The children too were weakening, especially Kirsty whose coughing reminded Caitlin uneasily of Brendan.

As they left the cottage William said: 'The *cailleach* had strange eyes, did you notice them, Mother?' He chuckled and patted Bran's head, 'Like his.'

William was right, thought Caitlin realising what had been troubling her about the *cailleach*'s eyes. Astonishingly young vivid eyes, in that ancient face. And not quite human. She shivered.

At the summit where the road descended into the snowy vale of Glen Etive, they stopped for a last look back. But the landmark, the overhanging crag with its solitary tree were no longer visible.

William shrugged. 'I expect it was a fairy place, and Bran was in league with the *cailleach*, who was a fairy godmother.'

'Or a guardian angel,' said Caitlin wishing she could have more of her help at that moment, for Liam was so weak he twice almost rolled out of the saddle, with a bout of coughing. She was horrified to see the snow spotted with his blood. 'We must stop and rest,' she said, helping him down, where he collapsed weakly on to the ground, his back against a boulder.

He seemed barely conscious but made no protest when she roused him again. Too weak to walk or, she suspected, to be entrusted with Kirsty whom she took from his arms, she insisted that he ride alone, ignoring protests that he felt stronger, a new man, with the rest.

'We must go on. We must be near the place the *cailleach* told us about. She said it was just a short distance.'

As their sorry cavalcade continued Caitlin realised that with Kirsty and William, there was a slender chance of reaching safety, but burdened with Liam, their progress was slow, careful, in case a sudden jolt made him lose more blood.

Caitlin's attention, however, was riveted on the fast-fading light. She had a new cause for terror, which she proposed to keep to herself as long as possible.

For some time now, she was aware that they were being followed. And not by Campbell soldiers. The sinister shadows were not redcoats, but grey shadows that blended with the darkening hills. Grey shadows, swift and lean, that kept steady pace with them.

Wolves.

'We must reach Dalness before dark.'

William ran ahead the top of the slope. 'That will be Etive down there,' he said hopefully. Reaching his side, Caitlin decided with a sinking heart, that it might indeed be Etive, but there were no landmarks of any kind, no shelter either. They would have to travel across open country with no protection against the wolves when they attacked.

The short winter day for travellers was almost done and still the grey shadows moved. At least on the brow of this boulder-strewn hill they would stand a better chance of holding out than moving across that snow-filled plateau.

Liam was swaying in the saddle, the exertion of riding had caused the wound on his head to open again, the bandage heavily bloodied. If they did not find shelter and rest, he would be dead before morning. And suddenly she wanted to give way, to fall down and scream out loud her fears, against relentless fate intent upon destroying them if not with Campbell swords, then with wolves.

What was the use of going on? Somewhere in the coming night, they were all going to die. If not from cold and starvation, then torn to pieces by the wild animals.

When darkness fell they would move in. It was only Bran's presence which had held them at a distance, that and daylight. But what was one dog against twenty hungry wolves? After Bran, maddened on blood, they would move in swiftly, attack and carry off the weakest, the smallest first.

Sobbing, she clutched Kirsty tightly to her breast. The pistol was useless without shot and they had not even man's most primitive weapon, fire, to keep them at bay. She fancied that already she saw their red eyes, growing closer, closer.

Bran came to her, as if conscious of her distress. Resting his head against her arm, he too cried quietly.

She put her arms around his neck. 'Find us another hut, any place where we can shelter.'

As if he had understood her words, he vanished up the hillside. A place of shelter, where the children could nestle into his warm body. That might just keep them alive until morning. If the wolves did not attack.

Oh dear God, help us, help us.

It was almost dark. Snowflakes had begun to fall again, soon there would be another blizzard raging around them, making further progress impossible.

'Let us rest here for a while.'

With William's help Liam dismounted and they led him to an inadequate boulder where he slumped down gratefully to the ground.

She took Kirsty into her plaid. The child was so weak, she seemed to be sleeping most of the time now. William took her hand and led her away from Liam.

'Mother, have you seen the wolves?'

'I have. But there is nothing to be scared about.' She tried to make her voice sound casual and firm.

'Is there not? I am glad, because they have been with us since we left the *cailleach*'s hut. I suppose they are keeping their distance because they are afraid of Bran.'

She squeezed his hand. 'Bran will protect us, never fear.'

One dog, against a hungry wolf pack? She saw the question unsaid in William's eyes as he asked: 'Where has he gone?' And running up the path he called: 'Bran, Bran.'

At last a distant bark.

'Wait, William.' Caitlin held him fast. Bran – or was it the wolf pack?

'It is Bran,' shouted William as the dog appeared and dragged at William's plaid. 'Look, he wants us to follow him.'

Liam had struggled to his feet. 'For God's sake, do not let the child go, Caitlin. It is almost pitch black out there.'

'I can take care of myself, sir,' said William stiffly.

Caitlin looked at dog and boy. 'Make sure you do.'

'I will keep whistling, Mother, like this, every few minutes, so that you will know we are not lost.'

Lost. Starvation. Wolves. How easy it would be to die in these hills –

'Mother,' William shouted. 'Bran has found us a cave. Just a little distance. We will be snug there. You take the horse and Kirsty, Mother.' And having taken command, he stretched out his hand to Liam. 'Come, sir, I will see you safe, you may lean on me.'

Surprisingly for once Liam did not argue. With Bran running a few steps ahead and waiting for them eagerly, they reached the cave. Off the main track, they could have searched and never discovered it on their own. As they huddled into the plaids and tried to settle for the night, Caitlin slept close in Liam's arms, for she thought this might be their last night on earth together.

If only they had fire. But even without the wolves, how could they survive? Liam badly injured, hungry, cold, the snow outside, the hungry pack biding its time. Sickened she thought that at dawn, the buzzards, the kites would move in and signal the end.

When during the long hours of that night, Liam

310

sometimes wakened from his fevered sleep, they talked softly and even kissed. Gentle kisses, passion would come later – if they lived, Liam thought, as he told her that Eunice was dead and Stephen had married.

'A minister's daughter from Perth. Alison by name.'

'I am glad, so glad,' said Caitlin.

'Eunice's death freed him. And we too are free now. We can have the rest of our lives together.'

Caitlin shivered, holding him close. Once before they had expected to have six nights of love and had but one. Now when they had discovered they were free to spend the rest of their lives together, was this also doomed to be one night, ironically with death at its end?

But to Liam's question: 'Where shall we go?' she answered: 'Ardarroch, perhaps. William inherits.'

'No. Not there.' Liam thrust the image away from him. How could he live unhaunted in the glen which he had once helped destroy? Hampered by a Campbell of Glencorrie as his father, hated, despised or living under a false identity, that was no way for William to begin his reign as Clan chief.

'Shall you go then to Glenlyon, to Fortingall?' she asked.

'Never. That is not for me, even if my name is not already posted as deserter. As for Glencorrie, it is Stephen's to do with as he wishes.' He paused before asking: 'Do we part then? You go as is your duty to Ardarroch and I make my way to Ulster or to some Lowland town where I may creep about unobserved. In some places, God knows, I may still have friends from my days of carrying Glenlyon's begging bowl. Or I could take ship to Ulster and seek refuge with the O'Rourkes there. Is this how it is to be then, Caitlin. You are silent, do I go one way and you another?'

She gave a sharp cry of protest, for she had no thought of further parting from him. Somewhere ahead of them lay a township but would it be a haven? Perhaps Liam would already be dead before they reached it or arrested by the Argylls, taken and shot. Had they met again merely to part in the eternity of death? She thought of the caterans, the drifting broken men who sheltered outlaws in their ranks. Men like Liam once noble, soon degraded, with a price on their heads. Was that what fate had in store? And then she thought of the good things, of the faith she had in God's

311

mercy that worked out men's destinies.

'I will stay with you, whatever happens. In life or in death, I will be your wife, Liam Campbell.'

At her side, Kirsty awoke: 'A nasty dream, Mama, send it away,' she wailed. Soothed and cradled by her mother's warm arms, she slept again.

'She is your image,' said Liam. 'I love her for that.'

'Good. She shall be your daughter.'

'Where is Bran, Mother?' William whispered.

'Out searching for food, I imagine. Even if he finds it we have no shepherd's cottage on hand this time.'

'We could never find it again, anyway, Mother.'

'Why do you say that?'

William smiled. 'You know why, Mother.' He stood up. 'I am going to look for him.'

Suddenly uneasy, Caitlin said: 'I will come with you.' Away from the cave they called his name.

'Listen. I heard something.' William raced down the little gully. 'Bran, Bran –'

Caitlin followed him quickly to where Bran lay on his side, whining gently. Her first thought was that the wolves had attacked him.

William shook his head. 'No, look at the tracks, just his own, he lay down to rest. He is old,' whispered William, stroking his head. 'Poor old dog.'

Caitlin knelt beside him, saw that the bright topaz eyes had faded as though he regarded them through a mist. His muzzle was white, his once silky hair harsh and brittle. A very old dog, trembling with age, and dying before their eyes.

'Do not die, Bran, do not leave us now,' sobbed Caitlin. But even as she spoke, his eyes glazed over. His tail flicked once and with a gentle whimper, he shuddered no more.

'Bran.' William touched the heart that was still.

'Why should this happen, now. Why? Why? Dear God, have we not suffered enough. Is there no beginning to your mercy?' She sobbed and William put his arms around her.

'He would have stayed with us, mother, but he cannot leave these hills. He belongs to Glencoe, to Ardarroch. His time had come to leave us, but he stayed a little longer to help us to survive, by finding us shelter.'

'Oh, Bran, Bran,' cried Caitlin. Life was suddenly all endings, a hopeless travail against suffering and grief.

William stood up. 'I am not going to leave him here for the buzzards and the eagles. Those wolves too, they are lurking about somewhere.'

'What can we do?'

'Take him back there,' he pointed to the way they had come. 'Bury him in the land that is his.'

'But how, William, how?' They exchanged glances. Bran was a large dog. Only a full grown man like Liam could have dragged him, in his health and strength.

William thought for a moment. 'We will lie him on a plaid and carry him between us.'

Caitlin followed him back to the cave where Liam lay motionless against the rock. Eyes closed, his hair and eyelashes frozen, he had the look of a dead man.

'Liam, Liam, not you too,' she cried, kneeling beside him. Was there no end to human endurance, no end to this agony? Was Liam to die? Had they found each other again only to be parted once more, and forever?

William shook Liam gently and his eyes flickered open. 'Good day to you, sir. How goes it with you?'

Liam summoned a smile. 'I am tolerably well, young sir. But tired and hungry and not very comfortable. The dog, did you find him?'

As he explained quickly, William took the plaid from the horse's back. 'You are not to die too, sir. That would make my mother very unhappy,' he added severely. 'We will get you to Dalness by and by.'

Caitlin shaped the plaid into a sling with knots at all four ends, so that they could drag Bran along in the snow in what would be his shroud. The task took longer than she intended, since she could not see clearly for her tears.

'I will attend to it, Mother, you get the Lieutenant a drink. I fear he is far from well.'

When Caitlin at last ran down into the gully, she found William alone, the plaid dangling. 'Where is he, what have you done with him,?'

William pointed: 'Over there, see.'

'Dear God, the wolves,' Caitlin screamed, for the grey pack had moved in quickly and crouched watching them.

She seized William's hand. 'Run, run back to the cave.'

'Mother, Mother, do not be scared. They are not wolves. Do you not see, they are the wild deerhounds.' His shout of laughter alarmed them. They rose suddenly and baying loped back towards the hills of Glencoe. Thirty, forty, she could not count them all.

'Look, Mother, look.' Caitlin stared, hand shielding her eyes against the sun. On a ledge high above the pack was their leader. A leader who could have been Bran, Bran as she had always known him, strong, vigorous. He looked back, bayed once, a sound of triumph and then the entire pack seemed to vanish with him into the mist.

William put his arm around her. 'No need for any more tears, Mother. Bran has found his own again.'

'Did you bury him then?' asked Liam, who had struggled to his feet once more. 'Poor beast.'

'We must have been mistaken, about him being dead, I mean,' said Caitlin. 'The wild deerhounds have been following us and he must have found that last strength he needed to go with them.'

'Even the dog has deserted us.' Liam's expression said so plainly. Caitlin shook her head. Exhausted with tears, some other time, she would tell Liam the story of Bran. Now, all that concerned her was reaching Dalness while she still had strength, and before the storm that already threatened came full blast upon them.

Kirsty had awakened reluctantly. 'Kirsty hungry.'

'We will be home soon, my pet,' said Caitlin, settling her sleepily into Liam's arms on the horse's back.

William ran ahead, down the slope and across the plateau. At last he reported a huddle of houses, smoke rising, about a quarter mile distant. Sniffing the air, they could smell the peat.

As they staggered down the hillside, a slow unsteady progress with Caitlin clutching the reins of a tired horse and Liam slumped in the saddle, hardly conscious, she heard herself praying out loud to that grey bitter sky: 'Dear Lord, do not let him die. Ask anything of me, but please let him live.'

The snow stopped and a glow of light beamed across the hills where the deerhound pack had disappeared. The light of hope, thought Caitlin, a sign that all would be well. And she remembered that other man she had loved who was now far beyond the veil of time. How, at the end of his life, he had touched her hair with a wasted hand and said: 'Each time I look at William I remember that as once Liam Campbell loved you – a Macdonald child of his sworn enemy – as his own flesh and blood, so too could I love this lad as my own. In this way, the blood debt between our clans was cancelled. Some day, Caitlin, when I am gone, perhaps that debt will be settled in full and for ever.'

She looked at William, who seeing the horse struggling over a bad patch, was at Liam's side, his hand on the saddle, supporting him.

Liam was aware of his presence and Caitlin thought he thanked him, called him, 'My son.'

She saw the face of the man in the child, and the child in the man, each mirroring past, present and future. One day, if God so willed, they would be safe and William would call Liam Campbell 'Father' and the dying wish of Brendan Macdonald would be fulfilled at last.

And the peace between Ardarroch and Glencorrie would flow out like a great cleansing river and wash away the stain of the great hate between Macdonalds and Campbells everywhere. They too would meet and shake hands and be brothers.

Epilogue

The story of Glencoe and its aftermath belongs to history. After the massacre came the rumours. First, there had been a battle between Campbells and Macdonalds but no mention of redcoats abusing Glencoe hospitality and their 'murder under trust'. Later, the story became an ambush in which Campbells slaughtered Macdonalds and their brave chief MacIan died sword in hand.

By the end of March 1692, with Argyll's regiment in Edinburgh en route for Flanders, there were other whispers: unbiased damning accounts from the soldiers who had been there, and Glenlyon, without shame, disporting himself daily in the Royal Coffee House in Parliament Close, proudly bragging: 'I would stab any man in Scotland or England without asking the cause, if the King gave me orders, and it is every good subject's duty to do so.' His intention; to apply to the Privy Council for reward for his regiment's good service.

From those same coffee houses, copies of the orders for the massacre from Hamilton and Duncanson fell into Jacobite hands. Suddenly every officer was on the lookout for a scapegoat. Colonel Hill in his lonely fort blamed MacIan for being tardy in taking the oath. If he had gone straight to Inveraray, Hill maintained, none of this would have happened.

On April 12 the story reached the *Paris Gazette* which informed its readers: 'the laird of Glencoe was butchered several days ago in the most barbarous manner.' Glenlyon and Hill were specifically mentioned as the perpetrators of this foul deed and on April 20, a full account appeared in London under the authorship of the Jacobite pamphleteer, George Leslie. Entitled: 'Letter from a Gentleman in Edinburgh to his friend in London after the Massacre', it was accurate in every detail and ran to four thousand words, including the publication of the Duncanson and Hamilton orders.

Meanwhile, at the first whiff of calumny, Breadalbane left London for his Scottish estates. 'It is a far cry to Loch Awe,' said he. The Master of Stair was in Flanders with his King and remarked: 'The affair of Glencoe was very ill-executed, but 'tis strange to me that means so much regret for a sept of thieves.'

The outcry continued, persistent enough for an enquiry to be called. But not until 1695 were Glenlyon, Drummond, Lindsay, Lundie and Barber judged 'guilty of a slaughter under trust'. Parliament recommended that they stand trial, but as the Argylls were then in Flanders, the King had no intention of sending them back. He took the traditional refuge of monarchs and blamed those who had 'misinterpreted' his orders. Loyal subjects anxious to please, hastened with assurances that His Majesty had been in a great hurry and had not read the order carefully before signing. Nowhere, however, did the King's behaviour before and after the massacre suggest that he disapproved of the cold-blooded plan to exterminate this small Clan of his Highland subjects.

Muddied waters had been stirred and Breadalbane found himself in Edinburgh Castle jail for the Achallader truce's secret clause with the Jacobites. He survived the experience, refusing to vote for the Union in 1707 and in 1715 declared his true colours by supporting the Jacobite Rising. He died at the ripe old age of eighty-two in 1717.

Argyll, with true Campbell ingenuity, had slid gracefully and discreetly out of the 'stramach' to emerge honoured as Duke in 1701. Two years later he died, aged fifty. The Master of Stair became Earl, but the signing away of Scotland's independence made him many bitter enemies. When he died aged fifty-eight, in his sleep, it was immediately suggested that he had taken his own life – in remorse for Glencoe.

King William's death in March 1702 had a fine touch of melodrama. He was thrown from his horse which had stumbled on a molehill and the Jacobites ever after raised their glasses to 'the little gentleman in black velvet' joyfully acclaimed as responsible for their archenemy's death.

Sir Robert Campbell of Glenlyon never returned to Scotland. He died at Bruges in 1696, an unhappy haunted man. Those who knew him whispered: 'MacIan of Glencoe hangs about Glenlyon night and day and you may see him in his face.' Sir Robert's son, John Campbell led Breadalbane's men into battle at Sheriffmuir, alongside the Macdonalds, where he declared to Glengarry: 'The only rivalry I shall have with a Macdonald is which of us will wreak upon yon ranks the injuries of our King.' The two men shook hands and took the field together.

As for Liam Campbell and Caitlin Macdonald, the history books record neither their names nor their further adventures, nor does the map indicate Ardarroch and Glencorrie. But this much is certain. There were only thirty-eight Macdonalds killed that night in Glencoe, less than one tenth of the population. Such small numbers suggest that the Clan was warned. History records that at 'least one officer – a Campbell – outraged by the inhuman order took the law into his own hands and warned the Macdonalds to make their escape.' And Liam Campbell, or someone very like him, was that man.

The Macdonalds returned to Glencoe and with support from their friends they slowly rebuilt the ruined glen. As for William Macdonald of Ardarroch, in due course he returned to his own again, as chief. He had not been a month in the glen when one morning he opened the door of the Tower to find a dog waiting outside. A stray, he thought at first, until the deerhound big as a pony, a smiling topaz-eyed creature, with a silky coat and a long curly tail, responded to his delighted recognition and answered, joyously barking, to the name:

'Bran!'

All Futura Books are available at your bookshop or newsagent, or can be ordered from the following address:
Futura Books, Cash Sales Department,
P.O. Box 11, Falmouth, Cornwall

Please send cheque or postal order (no currency), and allow 55p for postage and packing for the first book plus 22p for the second book and 14p for each additional book ordered up to a maximum charge of £1.75 in U.K.

Customers in Eire and B.F.P.O. please allow 55p for the first book, 22p for the second book plus 14p per copy for the next 7 books, thereafter 8p per book.

Overseas customers please allow £1.00 for postage and packing for the first book and 25p per copy for each additional book.